By
Tom Barber

*****

Return Fire
Copyright: Archway Productions
Published: 18th December 2013

The Sam Archer thriller series
by
Tom Barber

NINE LIVES

26 year old Sam Archer has just been selected to join
a new counter-terrorist squad, the Armed Response
Unit. And they have their first case. A team of
suicide bombers are planning to attack London on
New Year's Eve. The problem?
No one knows where any of them are.

THE GETAWAY

Archer is in New York City for a funeral. After the
service, an old familiar face approaches him with a
proposition. A team of bank robbers are tearing the
city apart, robbing it for millions.
The FBI agent needs Archer to go undercover and try
to stop them.

BLACKOUT

Three men have been killed in the UK and USA in
one morning. The deaths take place thousands of
miles apart, yet are connected by an event fifteen
years ago. Before long, Archer and the ARU are
drawn into the violent fray. And there's a problem.
One of their own men is on the extermination list.

SILENT NIGHT

A dead body is found in Central Park, a man who was killed by a deadly virus. Someone out there has more of the substance and is planning to use it. Archer must find where this virus came from and secure it before any more is released.

But he is already too late.

ONE WAY

On his way home, Archer saves a team of US Marshals from a violent ambush in the middle of the Upper West Side. The group are forced to take cover in a tenement block in Harlem. But there are more killers on the way to finish the job.

And Archer feels there's something about the group of Marshals that isn't quite right.

RETURN FIRE

Four months after they first encountered one another, Sam Archer and Alice Vargas are both working in the NYPD Counter-Terrorism Bureau and also living together. But a week after Vargas leaves for a trip to Europe, Archer gets a knock on his front door. Apparently Vargas has completely disappeared.

And it appears she's been abducted.

GREEN LIGHT

A nineteen year old woman is gunned down in a Queens car park, the latest victim in a brutal gang turf war that goes back almost a century. Suspended from duty, his badge and gun confiscated, Archer is nevertheless drawn into the fray as he seeks justice for the girl. People are going missing, all over New York.

And soon, so does he.

LAST BREATH

A Federal manhunt is underway across the United States. Three people have been shot by a sniper, and he's gone to ground somewhere in Washington D.C., his killing spree apparently still not over. As riots engulf the city and the manhunt intensifies, Sam Archer arrives in the city to visit his family.

Or so it would appear.

JUMP SEAT

A commercial airliner crashes into the Atlantic Ocean with hundreds of people on board. When another follows three days later, Archer and the rest of the team are assigned the case. At any moment, they know another plane could go down.

And to try and solve the case, Archer's going to have to go 35,000 feet up in the sky.

CLEARED HOT

A female CT Bureau detective and colleague of Archer's is shot in the head in an empty pool in Astoria. Archer learns she's been re-examining a strange case from seventeen years ago. On the morning of Tuesday September 11th, 2001, a FDNY firefighter showed up to work and committed suicide.

But no-one has ever figured out why.

TRICK TURN

At a pre-July 4th carnival in New York, an eleven year old girl is almost killed when a knife slams into a wall, missing her by a hair's breadth. No-one saw who threw the blade, but Archer and his NYPD team can guess why.

Her dead father was one of the most powerful mobsters in the city.
And someone seems hell bent on reuniting the girl with him.

NIGHT SUN

As Archer is sent to a federal prison to help transport an old foe to another facility, a situation erupts that leads to the escape of some other, extremely dangerous prisoners. One of them is an inmate with just six days left on his sentence.

But for a reason that quickly becomes clear, that's six days too many.

Also:
CLOSE CALLS

In a collection of three stories, familiar characters from the Sam Archer thriller series look Death right in the eye and don't blink first. Moments that forged the people they are today.
Moments they can never forget.
Their close calls.

HAND OFF
In this prequel novel, featuring two familiar characters from the Sam Archer thriller series, an investigation involving a dead famous athlete, another assaulted in a seedy strip club toilet and a vigilante going out at night delivering street justice draws the NYPD's attention.

Despite their junior status, Officers Matt Shepherd and Jake Hendricks are drawn into the case as quiet, unofficial investigators.

But also, as suspects.

For Nicola, Helen, Jodi, Claire, Clare and Mel at the
Tewkesbury Book Club.

ONE

Lying alone in the large bed, the dark-haired woman's eyes suddenly flared open.

She was on her left side, facing the balcony and as her sleepy brain recalibrated, she found herself staring out at the night sky through the open French windows. The thin curtains were fluttering gently, having been pulled back to allow what faint breeze there was to whisper into the room, the night hot and close, the street below quiet.

The bedroom was on the 2nd floor of the villa, facing a coastal road, and although there was the occasional noise from outside that wasn't what had woken her. Taking a deep breath, she pushed herself upright and ran her fingers through her hair, doing her best to rid herself of yet another nightmare.

Twenty eight years old, tanned and lithe, she had long black hair, hazel eyes and skin the colour of dark caramel, a perfect blend of her Brazilian and American heritage, her natural tan enhanced and made richer by her exposure to the Mediterranean sun over the last few days.

As the mists of sleep started to clear, she bowed her head and closed her eyes, taking a few deep breaths.

She was a tough woman, mentally strong, and until the last few months had never really had any trouble sleeping, at least not that she could remember. However, during the past four months and especially over the last seven days, her nights had been as fragmented as the aftermath of a glass vase dropped onto a hard floor.

There were two reasons for that.

The first was she was still having regular flashbacks from a job she'd worked on four months ago; employed by the United States Marshals service to protect a witness, she'd been trapped inside an apartment building in New York, the group she was hiding with being hunted by a team of determined and ruthless killers.

The second reason was a person.

And he wasn't here tonight.

She'd met him that day back in March after he'd been trapped in the Harlem building with her and he'd ended up saving her life. Since then, the bond that had developed between them during those intense few hours had deepened, and now they were both living and working together. She'd fallen for him hard and had been delighted when she'd found her feelings were reciprocated.

But right now things between them weren't good at all. They'd had a massive argument just before she'd left New York a week ago, which had started out as something pretty innocuous then developed into a full-on shouting match. She'd said some things in the heat of the moment that she now deeply regretted, and had spent all week wishing she could take them back. She'd been constantly checking her phone and email for missed calls or messages, but there hadn't been anything from him, not one word.

Opening her eyes, she glanced over at the empty space beside her.

In ten hours, she'd see him again.

And she genuinely didn't know if things were going to work out.

With those same thoughts squirrelling around in her head, just as they'd done all week, she slid out from under the covers, grabbed her cell phone from the bedside table and padded across the wooden floor to the door, quietly pulling it open.

The villa beyond was dark and quiet, the only other person in the house fast asleep. The young woman was dressed in a grey crop top and a pair of small grey shorts, light sleep-wear given the night time heat, and as she stood there she felt a welcome whisper of wind across her bare skin, fanning her for the briefest of moments.

She walked out of her room and moved down the twisting stairs slowly and silently. Arriving on the ground floor, she padded across the cool tiles and double-checked the front door was locked, which it was. Although there was no reason why it shouldn't have been, nevertheless she felt a quick moment of relief; the ordeal inside the Harlem housing block had left her with a variety of scars both mental and physical, and one of the former was an increased anxiety concerning security.

Standing there alone in the darkness, she saw the hands of a clock on the wall indicate it was 2:19am. Her flight home was at 10:30am, so she figured she could afford four or five hours more sleep before she'd have to rise, shower, grab a quick breakfast then take a cab to the airport.

Satisfied the house was secure, she quickly checked her phone again for messages or missed calls.

Nothing.

Tucking the phone into the pocket in the back of her shorts, she headed into the kitchen and poured herself a glass of water from the tap, her mouth dry

13

from the night-time heat. After taking a few sips, she tipped the rest away and retraced her steps, heading up the stairs quietly, moving back into the guest bedroom and closing the door behind her with a soft *click*.

Walking over to the bed, she slid between the thin covers, pulling the top sheet back over her body and looking out through the open French windows to her left again, at the moon and stars up in the night sky. His image reappeared in her mind and she started thinking about what she would say when she saw him at JFK, wondering which one of them would be the first to extend the olive branch. She so hoped she hadn't blown it.

Despite the heat, she shivered; as so often happened at night, all of her fears began to magnify, intensified by the quiet.

Maybe he doesn't want to reconcile, she thought.

Maybe we're done?

Shit; are we done?

Settling deeper into the pillow, she closed her eyes and tried to clear her mind.

The three men waited, giving her time to fall back to sleep.

Then a few minutes later, the door to the small bathroom behind her slowly opened.

The trio, all dressed in dark clothing, moved noiselessly into the bedroom. Standing together by the right side of the bed, they stared down at the woman lying between the sheets with her back to them, completely unaware that they were there.

The man on the left was holding a roll of duct tape, the man on the far right a case containing some equipment.

The guy in the middle was the leader. His hands were free.

As the other two looked at him, waiting for the order, the leader studied the woman in the bed, noting the delicious smoothness of her tanned skin and her complete vulnerability as she lay there with her back to them.

Then he turned and nodded to each of his companions.

Time to begin.

TWO

Five hours later and over three thousand six hundred miles away in New York City, NYPD 3rd Grade Detective Sam Archer suddenly jerked awake with a gasp.

Snapping upright in bed, he sat still for a moment, sweat gathered on his brow as he steadied his breathing. With his heart still thumping and his brain starting to clear, he instinctively reached to his left side protectively but his hand met nothing but empty sheets.

Then as his senses returned, he looked at the vacant space beside him.

And remembered she wasn't there.

Feeling the unpleasant effects of the nightmare start to fade, Archer realised he'd been shouting in the dream and wondered if he'd done the same in reality as he slept. Drawing the top sheet away, he pushed himself to his feet and walked across the room, opening his bedroom door quietly and stepping out into the hallway beyond. He was dressed in a pair of white boxer shorts, his body lean and tanned with a fresh scar on the left side of his lower torso. It was a warm summer night but he had the air conditioning working, keeping the apartment cool.

Further down the hall was another bedroom, the door to it slightly ajar. Walking forward silently, Archer looked inside and saw a small girl fast asleep in the bed against the far wall, furry toys surrounding her, a backpack dumped on the floor amongst some sheets of paper and colouring pencils.

He smiled as he watched her, his frame casting a shadow across the room that was reassuring, not threatening. Although she wasn't his biological child, the two were kindred spirits in several ways, one of them being that the girl had been suffering some nightmares herself lately. Thankfully, he saw that she was fast asleep tonight and didn't seem to be dreaming. She was a good kid, kind and thoughtful.

And how she'd ended up living with Archer was a story for which he was still trying to figure out the ending.

Taking a last look at the sleeping girl, Archer walked on down the hallway, grabbing a navy-blue plaid shirt from a hook by the front door on the way and pulling it on. Rolling up the sleeves but not bothering to do up the buttons, he walked into the kitchen, pulled open the refrigerator and took a litre bottle of water from the shelf, letting the door fall back and shut by itself. He then moved into the small sitting room to his right and opened the sliding panel to the apartment's balcony, stepping outside and drawing the frame shut behind him. It was the middle of the night but he wasn't ready to go back to sleep yet; not if all that awaited him were bad dreams and an empty bed.

Standing there alone on the 2nd floor balcony, he looked out into the distance. The apartment was in Queens, facing the west side of Manhattan, and lights in tall skyscrapers all over the city across the East River ahead were still shining brightly, the city that never slept staying true to its reputation. Observing the distant buildings, the busiest and most

17

intense island in the world, Archer smiled for a brief moment. He'd never tire of that view.

Turning, he took a seat in a wicker chair and shifted his attention to the street below. Every now and then a vehicle drove by, moving past the occasional lone figure of a pedestrian on the sidewalk making their way home, either a late Friday night or early Saturday morning depending on how you looked at it. It was a safe neighbourhood with affordable rent and you could walk around at any time of the night without any problems, totally contradicting New York's old reputation as a dangerous place to live.

However, concerns of that nature weren't something that Archer needed to worry about. Being an NYPD Detective, he carried his fully-loaded Sig Sauer P226 pistol and two spare magazines with him everywhere he went, both on duty and off. He'd learned the importance of that not too long ago when he'd been caught unarmed on the street in Manhattan; he'd been coming home from a gym workout and had almost been killed when he'd been swept up in a brutal ambush carried out against a team of US Marshals. Ever since then the handgun went with him everywhere, and that meant everywhere; when he did his laundry, went out to dinner, even when he went to the local dentist for a check-up on his day off. It was pretty unlikely that he'd get jumped as he was having his scale and polish, but Archer wasn't exactly a walking four leaf clover in terms of luck.

Opening the bottle of Poland Spring he took a cold sip, enjoying the light night breeze and the distant subdued sounds of the city. He'd lived in New York for over a year, having arrived from London in May

18

last year after making full use of the dual nationality his English mother and American father had given him, both of whom had now passed away. Prior to the move, he'd spent two years as an integral member of the Armed Response Unit, one of the two premier counter-terrorist teams in London. Constructed of two halves, a five person analyst team and a ten-man task force, Archer had been one of the four members of the Unit's First Team, the quartet charged with some of the most dangerous and high-risk situations in the city. The sheer nature of its work meant the ARU was never far from trouble, and although he'd only been with the team for two years, he'd seen a hell of a lot of action.

However, he'd always been curious as to what it would be like to be a cop in the Big Apple and had decided to grab the opportunity in May of last year, following in his father's footsteps who'd been an NYPD sergeant back in the day. After a helping hand from his old boss and the head of the NYPD's newly-formed Counter-Terrorism Bureau, Archer had ended up in a five-man detective team here in New York City. He was following in his old man's footsteps residentially too; he'd rented a place down the street a few years back and after his son had spent a week or so in the area two years ago, he figured it was as good a place as any to live in the city. Apart from the benefits of the comparatively cheaper rent, the apartment's location was also convenient for Archer's work. The NYPD Counter-Terrorism Bureau HQ was across Queens on Vernon Boulevard, a hundred yards or so from the Queensborough Bridge, and he could be there in less than ten minutes if he needed to be.

Often, that was the case.

19

As the thought of recent operations crossed his mind, he looked down at the neat scar across the lower left side of his stomach, partially hidden by the side of the shirt, a reminder of that day back in March when he'd been caught on the street without his weapon. A shard of glass from a grenade explosion had sliced right into him; it was one of many injuries he'd acquired in the last few years, including breaking his ankle twice, his nose once and suffering from a serious bout of pneumonia which had hospitalised him.

Archer had only been a counter-terrorist cop for three years, but the level of punishment he took on the job hadn't gone unnoticed. *You can take an ass kicking like no other,* his NYPD partner and friend Josh Blake had told him a few weeks ago. Archer hadn't argued; it was a running joke in the Department that he was harder to put down than the Road-Runner. Twenty eight years old, blond haired, blue eyed and in the best physical condition of his life, Sam Archer looked like an oil painting which an artist had completed then for some reason decided to damage. All the scars, cuts and broken bones his body had experienced were like rips and tears to the canvas. He'd been stabbed, punched, kicked, choked and shot at more times than he could remember and he'd thought he was going to die on several occasions, his number finally up.

However, he was still here, and the people who'd inflicted the damage weren't.

And that wasn't a coincidence either.

Examining the fresh scar on his stomach, he remembered that day, those brutal few hours he'd been trapped in a Harlem apartment block; it'd been one of the worst nights of his life but in another way, also one of the best. He'd almost died, and by all reasoning should have done given what had happened inside that building.

But he'd also met Alice Vargas.

Feeling the cold bottle of water start to numb his fingers, he placed it down as his eyes moved to the empty seat beside his where she would normally sit. Vargas was Archer's age, twenty eight, and apart from her dark looks and upbringing in LA, the two shared many similarities. She and Archer had fallen for each other hard soon after they'd first met that night in Harlem and once the situation in the building had finally been resolved, they'd spent more and more time together, particularly as they started working on the same team in the NYPD. Before long, what had been lying just under the surface between them had quickly caught fire. In the previous twelve months, Archer had struggled with the solitude that had started to define his life as a cop, but Vargas had completely changed that.

Three weeks ago, they'd taken a big step. Vargas had moved into his apartment here in Queens with her adopted daughter, leaving their previous place in Park Slope.

Sitting there alone, Archer's smile faded.

That was when the problems had started.

Vargas was the girl's adoptive mother, and before her guardianship the kid had been through some traumatic experiences in her short life, seeing things that most adults would never have to witness.

However, living with Archer seemed to be triggering issues for her, almost as if his constant presence somehow brought some of those dark

21

memories flooding back. Since she moved in at the beginning of the month the girl had started having terrible nightmares, often accompanied by fits due to her epilepsy, resulting in Archer and Vargas having their sleep constantly interrupted by blood-curdling screams that echoed around the building. The neighbours had started to complain too, with good reason, and then Archer and Vargas had both started suffering bad dreams as well, almost as if the three of them being in close proximity triggered some kind of chain reaction.

As the nightmares continued and the hours of sleep decreased, the tension in the apartment had started to build, and things had finally boiled over a week ago just as Vargas was leaving for a week-long trip to Spain; what had started out as a disagreement about something completely trivial had grown into a full-on shouting match, neither of them backing down, the argument fuelled by tiredness and frustration. Both of them had been fired up, letting it all out, and what they'd built over the past few months seemed to disintegrate in moments right before their eyes.

The moment Vargas had left, slamming the door, Archer had immediately started to regret what he'd said, but the damage had already been done. He'd thought about calling her, but figured she'd contact him when she was ready to talk. He hadn't heard a peep from her since, which told him she was still pissed.

Feeling the weight of his cell phone in the pocket of the shirt dragging the left side of the garment down, he took out the Nokia with his right hand and switched it on. Once it powered up, he saw he had several missed calls but no new messages.

He clicked onto the missed calls to see if they'd been from Vargas, but they were from Josh.

Shit.

Looking down at the phone, he suddenly focused on the present and frowned.

Josh's missed calls had come less than half an hour ago.

Glancing at the time on the screen, Archer saw it was *2:32 am,* not to mention the fact that the team were on leave for the week.

What the hell is he doing calling me at 2 in the morning?

Confused, he started to scroll for his partner's number. Maybe he'd pocket-called him by accident, or had had too much to drink.

But before he could find the number, Archer suddenly heard something through the balcony glass.

Three quick knocks on his front door.

He froze. The raps were slightly muffled through the glass of the closed balcony door but still carried an unmistakeable urgency.

Rising quickly from the wicker chair and sliding the balcony door back, Archer moved rapidly across the apartment, past the front door and towards his bedroom. Opening his bedside table, he retrieved his Sig Sauer P226 pistol, checking the chamber by pulling back the top-slide half an inch and seeing a round resting there in the pipe. It was the middle of the night, not the time people typically came calling, and Archer had learned the hard way to always to be on his guard.

The three knocks came again, quiet but urgent, and louder now Archer was inside the apartment. He moved forward, keeping the Sig by his right leg just in case the child in the bedroom had woken up and was watching him.

Passing her door, he glanced in and saw she was still asleep.

He walked up to the front door, then flattened himself against the wall and turned his head towards the frame.

'Who is it?' he asked quietly.

'Josh.'

Instantly relaxing and shaking his head as he exhaled, Archer opened the door and saw his NYPD Counter-Terrorism Bureau partner standing there. Thirty years old, African American, happily married and a father of three, Josh Blake was a unique mix, built like a tank yet with a calm and gentle temperament, totally unexpected from someone of his intimidating size. He also lived in Manhattan on the Upper West Side, which meant he was a long way from home, especially at this hour.

Dressed in jeans and a grey t shirt that couldn't have been smaller than an XL, he had a look of urgency on his face which Archer immediately noticed.

'Jesus Christ, you almost gave me a heart attack,' Archer whispered so the girl wouldn't wake up.

He pulled the door back so his NYPD partner could come in.

'What's wrong?'

'I've been trying to call you,' Josh replied quietly, stepping into the apartment.

'I just saw,' Archer said, pushing the door closed and locking it. *'Why?'*

Josh paused. Glancing over Archer's shoulder at the open door of the little girl's bedroom, he motioned for his partner to follow him.

The two men moved across the sitting room and Josh drew back the balcony door, Archer joining him and still carrying his pistol as Josh pulled the panel shut behind them.

'What's going on?' Archer asked, the two men standing face to face and talking normally now they were out of earshot.

Josh hesitated for a moment. 'It's Vargas, Arch.'

Still holding the Sig, Archer immediately tensed. Josh looked him in the eye.

'Something's happened.'

'What?'

'She's gone missing.'

THREE

Twenty minutes later, Archer gave Vargas' daughter a final hug and left her with Josh's wife Michelle at their home over on the Upper West Side in Manhattan. Pulling the front door shut quietly behind him and joining Josh on the front step, the two men strode towards the Counter-Terrorism Bureau Ford 4x4 parked by the sidewalk.

The smile Archer had forced when he'd said goodbye to the girl disappeared the instant he'd closed the front door.

After Josh had told him why he'd stopped by, Archer hadn't wasted a second asking for details, knowing his partner could explain on the move. Heading back inside as Josh went down to start the car, Archer had pulled on some jeans and sneakers then woken the little girl as he did up his shirt, telling her something had come up at work and that she'd be having a sleep-over at Josh's place. She'd become good friends with Josh and Michelle's three kids and had stayed there in the past so it wasn't an issue, especially as Archer had played up the adventure while quickly packing her bag and grabbed her epilepsy medication, the girl still half-asleep and not really understanding what was going on.

Once he'd gathered her things and locked up, he'd carried the sleepy girl still in her pyjamas downstairs and out to the Bureau Ford. Josh had then burned it over to his place on the Upper West Side, he and Archer not saying a word, saving it for when the child in the backseat was safely out of earshot.

Now just the two of them again, Josh fired the engine, released the handbrake and set off for the return journey to Queens, turning out onto Central Park West and heading straight for the Counter-Terrorism Bureau Headquarters just the other side of the Queensborough Bridge.

'How long ago?' Archer asked, his leg jiggling with nervous tension, looking ahead at the lamp-lit streets of the city as they flashed past.

'Anywhere after 11 o'clock last night, Spanish time.'

'Who was the last person to see her?'

'Her grandmother.'

'How did it go down?'

'Alice took her out to dinner and after they got back they said goodnight about an hour before midnight,' Josh explained. 'When she wasn't responding to any calls or knocks on the door this morning, her grandmother checked her room.'

He paused.

'Her bags and passport were still there, but Alice was gone. Left a real scene too.'

'What do you mean?'

'She must have put up one hell of a fight, Arch,' he said, just making it past a red light and accelerating to try and beat the next one. 'Both lamps were smashed and there was blood on the sheets.'

Pause.

'Alice's?'

'We don't know yet. The Department have a liaison stationed in Madrid and he's already got the Spanish cops running the samples for DNA. The results should come through in the next hour or so; if it's not Vargas' blood, we might be able to get a match on whoever abducted her.'

As Archer absorbed the news, Josh turned left at Columbus Circle and started heading east across Manhattan on 59th Street, the previous calm of the night now completely vanished, the shadowy Central Park rolling past their left side.

'Any ransom calls?' Archer asked.

'None.'

'Borders?'

'Her photo and vitals have gone out to European police departments. A Spanish forensics team dusted the bedroom, but it looks like whoever took her was wearing gloves. The only prints in there were Vargas', the maid's and her grandmother's.'

His leg still jiggling, Archer checked his watch, picturing the abduction in his head. 'Madrid is six hours ahead, so 11pm Spanish time is 5pm here. And her grandmother didn't discover she was missing until 8 o'clock the next morning.'

Josh nodded.

Archer swore. 'Jesus Christ, that's a nine hour window to get her out of the country. She could be anywhere in Europe right now.'

Josh didn't reply. The humming of the car's powerful engine filled the silence.

'How did you hear?' Archer asked.

'Shepherd. The Spanish authorities called the Department and he's ordered you, me and Marquez in. When I got there, he told me you weren't answering your phone so he sent me to get you immediately.'

'It wasn't switched on,' Archer replied. 'We're supposed to be on leave.'

28

'Not anymore,' Josh said, shaking his head grimly and speeding on towards the Queensborough.

They crossed the Bridge moments later and after a swift right turn and a quick ride down Vernon Boulevard, pulled into a space outside the Counter-Terrorism Bureau's HQ fifty yards from the water.

The building was located in an unassuming non-residential area, dominated by auto-shops and warehouses, an unexpected but intentionally-chosen location for what was the beating heart of New York's fight against terrorism. Stepping out, the two men slammed their car doors and strode quickly towards the entrance, and after buzzing themselves in, walked inside.

It was the middle of the night but the place was as busy as a Midtown office during the day, the staff and detectives working away in the large tech and analyst area to the left, their shift patterns ensuring the staff worked with the same clinical purpose, focus and efficiency at 3am as they did at 3pm. Not wasting a second, Archer and Josh turned right, moving into the field team's portion of the building, a series of desks and cubicles for the detectives who worked out of the Bureau.

As the two men strode past the detective pit, they heard a whistle from above and saw a member of their team, Detective Lisa Marquez, standing on a walkway and beckoning them up.

The moment he saw her, Archer felt the briefest moment of reassurance. Latina, thirty three and a single mother from the Bronx, Marquez looked as sharp as a cat considering it was the middle of the night. Archer had a huge amount of respect for her which was returned, the mutual high regard borne

29

from both having got each other out of some tight spots before. Some people had to work at being a police officer but others were born to it and Lisa Marquez was one of those; every part of her personality made her an effective cop, from her calm demeanour and resilience under pressure to her hatred of injustice and razor-sharp deduction. She was also Vargas' detective partner and the two had become close in the past few months; all in all, Marquez was damn good and Archer was glad she was here.

Like him and Josh, she was someone who wouldn't rest until they got Vargas back.

Arriving at the stairs, Archer and Josh took them two at a time, and once they reached the second tier, they turned and strode towards Marquez who was standing halfway down the walkway with a cup of coffee in her hand. Up on this level were a series of Conference Rooms the detective teams below used as operational command posts and she was outside Number 5.

As the two men approached her, she stepped forward to meet them.

'You made it,' she said to Archer, squeezing his shoulder supportively with her free hand once they joined her.

'What's the latest?' Josh asked.

'You're both just in time,' she said. 'Madrid's about to call us back.'

Turning immediately, Archer and Josh walked straight into the Conference Room, Marquez following but keeping the door open behind them. As they entered, Archer saw their team leader Sergeant Matt Shepherd sitting at the table in the room talking

30

with an analyst from next door who was working on a laptop. Brown haired, in his mid-thirties, over six feet tall and solidly built, Shepherd was a natural leader, cool, calm and measured and a man who'd been through more than his own share of battles.

He turned in his seat as the trio walked in, focusing on Archer.

'You're here,' he said. 'Good.'

'Josh filled me in, sir,' Archer said. 'Sorry I didn't pick up your calls.'

Shepherd nodded, waving his hand. 'We're supposed to be on leave. Only reason they got me was because of my landline.'

He glanced at Josh.

'Did you explain?'

'Yes, sir. Where are we at?'

As the three of his four detectives stood there, Shepherd motioned to the chairs around him at the table, his face grim.

'Take a seat.'

FOUR

The trio sat down, Archer and Josh on the left side of the table opposite Marquez, who took the empty chair beside Shepherd on the right. On the large screen on the wall ahead Archer saw a news-feed, the headline in Spanish, a number of police cars surrounding a villa in the centre of a small town near the sea.

It was already early morning there, six hours ahead, and the sun was glinting off the cars and windows of villas; Archer saw a scrolling headline in Spanish under the shot which he could just about translate but he focused on the images instead. He guessed the abduction of an NYPD cop would stand out from some of the run of the mill stories they usually had to cover.

'What's the name of the town?' Josh asked, studying the screen.

'Nerja,' Shepherd replied. 'An old fishing village turned tourist spot on the Southern coast. As you can see, local news has jumped on the story. We've been talking with Detective Travis, our contact stationed in Madrid. He's already driven down there and is now working closely with the regional police.'

He turned to Josh and Archer.

'He called whilst you were both absent. Apparently the cops interviewed a neighbour who said he heard a commotion coming from somewhere nearby last night which woke him up. He'd been drinking though, so isn't the most reliable witness, but said he heard some things being knocked over and smashed around.'

'He didn't investigate?' Josh asked, frowning.

'Said he thought it was a domestic dispute. Didn't want to get involved.'

'Did the man guess what time?' Archer asked.

'That was the one thing he was sure about. He said it was 2:30am on the nose.'

'How can he be so exact?'

'He remembers hearing the clock-tower down the street chime during the ruckus. Then he fell asleep.'

Pause.

'OK, so that's 8:30pm our time,' Marquez replied, checking her watch. 'From that moment until right now gives them five and a half hours to put distance between themselves and the villa.'

'Excuse me for asking, but why was she in Spain in the first place?' the analyst sitting at the table asked. Archer remembered his name was Ethan.

'Visiting her grandmother,' Archer replied. 'She's been ill. We're all supposed to be on leave for a week. Vargas used the time to go look after her while she's recuperating.'

As Ethan nodded, Josh turned to Shepherd. 'Still no ransom calls, sir?'

'Not here or to the Spanish police. Could be coming later though. Give us time to realise Vargas is missing and let us stew.'

There was a pause and they all watched the muted Spanish news footage in silence.

The tension in the room was palpable.

'Who the hell kidnaps an NYPD detective in Spain?' Marquez said. 'If you go down that path, you know you've got officers from both our Department and the Spanish force on your back. That's a lot of people invested in finding her; it doesn't make any sense.'

'Who's to say they knew she was a cop?' Josh replied. 'She wasn't on police business, so wouldn't have had her badge and she was abroad, which meant she wouldn't have had her gun. Whoever took her might not know who she is; this could have been a case of wrong target, wrong time.'

Beside him, Archer shook his head, staring at the screen.

'No way,' he said. 'This feels deliberate.'

He pointed at the news feed.

'Look at the height of the 2nd floor of the villa.'

The group all studied the shot of the property.

'That's quite a way up, next to a public street. Say this was an opportunistic break-in and kidnap; that wall would be a bitch to scale, let alone to get back down with a woman trained in self-defence resisting you. And going in from the front would have taken some significant effort too; Vargas would have sealed the house shut. Breaching the villa quietly, restraining her, then taking her away without anyone noticing would require some serious determination and pre-planning. Why not find an easier mark?'

There was a pause.

'Whoever took her definitely knows who she is.'

'But why kidnap her?' Ethan asked. 'Something from her past?'

'That's what I'm thinking,' Shepherd said. 'Pull up her file.'

Ethan's fingers quickly flickered across the keypad and a few moments later the news report was replaced by Vargas' police bio.

The file photo had been taken just a few months ago when she'd joined the NYPD; she was in official uniform looking straight at the camera, her black hair tied back neatly and a hint of a smile at the edges of her mouth. Archer felt his stomach clench as he saw the snap, Vargas suddenly joining them in the room, part of the team.

'3rd Grade NYPD Detective Alice Vargas,' Ethan read as the group all looked at her file on the screen. 'Twenty eight years old, born in Los Angeles to Elaine and Raul Vargas. Raised in Reseda, California.'

He scrolled down.

'Parents divorced soon after she was born; she lived with her mother and attended Reseda High School. Ended up working a 9-5 in LA for a few years then quit and signed up to the Police Academy when she was twenty five. Since then, she's former LAPD, Miami-Dade PD, a United States Marshal and currently NYPD.'

He paused, studying her history.

'Holy shit; all that in three years?'

'It's a long story,' Shepherd said. 'But including New York, that's four different career locations.'

He turned to his team.

'Four separate places to make enemies.'

'So let's start with the most recent, right here in New York,' Josh said. 'All NYPD detectives are potential targets.'

'I agree,' Archer said. 'But this isn't something from New York.'

'How can you know?'

35

'She works out of this Bureau and pretty much everything we do here is covert. Not much use being a counter-terrorist cop if the players on the other side know everything about you.'

'Plus she's only worked here for a few months,' Marquez continued, agreeing with Archer. 'We've all seen the cases she's been involved in. How much trouble could you stir up in that timeframe when the other side don't have a clue who you are?'

Shepherd turned to her. 'You're Vargas' partner out there in the field. Has she been caught up in anything unusual that you can think of? Anything at all?'

Marquez shook her head. 'Nothing. This can't be someone she's encountered in New York. Surely we'd have noticed anything out of the ordinary if it was?'

Shepherd thought for a moment.

'OK, so that's one option struck off,' he said. 'Let's move backwards chronologically. Before us, she was a member of the Marshals Service and Miami-Dade PD prior to that.'

'Her work in both seems to have been wrapped up too,' Ethan said, reading the file. 'There's a lot of history there, but no apparent loose ends.'

Shepherd, Josh and Marquez all glanced at Archer, who nodded, suddenly taken back four months.

'Yeah, I can vouch for that,' he said.

'So already that's three out of the four options void,' Josh said. 'Leaves us just with her time in LA.'

'She worked a squad car for two years after the Academy,' Ethan read, scrolling down on the file, everyone looking at it up on the screen. 'Partner was an older veteran called Alvarez.'

'Where was their beat?' Shepherd asked.

'Inglewood, then a few months in Chinatown before she was transferred to Miami.'

'A lot of gangs have links around the world,' Josh said. 'It's conceivable she could have pissed someone off and they tracked her down.'

'For what, issuing a parking ticket?' Marquez said, reading the file on the screen. 'Look at her record. It's innocuous.'

'But she shot someone,' Ethan said, pointing. 'Bottom of the screen.'

The team all focused where his finger was aimed. As he read the notation, Shepherd's eyes narrowed; Ethan was right.

'Open it up.'

Ethan tapped a few keys and the official LAPD police report appeared on the screen.

'Shootout in Chinatown,' he read. 'Vargas put two guys down. One of them had to have the lower portion of his arm amputated due to a later infection.'

'Cause of the gunfight?'

'They held up a liquor store,' Ethan read. 'Vargas and Alvarez were first to respond. Apparently these guys decided to bang it out on the street so they had no choice but to take cover and fire back.'

'She and her partner shot two gang members,' Josh said. 'There's motive.'

Ethan pulled up another window and searched for the incident, drawing up the report. Vargas's file was momentarily replaced by two LAPD profiles of the two gang members. They both had shaved heads and

37

tattoos on their necks, both with tear drops tattooed under their right eyes. Studying them, Archer knew that certain gang members were rewarded with a tear tattoo whenever they killed someone; it wasn't the smartest thing to do if you wanted to beat a murder rap, but it sure as hell sent a message to people who might be thinking about crossing you.

'Emilio Sanchez and Rodrigo Fuentes,' Ethan said. 'Both Surenos; Mexican Mafia.'

He pointed at the photo on the right.

'Fuentes is the one who lost his lower arm. But I guess it doesn't matter anymore.'

'Why?' Shepherd asked.

'He's dead. Stabbed to death in prison six months into his sentence. And Sanchez is doing life for murder at Pelican Bay.'

'Nevertheless Vargas still put two bullets in Fuentes,' Josh said. 'And after she dropped him, he went to jail for six months before he was killed. That's a lot of time to think about revenge; especially when you're sitting in a cell all day.'

'But he died some time ago,' Archer replied, unconvinced. 'And these guys are street bangers, not criminal masterminds. Even if they had friends who were determined to get revenge, there's no way they could track Alice down. Not from Miami to the Marshals service to New York, and definitely not to Spain.'

He shook his head.

'It's got nothing to do with them. They don't have the connections. For guys like this, LA is their entire world.'

Leaning forward in his chair, Archer cursed quietly, frustrated and worried as Ethan brought Vargas' file back onto the screen.

Four options from Alice's past, all seemingly dead ends. He'd been banking on this being a ransom case, but with no obvious suspects he realised Josh could be right.

Her kidnappers might not even know who she is.

No ransom calls. No witnesses.

And no trace of Vargas.

As the thoughts crossed his mind, Archer felt his stomach grip.

He was suddenly starting to feel a hell of a lot worse about this.

FIVE

'Let's take another look at the present, not her past,'
Shepherd said. He turned to Archer. 'She moved in
with you recently, right?'

'Yes, sir. Three weeks ago, from Brooklyn.'

'You seen anyone hanging around outside your
apartment lately?'

Archer paused, thinking about it. He'd been so
distracted with work and all the shit he and Vargas
were dealing with that he realised he hadn't been
paying as much attention as he normally would have.

'I don't think so. But it's New York; there're
always people on the streets.'

'Any of them catch your attention?'

'No.'

'Is Vargas well off? Financially?'

'Same as the rest of us.'

'Family connected?'

Archer shook his head. 'Mother died over a decade
ago and she never knew her father.'

Pause.

'I still think the kidnappers could be people who
only saw her in Spain this week,' Josh said, his
argument seeming more plausible by the second.
'People who never encountered her before.'

Behind his laptop, Ethan frowned. 'But like Arch
said, why would they go to so much trouble? And
why Vargas?'

'Trafficking.'

The word hung in the room as a silence descended.
Josh paused a beat.

'We have to consider the possibility. Exporting women is a growing problem worldwide, especially in Europe, and Vargas isn't exactly hard to look at.'

'It's possible,' Shepherd said eventually, glancing over at Archer. As he went to continue, the phone on the desk suddenly rang. Shepherd picked up the receiver, the other three detectives all watching as he took the call.

'Shepherd.'

He listened for a moment.

'OK, put him through,' he said, pushing the loudspeaker button on the phone and placing the receiver back on its base.

'Hello?' a voice said.

'Travis?'

'Speaking.'

'This is Sergeant Matt Shepherd, Counter-Terrorism Bureau. You're on speakerphone; as well as myself, there are three of my detectives and an analyst in the room. I'm leading the investigation into Detective Vargas' disappearance. What have you got?'

'Good news, sir; well, kind of. The blood test results just came back from the lab.'

'And?'

'There were four different types. Three have come back with a match.'

'Go on.'

'One of them was Detective Vargas.'

Across the table from Shepherd, Archer's knuckles tightened.

'The other samples belong to two men called Milo Stanovich and Ibrahim Payan.'

Shepherd frowned. 'Who are they?'

'*Slovakian immigrants living in the UK. Both men have extensive criminal records; they've each been convicted for prostitution, drug usage and sex trafficking.*'

'Age?'

'*Early thirties.*'

'Where are they based?'

'*Currently in London. The Metropolitan Police have been informed; apparently they sent officers to each man's last known address but there's been no sign of either of them. Wherever they are right now, they're laying low.*'

'Who's to say they're even in the UK?' Archer said. 'They could be anywhere in Europe with her.'

'*We considered that, but both men are back in the city.*'

'How can you be so sure?' Shepherd asked.

'*Stanovich ordered a pizza from a twenty four hour joint forty minutes ago. Paid over the phone using his bank card and took delivery on a street corner in South London. Police are checking the surrounding area and already have the delivery man in for questioning, but it's not looking promising. Seeing as the guy had already paid, the delivery man hardly spent any time with him. Just handed over the pizza and left.*'

'Shit.'

'*It looks like Stanovich didn't even pick it up though, so he couldn't have been arrested at the scene. His file says he's six foot five and has a shaved head, but the delivery guy said the man who collected the pizza was nearer six foot and had blond hair.*'

'And Payan?'

'He called his girlfriend just over thirty minutes ago saying he'd just got back from a trip and that he'd see her later today. Call was too quick to trace, but Met police are with her and her house is under surveillance. Judging by the timing of the two incidents, it seems likely they arrived back together.'

'So what's happening now?' Shepherd asked.

'Police in London are searching for Stanovich and Payan. When they find them, we should be able to get them talking and find Detective Vargas. Police here in Spain say abductions similar to this have happened before; most of the time it's gangs involved in the sex trade. The good news is the girls who are rescued are almost always found alive; they're not worth any money dead.'

Shepherd nodded. 'OK. Good work, Travis.'

'Thank you, sir. In the meantime the lab teams here are working on identifying the fourth blood sample. I'll call you the moment a result comes through.'

'Got it.'

Then he hung up.

While Travis had been giving his report, Ethan had located Stanovich's and Payan's files via Interpol and he pulled them up onto the screen, replacing Vargas' police file. Shepherd, Archer, Marquez and Josh saw two tough-looking men not dissimilar in type from the two gang members from LA but with different ethnicity and no tattoos on their faces.

On the left, Stanovich looked tall and lean, bags under his eyes and a bent nose no doubt broken in the past but never reset. In the other photo, Payan's eyebrows were criss-crossed with scar tissue like rough patchwork above dark expressionless eyes staring straight at the camera.

43

Both looked just what they were.

Menacing, dangerous thugs.

At the end of table, Archer sat totally still, studying the two men who'd snatched Vargas, searing their image into his brain.

They had no idea who they'd just pissed off.

'Our suspects,' Shepherd said, studying the mug-shots. 'Give me the vitals, Ethan.'

'Both were born in Bratislava and moved to the UK eight years ago. Stanovich is thirty two, Payan thirty three, and according to this they're old acquaintances. Like Travis said, they've been arrested numerous times for various offences and served time. The most recent on each file is eighteen months for trafficking and running a prostitution network in south London.'

'But they can still remain in the UK despite jail time?' Marquez said, frowning.

'Joys of membership of the EU,' Archer said. 'The government's probably paying their rent.'

'Do they have a history of going to Spain?' Shepherd asked.

'Not that I can see,' Ethan said. 'But it's hard to track movement around Europe these days.'

'Two known sex traffickers,' Josh said. 'I knew it. They were probably searching for targets to abduct; young attractive women who were alone or in pairs. Nerja's a tourist spot, so it's probably a good hunting ground for them. Vargas must have caught their eye.'

'And without her badge and gun, they wouldn't have any idea who she is and the connections she has,' Marquez added, now on board with the idea.

'This is progress, guys,' Shepherd said, looking at the pair of suspects. 'Now we've got two of our kidnappers.'

'I'll contact the Met,' Ethan said, reaching for the phone and picking up the receiver. 'Ask them to give us a rolling update as news comes in.'

Shepherd nodded. 'I want to know anything the moment they do.'

As he spoke, there was a knock on the open door behind them; turning, the group saw Lieutenant Franklin standing there, head of the Counter-Terrorism Bureau. He was a grizzled moustached veteran who was as tough as nails and a legend within the Department. They all started to get to their feet but he waved them back down, looking at the screen across the room.

'These are our suspects?' he asked, indicating he knew exactly what was going on.

'Yes, sir,' Shepherd said. 'Both are based in the UK.'

Turning to him, Franklin motioned to the walkway outside with his head. 'One moment, Shep.'

Shepherd rose and walked outside, shutting the door behind him and joining his boss on the walkway, their conversation a murmur on the other side of the door as Shepherd explained the situation and the leads they'd just been given on the two sex traffickers to his boss. In Shepherd's absence, Archer, Marquez and Josh continued to focus on Stanovich's and Payan's photographs and vital statistics.

'Can you print copies of their files?' Marquez asked Ethan, who nodded, his phone still clamped to his ear as he tapped away on his laptop.

45

Across the table, Josh turned to Archer, noting his partner's fixed stare as he studied the mug-shots.

'Thoughts?' he asked.

'I hope they've each written a will.'

As Josh went to reply, the door opened again and Shepherd stepped back into the room alone, Franklin already gone. He looked over at Ethan.

'Did you get through?'

'Any second, sir.'

'Do something else for me first.'

'What do you need?'

'Four seats to Heathrow on the first British Airways flight of the day out of JFK. Book them in Club Class on the Bureau's budget. Lieutenant Franklin wants us over there on the ground to help find these men and get Vargas back.'

'Club, sir?'

'Yes, as I said. He wants us rested and ready to go as soon as we arrive.'

Ethan nodded, ending his current call abruptly and pushing the operator line. Checking his watch and standing by the door, Shepherd turned to his three detectives.

'It's just past 3:15am. You three, go home and get a change of clothes, your passports and then get your asses over to JFK immediately. I'll meet you there.'

As the trio rose, he took a last look at the two sex traffickers on the screen who'd kidnapped Vargas.

'We're going to London.'

SIX

Just over an hour and a half later, Shepherd, Archer, Marquez and Josh were all together again inside JFK's Terminal 4 as the clocks inside the building ticked past 4:50am. The Terminal was subdued and quiet, none of the long queues so typical later in the day, but the British Airways booths had already been opened, checking in passengers for the 6:20am flight to London.

The four NYPD detectives had already collected their boarding passes, and were now moving through the security points that stood between them and the Gates on the other side. Watching Marquez and Josh walk through two rectangular metal detectors, Archer waited his turn in the queue.

He'd changed into light blue jeans, a black t-shirt and a checked grey and white shirt over the top, the first things that had come to hand in his wardrobe. After Josh had made a flash pit-stop at his own place to grab a bag and his passport, he'd driven Archer back to his apartment in Queens and waited as he gathered his own gear. Archer hadn't concentrated as he'd changed his clothes, working on autopilot, but as he'd pulled the shirt he was wearing from a hanger inside his closet, he'd seen Alice's clothes lined up neatly beside his and caught the scent of her perfume. Quickly closing the wardrobe door, he'd thrown a spare set of clothes into a holdall, secured his pistol and after grabbing his passport, had walked out of the apartment and re-joined Josh in the car, the two of them heading straight for JFK.

47

Just ahead, Marquez and Josh were both cleared through security and they joined Shepherd on the other side, the trio waiting for Archer and all dressed similarly to him. An official beckoned Archer forward, and he stepped through the rectangular detector, his bag, shoes and valuables placed on a grey plastic tray and going through the x-ray machine to his left. The scanner didn't bleep, satisfying the TSA team, and he was allowed to continue forward, the security team shifting their attention to the next person in line.

Despite the hassle, Archer felt reassured by the safety of the whole process as he pocketed his phone, wallet and NYPD badge then pulled on his black and white Converse shoes, tying the laces. However, at that moment he was less comfortable with the absent holster and Sig Sauer pistol that usually resided on his hip. Seeing as the NYPD quartet were travelling to another country, they'd each had to leave their side-arm behind at home.

Given the circumstances and the reason for their trip, Archer didn't feel especially comfortable about it and he knew the others would feel the same.

With his shoes back on, Archer scooped up his holdall and re-joined Shepherd, Josh and Marquez. The team then headed up a few steps into the inner heart of the Terminal, immediately surrounded by Gates, wandering travellers, Duty Free shops selling alcohol, fragrances and gadgets beside several overpriced news vendors offering refreshments at twice the normal price.

The place was subdued and quiet, just like the four NYPD detectives. Walking forward, Archer checked his watch. *4:57 am.* Their flight wasn't for another hour and twenty three minutes, which meant all they

48

could do now was sit and wait. He immediately set off towards a row of empty seats up ahead but Shepherd caught his shoulder and pointed to his left.

'Ethan booked us into Club Class,' he reminded him. 'Let's use the Lounge.'

Turning, Archer followed the others as they cut a direct path through the Terminal towards the entrance to the British Airways Lounge. A perk of their more expensive seats, the Lounge was a private, secluded area which provided privacy, space to work and complimentary food and drink. Arriving at the reception desk, they each showed a woman in a navy blue BA suit their boarding passes and passports. She welcomed them through with a smile that was impressively genuine for this time in the morning, but only Josh managed to match it as they passed her desk and walked into the Lounge.

There were about twenty other people sitting around the room, mostly businessmen and women reading documents or working on laptops, brought together for a brief spell before flying on to their various destinations around the world. A few had dozed off, that light kind of sleep that would be ended in an instant when a flight was called for boarding, whilst others were sipping drinks or eating the light snacks provided.

There were plenty of available seats and the quartet moved towards four armchairs centred around a low-cut polished table towards the back of the lounge, the typical police approach, keeping their backs to the wall and their eyes on the door. Placing their bags down, Josh and Marquez immediately headed over towards a coffee and tea selection across the room beside the complimentary food. As they both left, Shepherd's phone started ringing and he took the call, walking away and talking quietly to whoever was on the other end.

Momentarily alone, Archer took a seat and leaned back in a leather armchair, rubbing tiredness out of his eyes, the warm darkness of his apartment a distant memory now it had been replaced by harsh airport lighting and cold recycled air from the ventilation system. He felt like shit; ever since Josh had told him Vargas had been taken, his stomach had knotted up like an intricate Chinese puzzle and had stayed that way ever since.

What the hell was this about?

Whatever the reason Stanovich and Payan had kidnapped Alice, they'd taken her at 2:30am; she would have been fast asleep, the element of surprise helping to make their task easier, but it sounded as if she'd gone down fighting. Even though these men must have caught her off guard, she'd still managed to draw blood from all three, giving the investigating team plenty to work with.

Sitting there alone for the moment, Archer paused.

All three.

There was someone else involved here. The owner of the fourth sample that Travis said wasn't Vargas' and which hadn't yet been matched.

A third kidnapper.

As he considered the few facts he had, Archer tried to clarify his thoughts; the owner of the as yet unidentified blood sample was another mystery in a night already full of them. Everything had happened as suddenly as a fast-moving tornado hitting an unsuspecting Midwest town. Three hours ago he'd been fast asleep but was now on his way to the UK to track down two sleazy, ex-con sex traffickers who'd kidnapped his girlfriend.

Another nightmare.

But this time he was awake.

Sitting there alone, his foot tapped quietly with impatience as he checked his watch. He'd seen the Liam Neeson movies but he also knew the facts; every sixty seconds after a woman is kidnapped by men in the sex-trade is another minute closer to never finding her again. Although Stanovich and Payan were both apparently back in London, there was no guarantee at all that they'd brought Vargas to the city with them. They could easily have passed her onto someone else on their way through Europe, injecting her with substances to keep her compliant.

Or done something even worse.

Feeling bile rise in his gut, he forced his mind elsewhere, but despite his best efforts it kept conjuring up an image of Vargas tied up somewhere, bleeding and vulnerable, still dressed in those small grey nightclothes she wore, alone and scared.

Just hold on, Alice, he thought.

I'm coming for you.

Then his thoughts shifted to Stanovich and Payan. His already dark mood turned as black as pitch.

I'm coming for you too.

Ten feet to the left, Shepherd thanked whoever had called him and hung up, tucking the phone back into his jeans and walking over to take a seat beside Archer.

'That was Travis,' he said. 'Still no match on the fourth sample. Spanish police have been informed that we're heading to London and have asked that we keep them fully updated on any progress.'

51

Archer nodded but didn't reply, the silence filled by the quiet murmur of muted conversations around the room.

'There's something else too, Arch,' Shepherd said, settling back in his chair.

'What is it?'

'We're going to need a Command Post and base when we get to London, and a hotel room isn't going to cut it. Is there any chance your old colleagues could help?'

As Josh and Marquez walked over, each carrying two cups, Archer realised he'd been so focused on Stanovich and Payan that he hadn't given any thought to where they were heading.

London; his old stomping ground.

Checking his watch, he saw it was past 10am in the UK, and pulled his cell phone as Josh and Marquez sat down.

'Any news?' Josh asked, passing Shepherd a cup of coffee.

Taking the drink, Shepherd didn't reply, watching Archer who was looking at the screen of his phone. Reading a text message that had come in a few minutes earlier without him noticing, Archer fired back a quick reply then pocketed the phone, taking a cup of tea from Marquez.

'That was Chalky, one of my old team-mates,' he said to Shepherd. 'He's an officer at the ARU. He said we've got a Command Post ready and waiting for us after we land.'

'At your old HQ? Already? How did they know?'

'Apparently Ethan called ahead at Lieutenant Franklin's request and informed Director Cobb about the situation. He's very keen to help. He's offered us space at their base and the use of their resources to help apprehend Stanovich and Payan.'

'Great,' Josh said, drinking from his tea.

Shepherd nodded. 'That's good of him.'

Archer didn't reply, glancing at his watch again as he looked at the quiet Lounge around him, feeling impatient.

Just over an hour until flight time.

Now all they could do was wait.

*

Three thousand four hundred miles away, the sun had already come up over London on a bright July Saturday morning, but the light beating through the apartment window was giving the scarred Middle Eastern man with the broken nose a thumping headache.

His mood sour, the man took a mouthful of pizza, the act of chewing causing his face to throb with every bite; he was sitting inside an apartment in the south of the city with Milo Stanovich and a South African man who was standing near the window watching the street below. They had an open Dominos box on the floor beside them, half of the contents already eaten, not a typical choice for breakfast but convenient and providing the ample calories they were possibly going to need today.

Stanovich had paid for the food but the South African had picked it up. Finishing the crust of his second slice, the Middle Eastern guy squinted against the light coming in through the window.

'Draw them for me, will you?' he asked the South African. 'Feel like I'm being interrogated.'

By the window, the other man nodded and twisted the handle on the blinds; the room suddenly became darker. He then walked forward and took another slice of pizza.

'Breakfast of champions,' he said, his accent infused with a Johannesburg lilt, breakfast sounding like *blekfust*. Taking a bite, he bumped Stanovich's shoulder with his other hand. 'You not hungry, Stan?'

Stanovich didn't reply. Chewing and stepping back, the South African shifted his attention to the man with the broken nose.

'How's the beak?'

'Think the bitch broke it,' he replied, gently feeling the swollen surface.

'You bled out, right?'

He nodded. 'The cops will be all over the samples by now.'

Breathing in through his mouth, he shifted his attention to Stanovich.

'That means they're going to be looking for us.'

Stanovich stayed quiet. He'd been that way all morning, keeping his thoughts to himself. The Middle Eastern man took a bite of pizza, leaving a smear of oil across his lip.

'That means we need to be ready for when they come.'

Stanovich looked at him for a moment but didn't respond. The guy with the broken nose looked up at the South African, who took another bite of pizza and checked his watch.

It was 10:04am.

Then they both glanced at a holdall full of equipment sitting next to them on the floor beside the pizza box.

The Middle Eastern man took a last bite and tossed the half-eaten crust at the open box, his bad mood overpowering his patience.

'Enough pizza. Time to prepare.'

SEVEN

The British Airways Boeing 747 left New York right on schedule at 6:20am. Located towards the front of the plane, the Club Class seating was separated into spacious pods, positioned in pairs with screens between the seats to afford some privacy.

Archer and Josh were in a pair of seats on the left of the cabin, Marquez and Shepherd in the middle of the cabin with an aisle either side. Despite what lay ahead and the fact that they were flying into daylight hours, Josh and Marquez managed to doze off early in the journey, their bodies making up for the sleep they'd missed during the night. Beside the sleeping Marquez, Shepherd was hard at work, studying Stanovich and Payan's files whilst taking occasional sips of strong coffee, figuring out a plan of action when they arrived in London.

In his seat by the window in the pod beside Josh, Archer was also awake, looking through the small gap in the blind at the white clouds and Atlantic Ocean far below. Now they were in the air, time seemed to have slowed right down. Seeing as they were flying into a different time-zone, the flight was due to land at 6:15pm UK time which meant they'd have lost half a day, twelve more hours to move a kidnapped woman whose current location was still a mystery. Although he knew worrying about it wouldn't do anything to help their situation, he felt that radius of where Vargas could be widening every second.

Twelve hours.
Shit.

By the time they landed, she could be almost anywhere.

Feeling restless, Archer unclipped his seatbelt and rose, walking down the cabin towards the partition between Club Class and Premium Economy. The curtains on both aisles had been drawn across, allowing passengers some further privacy, and a stewardess was standing in the space between, placing several stubby cans of Heineken onto a tray from a compartment and tucking plastic glasses on top.

She smiled when she saw Archer, her uniform as pristine as her make-up.

'Can I get you something, sir?'

He shook his head, forcing a smile in return. Continuing with her work she pushed the compartment closed and moved down the cabin with the drinks, disappearing down the aisle on the opposite side.

Turning, Archer stood with his back to the curtain and folded his arms, watching the cabin in front of him. Including Josh and Marquez, three or four other people were asleep, another absorbed in a movie, two others working on laptops. Despite how anxious he felt, he was reassured that his colleagues were here with him; he thought back two years to another plane journey, that occasion flying in the opposite direction from London to New York. Someone had killed his father and he'd spent a dangerous week tracking that son of a bitch down; although he'd had a degree of assistance he sure could have used Shepherd's, Josh's and Marquez' help back then too.

The plane suddenly shuddered as they hit a brief patch of turbulence, the movement waking Marquez, who stirred. As she opened her eyes, came to and stretched, she noticed Archer standing further down the cabin and smiled. After a quickly-stifled yawn and smoothing down her hair, she unclipped her seatbelt, rose to her feet and walked down the aisle to join him, getting some blood flowing through her legs.

'Can't sleep?' she asked, the two of them standing near one of the main exit doors of the plane.

'Not right now.'

She paused for a moment, working her ankles. 'How are the dreams?'

He looked over at her, surprised. He hadn't slept for a second, so she couldn't have seen or heard him struggling with nightmares.

'Vargas told me,' Marquez added, seeing the look on his face.

'Yeah. They're still there.'

'What happens in them?'

He thought for a moment. 'I'm stuck somewhere. There's no way out. I know something is coming to kill me, but I can't move, like I'm caught in treacle. It's coming closer and closer, but I'm trapped. I'm thrashing and shouting, but there's nothing I can do. Then it goes black.'

Marquez watched him closely and he forced a smile.

'Gee, I wonder what that stems from,' he said.

There was a pause.

'Two weeks ago I tried to go up the Empire State with Vargas and her daughter but I couldn't even get into the lift. I've never headed towards an exit so fast. It's been four months since that night and it still freaks me out when I have to enter a tall building.'

He shook his head.

'Bit of a handicap in New York, right?'

'Don't beat yourself up,' she said. 'That was one hell of an ordeal you guys went through. To bounce straight back from that into an everyday routine was never going to be easy. It'll get better in time.'

She paused.

'And everyone's afraid of something. It isn't sensible, or rational, it's just what it is. Fear's nothing to be ashamed of. It doesn't make you a coward; it's what makes you human.'

Standing beside him, she looked down the cabin and smiled, nodding at Josh.

'He's terrified of spiders,' she said, looking at Archer's partner who was fast asleep, his large frame almost overflowing the seat in the pod. 'Put him up against big dangerous suspects resisting arrest and he won't even breathe heavy. But tell him there's a spider anywhere near him and you watch him jump around like a schoolgirl on Halloween.'

Archer glanced at her and grinned. 'Are you serious? I never knew.'

'He keeps it quiet. You know what some of the guys are like in the Bureau; he'd be finding spiders everywhere.'

Still smiling, Archer turned his attention to Shepherd, who was awake and studying Stanovich and Payan's files, lost in concentration with his back to them.

'I can't imagine much frightens Shep,' he said, lowering his voice even though it was unlikely he'd hear over the noise of the aircraft.

'Horses.'

'What?'

'Horses, I swear to God. I took a call with him once to Central Park and discovered that little secret when a series of horse-drawn carriages rolled by.'

This time Archer laughed. 'Where the hell does that come from?'

'God only knows.'

'So what are you afraid of?' he asked her.

She didn't reply. Turning, he watched her smile fade.

'Hospitals.'

Archer paused.

'Why?' he eventually asked.

She thought for a moment, then forced a smile.

'That's a story for another day.'

Standing beside her, Archer didn't push it, feeling guilty that he'd stirred a memory in her that clearly made her uncomfortable. He glanced at his fellow detective and close friend; Marquez was a tough, guarded woman and there was a lot about her he didn't know.

He treasured his own privacy but she valued hers like solid gold.

'What's the most afraid you've ever been?' he asked quietly.

She paused, considering it. 'Four months ago. Had a gun pulled on me from behind. Thought that was it.' She nodded at Josh again. 'Thankfully he showed up just in time.'

'He has a habit of doing that.'

'What about you?'

'When I was a kid,' Archer said. 'Eight years old.'

She tilted her head, surprised. 'Not something from when you were a cop?'

'This was way worse.'

'What happened?'

'I was with one of my friends in a park in London, goofing around on a Sunday. His older brother had told him about a trick the night before that we thought was cool. Mix some strips of aluminium foil with bleach, seal a bottle and shake it and you've got a home-made cracker bomb.'

He paused.

'We were going to try it out there in the park. Apparently there was about a ten second gap between shaking the bleach before it reacted with the foil and went off, so we shook it up, left it on the grass and took off for cover to watch.'

He shook his head.

'But the groundsman saw us do it and ran over. We tried shouting at him to stop but he kept coming closer, walking right up towards the bottle. I stepped out from where we were hiding and started running towards him but it was too late. The bleach blew up right in front of him.'

He paused.

'I'll never forget running over and seeing him just lying there, burning chemicals all over his face and arms. My friend ran for help. When an ambulance came they took the man to intensive care. It was touch and go whether he was going to make it, and I stayed there all night with my mother waiting for the man to wake up.'

He exhaled, taken back twenty years.

'Longest night of my life. Every second, I thought that nurse was going to reappear telling us that he died.'

'Did he make it?' she asked.

Archer nodded. 'He pulled through.'

'What happened to him?'

'I don't know.'

He paused, lost in thought.

'That was the most afraid I've ever been. Well, until today I guess.'

'We'll find her.'

'If she's still alive.'

'Hey; don't even think that. Not for a second. She's a fighter, Arch. She'll hang in there. And last time you were dealing with it all on your own.'

She motioned to herself then Josh and Shepherd.

'This time you have us. And we're not going anywhere until we get her back.'

Another period of silence followed. Then Marquez checked her watch.

'We're landing in an hour. I need to fill out the immigration card.'

Beside them, a wicker basket had been left on top of the counter to their right, some sandwiches in packaging and muffins wrapped in plastic resting in the centre. Taking a sandwich, she passed it to him.

'Eat something. You're gonna need the fuel.'

'I had breakfast.'

'No, you didn't.'

He smiled as Marquez waited, undeterred. Then he took the food.

'What would I do without you?'

'Get trapped in a building with a load of people trying to kill you,' she said. 'Probably.'

Squeezing his arm, she walked away back down the aisle to her seat, pulling a pen from her pocket.

Hospitals, he heard her voice echo in his head as he watched her go.

*

They landed right on time at Heathrow, 6:15pm UK time, the English weather outside the window similar to that back in New York, bright and warm with the early evening sun casting a golden glow over the airfield as they touched down. Once they taxied into Terminal Five and the pilot thanked the passengers over the intercom for flying with the airline, the four NYPD detectives unclipped their seatbelts, grabbed their hand luggage and then made their way off the Boeing jet, quickly heading towards Immigration.

Given Archer's dual nationality, he was through to the other side swiftly and waited for the other three to pass through the Non-UK and EU nationals aisles and join him. They did so before the main queues had really started to form behind them, another benefit of a seat further up the plane, and as the trio joined up with him he saw the focus on each face, matching his own.

Now through Border Control, the group navigated their way towards an automated exit that led into the large glass Arrivals Hall of Heathrow Terminal Five. As they walked through the double doors, they saw a line of eager people behind a long barrier to their left, some family members waiting for loved ones, business people waiting for colleagues and chauffeurs holding up signs for clients.

Then, to his surprise, Archer saw two people he recognised. They were standing in the middle of the hall, both looking up at the flight board, Danny White, aka Chalky, and Ryan Fox, members of the ARU's First Team and two of Archer's closest friends.

Chalky was Archer's age, twenty eight, and although a similar build to his best friend he possessed very different colouring, with brown eyes

63

and dark hair. As it was summer he was tanned, making him look almost Mediterranean and a real contrast to Fox beside him, who was five years older, had sandy blond hair and was whippier, almost a physical representation of his animal name-sake. Both men were naturally light-hearted and always good company, but they were also as tough as nails. Each had taken bullets for the Unit before, and although he'd absorbed a huge amount of punishment in the last several years Archer had never been shot, so in that regard both old friends had something on him which they never failed to remind him.

Archer saw they were both dressed in jeans and a navy blue polo shirt with the ARU logo in white on the left side of the chest, police uniform but not their tactical gear. Each also had his sidearm, a Glock 17 in a holster on his hip, which meant they must have cleared their presence with the Heathrow police before they entered the building. Turning, Chalky suddenly saw the NYPD quartet and hit Fox on the shoulder, who popped a last piece of a chocolate bar into his mouth and swivelled to face the approaching four detectives, stuffing the wrapper into his pocket.

Archer took the lead and the two groups met up beneath an Arrivals board.

'Look who's back,' Chalky said, giving Archer a bear hug. 'Twelve months on and still so damn ugly.'

Briefly returning the hug, Archer stepped back, waiting for the mocking comment that normally followed.

'That's it?' he said. 'No more insults?'

'I'll let you off today,' Chalky said.

Once Archer and Fox exchanged a similar greeting, Archer turned to make introductions.

'Guys, this is Chalky and Fox. You two, this is Josh Blake, Lisa Marquez and Matt Shepherd, our NYPD sergeant.'

They all shook hands and exchanged greetings. Apart from Josh and Chalky, none of them had met each other before and it was a surreal moment for Archer as his past and present suddenly collided.

'Your analyst called and gave Cobb a full debrief,' Chalky said to Shepherd after shaking his hand. 'We've just been stood down after a month-long operation so we're free to help unless a major threat comes in. Cobb's volunteered our HQ for you to use as your base.'

'He's got a number of our team working on this already,' Fox said. 'And he sent the two of us over here to pick you up.'

'We appreciate it,' Shepherd said, nodding to the two men. 'Thanks.'

'Any progress on Stanovich and Payan's location?' Marquez asked.

Fox nodded as he turned and headed towards the exit, the group walking with him.

'The Met took a call forty minutes ago from Stanovich at 5:50pm. It was diverted to us.'

'What did he say?' Archer asked.

'Apparently he has Vargas somewhere in the city. He knows that she's an NYPD detective too; he wants two million pounds by 8pm or he kills her.'

'Proof of life?' Archer asked.

Fox shook his head. 'Afraid not.'

'You get a trace?' Shepherd asked, as they approached the exit to the Terminal.

'We did. He called from a housing estate in Brixton,' Chalky said. 'It's a neighbourhood in the south of the city on the other side of the Thames. Cobb sent the rest of the task force over there to take him down.'

He turned to Archer.

'Porter's leading the raid.'

'So are we heading over there?' Marquez asked.

Chalky shook his head. 'Our guys will handle it. Cobb wants us all back at HQ. Now you're here, we'll set up a command post and get a real time update.'

The NYPD team all nodded, pleased there'd been a development and moved through the doors quickly, not wanting to waste a second. As he followed Chalky and Fox with the others towards the short-stay parking area, Archer pictured his old friend Porter and the rest of the task force guys preparing to breach Stanovich's location.

By the time they were done with him, the Slovakian would be begging to hand Vargas back.

EIGHT

Across London at the Brixton council estate, an ARU task force officer nicknamed Shifty was tucked in close to a wall inside an apartment adjacent to the one Stanovich's ransom call had originated from.

Dressed in street clothes so as not to attract suspicion when he'd arrived with another officer ten minutes before, Shifty had made a tiny incision through the wall with a special drill designed for the purpose and had fed a miniature fibre-optic camera on the other end of the wire through the gap. The apartment behind him was quiet and empty; the two residents had been ushered outside, both now sitting in an unmarked police car and being reassured by two undercover Met firearms officers who'd arrived as back-up.

Alone in the apartment, Shifty was holding a small portable screen in his hand; there was a movable control stick on the box with a wire connected to the side that led into the wall beside him.

Controlling the angle of the feed with the stick and working silently, he studied the screen in his hands.

He saw a man standing with his back to the wall inside the living room. The room around the guy was rudimentary in its furnishings, several chairs and an old couch; there was a landline phone sitting on a table beside him but there was no sign of anyone else in the apartment, no indication that the missing detective was here.

Shifty studied the screen. The man next door was lean and tall, dressed in white Adidas tracksuit

67

trousers and a matching zipped-up top, early evening sun filtering in through the windows behind him, an old pizza box beside his left foot.

He was also about six foot five with a shaved head. Milo Stanovich.

Got you, you son of a bitch, Shifty thought.

Keeping hold of the screen with his left hand, he slowly slid his hand to a pressel switch by his sternum, hooked up to a Velcro microphone already strapped around his neck and connected to the earpiece tucked into his ear.

'This is Shifty,' he whispered. *'Eyes on the living space.'*

'What do you see?' Porter's voice asked, the ARU sergeant and head of the task force.

'Stanovich is alone, far end of the room, back to the window.'

Shifty paused, studying the screen in his hand.

He gently increased the focus on the suspect, searching for any evidence of handguns or knives.

'Could be carrying a weapon, but I can't see one.'

'Any sign of Detective Vargas?'

'No. Not yet.'

'Spitz, report,' Porter said.

'I'm the other side. She's not in the bedroom or bathroom. Looks like Stanovich is the only person here.'

'The front door?'

'It's clear, Port. No tripwires or traps.'

Down in the car park, Porter heard this and nodded.

They were good to go.

Sitting in the front passenger seat of a 4x4 BMW, he and the two other men in the car with him were dressed in their combat police gear, navy blue fatigues, black boots and bulletproof tac vests carrying stun grenades, pliers, plastic handcuffs and spare ammunition for the weapons they were carrying. Each man had a Glock 17 slotted into a holster clipped around his thigh and the officer in the back seat was cradling a Remington 12 gauge shotgun, Porter and the other man armed with a Heckler and Koch MP5 sub-machine gun.

There was another ARU BMW parked beside them in the apartment block courtyard with three other officers dressed in the same gear sitting inside.

All of them were looking at Porter, waiting for the order to move.

He checked his watch; 6:29pm. Stanovich was demanding the money by 8pm, so they had an hour and a half at their disposal. He and the other guys had all been at the Unit this morning when the call came in from the Counter-Terrorism Bureau in New York informing Cobb that an NYPD detective had been kidnapped and the two perpetrators were thought to be in London. Porter had been in Cobb's office with him when he received the call and both men had been confused as to why it had been directed to them, a counter-terrorist unit.

Cobb had been about to redirect the man to CID when the American analyst had revealed that the kidnapped NYPD detective they were trying to locate was both a team-mate of Sam Archer and his girlfriend, which is why he'd called them specifically. He'd added that four detectives from the Bureau, including Archer, were already on their way to London on Lieutenant Franklin's orders.

And the analyst had asked if the ARU could help.

The decision was already made before the man hung up; although the Unit had their usual work to attend to, MI5, the Met and SCO19 could more than cover it at the moment and Cobb was determined to do what he could. To everyone who'd known him from his time there, Archer's memory lingered large in the Unit but Cobb and Porter particularly held their old colleague in special regard.

He'd saved their lives once and neither man would ever forget it.

When he'd passed all this information on to the rest of the ARU, Cobb had received his team's unanimous support in doing what they could to assist the NYPD team headed their way. Nine hours later, Porter leaned forward and looked up at the 2nd floor of the apartment block. Seeing as the ARU was a counter-terrorism Unit sex-traffickers weren't their usual target, but the Slovakian man upstairs in 2F had kidnapped Arch's girlfriend and threatened to kill her, which was the biggest mistake he'd ever made.

Porter pushed the circular switch on the front of his tac vest, the other officers waiting for his call.

'Listen up,' he said. 'We move fast and clean. She's probably hidden in there somewhere, so clear every room quickly. Once he's in cuffs, we'll find her.'

He turned to the officer in the back seat behind him holding the shotgun, but still held down his pressel switch so the other guys could hear his orders.

'The door might be reinforced, so Mason, you'll blow the lock. I'll take point. Hold your fire unless he makes a move but get him in handcuffs ASAP. We need this guy alive to find out where he's hidden the girl.'

Mason nodded; Porter paused.

'Go.'

The car doors immediately opened, the six officers stepping out, closing them quietly then moving to the stairs. They climbed them quickly, the stairwell filled with the sound of boots on concrete, Porter moving behind Mason who was at the front of the line and carrying his shotgun with a breaching round in the chamber.

As the group arrived on the 2nd floor, Spitz and Shifty appeared from the apartments either side of Stanovich's, each man in plain clothes but wearing a tac vest and also carrying a fully-loaded MP5 with a Glock strapped around their thigh like the others.

Moving smoothly and quietly, the eight-man team came to a halt outside the apartment, several curtains on grille-covered windows elsewhere in the block flickering as residents watched.

Kneeling to one side of the door, Mason didn't wait a second.

He put the shotgun against the lock immediately and fired.

The blast annihilated the mechanism and the door was smashed back a moment later, the counter-terrorist police team piling in through the door one by one in a well-practised drill, looking down the sights of their weapons and already familiar with the layout of the place from the schematics they'd studied minutes earlier.

'Police!' they all shouted. *'Get down!'*

As three of the officers split, checking the other rooms for Detective Vargas, Payan or any other occupants they might have missed, Porter took the lead, training the sights of his MP5 on the tall frame of Stanovich clearly visible through the open door to the sitting room.

The Slovakian hadn't moved since they arrived, standing right where Shifty had said he was in the sitting room with his back to the wall. He'd been taken completely by surprise and his eyes were wide with fear as he stared at the police team, nothing around him save a table to his right and an old pizza box on the floor to his left, the room stinking of sweat and greasy food.

'Get your hands up and get down on the ground!' Porter bellowed, the sights of his MP5 on the man's chin, aiming at the brain stem.

Staring at them, Stanovich didn't move, keeping his hands by his side.

Sweat glistened on his brow and neck, having already stained the collar of the zipped-up tracksuit top.

'I said get your hands up!' Porter ordered again, Mason beside him with his shotgun trained on the sex-trafficker, the two men covering the Slovakian.

'Do it!' Mason bellowed.

'I can't!' Stanovich whispered in an Eastern European accent, looking at the two men with wide desperate eyes. *'Help me.'*

Looking at the man's face through the sights of the MP5, Porter suddenly paused.

Stanovich stared back at him, his eyes as wide as dinner plates.

He was standing rigid, just as if he was on a parade ground and had been suddenly called to attention.

Something about this was wrong.

As Mason kept his shotgun on the man and the rest of the team cleared the residence, Porter stared at the Slovakian.

Then he stepped to the side, looking behind the tall suspect. There was nothing back there.

But then something caught Porter's attention.

Tilting his head, he saw two strands of something reflect the dying sunlight from the window. They glistened like the fine threads of a spider's web.

Peering closer, Porter saw they were two thin translucent wires. One end of each was hooked around Stanovich's wrists.

The other ends were attached to the radiator behind him below the window.

Porter froze, staring at them. The wires were drawn tight, almost at breaking point, and vibrated slightly as Stanovich shook with fear.

'Clear!' someone shouted from the bathroom.

'Clear!' another voice called from the bedroom.

Porter didn't respond, moving back and focusing on Stanovich. His tracksuit top was zipped up all the way, despite the heat.

It was concealing something underneath.

'Open it,' Porter said quietly, not taking his eyes off Stanovich, Mason keeping his shotgun on the man's head.

'I can't,' Stanovich whispered again, sweat running into his eyes as he looked down at his hands tied to the radiator with the threads.

As the other officers joined him, keeping their weapons trained on Stanovich, Porter stepped forward slowly, keeping his MP5 trained on the man with his right hand.

He used his left to unzip the garment, Stanovich quivering as six more weapons were aimed at him from just a couple of feet away as the rest of the task force joined Porter and Mason.

As the zip reached the bottom, the two sides of the tracksuit top parted.

And Porter froze.

Stanovich was wearing a vest packed tight with TNT and several rectangular bags of thick nails.

'Holy shit!' Mason said, staring at the explosives.

Examining the device, Porter saw the thin translucent wires wrapped around Stanovich's wrists and the radiator were leading into a detonator stuck beside the red sticks of TNT.

And a light on the front was glowing red.

Porter's attention snapped up to Stanovich's face, who was trembling, the wires connecting him to the radiator at breaking point.

'Look,' Stanovich whispered, his eyes darting to Porter's right.

The ARU sergeant snapped his head over his shoulder and saw a circular webcam mounted on the wall behind them to the right, aimed directly at the Slovakian.

They were being watched.

'Everybody out!' Porter shouted, turning and pushing his men towards the door immediately.

Across the city, the Middle Eastern man with the broken nose was watching the webcam feed from a laptop inside a car, a detonator resting beside the keypad. Beside him, the South African was also observing the screen from the driver's seat.

74

Seeing the police task force turn and run for the door, they both smiled.

The trap had worked.

'Goodbye,' the Middle Eastern man said quietly.

And a split-second later, he pushed the detonation switch.

NINE

The two cars made it to the ARU HQ in just over thirty minutes; the journey should have taken longer due to the Saturday early-evening traffic but Chalky and Fox activated the police lights in the front and rear fenders of their two BMWs, clearing a path as vehicles moved out of their way. Archer and Josh rode with Chalky, Shepherd and Marquez with Fox, and the conversation in both cars was minimal, everyone saving their energy and focus for what was coming next.

In the lead BMW, Chalky eventually pulled to a halt in front of a white barrier outside the ARU headquarters in the north of the city. To the left of the barrier was a guard hut and the grey-haired man stationed inside pushed a button to lift the bar, giving Chalky a thumbs up which he acknowledged with a nod. With Fox close behind, the two cars drove in and parked side by side in a couple of empty spaces on the left, ten yards or so from the front of the building.

Everyone stepped out, slamming the doors, and then followed Fox and Chalky as they took the lead and headed towards the entrance. As Archer walked behind them, memories suddenly flooded back as he looked up at his old home, feeling as if he'd just found a stack of old photographs hidden away that he hadn't seen for a year. He hadn't been back since he left last May but the ARU HQ hadn't changed. It was a two storey building shaped in a reverse L, the Operations area on the 1st floor and the interrogation cells, locker room and gun-cage on the ground floor, along the long corridor that led towards the rear of the building.

Although the Unit had only been in existence for three years, they'd been attacked here in the past, so an urgent redesign of the building had taken place just before Archer had left which meant it was now more like a fortress, each section designed as an isolated unit. Every pane of glass was bulletproof, a guard stationed on both the gate and inside the entrance and a well-stocked armoury to provide sufficient firepower for the ten task force officers who worked out of the Unit.

Glancing up as he walked, Archer caught a glimpse of one of the rotors of the Unit's black helicopter. The sight of the vessel stirred a memory from a rainy night in April the year before and he subconsciously touched a thin jagged scar hidden under his hairline that ran from the middle of his brow down to his left temple.

'Home sweet home,' Chalky said as they approached the door.

Behind him, looking up at the chopper's rotor, Archer didn't reply.

As Fox pulled open the front door and the group walked inside, Archer saw a Perspex glass panel had been set up between the entrance and the access to the rest of the building beyond, an extra precaution to prevent unwanted intruders. An officer he didn't recognise was sitting behind a desk, protected by another layer of bulletproof glass. The man looked young and friendly but also brisk and professional, brown haired, somewhere in his mid-twenties.

Seeing the group, the man pushed a button and the panel blocking off the interior of the building slid back.

'This is Lipton,' Chalky said, the man raising his hand in welcome as the group nodded a greeting to him. 'Any progress, Lip?'

He nodded. 'You better all get up there. Something's happened.'

'In Brixton?'

'I'm not sure. But I heard the commotion from down here.'

Without a word, the group walked up the stairs quickly, and after arriving on the second level they walked down a short corridor parallel to the car park, entering the Operations floor.

Up ahead on the right was the tech area, a hub of desks, computers, screens and expensive equipment where the analyst team resided. A series of monitors were mounted on the walls, a large centred widescreen dominating the space amongst a series of smaller ones. To the newcomers' left through an open door and overlooking the car park was the Briefing Room where the ten-man task force normally gathered, using it as their rec space between operations. Right then Archer saw it was empty, all of the task force apart from Chalky and Fox taking part in the raid at Stanovich's address in Brixton.

To their immediate right was Cobb's office, a room walled with reinforced bulletproof glass which oversaw the tech area, but at that moment he wasn't inside. Directly ahead, Archer saw his old boss standing with the analysts, his back to the newly-arrived team and as yet unaware of their presence. Forty one years old, six foot two inches tall and Director of the ARU, Cobb looked as he always had, smartly dressed in a sharp dark suit and wearing

78

polished black shoes, his dark brown hair expensively cut and combed neatly back.

Although he had his back to the newcomers, Archer immediately registered Cobb's tense body language. Everyone in the room was focused on the main television screen and were watching it so intently that none of them noticed the newcomers arrive.

Archer's eyes immediately flicked up to the screen.

The images were an aerial view from a chopper, hovering above a council estate tower block.

And one of the apartments was on fire.

*

'It was a trap,' the lead analyst Nikki said moments later. 'And we walked right into it.'

The newcomers had moved forward into the tech area, Cobb realising they'd arrived; he shook hands with Shepherd quickly, nodding to the others, but immediately returned his attention to the screen, no time right now for extended welcomes. Standing beside Shepherd and Cobb, Archer made eye contact with Nikki; a slender, dark-haired thirty year old wearing a slim pair of glasses over her nose. She managed the briefest of smiles as their eyes met but looked just about as worried as Archer had ever seen her.

'A trap?' Chalky said. 'What do you mean?'

'Stanovich was waiting inside for them,' Nikki said. 'When the guys were all in the apartment, the entire place blew.'

'Was Vargas inside?' Archer asked.

'We don't know.'

As Chalky stared at her, everyone else looked at the screen; below the footage of the burning apartment was a gut-churning headline.

Breaking: Large explosion at Brixton council estate. Members of counter-terrorist police team feared dead.

'Casualties?' Fox asked.

'All,' Nikki said. 'And two fatalities.'

'Who?' Chalky asked quickly.

'Mason and Spitz,' Cobb said quietly.

Staring at his boss, Chalky didn't reply. Beside him, Fox and Archer were just as stunned as he was. They'd each known Mason and Spitz for a long time; Chalky and Fox had left them in the Briefing Room before they'd headed to the airport.

Now they were gone.

'Wait a moment,' Shepherd said, confused and looking at the news report. 'Stanovich was inside when it blew?'

Nikki nodded. 'But listen to this.'

She tapped a few keys and playback of the raid sounded around the Operations area. It was normal procedure to record the radio chatter and exchanges on raids and armed entries so there was no confusion during the debriefs and filling out of reports; it was also insurance in case their procedure was challenged later.

The moment the recording started, the room became completely silent.

'*Police!*' they all heard. *'Get down!'*

There was a flurry of activity, the sound of pounding feet and doors being breached, orders being shouted.

'Get your hands up and get down on the ground!' a voice shouted.

Porter, Archer instantly thought.

A gentle giant, known for never swearing, and an old friend.

'I said get your hands up!' Porter repeated.

'Do it!' someone else shouted.

Pause.

There was some smashing and faint murmuring.

'Open it,' Porter's voice ordered.

'I can't.'

There was another pause, and a rustle.

No one in the tech area moved, listening to the recording.

Pause.

'Holy shit!' the second voice said.

'Look.'

Pause.

'Everybody out!' Porter's voice shouted.

There was a sound of fast movement.

And a terrifying blast a split-second before the recording went dead.

'Stanovich knew we'd trace the call,' Nikki said, turning in her chair to face them after a small period of silence. 'He must have rigged the property to blow once our guys were inside.'

'But he was in there too,' Marquez said, shaking her head. 'Why the hell would he kill himself if he knew you were coming? Why not booby-trap the apartment and leave?'

'Nik, can you run the tape back?' Archer suddenly asked.

She nodded. 'To where?'

'Just after they entered. When Port ordered Stanovich to get his hands up.'

She turned to the screen and traced back to the entry, then ran the recording again.

'Get your hands up!'

'Do it!'

Following the two orders and amongst the smashing and shouts of *Police*, there was a whisper of sound.

Someone had said something.

'Pause,' Archer said.

'Who was that?' Josh said, as Nikki stopped the tape. 'Stanovich?'

Archer looked at Nikki. 'Can you rewind and isolate?'

She nodded, winding the recording back. Tapping away on her keypad, she cleared the police shouts and background noise, leaving just the faint murmur.

'Here we go,' she said, hitting *Play*.

The recording ran through again but with only the faint murmur; however, it was still too quiet to be distinguishable. The group all frowned as they strained to hear, missing what was said.

'Amplify, Nikki,' Cobb said, standing beside Shepherd with his arms folded.

She rewound, tapped a few more keys then ran the recording again.

This time it was loud enough.

'I can't,' the amplified whisper said. *'Help me.'*

'That's Stanovich,' Nikki said, pushing *Pause* again as the others nodded in agreement.

'Help me?' Josh said. 'What the hell is he talking about? He's the one who kidnapped Vargas and

82

threatened to kill her. What did he expect your guys to do?'

No one replied. The news feed was still focusing on the blasted-out apartment, smoke continuing to billow up into the sky, the circling helicopter capturing the footage.

As more thoughts and questions raced through his mind, Archer stared up at the screen.

Eight of his friends had just been taken out in the blink of an eye, two of them dead, and one of Vargas' kidnappers had just killed himself.

And he didn't even want to consider the possibility that Vargas had been somewhere in that apartment.

As Chalky and Fox stood there silently beside him, everyone watching the screen, Archer heard Stanovich's whisper echo in his mind.

I can't.

Help me.

Stanovich was dead.

So where the hell was Payan?

TEN

At that moment in a house across North London, Ibrahim Payan was sitting pushed up against a wall, staring down at a silenced pistol that was jammed into his mouth. Having been on the wrong side of the law for almost his entire adult life Payan wasn't a man who scared easily, but at that moment he was beyond terrified, doing his best to breathe around the greasy oiled barrel of the suppressor as his eyes readjusted to the light.

He was sitting inside the sitting room of some house he'd never been in before, bound to a chair, his arms and feet strapped to the frame. He'd been here for over a day; yesterday afternoon he'd unlocked his apartment and walked straight into an ambush, three men lying in wait for him. One shoved a pistol into his face, a second closed the door behind him and the third hit him over the back of the head hard before he could react.

Dazed and groggy, he'd tried to fight back, but he'd been pinned down and injected with something, passing out moments later.

He'd woken up this morning, duct-taped to a chair with a strip of tape over his mouth and a cloth bag over his head. He'd strained at the binds, trying to loosen them, but they were too tight and he'd soon given up realising it was hopeless, spending the rest of the day fighting to breathe inside the confines of the bag.

Only one person had come into the house all day, and that was early this morning. Pulling the bag and gag off, the man had withdrawn Payan's phone and ordered him to call his girlfriend and tell her he'd been out of town for the night but would see her later. The temptation to somehow use the opportunity to ask Mischa for help had been enormous, but the razor-sharp flick knife to his throat had persuaded him otherwise.

After that brief conversation, the man had replaced the tape, put the bag back over Payan's head and departed.

No one else had entered the house all day.

However, someone had arrived a minute or so ago. Payan had heard the lock being opened on the front entrance, a brief sound of cars on the street outside, then heard the sound of the front door being closed, followed shortly by footsteps walking into the room. Just seconds ago the bag over his head had been pulled off, his eyes burning from the sudden light, but before they could adjust the suppressor to a silenced pistol was shoved into his mouth, the silencer grinding against his lips and teeth as it was rammed inside.

As his eyes adjusted to the light, he saw two men standing in front of him, neither of whom he'd ever seen before. The one holding the pistol was Middle Eastern and somewhere in his thirties; he was brown-skinned, his face a woven patchwork of scar tissue, the texture patchy and translucent from what looked like horrific burns. The man was dressed in cream-coloured khakis and a loose black shirt, the sleeves rolled up and revealing more of those disfiguring scars.

Looking at his face, Payan saw dark rings under the man's eyes, the cause of which looked to be a badly broken nose. He had a strip of tape over the top and it was swollen and bruised. The guy stared down at Payan impassively, his knuckles tight around the grip of the pistol.

Beside him, his companion didn't have the same burn scars or broken nose but he looked just as tough and uncompromising; he was blond and stocky, dressed in a dark shirt and khakis with a pistol in a holster on his hip. Wearing a thin set of latex gloves, he was sitting on a chair just to the side of Payan and was dialling a number into the landline beside them. He also had his sleeves rolled up in response to the early evening heat, revealing thick tanned forearms ridged with muscle and criss-crossed with a variety of scars.

His heart racing and struggling to breathe around the suppressor, Payan watched the blond man finish dialling a number. The guy then pushed the loudspeaker button and held up a piece of paper with instructions written on the sheet, pointing at it and looking straight into Payan's eyes.

'When they answer, you say this,' the man said, his accent South African and gravelly. 'One wrong word, you die, my friend.'

The man with the burn scars and broken nose pulled back the hammer on the pistol to emphasise the point, and Payan's eyes widened in terror. As the call connected, the man kept the pistol where it was then pulled it out, Payan immediately taking deep lungfuls of air.

The Middle Eastern guy then held the silencer an inch from the terrified Slovakian's face, pushing the suppressor into his forehead.

'One wrong word,' he repeated, echoing his partner's warning as Payan looked at the sheet of paper in the South African's hand.

At the ARU HQ, the group was still gathered in Operations and watching the news feed when the phone on Nikki's desk started ringing.

She scooped up the receiver in one smooth motion, not taking her eyes off the television above her desk.

'Carter.'

A beat later, she froze.

Turning to Cobb immediately, she pointed to the receiver and then at Payan's mug-shot quickly on her computer screen, catching everyone's attention. As she started a trace on her computer keypad with her left hand, she pushed the button for the loudspeaker with her forefinger and placed the phone back on the cradle.

'Can you repeat that?' she said.

'You...heard me,' a man with an Eastern European accent said. *'Did you like...what I left you...in Brixton?'*

Payan, Archer thought, standing beside Fox and Chalky.

The second kidnapper.

A complete silence fell over Operations as everyone in the room listened intently to the call, the report on the television playing silently on the screen above their heads.

'Is that Payan?' Cobb said.

'Yes.'

'All we want is to get Detective Vargas back. We'll do what you say. What do you want?'

'Stan...Stanovich told you what I want. Money. I...knew you'd try to kill...me. I had to send a...message.'

87

Looking at Marquez, Archer frowned. The man had a bizarre, monotone way of talking; his speech was staccato and abrupt, as if he was struggling with the words, delays between the sentences.

At her desk, Nikki turned to Cobb and held up her fingers, mouthing *ten seconds*. On the computer screen behind her, Archer saw the numbers of the software she was using counting down beside Payan's mug-shot, the red circle tracking the call contracting by the second.

As he looked at the map, his stomach jolted.

The call was coming from somewhere nearby.

'So you want two million pounds?' Cobb said, watching the trace countdown and speaking slowly. 'Tell me where and how we can deliver that to you.'

'I'll...call you b...back with an account n...number.'

'Wait!' Archer said, as Nikki frantically motioned at them to keep talking.

Pause.

'Let us talk to Vargas. A proof of life.'

He paused.

'If you want us to do what you want, we need to know that she's OK.'

There was a pause followed by some kind of shuffling noise.

Then the call went dead.

'Did you get it?' Cobb asked Nikki as they all stared at her screen.

'Yes, sir,' Nikki said, checking the screen and looking at the tight red circle drawn in up close on the city map. 'He's in Hendon. Fifteen minutes from here.'

'Call EOD and SCO19,' Cobb ordered two of the other analysts. 'I want them both at the scene immediately. Warn them that the house will probably be rigged up with explosives just like the other.'

As Nikki studied the map and the other analysts got to work, Archer leaned forward and noted the address. Without a word, he turned and quickly headed for the stairs, not waiting for orders and intent on finding Vargas himself.

Cobb saw him leave and guessing where he was headed, turned to Fox.

'Give him a lift.'

'Yes, sir,' he said, turning and following Archer.

Beside Cobb, Shepherd turned to Marquez and Josh. 'Both of you go with them. And this time we need that son of a bitch alive.'

Inside the house in Hendon, the blond South African rose from his chair and stuffed the piece of paper into his pocket, having ended the call. The Middle Eastern man with the burn scars didn't move, keeping the silenced pistol an inch from Payan's face.

'Did they get it?' he asked.

'They got it,' the South African said, checking his watch. 'You heard them trying to keep us on the line. They'll have the trace.'

The Middle Eastern man smiled.

'It's game time,' he said. 'Call Finchley and tell him to let the bitch loose. The cops will be so distracted they'll never realise what she's doing.'

The South African nodded, pulling his cell phone and scrolling for a number as he turned and headed for the door. Watching him go, Payan remaining strapped to the chair, staring at the pistol an inch from his face.

'I did…what you asked,' the Slovakian managed to get out, staring up at the silencer for the handgun. 'You should let me go.'

The man with the broken nose looked down at his captive for a moment.

Then he grinned, the grafted skin on his face crinkling up and gathering around the dark rings under his eyes.

'You're not going anywhere.'

ELEVEN

Less than a minute later, an ARU BMW carrying Fox, Archer, Marquez and Josh was weaving through North London, heading for Hendon. Behind the wheel, Fox had begun the journey at his normal relentless speed, the lights on the front and rear of the car activated and traffic moving out of their way hastily as he cut his way through as if he was going for pole on a race track, but before long their progress became stop-start. As Nikki had said, Hendon was normally a fifteen minute journey but unlike the journey from the airport, the streets were narrower here and clogged with evening traffic, the thick congestion meaning a lot of vehicles in front had nowhere to go to get out of the way of the police car.

In the front passenger seat, Archer sat impatiently as the journey passed by agonisingly slowly, willing the BMW to find a way through. There was no other police vehicle following them; Shepherd had remained behind at HQ with Cobb, the two men finally having a chance to trade information, and Chalky had stayed too. Archer knew his best friend better than anyone and he'd seen from his face how hard he'd taken Mason's and Spitz' deaths. Chalky had always been the loose cannon beside Archer's straight shot, which was one of the reasons they were such good friends and worked so well together, but that joviality and light-hearted nature had a flip-side that not many people saw. Death devastated Chalky; it always had done. It was an unexpected side to his friend that was endearing but also hard to watch.

As Fox worked his way through the streets, the journey still stop-start despite the flashing police lights, he made a left turn and they suddenly found themselves at the back of another stream of stationary traffic.

'Shit,' he said, pressing the button to call Nikki, using the hands-free equipment.

As she answered, Archer looked at the panel terminal inside the car and saw their position on the map.

'We're only halfway there, Nik,' Fox said, the call on speakerphone so all four in the car could hear. 'Traffic's a bitch.'

'It's OK; SCO19 and EOD are almost at the scene. They'll clear the area and set up a perimeter. I told Brookins you're on your way so he's expecting you; he's going to rig up a command post with EOD and assess the situation. No one's just going to walk into this one.'

Fox nodded. 'I'll call you back.'

Ending the call, he cursed, looking at the traffic ahead.

'This is taking too long.'

'Tell me about it,' Archer muttered beside him.

Back at the ARU's HQ, the time was just approaching 7pm. The barrier at the front entrance had been lowered now Fox and the other three had left, everyone else still inside the building, the car park lined with vehicles but empty of human activity.

As the setting sun reflected golden light off the windows of the surrounding office buildings, a black Ford drove down the street and pulled up outside the

ARU's front barrier, coming to the end of a journey that had started across town in Kensington.

There were two people in the car, a man and a woman. Reaching across from his seat behind the wheel, the man slipped his hands inside the woman's coat for a moment, then withdrew his fingers and tightened the belt.

In the passenger seat, ARU analyst Jenny Beckett sat there in silence staring straight ahead, her eyes red rimmed from tears, her lip trembling.

'Get out,' the man ordered.

Beckett hesitated for a moment.

The man stared at her.

Then she pushed open her door and stepped out unsteadily.

The moment she shut the door, the Ford moved off down the street, turning and disappearing out of sight. Watching it go, Beckett turned and looked at the ARU building. It was a summer evening but even so, she was wearing a well-cut thin cream overcoat over her dark trousers and white shirt. Given the heat, it was a somewhat odd choice of clothing, but she'd always dressed stylishly and tonight was no different.

Feeling as if she was about to faint, she walked forwards slowly and approached the gap beside the barrier, her high heels clicking on the concrete.

The guard on the front gate, a pleasant fifty four year old man called Wilson, nodded when he saw her.

'Evening Jen,' he called through the glass.

She didn't even notice him, walking slowly past his hut. The distance to the front entrance of the building wasn't far, but at that moment it stretched out in front of her as if it would never end.

She paused for a moment, trying to gather herself and not break down, and then continued on, thinking of her children as she began the walk across the car park towards the ARU HQ.

By the time the ARU BMW turned onto the residential road outside the house in Hendon, the four people inside saw that the EOD and SCO19 teams had already established themselves on the street, setting up a defensive perimeter and surrounding the house where the call from Payan had originated. EOD was the city's bomb disposal unit, SCO19 the other main counter-terrorism task force; both units were highly professional, more than a match for a single Slovakian sex-trafficker.

The SCO19 team was surrounding the house, the street already cleared of pedestrians who were being held back behind hastily drawn-up tape. EOD were beside their truck in the road, a group of their specialists gathered together beside SC019 in a command post, set up between two cars and facing the house.

Passing through the police cordon in the BMW after showing his ID, Fox drew to a halt and the group stepped out, the three NYPD detectives following Fox who strode towards the burly SCO19 sergeant at the command post beside the bomb-disposal team on the street. Archer recognised the man, remembering his name was Brookins and as they approached him, he paused in his conversation with the EOD lead specialist and turned.

'Hey Foxy.'

'Hello, Sarge.'

Looking at the group with him, Brookins spotted Archer.

'Holy shit, long time kid,' he said. 'Haven't seen you for a while. Where've you been?'

'Joined the NYPD.'

'What?'

'Long story. But that's why we're here. The kidnapped detective is one of ours.'

As Brookins digested this information, Marquez and Josh looked over at the house.

'Is he still in there?' Marquez asked.

'Unknown.'

'He isn't talking?' Fox asked, examining all the activity on the street, pedestrians and residents on both sides being herded further back as Met officers secured the area. 'You must have got his attention by now.'

'We tried the phone but no one's picking up,' Brookins replied. 'We figure he could very well have your detective in there somewhere.'

He jabbed a thumb towards the EOD team to his right, who were busy getting their equipment ready.

'Bomb disposal are going to get us a better look inside. I've got four guys covering the back in case he tries to bail out.'

'What about fibre optics?' Josh asked.

Brookins shook his head. 'After what happened in Brixton, I'm not risking any of my men going that close.'

He paused, realising what he'd said.

'Commiserations, by the way.'

Fox nodded.

'I heard some didn't make it.'

95

'Mason and Spitz.'

'Christ.'

Beside them, Archer had gone quiet, focusing on the house ahead of him. The properties each side were still being cleared, residents being rushed out as members of the SCO19 team gathered at various vantage points, aiming their weapons at the property where they believed Payan was holed up. The officers were garbed in their assault gear, armour, helmets and weapons but were staying back in case this was another trap and the house was booby-trapped with explosives.

Looking behind him, he saw two SCO19 sharpshooters were positioned on the 1st floor of two houses across the street, their rifles aimed at the front door. As Brookins resumed his conversation with Jameson, planning their approach, Archer turned back to Marquez and Josh to his left.

'What do you think?'

Marquez didn't reply for a moment, examining the other houses on the street.

He recognised that look on her face.

It was mirroring his own thoughts.

She shook her head, studying the scene. 'This feels wrong.'

'How so?' Josh asked.

'I don't know. But it just does.'

As Josh looked at her, Archer glanced around.

Everyone was fixated on the front of the property, the setting sun reflecting off the windows of houses along the street.

Kidnapping Vargas and getting her out of the villa undetected had required some serious skill, nerve and pre-planning. But then the same people did something as amateurish as calling the police long enough to give them a trace and then hide out in a house with no escape routes?

It's too easy, he thought, scanning the surrounding area.

Marquez was right.

Something about this felt off.

At the ARU HQ, Beckett was now almost at the entrance. Her raincoat was thin but she was sweating profusely, each footstep making a quiet *click* as her stiletto made contact with the concrete. She saw the entrance was now only ten yards away, illuminated by the golden light of the setting sun.

And as she drew nearer to the front doors of the building she caught her breath, knowing this was the last time she was ever going to see them.

TWELVE

On the street in Hendon, the EOD team had just finished their preparations and were ready. One of their specialists turned and gave a thumbs up to Brookins at the command post, who picked up his radio.

'Baxter, report.'

'We're in place, sir. Back of the house is clear.'

'Swan, blow the charge! I repeat, blow the charge!'

Fifteen yards to the left side of the house, one of the SCO19 officers was holding a clacker for some small charges he'd already placed on the hinges and lock on the front door of Payan's hideout.

Acknowledging the order over his radio, he pressed the detonator.

The charges went off with a loud *crack* and blew the door off cleanly, revealing the entrance hall of the house as the frame fell backwards onto the front steps. With SCO19's weapons trained on the doorway, an EOD specialist in a blast suit immediately moved forward with a remote-controlled bot in his hands, walking over the front lawn and approaching the open doorway.

Standing beside Marquez, Josh and Fox as they all watched the guy move forward, Archer was feeling increasingly uneasy as he observed the specialist approach the house. For EOD, normal protocol was to send a bot like the one the man was carrying into an uncertain situation, a remote-controlled vehicle fitted with cameras, microphones, sensors and moveable pincers to give the specialists a good idea of what they were dealing with without compromising their safety. If it had been flat ground, Archer knew the bomb-disposal team would have just sent the bot down, but the front doorway to the property was up a couple of steps, which meant in this situation it needed to be placed inside.

The atmosphere was tense as the specialist arrived outside the house. He made it to the entrance and placed the bot down inside the property. Despite his protective suit, the specialist was well within the blast radius if the house was baited with explosives as in Brixton.

But it didn't blow.

As the specialist immediately retreated, the bot now in place, Archer's attention turned to the EOD leader, Harry Jameson, standing to his right just past Fox and Brookins. He was looking down at a screen in his hands, similar to the one used by the ARU and SCO19 for fibre optics.

'Wally's in position,' Jameson said. 'Here we go.'

Beside him, another specialist was holding a control box and he pushed the stick forward.

Looking over at the residence, Archer and the others heard a faint whirring noise.

And they all watched as the bot dubbed Wally slowly disappeared into the house.

At the ARU HQ, Beckett pulled open the door to the entrance and approached the barrier between her and the interior of the building. Behind the glass booth beside it, Lipton looked up and smiled.

'Evening, Jen,' he said, his voice slightly muffled by the protective screen. 'Where've you been?'

'Doctor.'

'Everything OK?'

99

'Yes,' she replied, so quietly it was almost a whisper.

'There've been some developments. You'd better go up and see for yourself.'

She didn't reply as the door slid back, and she walked forward towards the stairs, her legs barely holding her up now she was in the building.

Shakily, she started to make her way slowly up.

'Structure looks clear,' Jameson said, examining the screen as the specialist beside him controlled Wally. 'Don't see any explosives.'

Brookins, the NYPD group and Fox watched silently, the SCO19 officers in position with their weapons trained on the property.

'Any sign of Payan?' Brookins asked. 'Or the woman?'

'Neither, yet,' Jameson said.

There was a pause, everyone waiting. Beside Jameson, the specialist with the controls continued to skilfully manoeuvre the bot, checking the screen in Jameson's hands as he did so.

'Wait,' Jameson suddenly said.

'What is it?' Brookins asked.

'We've got something in the sitting room.'

Tilting his head, Jameson peered closely at the screen.

He frowned.

'What's wrong?' Fox asked.

Jameson tilted the screen so Brookins, Fox and Archer could see.

'I wasn't expecting this.'

'What?'

'Payan's dead.'

As Fox and Brookins both frowned and peered over at the screen, Archer looked around the street again, all his instincts on high alert.

Then, out of the corner of his eye, he saw a tiny hint of movement.

A small red dot had suddenly appeared on Marquez' chest.

THIRTEEN

On the 1st floor of the ARU headquarters, Chalky was standing alone inside the Briefing Room, quickly drinking a thick double espresso from the coffee machine in the corner as he waited for the machine to pour a second cup for Shepherd.

As he waited, he felt the emptiness of the room around him, and was doing his best not to dwell on what had happened to Mason and Spitz. He'd been very good friends with the two dead officers; they were tough and decent men with whom he'd shared a great rapport. Both of them had been great characters. Mason had beaten cancer as a teenager, going on to become an elite cop and devout family man; as his thoughts turned to Spitz, Chalky smiled as he remembered when he'd been a groomsman at Spitz' wedding last year. During the first dance with his new wife, Spitz had managed to get his foot tangled in his bride's wedding gown. Panicking, he'd lost his balance, and they'd both tumbled off the dance-floor, taking a table with them as they fell and sending glasses and plates of food everywhere.

His brief smile faded. Swallowing the lump in his throat Chalky finished making the coffee, channelling his emotions into a white-hot desire to take down whoever was responsible for all this.

Stirring two sugars into Shepherd's drink, he looked over through the open door at the Operations area in front of him. The American sergeant was standing side by side with Cobb in the tech area having just finished a brief conversation in Cobb's office; the two men were now watching the situation unfolding at the house in Hendon.

102

Draining his espresso and throwing the cup in the rubbish bin, Chalky picked up Shepherd's steaming coffee and walked forward to the door. As he did so, he sensed movement to his right and saw Beckett, one of the analysts.

She was coming down the corridor from the stairs.

Chalky paused. She may have heard the bad news concerning the task force already, but he felt he should tell her what had happened to Mason, Spitz and the rest of the team, just in case. They all worked closely together and he knew she'd take the news just as hard as the rest of them.

'Hey Jen,' he said, moving out of the doorway to join her.

Focusing on the Operations area, her attention suddenly snapped onto him and he stopped in his tracks.

Her red-rimmed eyes were as wide as saucers, her hair slightly tangled. Her lip was trembling, sweat sheening her brow, her body shaking like a leaf in the wind.

She looked absolutely terrified.

'Jen?'

Seeing the red dot on Marquez and realising instantly what was happening, Archer reacted a split-second before the sniper fired.

He ducked and shoved Marquez hard, straight into Josh. A split second later, there was a *whizz* as a bullet missed her head by a fraction of an inch, hitting a post-box on the pavement behind her as the echo of a gunshot from somewhere followed a moment later.

As Marquez and Josh fell to the ground and everyone froze as they heard the weapon's report, Archer spun back to Fox and Brookins to warn them.

To his horror, he saw Fox had a red dot on his forehead from another angle.

'Get down!' he shouted, dragging his old team-mate to the ground.

Before they hit the concrete, there was a *thump* and Brookins was knocked sideways, blood spraying into the air as he was hit in the upper arm, the bullet's trajectory going straight through where Fox's head had been.

As Archer and Fox hit the deck hard, hidden behind the front of an SC019 car, Archer saw Brookins drop as everyone started to dive for cover, the SCO19 officers swinging their weapons around trying to find the source of the gunfire.

'Two snipers!' Archer shouted, ducking as another round suddenly punched through the car he and Fox were using as cover, exiting just above their heads.

'Jen, what's wrong?' Chalky asked, staring at Beckett.

She tried to reply, her mouth working, but the words wouldn't come out. No one else on the 1st floor had seen her yet, everyone in the tech pit concentrating on something that was going on in Hendon, some of them talking hurriedly, all of them transfixed to the feed.

Not paying them any attention, Chalky was totally focused on Beckett. He noticed she was wearing a cream-coloured coat which was odd on such a warm evening, her hair damp with sweat.

The coat seemed slightly bulky.

He looked up at her and she stared back wordlessly, still unable to speak.

Following his gut instinct, he placed the cup on the floor and stepped forward quickly, undoing the belt on the garment and drawing it open.

The moment he parted the sides, his eyes widened in horror.

Beckett was wearing a vest packed with TNT, hooked up to a timer counting down in constantly changing red numbers.

00:19.

00:18.

00:17.

Working the bolt on his M40A5 rifle, the Canadian sniper with the call-sign Grange focused the scope on where the group from the ARU and NYPD had been standing, but they were now out of sight, huddled down behind two cars for cover, the element of surprise gone, his chance blown.

'Shit!'

As the SCO19 officers turned in his direction, trying to locate him, he put the scope on the car just about where he figured the black NYPD detective's head was and pulled the trigger.

At the ARU HQ, Chalky reacted instantly, dragging the coat off her body in one fluid motion then quickly examining all sides of the bomb vest. It was black, framed by a thick metal casing that ran over her shoulders and hugged her body tight, two padlocks through slots on the metal sealing it in place.

Bars of TNT were tightly packed all around the garment, more than enough to cause catastrophic damage and kill everyone in the room.

00:16.

00:15.

He grabbed the metal frame of the vest and tried to lift it, but it was no use.

The damn thing was firmly locked in place by the padlocks.

'Just hang on!' he told her.

She was shaking, looking as if she was about to pass out.

'Hang on!'

Others in the room, transfixed on the feed from Hendon, heard the urgency in his voice and turned. Seeing Beckett standing there in the vest, two analysts immediately leapt to their feet in horror and backed away, causing Cobb, Shepherd and Nikki turning to swing round to see what was going on.

Chalky didn't pause for a second, fighting with the two thick locks on the vest while keeping his eyes on the timer.

00:12.

00:11.

It was no use.

They were locked tight.

As everyone stayed low and SCO19 located the twin snipers and returned fire, Archer saw Marquez duck as another bullet tore through the car she and Josh were behind, missing her head by an inch and leaving a black hole in the side of the vehicle.

As they were showered with smashed glass from another bullet, Archer realised something significant as he looked over at the pair.

Despite SCO19's return fire, the snipers' own fire was concentrated purely on them.

The NYPD sergeant Shepherd reacted first, running forward to try and help Chalky as Cobb raced across the level and ripped open the door to his office, which had bulletproof glass windows.

'Everybody inside now!'

As the analysts scrambled across the room, Chalky pulled his Glock and held onto Beckett firmly with one hand as he put the barrel against one of the locks. He fired twice, Beckett jolting and whimpering in fear from the force of the shots; the bullets blew the thick padlock off and buried themselves into the far wall behind them.

As Shepherd ripped the steel hook of the lock clear, Chalky put his Glock against the second lock and fired again, pulling the hook away after the lock dropped off.

'Hurry!' Shepherd said, as Beckett stood immobile, unable to move.

00:07.

00:06.

The two men undid the clasps, loosened the vest, and quickly pulled it over Beckett's head as fast as they could. Laying it on the floor, Shepherd grabbed Beckett as Chalky pulled the Briefing Room door shut behind them.

Holding her up, the two men ran for Cobb's office, throwing themselves through the open doorway.

107

Standing beside the frame and waiting for them, Cobb shut and secured the door as soon as they were inside.

Taking cover as bullets ripped through the window and into the room around him from the SCO19 officers who'd established his firing point, Grange was already on his way out of there.

'Abort!' he shouted to Stockwell over his cell phone as he ran for the door. *'Abort! Get the hell out of there!'*

Going through the open bedroom door and ditching the sniper rifle, he sprinted through the empty house, out through the back door and leapt over the fence. He saw Stockwell appear from behind the back of a house at the other end of the street, and they both ran towards a car parked halfway down.

Reaching it at the same time, both men climbed inside and Stockwell fired the engine, roaring off down the road in the opposite direction from the police cordon.

'Shit!' Grange shouted in frustration, as Stockwell got them out of there. *'Shit!'*

At that moment across town, the timer on the vest hit *0:00.*

A split-second later, the entire second level of the ARU HQ exploded. The blast rocked the whole building, smashing out the glass on Cobb's office, and throwing everyone inside across the room, spraying them all with fragments of bulletproof glass and debris. The force was unbelievable, like an invisible tsunami of pressure, flinging them around as if they were rag dolls, and the floor was suddenly filled with a black pungent smoke, large parts of the immediate area on fire, the windows of the Briefing Room completely smashed out.

The lights on fire alarms on the ceiling were flashing but no one lying on the floor could hear the sirens.

Most were unconscious.

And no one was moving.

Having been punched into the far wall, hitting it with incredible force before landing on the floor, Chalky opened his eyes and gasped for air. Beckett and Shepherd were both lying beside him in limp heaps. Coughing and trying to breathe through the smoke, he crawled over and checked Beckett; he saw a thick shard of bulletproof glass buried in her back, blood already staining her sweat-stained white shirt.

Coughing again and unable to hear anything, Chalky looked around and saw no one else was moving in the smoky silence, hot blood stinging his eyes as it streamed down from a cut to his head and dripped onto the floor in front of him.

Cobb, Shepherd and all the analysts were down.

And the entire 1st floor of the ARU building had been destroyed.

FOURTEEN

Less than ten minutes later, Archer joined Marquez, Fox and Josh outside the house in Hendon, stepping back through the gap where the front door used to be and walking onto a small patch of grass to the right of the entrance.

'Everyone OK?' Archer asked as he joined the other three. They nodded; each had been nicked and cut by pieces of smashed glass from the car windows, their clothes dirtied by diving to the ground.

All of them were well aware how close they'd come to being killed. They'd stayed down behind cover for five minutes or so until SC019 cleared the two residences where the sniper fire had come from. The officers had found two abandoned rifles, two open back doors, four dead colleagues and not a trace of either shooter. The scene had now been restored to a semblance of calm, the sudden assault on the police teams having taken everyone off guard, but the remaining SCO19 officers looked pretty grim as they guarded the street, a back-up team clearing every house in the immediate vicinity. Three ambulances had arrived earlier and Archer saw one of them suddenly take off, siren blaring as it carried Brookins to hospital; however, the other two hadn't left yet.

One of them was being loaded up one by one with the four dead officers before taking them to the morgue.

'Jesus, Arch, I owe you a beer,' Josh said to Archer quietly, watching the ambulance crews work.

'Make it two,' Fox added.

Archer didn't reply, looking at the scene around him. 'How's Brookins?'

'Stable,' Fox said. 'Different story from the other four guys.'

A short silence fell, the group watching the medical team and feeling exposed standing there in the garden.

'Two shooters,' Archer said. 'What kind of rifles did they use?'

'M40A5s; bolt action and bipod, with laser-sights. They're already on the way to the lab for prints, but tracing the weapons will be hard. The serial number on each has been burnt off with acid.'

'And they just ditched them?' Archer said.

Fox nodded.

'What about witnesses when the snipers escaped?'

'None. Street camera CCTV from around back is being checked, but the four SCO19 guys who were guarding the back entrances were all shot in the head and dumped in the kitchen of each house, keeping them out of sight.'

'We didn't hear any rifle reports before we were attacked?'

'The foursome were all hit with a silenced .22 handgun; each took a single round to the head. It's no wonder we didn't hear anything; someone could fire a weapon like that in the same room as you and you wouldn't hear the report.'

Archer looked at him and thought back to the sequence.

'One of the officers called in an update moments before Swan blew the front door; they must have

111

been killed less than a minute before the attack. The two snipers moved in fast and timed it to the second.'

'And the homeowners were already evacuated,' Marquez said. 'They killed the four officers, breached the back doors of both houses, moved up to their firing points and set up, all in the space of sixty seconds or so.'

She paused.

'Jesus. These guys were clinical.'

'And they abandoned the rifles,' Archer said. 'That means they aren't exactly struggling for cash or concerned about us tracing the weapons.'

'Their cheeks must have touched the stock on each rifle when they aimed,' Josh said. 'Could have left samples of DNA.'

'It's tenuous,' Fox said, unconvinced. 'And if so, it could still take weeks to get a result.'

With their backs to the house, the group all looked around the street, the light fading now the sun was disappearing over the horizon. It was a beautiful sunset, an odd contrast to the events of today, especially as at that moment two paramedics finished loading the last dead SCO19 officer inside the ambulance; once he was in, they slammed the doors and then walked to the front of the vehicle.

'How the hell did you realise what was about to happen?' Josh asked Archer.

'I knew something was wrong when they said Payan was dead; it seemed almost stage-managed.'

He glanced at Marquez.

'Then I turned and saw a red dot on your chest, Lisa. Then you, Foxy.'

'And they kept trying, even when we hit the ground,' Marquez said. 'Their fire was exclusively aimed at us. Not SCO19, or EOD.

She paused.

'Just us.'

'Any sign of Alice inside?' Josh asked Archer.

Archer shook his head. 'I couldn't look thoroughly, but the team in there said no. Just Payan's corpse.'

As he spoke, the group became aware of a rattling sound as something was wheeled up the path; turning, they saw two paramedics from the remaining ambulance wheeling a gurney towards the house to collect Payan's body. Watching them pass and approach the entrance, Josh swore.

'So now two of Vargas' kidnappers are dead.'

'You think someone betrayed them?' Fox asked the other three.

'How do you mean?' Josh asked.

'Used them to kidnap Vargas and then screwed them over? Killed them both then made off with her?'

'If they did that, why go to all this trouble and put themselves at unnecessary risk?' Marquez said, looking over at the aftermath of the sniper attack. 'Why not just whack the two guys then disappear? Why come after us?'

She paused.

'Something about that call Payan made bothered me the moment I heard him start talking.'

'Why? Fox asked.

'His speech didn't sound right.'

'He's from Bratislava and a low-life. He's not going to speak like he lives at Downton Abbey.'

'No, she's right,' Archer said, looking at Marquez. 'I know what she means. I thought that exact same thing. It sounded forced. Stilted.'

'Like he was under duress?' Josh said.

Archer nodded. 'And Stanovich said he couldn't put his hands up just before the apartment in Brixton blew; we all heard the recording.'

He paused.

'Someone used them to try to get to us.'

'So now what the hell do we do?' Fox asked. 'Wait on the CCTV and hope we can ID the snipers or lift a print from the rifle?'

'There's another possible lead,' Marquez said, looking at Archer who nodded.

'Which is?'

'There was a third kidnapper in Spain. Stanovich and Payan were only two of them.'

'How do you know?'

'The lab. Alice busted them up and they bled at the scene before they took her away. Spanish Forensics found four different blood types and took them straight to the lab. Vargas, Stanovich and Payan were three of them.'

Fox frowned. 'You said Vargas drew blood from each of them?'

Archer nodded, noticing his old colleague's expression.

'Why? You think she didn't?'

Fox glanced at the house. 'I took a quick look inside at Payan's body before Forensics took over.'

'So?' Josh said.

'He didn't have any marks on his face or neck other than the gunshot wound.'

'*Shit!*' the Middle Eastern man with the broken nose said, hitting the dashboard of the car in frustration. He was listening to a report down the other end of the phone as they sped down the street, the South African man beside him at the wheel. 'What the hell went wrong?'

'*They moved just as we fired,*' Grange explained on the call. '*The blond cop pushed the woman and black guy out of the way. We kept firing but couldn't put them down.*'

'Are you kidding me? Where are you?'

'*Heading for the River. We already changed the plates. The cops won't find us.*'

Beside him, the South African turned onto another street. Peering ahead, the Middle Eastern man looked into the car park of the ARU headquarters and saw flames and smoke billowing out from the destroyed upper level.

So far, so good.

'Wait a minute,' the South African said, frowning and peering closer, the car slowing to a halt. 'What the hell?'

'What?' the Middle Eastern man asked, interrupting his conversation on the phone.

'Front door.'

They both saw people being helped out, several being carried but others managing to walk with assistance.

As they watched, a woman was being lifted out between two paramedics.

Both men stared in disbelief as they recognised the female analyst they'd chosen so carefully for the bomb vest. She looked in bad shape, suspended between the two men who were supporting her, but she was obviously still alive. Given the amount of explosives that had been strapped to her, she should have been pure vapour by now.

'Holy shit,' the South African said. 'How the hell did she survive?'

The Middle Eastern man didn't reply, his mood darkening by the second as he watched the woman get lowered face down onto a blanket on the ground, some waiting paramedics immediately tending to her.

'Finchley and Portland must have screwed it up,' he said quietly. 'They didn't lock the vest on tight enough.'

Pausing for a moment, he closed his eyes, taking a breath to try and stay calm through a thumping headache. Then he returned his attention to the call.

'Both of you, get off the street,' he ordered. 'Fall back to the safe-house right now and stay put until I get there. And you'd better hope the boss hasn't seen the news.'

A moment later, he ended the call as the South African put his foot down and they headed off down the street, taking the next right turn and leaving the burning police building behind as they disappeared out of sight.

FIFTEEN

In Hendon, Archer, Marquez, Josh and Fox walked past Wally into the sitting room where a four-man Forensics team was gathered around Ibrahim Payan's corpse.

The Slovakian was slumped forward in a chair, his arms and ankles taped to the wooden frame, the room smelling unpleasantly of sweat and the contents of his vacated bowel. Dressed in tracksuit bottoms and a sweat-stained t-shirt, blood was spattered on the white wall behind the dead man from a gunshot wound to his forehead. A solitary shell casing was lying on the carpet to the right, a small copper shape on the carpet. The investigators were taking photographs of the scene, inspecting the dead man's body and checking for trace evidence before they moved him onto the waiting gurney to take him to the lab for analysis.

'What happened, guys?' Fox asked as they joined them.

One of the pair who was studying Payan's body rose and turned to the newcomers, his partner continuing her work.

'Most of it's pretty clear,' he said. 'Single shot to the head, from about half a foot away. Shell casing's from a .22 handgun.'

He knelt down, indicating the angle.

'Shooter was up close. Neighbours didn't hear a thing, so the weapon must have been suppressed. At that calibre, the shot would have been so quiet that someone upstairs in the house wouldn't have heard it. '

'What about other wounds?' Marquez said.

The man lifted a gloved hand to the back of Payan's head. 'He suffered blunt force trauma to the back of his skull, but it didn't draw blood. Clean blow. He's got a bump here the size of a small egg. Whoever subdued him whacked him over the head with something then probably gagged and tied him up before he could recover.'

He then pointed at the dead man's mouth, touching the skin gently. As the man gently withdrew his finger, Archer saw thin white sticky strands.

'There are traces of glue here from a strip of tape. He's also got some oil residue on his lips and teeth.'

'From the pistol?' Josh asked.

The man nodded. 'Someone pushed the barrel into his mouth hard. No outright cuts, which meant there must have been a silencer on the weapon otherwise the sights on the pistol would have left marks on his lips and maybe damaged his teeth. But there's oil there, which means the handgun used was suppressed and recently cleaned.'

'That's a hard weapon to acquire,' Fox said.

The investigator nodded. 'Don't get many silenced handguns on the streets in London. Whoever killed this man did a clinical job.'

Kneeling to join the investigator, Archer tilted his head and peered up at Payan's face. The dead Slovakian's eyes were still open, his body slack and held to the chair by the binds. Fox was right. He didn't have a broken nose or black eyes, and no scratch marks or any sign of damage to his face or neck; nothing that would have drawn blood.

Rising, he looked at the bump on the back of Payan's shaved head; he saw the lump, but no cut.

He turned to the investigator. 'Could a fist or elbow have inflicted this?'

'No way. You'd break bones hitting someone there that hard. It was something heavy but with a flat edge, like a piece of wood. Anything sharper would have cut him open.'

'They jumped her whilst she was asleep,' Marquez said, reading his mind. 'She wouldn't have had a chance to grab a weapon that heavy to fend them off.'

'Are there any other wounds on his body?' Josh asked.

The man nodded. 'We found something else. But it's weird. Look at this.'

Still on one knee, the man gently slid up the sleeve of Payan's tracksuit top with his gloved hands, all the way past the elbow.

'See?' he said, pointing to Payan's right forearm.

The group saw there were two puncture wounds on a prominent vein on his arm, an inch below his bicep. There were a couple of trickles of dried blood on the pale skin over an old tattoo, the rivulets crossing each other.

'Twin needle marks,' Marquez said. 'Was he using?'

The investigator shook his head. 'I don't think so. There're no other track marks on either arm or between his toes. I read his file on the way here; although he has a history of cocaine abuse, there was no record of any heroin use or any other injectable substance.'

'Could the killer have drugged him?' Josh asked. 'To keep him quiet?'

119

'It's very possible. He's a big guy, and wouldn't have been easy to transport once he came round from the blow to the head. When we get him to the lab, we can check his blood and run some tests.'

'Two puncture marks,' Archer said. 'Not one.'

'Whoever injected him may have been sloppy,' the investigator said. 'Had to puncture the vein twice to inject him.'

Marquez shook her head. 'Whoever did this killed four SCO19 officers silently then came with an inch of adding us to that list. These people aren't sloppy.'

Archer nodded, studying the needle marks.

'Could one of these punctures have been to take a blood sample?' he asked.

The investigator frowned. 'A blood sample? Why?'

'Someone obviously popped a needle in him twice. Say the first time was to drug him and the other was to take blood. Is that a possibility?'

The man shrugged. 'I suppose. But unless it's some kind of fetish for the killer, I don't know why anyone would do that. I guess this man could have a rare blood type which could potentially be worth a small amount of money. Not worth going to all this trouble though.'

Still on one knee beside Payan, Archer glanced up at the others.

All three realised what he was thinking.

'Hold on,' Josh said. 'You think someone planted his blood at the villa?'

Archer nodded. 'And they planted him here for us. As bait for the snipers.'

Before anyone could comment, there was a sudden commotion in the hallway by the front door as someone ran into the house.

'Fox?' a voice called. *'Ryan Fox?'*

'Yeah?' Fox shouted, turning towards the door.

A SCO19 officer ran into the living room; as he rose, Archer saw from the name tag on his tac vest that it was Swan, the man who'd blown the front door off earlier.

'What's wrong?' Fox asked.

'We're picking up a report from something across town,' Swan said. 'You need to see this.'

He moved across the living room, switching on the television. Picking up the remote from on top of the screen, he switched it to BBC News 24 then stepped back. Everyone in the room paused in what they were doing, and watched as two latest *Breaking News* headlines scrolled under the two newsreaders in the studio. One of them was running with what had just happened here in Hendon.

But it was the other that caught everyone's attention.

Breaking News: London counter-terrorist police headquarters hit by bomb blast.

Many casualties from explosion.

The moment he read it, Archer's blood ran cold. As everyone else stared at the screen, he looked back at Payan.

They planted him here, his mind echoed.

As bait.

SIXTEEN

Given some slightly lighter traffic, Fox got the group back to the ARU HQ in almost half the time it had taken them to get to Hendon, and they could see the smoke in the distance well before they got within sight of the building.

As the car made a final turn and sped down the street towards the now cordoned-off area, the first sight that greeted them was a car park full of ambulances, along with two fire engines and eight or nine busy paramedics tending to the injured in what looked like a makeshift triage post outside the front of the building. The place was a hive of activity, the upper floor of the HQ still burning in parts as the two fire crews tackled the flames inside.

Everyone in the car sat in stunned silence as they pulled up outside. Half an hour ago, there hadn't been so much as a crack in a window here.

Now the upper half of the building was virtually destroyed.

The front barrier was already lifted, presumably to allow emergency personnel in and out of the car park, with two armed Met police officers stationed there as a nod to security. After Fox and the others showed them their ID, the officers let them through and Fox parked in an empty space well away from the triage point; a moment later, everyone jumped out of the car and quickly moved towards the front of the building.

Marquez and Josh spotted Shepherd who was being wheeled on a gurney towards a waiting ambulance and immediately ran over to him. He was

122

unconscious, blood staining the side of his head; just beyond him was Cobb, who Fox headed for. The ARU Director was also out cold and strapped onto another gurney following closely behind Shepherd's, his head in a brace, his suit burned and stained with blood.

Staying by the car, Archer didn't move, staring at the scene around him.

The upper level of the ARU base had been severely damaged by an explosion; all the windows had been blown out and large sections of the upper wall were missing, revealing the interior of the 1st floor. Through the gaps he could see fire-fighters inside the Briefing Room and Operations working a hose, the smoke starting to lose its intensity as they got the flames under control. By the front doors, he was relieved to see Lipton and Wilson were unhurt, presumably because they'd been at their posts away from the Operations floor; they were moving around the injured, offering reassurance where they could but both looking totally shocked by what had happened.

Rapidly scanning the hive of activity for Chalky, Archer felt another moment of relief as he spotted him sitting on the kerb away to the left all by himself, no paramedic with him. He was holding a white bandage to the back of his head, staring straight ahead with an unfocused gaze. His forehead and cheeks were stained with smoke and blood, as were his navy blue polo shirt and light blue jeans.

Archer immediately ran over and dropped to one knee beside his friend. Chalky slowly turned his head to look at him. Up close, Archer saw that the side of his face was cut and scratched from pieces of glass.

However, judging by the devastation around him, he'd got off lightly.

'You're back,' Chalky said quietly.

Asking him if he was OK was a redundant question, so Archer just held his shoulder and looked him over, noting that other than the wound to his head and some other small cuts on his face, arms and body, he looked in much better shape than most of the others.

'What the hell happened, Chalk?' he asked. 'Who did this?'

'Beckett,' he said quietly. 'Wearing a vest.'

'A vest? Like a bomb vest?'

'Yeah. A vest.'

'Was she already in the building?'

'She…arrived late. I saw her. Something was wrong.'

He paused.

'She was scared.'

Chalky paused again, trying to gather his jumbled thoughts.

'It was…locked onto her.'

'The vest?'

He nodded, talking slowly.

'Locked onto her,' he repeated. 'Metal frame. Two…padlocks. I shot them off.'

As Chalky paused, switching hands to hold the blood-stained bandage to the back of his head, Archer looked over at Beckett, who was lying face down twenty feet away with two paramedics tending to her. Fox was kneeling beside her, talking with her quietly and holding her blood-stained hand. Although Archer hadn't known her for long before he left, they'd got on well enough and he'd liked her;

124

she'd started working at the Unit six months before his departure and he knew Nikki rated her highly, regarding her as one of her best analysts. He also remembered her work area had been decorated with photos of her twin sons who'd been around eight or nine years old at the time, her pride and joy.

No way would she have done something like this by choice.

'I'm going to go talk to her,' he told Chalky, who didn't respond. Patting his friend's shoulder again, Archer rose, moving over quickly to join Fox, passing a paramedic on the way who was heading straight for Chalky to check up on him.

Archer knelt beside Beckett, the opposite side from Fox who was now talking quietly with the paramedic treating her. The wounded analyst was lying with her face turned towards Archer; she was still conscious, blood staining her face, her clothes singed and her hair matted and tangled.

'Who did this, Jen?' he asked her quietly.

She paused.

'Two men.'

'They put the vest on you?'

She nodded slowly, her lip trembling.

'If I didn't, they were…they…'

Tears welled in her eyes.

She blinked, causing them to spill down her face onto the blanket under her right cheek.

The man tending to her interrupted his conversation with Fox and shifted his attention to Archer.

'Hey. Leave the questions for later.'

'What were they going to do, Jen?' Archer continued, ignoring the man.

'My sons,' she whispered. *'They were…going…to…kill them.'*

'Who were these men?' Archer asked.

'I don't…know. But…they sounded…'

'They sounded like what?'

'Australian.'

Archer paused. So did Beckett, blinking slowly as whatever the paramedics had given her for the pain kicked in.

'And they have my boys,' she whispered.

'I'll get them back.'

As he spoke, a gurney was rolled over and after lifting her carefully onto it she was wheeled away towards the back of a waiting ambulance. Rising, Fox and Archer watched her go, Beckett's words echoing in Archer's mind.

They sounded Australian.

And they have my boys.

Turning, he saw Nikki being patched up by a paramedic as she sat on the kerb near the front entrance. One of her arms was in a sling, her face screwed up in pain as the medic gently felt her shoulder, trying to assess the damage. Beyond her, Marquez was standing with Josh as they stared at the devastation around them. As Fox moved off to talk with Lipton and Wilson, Archer headed over to Nikki quickly, kneeling beside her, Josh stepping forward to join him as Marquez pulled her cell phone and turned away to make a call.

To his relief, Archer could immediately tell from Nikki's eyes that she was focused and with it, not half-concussed like Chalky or badly wounded like Beckett. She'd lost her glasses, her hair was tousled and she had two small cuts on her left cheek as well

126

as the busted-up shoulder but apart from that she looked OK, and as alert as ever.

'Still with us?' he asked.

'Just about,' she replied, making eye contact with him. 'Glad you're back.'

Without her glasses, she looked different, more vulnerable somehow. He saw her glance over to her right as the ambulance carrying Beckett moved off, headed for the exit. Her eyes followed it out of the car park.

'Did she tell you what happened?' she asked.

He nodded. 'Two men locked a bomb vest onto her. Said if she didn't do as they instructed they were going to kill her kids.'

'A locked bomb vest?' Josh said. 'How did they get it off?'

'Chalky shot off the locks,' Nikki said. 'He, Shepherd and Jen just made it into Cobb's office where we'd all taken cover before it detonated.'

'She thinks they were Australian,' Archer added.

'Australian?' Nikki repeated, frowning. 'Why the hell would two Aussies want to strap a bomb to her?'

'I don't know,' Archer said quietly.

Nikki looked Archer and Josh up and down, noting they too were looking a bit rough. 'What happened to you?'

'Payan was a lure. Two snipers tried to take us out.'

'What? All of you?'

He shook his head, looking at Josh. 'Just us.'

Turning his head, Archer looked over at Chalky, who was still sitting where he'd left him, a paramedic examining the back of his head. All the other wounded were being transported into

127

ambulances, getting them off site and on their way to hospital.

'Whoever put the vest on Beckett used her sons as the incentive,' he said. 'That means they're holding them somewhere. I'm going to find them but I need your help, Nik.'

The man examining her shoulder heard this.

'Not now,' he said. 'She's broken her collarbone and will be in shock. She needs to go to the hospital to be properly checked over.'

'We need Beckett's address,' Archer said to Nikki, undeterred and laser focused. 'Do you know where she lives?'

'Not off the top of my head. But I can get it.'

'You need to go to hospital,' the medic insisted.

'I'm staying,' Nikki said.

'No way.'

'I'm staying,' she repeated, more firmly. 'This is important. I can get checked out later.'

She motioned to her injured arm.

'Just give me some strong painkillers and I can manage.'

The paramedic stared at her for a moment, Archer and Josh waiting silently beside him. Then he shrugged, reached into the open bag on the ground beside him and withdrew a white capsule. Opening it, he tipped it into his palm and shook out two tablets.

'Take these,' he said, offering them to her. Once she popped the painkillers into her mouth he opened a bottle of water and passed it to her. 'And two more every four hours until you can get to the hospital.'

Knocking the tablets back and swallowing them with a gulp of water from the bottle, Nikki nodded her thanks to the man, pocketed the capsule and rose gingerly. Archer took hold of her uninjured shoulder to steady her as Josh stood up beside them; Nikki swayed for a moment than regained her balance.

'One last thing,' the paramedic said to her, closing his bag and rising too. 'You're still in shock. Try to stay seated, stay calm and avoid raising your heart-rate.'

'It's a bit late for that,' Nikki replied, looking at the damage and devastation around her.

*

Moments later, Archer, Nikki and Josh walked up the undamaged stairs to the 1st floor. As he'd entered the building, Archer had immediately noticed that the ground floor was pretty much unaffected, but now up the flight of stairs, he saw that despite all the extensive remodelling and repairs the HQ had undergone the year before, the 1st floor was a different story.

It looked as if it had been hit by an air strike.

Walking down the corridor, he, Josh and Nikki saw that the whole place was blackened and stank of wet ash and smoke. Large sections of brickwork in the Briefing Room had been blown out making the outer wall resemble one of those wartime pictures of houses damaged from the Blitz, the interior of the 1st floor now revealed to the outside world.

As they passed Cobb's office to their right, they saw papers and bits of glass everywhere mixed with bloodstains, shoes and pieces of clothing. Two filing cabinets had been smashed over onto one side, their contents partially strewn across the floor, the papers fluttering in the wind that was now blowing through the large gaps in the walls. The smell of smoke was

129

overpowering and Archer, Josh and Nikki covered their mouths as they entered what was left of Operations, their feet crunching over pebbles of broken glass.

Up ahead, they saw a group of firemen kill the water supply on their hose, having just put the last patches of fire out. They seemed to be finishing up and the one at the back turned as he heard Archer, Josh and Nikki walking over the broken glass.

'No way,' he ordered. 'Get back downstairs. You can't come up here. It's not safe.'

'I need to get to my computer,' Nikki said.

'Good luck with that,' the fire-fighter said, pointing at the tech area. Looking across, the trio saw everything not secured to the wall or floor had been annihilated by the explosion, all the computers smashed to pieces, their intelligence post destroyed. Archer knew that all of their data was backed up on servers located elsewhere, but Nikki would still need something to access the system.

'My laptop, then,' she said, pointing with her good arm, undeterred. 'It's in a protective case I had by my desk, so it might be OK if we can find it.'

'I don't care if it's locked in a vault. My job is to keep you safe.' The fire-fighter motioned to the blackened space around him. 'It's too dangerous up here.'

'It's vital. Please. It might help us identify who did this.'

The fireman hesitated, then glanced over at where she'd pointed; as his companions started to pack up their gear, the man shook his head then walked over to the tech area. He looked around for a moment, then walked over to the far wall, bent down and picked up a battered silver-coloured case.

'This?' he called.

'That's it.'

He walked back towards Nikki and passed the case to her.

'There. Now go.'

The group turned and headed back the way they'd come, but Nikki paused when they drew level with what remained of Cobb's office.

'Let's see if it's still working,' she said.

Seeing as she was struggling with just one arm, Josh helped her, taking the case, opening it and revealing a laptop tucked inside. He pulled the screen up and they saw it was still intact.

'Here goes,' Nikki said, pushing the power button as Josh held it in front of her.

The laptop switched on.

It powered up fast and Nikki logged herself in, the process slowed by having the use of just one hand and needing to peer closely at the screen, hampered without her glasses.

'Shit, this is going to take me longer than usual,' she said, looking around for somewhere to perch. 'I've got one hand and crappy eyesight. I need to sit down.'

'I wasn't joking!' the lead fire-fighter suddenly called again from behind them. *'Get downstairs now!'*

Josh closed the laptop and slid it into the case but before the trio started to make their way to the stairs, Nikki suddenly turned and ducked into Cobb's office, stepping through a gap where a pane of bulletproof glass used to be.

131

Archer and Josh paused, watching as she rummaged through the folders spilt from one of the filing cabinets. Impatiently discarding those she didn't need, she eventually found the one she wanted and rose, re-joining Archer and Josh as she clutched the green folder in her hand.

'Let's go downstairs to the interrogation cells,' she said. 'We can use the ground floor as a base.'

'Will it be OK?' Josh asked.

She nodded. 'Each section of the building is a separate pod. It's designed to remain intact in case of something like this.'

'What's in the folder?' Archer asked.

'You'll see.'

SEVENTEEN

Shortly afterwards, Archer finished a brief conversation with the last remaining paramedic in the car park and then walked back towards the building as the man jumped into an ambulance and drove off.

Marquez was standing by the front doors, having made a quick call to the Counter-Terrorism Bureau back in New York to let them know what had happened to Shepherd. Joining her, Archer turned and they both watched the vehicle move out of the car park quickly; it passed Wilson and Lipton who were standing by the front gate, both of them talking quietly with the Met firearms officers stationed there and both now armed with MP5s and Glocks as well as wearing a bulletproof tactical vest. Archer noticed that Wilson appeared to be OK but Lipton still looked shaken and was having a cigarette to steady his nerves; he was on duty but no one was picking him up on it. Considering what had just happened, he could be allowed a quick smoke.

Before he'd left his post, Lipton had locked open the Perspex screen by the front desk to allow ease of access for the fire-fighters. Re-entering the building and passing through the entrance unhindered, Archer and Marquez continued walking straight ahead and pulled open another door, heading down the long corridor of the reverse L towards the interrogation cells. A third of the way down, they both turned right and joined Chalky, Josh, Fox and Nikki inside one of the cells, the only other people left standing. The room was rectangular and bare save for a table and two chairs, three of the walls concrete, the fourth on

Archer's left a long one-way mirror with a viewing area on the other side for personnel to observe interrogations anonymously.

Sitting at the desk in the middle of the cell and with her back to the far wall, Nikki had her laptop on the table in front of her. Chalky was in the other chair beside her, still looking pretty rough but sitting quietly and watching Nikki work. That last paramedic Archer had spoken to had wanted to get Chalk to the hospital and under supervision, saying he had a suspected concussion but just like Nikki, Chalky had refused, demanding to stay.

Archer shut the door to the room and observed the group for a moment.

Then there were six, he thought.

'How's it going out there?' Nikki asked.

'All the injured are on their way to hospital,' he replied. 'Lipton and Wilson are just about to take over from the two Met guys at their posts.'

'How's Beckett?'

'Not so good. There's a piece of glass in the top of her back the size of a drinks mat. I also just spoke to the fire-teams and told them it was crucial we continued to work down here.'

'They didn't object?' Josh asked.

'Started to. They agreed with a bit of persuasion, providing we remain on this floor and don't try to go upstairs again.'

A silence fell, which Archer used to assess their current status.

It wasn't good at all.

The NYPD team had only been in London for less than two hours but the situation had deteriorated at a shocking pace, moving from bad to critical faster

134

than anyone could have possibly imagined or anticipated. In the past hour the ARU had lost over eighty per cent of its team, two of them dead, many others critically injured, and the two Slovakian suspects the NYPD detectives had come here to apprehend had been murdered.

There'd been three separate well-planned attacks, the ARU Operations area had been destroyed, and Nikki and Chalky were both wounded along with many others, including Cobb and Shepherd. Archer could also see that Josh and Marquez were jet-lagged, stressed and confused, not to mention feeling vulnerable without their firearms and in a foreign city where they'd been on the ground for less than two hours and had already had someone try to kill them.

He glanced at his watch. *7:31pm.* Madrid was an hour ahead of London, which meant judging by the ruckus the neighbour heard at 2:30am Alice had been kidnapped a full eighteen hours ago.

And the cherry on the top of all this was that no one still had any idea where the hell she was or what this was all about.

'So what now?' Fox asked, breaking the silence in the room. 'Where do we go from here?'

'Before we do anything, we need to establish a chain of command,' Nikki said.

Archer nodded. 'We're on your turf. With Cobb out of action, you're technically in charge, Nik.'

She shook her head immediately. 'No way. I'm only working at fifty per cent; one arm and shitty eyesight.'

'It's protocol.'

'Stuff protocol. Despite what's happened, technically this still isn't our operation,' she said, standing her ground. 'Vargas is your missing person. One of you needs to take charge.'

'I say Arch,' Josh said.

'Me too,' Marquez said.

'Me too,' said Chalky.

'And me,' Nikki said.

Archer looked at the group, the tables immediately turned on him.

'I have an emotional involvement in this case,' he argued. 'We need a cool head.'

'That's exactly what you have,' Nikki said.

'We're the same rank,' Archer said, turning to Marquez and Josh. 'We should draw straws.'

They both shook their heads.

'It has to be you,' Marquez said. 'You're the only one who has experience both working here and with our Department.'

'And no-one on the planet is more invested in finding Vargas than you,' Josh added. 'You're in charge, Arch.'

He looked at them for a moment, then sighed and relented.

'Fine.'

'By the way, I thought we had a detective stationed here?' Josh said. 'The exchange for you, Arch.'

Nikki nodded. 'Detective Slater. She's been loaned to Scotland Yard working another case. It's just us on this.'

As she spoke, Marquez' cell phone suddenly rang; she took the call, motioning *one minute* with her finger, and opening the door stepped outside, pulling it shut behind her. As she left, Archer turned to the rest of the room.

'OK, so let's think for moment and assess this thing. We came here for Stanovich and Payan, two of the three people we'd definitely placed at the villa where Vargas was abducted last night. Now both guys are dead; judging by Porter's radio recording before the blast in Brixton and what happened in Hendon, it looks pretty obvious that they were both coerced into making the ransom calls. Someone used them to come after us.'

He focused on Nikki.

'After the ambush, we made it into the house and saw Payan. He was duct-taped to a chair and had a bump on the back of his head the size of a squash ball. Forensics found grease on his lips and teeth from a suppressed .22 pistol and two puncture wounds from a needle on his arm.'

She frowned. 'Recent?'

Archer nodded. 'He got busted for coke before, but never heroin. I think they drugged him to transport him quietly and also took a sample of his blood.'

'Why would they do that?'

'Let's say whoever killed the two men took vials of their blood after kidnapping and restraining them. Then they went to Spain and abducted Vargas, leaving the blood samples at the scene as if she'd drawn it from them as she fought back. Shit, they might even have smashed up some of the room to make it look like she put up a huge fight. Stanovich and Payan were both men with history and police records here. Whoever did this to them knew we'd ID them quickly and immediately come looking to get Alice back.'

137

The others stayed silent, listening.

'We fell for it hook and line thinking they took her, and raced straight here looking for them both.'

He paused.

'And less than ninety minutes after we arrive, everyone apart from the six of us is either dead or badly injured. Twelve casualties and two fatalities, not including the four SCO19 boys who died.'

'In Hendon?' Nikki asked.

Archer nodded. 'The snipers whacked them a minute or so before they tried to drop us. And we didn't hear a thing.'

'So Stanovich and Payan weren't connected to Vargas' disappearance at all,' Josh said.

Archer shook his head. 'No. And whoever actually took her knows exactly who she is. She was specifically targeted. All these attacks indicate they want to put us out of action for good.'

There was a short silence as the penny dropped.

'Holy shit,' Josh said. 'We've been played.'

'Like an accordion,' Archer said. 'And Stanovich and Payan were thugs; both of them were as hard as nails, ex-cons who made a living out of exploiting young women and running gangs. But whoever killed them handled them both with ease. Neither guy would be easy to intimidate, but on Porter's recording and Payan's phone call, it sounded like they were about to piss their pants. Whoever these people are, they also just took out eighty per cent of a counter-terrorist police team without giving us so much as a hint as to their identity.'

No one replied.

'Whoever really took Vargas and is responsible for all this is extremely dangerous.'

'And now we've got two more hostages to worry about,' Josh continued. 'Beckett's kids.'

'What did she say when you spoke to her?' Chalky asked Archer.

'Two men strapped the vest onto her and sent her here,' Archer said. 'She thinks from their accents that they were both Australian. Told her that if she didn't do exactly what they said, they'd kill her sons. And the only reason anyone who was on the 1st floor is still alive is because of you, Chalk. How did it play out?'

Chalky thought for a moment as he recalled the events of earlier. 'I was in the Briefing Room. Beckett appeared, looking like she was about to faint. She was wearing a coat with a belt which I thought was weird given the hot weather. She was so scared she couldn't even speak. I followed a hunch, opened up the coat and saw she had more explosives strapped to her than a demo team uses on a bridge.'

'What kind of explosives?' Josh asked.

'TNT, on a timer. When I saw the vest, we had nineteen bloody seconds and no-one else had even noticed; they were all watching you lot in Hendon.'

'Perfect timing,' Nikki said. 'Immaculate even. Distract the entire team with a fake ransom call and stay on the line long enough to give us a direct trace. Whilst everyone is preoccupied with the situation in Hendon, send Beckett in strapped with enough TNT to blow the building in half and take the entire intelligence team out too.'

'And they knew some of us would go to Hendon,' Archer added. 'They were right there ready to mop us up.'

The conversation suddenly halted, the very few pieces that they had of the puzzle sliding into place.

The group realised they'd been completely duped.

'Jesus,' Josh said quietly. 'This was planned down to the last detail.'

'But who the hell is doing it?' Fox asked.

EIGHTEEN

Across London, the two men who'd strapped the explosives to Stanovich and killed Payan were standing side by side inside a dark 12th floor office in front of their employer.

They were nervous and on edge which was an unusual feeling for them both, but they'd messed up badly in the last hour and knew their employer didn't deal well with failure. The Middle Eastern man on the right with the burn scars and broken nose was known as Holloway today; he was also the man who'd led the kidnap last night in the Spanish town. Breaching the villa had been easy enough, scaling the side of the house quickly with two of his men and reaching the balcony of the room where the bitch was staying. They'd been about to go in and take her, but had heard her get out of bed, open the bedroom door and move off downstairs. He and his men had used the opportunity to enter the bedroom and hide out in her bathroom.

Waiting for her to return.

The hard part done, they'd heard her re-enter the room a minute later and go back to bed, but the three men stayed where they were for a while, letting her drift back to sleep.

Then they'd moved in.

Holloway had assumed she'd be easy prey but the bitch had fought like a wildcat, breaking his nose with her elbow and opening it up like a geyser as he, Covent and Wood had struggled to restrain her. None of them had anticipated such determined resistance and it had resulted in his blood leaking all over the

141

sheets and floor as the men with him finally gagged and tied up the woman, Wood hitting her over the head to daze her, the blow drawing blood.

As soon as she was bound and under control, Holloway knew they had to get the hell out of there; the woman had made a lot of noise. With no time to spare and too much of his blood on the sheets and floor to get rid of quickly if at all, he'd scattered Stanovich and Payan's samples as planned then left, heading to Malaga and a private jet their employer had hired.

Standing in front of that employer in the office, he silently cursed himself for his carelessness. He'd assumed that the NYPD detective would be easy to subdue, but he should have taken into account that she'd be well-trained and would have been versed in self-defence; as a result of that complacency, his blood had been left in the room and he knew that a half-competent Forensics team would soon be able to pull an ID.

That could be a big problem.

Beside him stood the South African who was known today as Piccadilly; he was Holloway's second-in-command and a clever son of a bitch, the three-pronged attack on the ARU and NYPD search operation his idea. However, he was remaining silent too, carefully watching the woman in front of them as she leaned back against the front of a desk.

Holloway and Piccadilly were both tough, hardened killers but their employer was a legend. Propped against the wood, her hands behind her back, she was only five foot two and dwarfed by the two men in front of her but nonetheless easily dominated the room. Every inch of her small frame emanated pure confidence, power and menace. She had hard brown eyes, dark hair streaked with silver and lined skin that was as tough as leather from years of exposure to hot sun. Both men knew all about her reputation and how she handled people who crossed her.

She wasn't someone to disappoint.

A laptop on the desk beside her was closed, but the light on it was glowing green which meant it was switched on.

Possibly meaning she knew from a news website what had happened.

'I just saw the news,' she said quietly, answering Holloway's silent question. 'On the internet.'

Shit.

'Three separate incidents were dominating the headlines. Two bomb attacks and a sniper ambush in Hendon.'

She paused.

'The report said only two ARU officers died in Brixton. But the rest are still alive and have been taken to hospital.'

Pause.

'Apparently no one died at the police station in the blast. And four men were killed in Hendon, yet none of them were the targets.'

She spoke slowly, emphasising the words.

'Explain yourselves.'

'The rest of them are down and not operational,' Holloway said, focusing on the few positives. 'Their intelligence floor was wrecked. They're out of the game.'

'Only two are dead.'

'So far,' Piccadilly said.

Pause.

She didn't move, continuing to look at the two men in turn.

'How badly are the rest wounded?' she asked.

'We don't know.'

'What happened in Hendon?'

'A group of them headed over there, just as we expected. Grange and Stockwell were in place, but they missed.'

'They missed?' she repeated, staring at him. Silence.

'I'd assumed I was spending all this money employing professionals, not a bunch of girl guides,' she said. 'And I'm struggling to understand how anyone could have survived the bomb at the police headquarters.'

'So are we. Finchley and Portland screwed up,' Holloway continued, eager to shift the blame off themselves. 'They put the explosives on the bitch and delivered her, but someone inside must have managed to pull the vest off. They can't have locked it on properly.'

'So where are Finchley and Portland now?'

'Upstairs; with Covent, Wood and Camden.'

The woman thought for a moment. 'How many of the search operation are still standing?'

'I'd say five or six. Grange said there were three NYPD cops and one ARU guy on the street in Hendon. Possibly a couple more from their base.'

'They're going to be looking for the missing detective. And if the analyst survived, she might describe the men who put the vest on her. That's not helpful.'

She flicked her cold dark gaze onto Holloway. He saw her eyes focusing on his broken nose.

144

'And you bled at the scene.'

He paused. 'She put up more of a fight than we expected.'

The woman studied him for a moment, almost as if she was deciding his fate.

'I suppose I should have allowed for this,' she said eventually. 'They're trained after all. Apparently I underestimated them and overestimated you. Wiping them all out within an hour was obviously too much to ask.'

She kept staring at Holloway.

'But we both know what's on your file. If they have your blood, they'll soon find out who you are.'

'But that might work in our favour.'

She waited. 'How.'

'Like you said, we've both seen my file.'

Holloway smiled.

'And that means I know where they'll be going next.'

NINETEEN

'So two anonymous Australian men forced Beckett to wear the vest,' Josh said, still inside the interrogation cell with the rest of the group minus Marquez. 'They used her kids as a threat, which means they must have apprehended them at home or coming out of school.'

'Not school,' Fox said. 'It's a Saturday.'

Thinking, Archer turned to Nikki. 'Is Beckett married?'

'Separated. Husband left four years ago. He lives in Germany.'

'She wasn't here earlier but the rest of your team was. Was that planned?'

'Yes. Today was one of her two days off a week. My staff's free days are on a rota system.'

'So she's a single mother with two kids on her day off from work,' Archer said. 'A smart choice. Out of everyone who worked here, she'd be one of the best targets to choose. Easy to coerce using her kids and no one would notice her absence as it was her day off. She could walk in here without being challenged whenever she liked.'

'And confronting her at home would be pretty easy,' Josh said. 'These people clearly did their homework. They'd know she'd be alone, no husband, no boyfriend. Hell, no one around to interfere.'

'I've got her address,' Nikki said, twisting the laptop with her good hand and showing the screen to the group. 'She lives in an apartment building off High Street Kensington.'

Archer looked at her, surprised. 'That's an expensive area.'

'Her family are well-off.'

'Someone needs to head over there to check it out,' he said, turning to the others. 'See if these Australians left any sort of trace or if they ditched the boys once Beckett did what they asked. They could still be there.'

'I'll do it,' Fox said, stepping forward and peering at the map on the screen.

'I'll come with you,' Josh said.

As Fox noted down the address, the door to the interrogation cell opened and Marquez stepped back into the room, tucking her phone into her pocket and shutting the door.

'That was Detective Travis in Madrid,' she said. 'He had good news.'

'Which is?' Archer asked.

'A match came through for the fourth blood sample from the villa.'

'Who?' Josh asked.

'Former Staff-Sergeant Dashnan Sahar; goes by the name Dash according to the notes on the file. Ex-grunt; was a commando in the Afghan National Army for six years.'

'Record?' Archer asked.

'Pretty good. His service career ended several years ago, but Travis said there's nothing on file to suggest he was any sort of trouble-maker. He did his time then left and appears to have dropped off the radar. Nothing's been heard from him since.'

'What does this guy look like?' Fox asked.

'Travis said Spanish police have sent his file through,' she said to Nikki. 'But that explains why it

147

took longer to find. He's not an ex-con; he's ex-military.'

Turning her laptop back to face her, Nikki typed as fast as she could with one hand but it took her longer than usual; the group waited as she worked.

A few moments later, she tapped two more keys and nodded.

'Here we go.'

She turned the laptop round and they all moved forward to get a closer look at the screen. The photo was an official army one and they saw a brown-skinned man with jet black hair and dark eyes wearing a green beret and looking straight at the camera. He looked professional and tough, his black hair neatly combed and his face stern. Glancing at his vital statistics, Archer saw the man was six foot three and two hundred and ten pounds.

'Big guy,' he said.

Beside him, Josh frowned. 'So what the hell does he want with Vargas?'

'Are you sure there isn't any more information since he left?' Archer asked. 'Anything at all we can use? We need to find this son of a bitch.'

Nikki spun the laptop. 'Give me a sec.'

She worked away with her good hand, peering closely at the screen. The group waited.

'His military file is done and dusted, but there's something else here.'

'What is it?' Marquez asked.

Nikki double-clicked the mouse. 'A medical report from a hospital in Kabul. Dated February last year, seventeen months ago.'

'A medical report?' Fox repeated. 'What does it say?'

148

'He spent several months having treatment after being brought in suffering from severe burns,' she read. 'Seventy per cent apparently. Another guy came in with him at the same time with similar injuries. He was a Brit. Former Sergeant Michael Bernhardt; ex 2 Para.'

'Where does this other guy live?' Archer asked. 'In the UK?'

She tapped some keys, searching the man's name through all the databases.

'Apparently,' she said. 'He's been out of the army for six years; worked for a private firm called *Shields Security* afterwards for half a year but that's the last entry on his file. Last known address is in Tottenham.'

'Photo?' Archer asked.

Nikki turned the laptop and the group saw another photo, a blond man who could only ever have been a soldier, square faced and with hard eyes.

'He's not the one we want, but he's a start,' Nikki said. 'And if these guys were brought into hospital together both suffering burn wounds, it could well mean they were involved in the same incident.'

'Not necessarily,' Josh said. 'The hospital was in Afghanistan's capital. Maybe they were two strangers caught up in a bomb blast?'

'So where were all the other victims,' Archer said, shaking his head. 'Two ex-soldiers with no documented history for at least the past four years.'

He nodded at the screen.

'These two knew each other.'

'Bernhardt lives pretty close by,' Nikki said. 'If we can find him, he might be able to throw some light on what's going on here. It's a long shot, but it's all we've got.'

Archer nodded. 'I'll go over to his place and check him out.'

'Me too,' Marquez said.

Archer shook his head, turning to her. 'You need to stay here, Lisa.'

She looked at him, surprised and indignant. 'Are you kidding me? Why?'

'Because those snipers know they missed. And it's almost certain that they'll be coming back to finish the job.' He looked at Chalky, who was still quiet and slightly out of it. 'He isn't ready for that yet.'

'We've got Wilson and Lipton,' Nikki said.

'With all due respect, that might not be enough.'

Marquez thought for a moment and then sighed and nodded.

'OK. But if they do try again, what am I supposed to use to defend us, a nightstick?'

Before Archer could reply, Nikki reached forward and opened the folder she'd brought down from Cobb's office. A moment later she slid some documents she'd extracted from the file across the table.

'These are official authorisations,' she said. 'Take a look.'

As Josh, Archer and Marquez each stepped forward and checked the documents, Archer scanned his copy. There were two pages stapled together, the back page with a notary seal and a signature on a dotted line, a space left for another below.

'Cobb has already signed them. We're a paramilitary unit; in times of extreme crisis, we have the power to authorise weapons use for whoever we want, and this situation most certainly qualifies.'

'These are kosher?' Archer asked.

'Completely. Cobb drew them up when he found out you were coming, just in case. And don't forget the Prime Minister ordered the formation of this Unit. He gave Cobb wide-ranging powers. You're covered.'

That sealed it. Fox pulled a pen from his pocket, passing it to Josh, and they each took turns to sign their own named document. When that was done, Fox opened the door and turned right, Josh and Marquez close behind as they headed down the corridor straight towards the gun-cage. Passing his signed form back to Nikki, who slotted them into the folder, Archer looked over at Chalky, who'd been uncharacteristically quiet throughout the conversation, just sitting and listening to the exchanges.

'You'd better stay here too for the moment, Chalk.'

He nodded. 'Will do.'

Turning, Archer headed for the door.

It was time to start fighting back.

TWENTY

Inside the 12th floor office across the city, Holloway, or former Staff Sergeant Dashnan Sahar as he was otherwise known, had outlined his new plan, fully acknowledging their unexpected lack of success but providing a solution.

In front of him, the woman had listened in total silence, her face expressionless. Having said his piece, a silence fell as Dash waited for her verdict.

She looked at him coldly. 'You think that will work?'

'Yes. And we'll finish what you hired us to do.'

She thought for a long moment, assessing this new plan.

'Very well. Both of you go. But before you do, send Finchley and Portland down here immediately and escort them in.'

Holloway nodded. 'Of course.'

'And don't fail me again.'

Turning, the two men walked out of the room, relieved to be out of her presence. Walking across the empty office building floor and approaching the lifts, Dash pulled his phone and called a saved number as Piccadilly walked beside him.

'Yeah?' Finchley said.

'Both of you, get down here now,' Dash said. 'She wants to see you.'

Ending the call before the Australian could answer, Dash came to a halt in front of the lifts and waited, Piccadilly beside him, the pair watching the illuminated floor indicators above their heads. A few moments later, one of the two lifts started rising, heading up from the lower floors after being called from above. As he and Piccadilly waited, Dash dialled another number, hearing the lift move past their floor and stop on 16.

'Yeah?' one of his other men, Notting, said.

'Where are you?'

'Outside the CCU at the Royal Marsden with Regent. The ARU task force officers were brought in earlier. Want us get in there and finish the job?'

'No. I've got new orders.'

'What are they?'

'Get over to Beckett's place. Call Grange, and tell him and Stockwell to join you. The analyst from Kensington somehow survived the blast; a handful of the cops are still alive too and someone's definitely going to be checking out where she lives.'

'What about Finch and Portland?'

'They're back here. Just take care of it.'

'Roger.'

Dash ended the call just as the lift arrived, the doors parting. Portland and Finchley were standing there, the two Australian men who'd broken into Beckett's apartment, taken her kids and strapped the vest onto her. Both were Caucasian, dark haired, unshaven and tanned; they were dressed the same as Dash and Piccadilly, khakis and shirts which covered the pistol each man had in a holster on his hip. Finchley had a sour look on his face, a scar running across the left side of his mouth from some altercation long ago; beside him, Portland was expressionless.

'What does she want?' Finchley asked.

153

'There's been a change of plan,' Dash said, motioning for the two men to step out and follow him.

As they walked forward, Piccadilly quietly fell into step behind them, making sure they couldn't double back.

The two newcomers followed Dash towards the office. As he opened the door and the men walked inside, Finchley and Portland saw their female employer standing in front of a desk, looking straight at them, her hands behind her back. Piccadilly closed the door behind them quietly and stepped to one side.

'What's going on?' Finchley asked.

'Which one of you delivered the woman to the police station?'

They looked at each other.

'Me,' Finchley said, jerking his head at Portland. 'He was taking care of the kids.'

Before either man could move, the woman whipped her arm around from behind her back.

She was holding a nail gun; dropping, she pushed the gun down and fired twice, the weapon giving off two fast *cracks* as she put a nail through each of Finchley's feet. The Australian screamed in pain and fell to the floor, clutching his feet and the twin nails embedded in them. As Portland jerked back, she turned the nail gun on him and held it steady, stepping forward and pushing it up into his face.

'Don't move,' she screamed at him.

As Finchley writhed on the floor in agony, Dash knelt down and punched him in the face twice, stunning him. After taking his pistol and tossing it across the room he and Piccadilly quickly bound the man's feet and wrists, blood leaking out from the injured man's feet, his shouts turning into muffled moans as the duct tape was pulled tight across his mouth.

Piccadilly hit him once again for good measure, then he and Dash dragged the bound man out of the room and into another office next door. Behind them, Portland stayed exactly where he was, looking at the nail gun pushed up against his chin, his hand frozen mid-way to the pistol tucked into the holster on his hip.

'You failed me,' the woman said at him, her finger poised on the trigger. 'They were all meant to die.'

'I'll make it right,' Portland said quickly. 'Whatever you want me to do, I'll do it.'

'No-one at the ARU building died,' she screamed, the nail gun shaking in her hand. 'No-one.'

'That was his fault,' Portland shouted back in desperation. 'They must have got the vest off her somehow before it detonated.'

'Do you care what happens to him?' she screamed.
'No!'

Shaking with anger, she kept the gun on him for a few more moments. Then she lowered it, just as Dash and Piccadilly returned from the office next door.

'He's ready for you,' Dash said.

'Good. Now get out of my sight and finish this.'

Nodding, the two men immediately moved to the door. Portland didn't dare move, frozen to the spot.

'Go with them,' she said quietly.

He looked at her for a moment, then nodded and walked rapidly out of the room.

Now alone again, the woman waited for the men to leave.

Once they were gone, she walked out of the main office into the open space of the 12th floor and turned left, moving into another office whilst still carrying the nail gun.

This second smaller office was still in the process of being refurbished, planks of wood ready to be planed leaning against the wall and some carpentry tools left in the corner of the room ready for Monday morning. The workmen had stacked their equipment neatly in the far corner; there were some saws and bags of nails sitting beside a rubbish bin full of discarded food wrappers and drinks cartons. This was where she'd found the nail-gun earlier, a pleasant surprise.

The Australian ex-soldier who'd failed with the bomb vest was lying in the middle of the floor, tied up, his eyes bulging with terror when he saw the woman enter. Plastic sheets were hanging down around the room to protect the paintwork against the dust from the carpentry, but as it was the weekend none of the workers had been here today, leaving the floor completely unoccupied, much like the rest of the building.

She shot him twice more in the legs; as he writhed in agony and moaned under the duct tape, the woman carefully laid down the nail-gun and pulled on a set of carpenter's overalls. When that was done, she put on a white mask to cover her face, almost as if she was preparing for an operation.

Which in a way, she was.

Then she closed the blinds, leaving her alone with the bound and wounded man, the room darker but

156

with just enough light to see. She turned to face him, and her eyes narrowed over the top of the mask.

'As you may have heard, I don't deal well with failure. Unluckily for you, I'm extremely disappointed. And you're going to pay for that.'

He watched as she picked up a power saw.

'I have a particular method with these things. I like to start on the feet and work my way up an inch at a time,' she said.

Staring at her in terror, he saw the skin around her eyes crinkle as she smiled.

'One man made it halfway up his thigh. He was a Russian though; a tough bastard. They always are. Let's see if you can beat his record. I have a feeling you won't.'

Finchley watched in horror as the woman turned on the saw, his muffled screams instantly lost under the shrieking whine of the serrated blades.

TWENTY ONE

Across London, Archer was already on his way to
Bernhardt's address in Tottenham, making good time
in Cobb's expensive silver Mercedes. Fox and Josh
had headed off a minute or so before, both armed
with Glocks and Fox with an MP5, the two men
taking the last remaining ARU BMW left in the car
park. The other had been badly damaged in the
explosion, a piece of wall falling through its roof,
and the other two vehicles the task force had used to
get to Brixton hadn't been returned yet.

Archer had needed a vehicle and Cobb's Mercedes
had immediately caught his eye. Telling himself his
old boss would understand, Archer had taken the
keys from the ARU Director's desk drawer upstairs,
finding them where he knew Cobb kept them and
smiling when he saw the set resting on some papers
beside an unopened bottle of quality Scotch. Having
already armed up in the gun-cage, he'd sprinted back
out to the car park and climbed inside the Mercedes,
firing the engine and taking off.

Now shifting down the street he swerved, just
avoiding another car that pulled out in front of him
without warning and feeling a sudden jolt of high-
voltage nerves. He knew that if he even put a scratch
on this thing it wouldn't matter if anyone else was
trying to take him out, Cobb would do it for them.

As he drove on, he kept his right hand on the wheel
and adjusted the ear piece hooked around his ear
with his left. Whilst in the locker room by the gun-
cage, Archer had pulled on a black ARU tactical vest
over his black t-shirt. The bulletproof garment
provided him with various tools, plastic cuffs, smoke

and stun grenades and a headset consisting of an earpiece and Velcro microphone which was already strapped around his neck; the equipment was now connected to his Nokia, which was tucked inside the left breast slot of the vest, and would give him quick hands-free communication with Nikki back at HQ.

Beside him on the passenger seat was a fully loaded Heckler and Koch MP5. Given the totally unexpected events of the day, Archer already felt more reassured to have it sitting beside him, like a workman reunited with his tools. The MP5 was his favourite sub-machine gun and although he hadn't used one recently, he'd spent countless hours on the range with the weapon in the past. Light, portable and accurate, it could fire eight hundred rounds a minute with quick magazine changes and was the sub-machine gun of choice for most of the counter-terrorist police and paramilitary teams around the world. With a fully loaded Glock pistol also tucked into a holster clipped around his thigh and spare magazines on his tac vest, Archer was good to go and feeling ready to handle anything that came his way.

As he paused at a red light, he checked his rear view mirror, looking for anything suspicious, either people or cars, anyone who looked as if they might be following him. Satisfied he was alone, he glanced at the clock on the dashboard; *7:51pm*, fast moving on towards nineteen hours since Alice had been kidnapped.

By a team of men who for some reason had just tried to kill every member of her search party.

Willing the light to turn green, Archer thought back to something that had been said when he and the other NYPD detectives had arrived at Heathrow.

Chalky had mentioned that Stanovich had made a ransom call demanding two million in cash, but that the Slovakian had also claimed Vargas was in the city. Given what they now knew Stanovich had clearly been under duress when he made the call, but Archer was clinging onto the possibility that what he'd been instructed to say was true, a slip up by the real kidnappers, meaning Vargas really was somewhere in London.

Taking his phone from the chest pocket of the vest, Archer scrolled for Nikki's number and called her. He slotted the phone back into its home as the lights turned green, pushing his foot down on the accelerator as the call rang twice and was then answered.

'How are you doing, Arch?' she said, down his earpiece, the connection perfect.

'I'm almost there, Nik' he said. 'Give me the lowdown on this guy.'

Former 2 Para Sergeant Michael Bernhardt. Thirty six years old, left the army six years ago. He saw action predominantly in the Middle East, fighting in Iraq and Afghanistan. No record since he left, but if he showed up in Kabul covered in burns last year then I suspect he was probably out there working as a contractor of some sort. A lot of ex-army guys are.'

'Anything since?'

'Nothing of importance. And remember, we don't know much about this man. His allegiances are unclear.'

'How are Foxy and Josh doing?'

'They're almost at Beckett's. But be careful, Arch; as I said, this man has some kind of history with

160

Dash. You might not get a warm welcome. In fact, it could be just the opposite.'

'Will do.'

Archer ended the call and focused on the traffic ahead, now just six or seven minutes from his destination.

Across the city, Fox and Josh had just arrived outside Beckett's apartment building, pulling into an empty space down a side street right beside the large gate blocking the courtyard off from the road.

Now the sun was going down, the light was matching their mood, growing darker by the minute as shadows slowly started to descend over the city. There were a couple of people on the street around them, but the place was generally quiet, the focus of activity on the High Street at the end of the road. Nevertheless, the two policemen were alert and not taking any chances, scanning everything around them as they drew to a halt.

In a situation like this, they couldn't be too cautious.

As Josh examined the street then peered up at the apartment building beyond the gate, Fox called Nikki using the tablet inside the car that had synced to his phone.

'How's it going?' Nikki asked, her voice filling the car.

'We're here,' he said. 'About to head up.'

'I contacted the Met and explained the situation. Back-up has been dispatched just in case. Two firearms teams are on their way; they'll be there shortly.'

161

Fox glanced at Josh, who was quietly checking the chamber of his Glock.

'We're not hanging around. They can follow us up when they get here.'

'OK. Be careful.'

Fox ended the call, then reached behind him and grabbed his MP5 from the back seat.

'Let's move.'

Stepping out of the car, Fox slammed the door and locked it; then the two men moved through the pedestrian entrance connected to the main gate securing the courtyard, heading towards the front doors of the building. There was no one else around and they moved fast, Fox scoping out some residents' cars parked neatly in bays to their right as Josh checked over his shoulder, making sure they weren't being followed.

A dark haired man was leaving the building as they approached and Fox managed to catch the door just before it shut behind him. The guy didn't even notice them, his head down as he read something on his smartphone, which was just as well considering Fox and Josh were both carrying weapons. The two policemen examined the man as they passed but he was obviously unarmed and didn't look suspicious, just a resident heading out and totally absorbed in what he was doing.

Turning their attention to the lobby, they saw there were two lifts to their left and a stairwell fifteen feet away to their far right. It was a smart place in a wealthy area; clearly Beckett's family money had come in handy. There were worse places to live.

As Josh pushed the button for the lift, Fox checked around them, his hands tight on his MP5.

By all logical reasoning, Beckett should have been dead by now, unable to tell anyone who had locked the vest onto her and why. It was summer and a Saturday, so Fox figured Jen might have been out with her sons today, but these men would have needed to confront her somewhere they knew she'd be alone, somewhere they could easily grab her sons and strap the TNT onto her without fear of being seen or heard.

He watched the floor indicator tick down; a moment later, one of the lifts arrived with a *ding*.

Fox was a professional, and knew how he would get that sort of thing done.

Whoever strapped the vest onto Beckett would have done it upstairs.

Outside in the courtyard, the dark-haired man who'd been studying his phone slowed as he approached the gate. He was thirty four years old and American.

And his call-sign was Notting.

Stopping in his tracks, he turned and pushed *Redial* on the phone, looking back at the building.

'Yeah?' Regent said.

'Two of them just walked in; black guy and a white guy. One has an MP5, the other a pistol. You in position?'

'Yeah.'

'I'll follow them up and cut them off. Grange and Stockwell will be here any second too. No mistakes this time.'

'Got it.'

Hanging up, Notting walked back across the courtyard towards the building, slowing as he approached the doors. He saw as he'd expected that

163

the two cops who'd just passed him were no longer in the lobby.

Already on their way upstairs.

Pulling out the analyst's key, he opened the door then locked it behind him, rattling the handle to make sure it was sealed then breaking off the key in the lock to stop anyone else coming in or leaving.

Turning, he checked the ticking red number display above one of the two elevators.

2.

3.

4.

He quickly moved over to the maintenance closet across the lobby, opening the door and withdrawing two items he'd placed in there earlier when he'd seen the two cops arrive. When that was done, he stepped into the other empty lift and pushed the button for 4, feeling his heart rate increase, pumping him up for what was about to happen.

Little did the two cops upstairs know they had less than thirty seconds to live.

TWENTY TWO

In the other lift, the journey up to 4 was brief. Once it *dinged* on arrival and the doors parted, Josh and Fox stepped out, turning left onto the main corridor of the 4th floor and clearing either side with their weapons.

The corridor was empty and quiet. The floor was carpeted, golden lights incrementally lining the hallway, and they both saw from the apartment letters on doors in front of them that 4H would be to their right.

Satisfied all was clear, the two men turned and started to make their way quickly towards Beckett's apartment. However, as he walked beside Fox and gripped his Glock double handed, Josh frowned as the sequence of their arrival moments ago replayed in his head.

Something hadn't been right.

Inside *4H*, Regent was standing in the hallway of Beckett's apartment, a Benelli twelve-gauge semi-automatic shotgun buried in his shoulder and aimed directly at the door.

A thickly-bearded guy with huge forearms and hands, he'd loaded seven shells inside the twelve-gauge and the fingers of his right hand were curled around the grip, his forefinger nestled on the trigger. The Benelli was a vicious weapon that required no pumping to reload and could fire seven or eight shells with the speed of a pistol. He knew back home in the United States that it was one of the top firearms people selected for home defence, which

165

was pretty ironic right now; weapons like this were extremely difficult to source in the UK, but men like him had all sorts of connections and friends in the kind of places that not many people liked to go.

The apartment behind him was empty. The two kids were long gone, picked up by Finchley and Portland and taken to the team's safe-house as soon as their mother had been sent to her death. It would have been easier to kill them both once the analyst had gone, but their employer had given them strict instructions to bring the kids in alive, an insurance policy in case things went wrong.

In hindsight, he could see that had been a sensible move; somehow, the ARU bitch had survived. Regent had heard the announcement of the explosion on the radio as he sat in the car outside the Royal Marsden with Notting and all seemed to have gone according to plan. However, the report that had followed shortly afterwards stated that although there'd been a number of injuries, some of them serious, no one caught in the police station blast had been killed.

Although that was a blow, Regent and his companions were used to adapting to a rapidly changing situation and on the positive side, the ARU's ability to operate was now severely compromised.

Feeling a buzz of anticipation, he kept his focus solely on the door, the weapon aimed straight at the wood. Two of the cops were on their way up, and Notting was following to block them off, the two Canadian snipers arriving any minute to make doubly sure that between them these guys didn't make it out alive.

166

The moment he heard the two men outside the door, Regent would pull the trigger and repeat until the weapon was empty.

He grinned, settling into the Benelli.

Once he was done, all that would be left of the two men would be pieces in the air like an old-fashioned ticker parade.

Outside in the corridor, following a couple of steps behind Fox, Josh thought about the man they'd passed downstairs. There was something about the guy that was bothering him. Something Josh had noticed as they passed.

But what the hell was it?

He replayed the scene in his mind. As Fox had caught the door to enter the apartment building and the man walked past them, Josh had seen the man's eyes flick up from his phone. If Josh hadn't been looking at him, he'd have missed it.

The guy hadn't reacted to the sight of the weapons in their hands at all.

Due to the different gun laws back home, civilians in the US were used to seeing cops carrying guns, but he knew people here weren't. Archer had told Josh about the restrictions on carrying firearms in the UK but the man he and Fox passed downstairs hadn't batted an eyelid.

Now just a foot from 4H, he suddenly grabbed Fox's arm, stopping him in his tracks.

Startled, his MP5 tucked in his shoulder, Fox turned and looked at him.

'What?' he whispered.

Josh went to reply, but the elevator behind them suddenly *dinged.*

167

The two policemen twisted towards the sound.

A second later the man from downstairs suddenly reappeared; this time his head was up.

And the phone he'd been holding was gone.

He was now carrying a thick twelve gauge shotgun, which he was already lifting it to his shoulder to aim straight at the two cops standing there unprotected in the middle of the corridor.

And Josh and Fox both realised that they'd just walked straight into another ambush.

TWENTY THREE

Josh Blake hated guns. For a police detective who was required to carry one as part of the job, that was pretty unusual and not something that many of his colleagues were aware of. In fact, he disliked all forms of violence and would always attempt to talk his way out of a confrontation rather than just wade in. He'd always regarded carrying a handgun as a necessary evil, and had only fired his weapon on duty a handful of times in almost a decade of service; the last occasion had been in March when he'd saved Marquez' life.

But he was also a man who despised those who thrived on violence, people who used it to intimidate and hurt others. That's why he'd become a cop and why he could end a life like the man who'd been about to kill Marquez and not be haunted by it.

And he knew without doubt in that split second that if he didn't use the gun in his hand, he was going to die.

Having already suspected something was wrong, he reacted before Fox. With blistering speed for a big man, he snapped his Glock up and fired twice, the reports of the two gunshots echoing down the corridor as the muzzle flashed.

The double-tap missed the man carrying the shotgun by half an inch, but forced him to duck back and use the edge of the wall boxing the lifts for protection. Beside Josh, Fox reacted a split-second later and let rip with his MP5, squeezing off two three-round bursts and kicking chalk and plaster up from the expensively-decorated wall as the trio of

169

spent shell casings jumped out of the weapon, falling to the floor beside him.

Suddenly, the deafening blast of a shotgun echoed behind them from Beckett's apartment. A huge hole appeared in the door behind the two cops, taking them both completely by surprise. They instinctively recoiled and threw themselves against the wall as more blasts followed, the door disintegrating as the shots pounded the frame to pieces with shocking power, splinters filling the air. The shells smashed through the wood and blew apart the corridor wall immediately beyond, the air misted with debris as if the wall had been hit by a cannon, just the outer remnants of the doorframe remaining.

'Jesus Christ!' Fox shouted, half-deaf but maintaining fire down the corridor at the gunman by the lifts in an effort to pin him down and buy them some time.

The man tried to retaliate but Fox stitched a three round burst into the wall by his head, successfully keeping him back. Squeezing off another double-tap himself, Josh barely heard the Glock fire, pretty much deafened from the shotgun blasts that they would have walked straight into.

Blinking as dust and wood particles stung his eyes, he focused on Beckett's apartment as Fox continued to keep the man down the corridor at bay with the MP5. Edging forward fast, Josh went to fire through the door then realised Beckett's kids could still be inside. However, he and Fox had to move; they were boxed in by two shotguns and if they stayed where they were they'd be ripped apart as if they were being fed through a paper shredder.

Suddenly, the fire inside the apartment ceased. Whoever was inside was reloading.

Or so Josh hoped.

'Let's go!' he shouted.

Taking advantage of the brief lull in fire, he and Fox raced past the destroyed door, half-expecting another barrage of fire to blast them as they were briefly exposed to whoever was inside.

They made it just before another hole appeared in the wall beyond the damaged door, spraying fragments of plaster into the air.

Once past the doorway, Fox turned and fired back down the corridor again at the guy by the lifts, then followed Josh as they raced for the fire exit at the end of the hallway.

They smashed through the fire door, just entering the stairwell as the metal-reinforced door took a shotgun blast, clanging loudly from the impact.

Just missing them, Notting ran down the corridor after the two men, Regent appearing out of the analyst's apartment ahead with his Benelli in his shoulder as Notting raced towards him.

'This way!' he shouted without breaking stride, the two men sprinting down the corridor and smashing open the fire exit.

As they entered the white stairwell, they heard the two cops running down the flight a floor below.

Notting caught a glimpse of the pair and traced them with his Benelli, pulling the trigger.

Josh and Fox hurtled down the flight as the wall behind them exploded from another shotgun blast. Fox made it to the ground floor first, running for the front door and turning the handle as he rammed into it, but the door was locked. Not wasting a second he

171

fired a burst through the glass and ran through the shattered gap as Josh followed hard on his heels, their feet crunching over the broken glass.

Sprinting across the courtyard, knowing they only had seconds before the two gunmen made it to the lobby, Josh saw Fox suddenly turn and fire back at the doorway, providing cover fire as Josh ran past him, the shell casings from the MP5 tinkling to the concrete courtyard as Fox unloaded with the sub-machine gun.

Josh made it to the gate then turned, taking over, aiming his Glock double-handed at the two men with shotguns who'd just appeared in the lobby, forcing them to pull back.

'Move!' he shouted, emptying his handgun at the entrance as Fox raced past him, not slowing as he made it through the gate and to their car, reloading his MP5 on the run.

As Josh kept the two gunmen at bay, Fox pulled out the keys and unlocked the car, still ducking low.

However, the BMW and the tree right behind him suddenly ate a violent burst of machine gun fire, taking him completely by surprise and forcing him to dive to the ground.

Peering round the wheel arch, he saw two gunmen aiming over the top of a BMW parked further ahead of him down the street, firing on him with automatic weapons. He fired back from under the car with the MP5, then leaned up and ripped open the driver's door. Climbing inside and keeping low, he looked back at Josh, who was still the other side of the gate and edging back whilst holding off the other two.

'Let's go!' Fox shouted, firing the engine.

Josh fired twice more towards the men taking cover in the front entrance, his pistol clicking dry, then turned and ran for the car. He went for the near side, yanking open the rear door as the two gunmen with shotguns ran out into the courtyard through the smashed lobby doors.

'Shit!' he shouted, throwing himself inside just as the car took a shotgun blast, smashing apart the near-side rear headlight, pieces of it flying into the air, quickly followed by fire from the two men behind the BMW ahead as the gunshots echoed around the street.

'Go!' he bellowed, lying on his side and reloading as he was sprayed with smashed glass from the window above his head.

Fox didn't need to be told twice and was already flooring it, the BMW's tyres biting down on the tarmac and propelling them forward with a squeal of rubber. As the car took another shotgun blast from the right side, Josh's open door hit a parked car and slammed shut as they took off down the street.

Up ahead, Fox saw they were closing down on the pair behind the BMW with the assault rifles; their fire would shred them to pieces and kill them instantly. As Josh covered their other side and fired through the smashed out rear window at the men running across the courtyard, Fox kept his left hand on the wheel, laid his fully-loaded MP5 across his forearm and ducking low, opened fire on the two gunmen behind the car, keeping his foot down as the car roared towards them.

He'd changed the selector to automatic and the MP5 let rip, draining the clip, the ferocious burst of fire smashing through the passenger window, forcing the two gunmen armed with the assault rifles to take

173

cover as the bullets ripped into their car, giving Fox and Josh a brief opportunity to get past. As the weapon clicked dry, shell casings littering his lap and scattered in the well by his feet, Fox lifted his head to take control of the car and check his rear view mirror but immediately ducked as a burst of gunfire smashed into the headrest immediately behind him.

Spinning the wheel and weaving the car in a fast zigzag so they were harder to hit, the shot-up BMW continued down the street at a ferocious pace as they continued to eat more gunfire.

Seeing a street on their left, Fox then took a hard screeching turn and drove them away from the four man ambush, he and Josh both bleeding from flying shards of glass but against all the odds, still alive.

As they sped away from the scene, wind whistling through the smashed out windows of the ARU BMW, Josh checked through the shot-out rear window behind him in the back seat and sucked in huge lungfuls of air as his adrenaline started to dump. Behind the wheel, Fox had activated the fender lights to give them a clear run back to base.

However, suddenly they started to lose speed.

'What's wrong?' Josh asked, turning to look over his shoulder at Fox. *'Keep going!'*

Fox didn't reply.

Josh watched as his head started to tip forward.

Then the ARU officer suddenly slumped against the window to his right.

The car slowed and started to veer out of control. Realising what had happened, Josh reached forward and grabbed the wheel to steady the car as the BMW shuddered to a halt, Fox's foot off the pedal. Josh

174

pushed open the door to his right, leapt out and yanked open the driver's door, catching Fox as he fell.

He'd been hit in the body, a round getting through the armpit area of the vest, and blood immediately stained Josh's own vest and arms as he caught the wounded man.

'Oh shit, Fox!' he said.

Knowing they had to get the hell out of there, the gunmen on the street beyond no doubt hard on their heels, he eased Fox over to the other seat as gently as he could then jumped behind the wheel. After slamming his door he restarted the stalled engine and took off, checking the rear view mirror to make sure they weren't being pursued. Beside him, Fox was still conscious but only just, blood staining the seat and the side of his navy blue polo shirt.

'Hang on, bro,' Josh said. *'Just hang on!'*

Whoever those men were, they'd known the police were coming. They'd been immaculately prepared and lying in wait, which meant they could have another team doing the same at Bernhardt's.

Warn Arch, Josh thought as Fox started to wheeze beside him.

Warn Arch.

As the car roared on down the street, Josh withdrew his cell from his vest and called Archer, most of the pedestrians they passed stopping to stare at the shot-up police car as it raced past. There was no response; cursing, Josh quickly looked down and saw his US provider wouldn't call the number on the UK network.

'Shit!'

175

Throwing it to one side, he swerved around a car in front and reached over as far as he could for Fox's phone. The ARU officer had now passed out and was slumped against the passenger door, out of reach. Stretching across whilst keeping his eyes on the road ahead, Josh grabbed Fox's vest and pulled him upright, then reached for the cell phone in his tac vest.

They'd only just made it out of there alive, but not unscathed. Fox needed medical attention immediately.

And unlike the two of them, Archer was going in all by himself.

TWENTY FOUR

In Tottenham moments earlier, Archer had pulled to a halt on the street at the back of Michael Bernhardt's house. Switching off the engine he looked up at the property to his right, a small semi-detached place, two floors and possibly with an attic for a third.

It was in a residential area, not on the high street, and was relatively quiet save for a group of youths gathered on the pavement a few doors down, several on bikes, all of them in tracksuits and hoodies. As it was now 8pm the light had almost faded for the day, the city slowly taking on a shroud of darkness that would only be broken by street and house lights.

Archer glanced at the kids and saw they were drinking, two with cans of beer and another passing a bottle of vodka around. They whistled and shouted at a couple of women across the street who ignored them; one of the youths hurled an empty bottle in their direction which smashed on the pavement and the two women scurried for safety as the youths laughed and jeered.

Grabbing his MP5 from the passenger seat, Archer climbed out of the Mercedes, slammed the door and locked the vehicle; then keeping the sub-machine gun on the right side of his body, he headed towards a side alley leading to the front of the houses on the other side of the street. As he crossed the road, the group of teenagers immediately spotted him in the police vest; one of them wolf-whistled, two others shouting insults, full of false bravado from the booze. Turning his head to look at them as he approached the alley, Archer's eyes narrowed, but he ignored them and focused on the task ahead.

He had bigger fish to fry tonight.

Moving down the narrow path, he slowed when he reached the other end, checking each way to make sure no-one was lying in wait. Seeing the road was clear, he walked out onto the street in front of the house. Heading to the front door, he quickly knocked twice, stepping to one side and examining the street around him again.

It was all quiet.

Vargas' kidnap, the sniper attack and the two explosions in the past few hours had left him on edge, especially given that he had almost no idea who was responsible for all this and where they were likely to strike next. All he currently knew was that an Afghan National Army ex-soldier called Dash was one of them, and the man who lived here had suffered the same burn wounds as him at the same time last year.

As he took the safety off his MP5 and waited for Bernhardt to answer, Vargas flashed into his mind again.

Just hang on Alice, he thought, glancing over his shoulder at the quiet street and feeling the seconds constantly tick by.

He went to knock again but then heard movement inside the property.

'Who is it?' a voice called.

'Police,' Archer said, standing to one side with the sub-machine gun on the door. 'I need to talk to you, sir.'

He waited, his finger on the trigger and standing to the side of the door.

After a long pause, it opened.

A man somewhere in his early forties stood in the doorway looking at Archer and the MP5 in his hands. His appearance was extraordinary; he had brown hair, stubble on his cheeks over pale, patchy skin, but he'd obviously suffered severe burns on his face, arms and neck at one time, the skin gelatinous and translucent like thin baking paper.

He looked startling but Archer's surprise was distilled by scanning him for any sign of a weapon.

He seemed clean.

'Michael Bernhardt?'

'That's me,' he said. 'Who the hell are you?'

'My name's Sam Archer. I'm an NYPD detective working a case here.'

'Mind lowering that thing?' Bernhardt said, looking at the MP5, which although resting in Archer's hands was pointed at Bernhardt's navel.

Archer nodded, moving his aim off the man but keeping his finger on the trigger.

'I need to talk to you about someone, sir.'

'Who?'

'Dashnan Sahar. According to our files you and he had some…interaction last year,' he said, focusing on the man's face and avoiding reference to his burns.

As he said Dash's name, he saw a quick glimmer of recognition.

'So you do know him.'

Bernhardt nodded. 'I knew him. But what's this about?'

'It's a long story,' Archer said, glancing over his shoulder quickly and feeling exposed. 'And I need you to come with me right now.'

179

'You got ID?'

Archer nodded, withdrawing his NYPD badge with his left hand and showing it to the man. Bernhardt peered at it and frowned again.

'You have no jurisdiction here. Is this a joke?'

'No, it's not. You can confirm my credentials back at our HQ. I'll explain on the way.'

'We can talk here.'

'It might not be safe,' Archer said. 'And we need to go right now.'

Bernhardt stayed where he was, frowning. 'Are you messing with me?'

'No, I'm not.'

The urgency in Archer's words, the fact he was carrying a weapon and his serious manner finally spurred a response. After looking at him closely for a moment, Bernhardt relented and nodded.

'OK, I'm intrigued. I'll come. Give me two seconds to fetch my phone and lock up.'

As he headed back inside, Archer walked forward and kept eyes on the former soldier, not wanting to let him out his sight in case he changed his mind or tried something if he was somehow involved in what was going on. Bernhardt was aware of his presence but didn't say anything, locking the back door and pocketing a Samsung from the kitchen counter before grabbing a shirt on the way as he walked back towards the front door.

Standing there in the hallway as the man approached him, Archer suddenly felt his phone purr in his vest. Using his hand's free mic and earpiece, he pushed *Answer.*

'Archer.'

'Arch, it's me!' Josh said, sounding out of breath, urgency in his voice.

'What's wrong? Are you alright?'

'Where are you?'

'Bernhardt's,' he said, as he stood in the hallway beside the former Para, who was now ready to go.

'It was an ambush! Fox and I only just made it out! Get the hell out of there!'

Before he could react, Archer suddenly heard a screech of tyres from the street outside.

Spinning round, he checked out of the door and saw a black car coming down the street fast from the right, the windows already down and three men inside.

Two of them saw him in the doorway.

And a moment later, they both raised assault rifles from inside the vehicle as they slammed to a halt.

'Back!' Archer shouted, pushing Bernhardt down the hallway and kicking the door shut.

An instant later, a barrage of assault rifle fire ripped into the front door, splinters of white wood blown into the air around them. Archer and Bernhardt scrambled back fast as the bullets chewed up the entrance but the flimsy door couldn't withstand the barrage of gunfire and swung open, exposing Archer and Bernhardt to the street again.

Still on the floor, Archer swung his MP5 around and fired back through the now open door at the car on the street. The three guys inside jerked down and the man behind the wheel quickly reversed out of Archer's narrow line of fire, Archer's bullets smashing out the front headlights and ripping more

181

holes in the front door as the car disappeared out of view.

Archer used those valuable seconds to get back to his feet, glancing behind him to see Bernhardt had done the same. Through the open damaged door hanging on its hinges, they both heard three car doors open and slam, the trio coming for them.

Keeping the unarmed Bernhardt behind him and his MP5 trained on the door, Archer turned to the former soldier and looked at the closed kitchen door.

'Back door!' he said urgently.

'There's a wall!' Bernhardt replied, staying where he was. 'It's too high to get over from here. We're boxed in!'

Outside the house, Dash, Piccadilly and Portland couldn't believe their luck as they moved to the front entrance quickly but cautiously, none of them wanting to take a round from the blond cop's MP5. They'd timed it to perfection, the detective bitch's boyfriend obviously having only just arrived, Bernhardt still there with him.

This was a golden opportunity.

And they had to make it count.

As his back hit the wall to the right of the door, Dash heard a noise and glancing to his left, saw the door to the immediate neighbour's house open, a woman stepping out clearly wondering what the noise was. The moment she saw the three armed men, she jerked back inside and slammed the door, locking it behind her. She'd be straight on the phone to the police.

They had to handle this immediately and get the hell out of here.

Turning his attention to the entrance as another short spurt of gunfire from inside the house ripped through the remaining wood, Dash saw the door had already been half torn apart by their gunfire. Each man was carrying an AR-15 assault rifle and had spare magazines in his pockets, joining the Ruger pistol they each had in a holster tucked under their shirts.

Pulling a stun grenade from his left pocket, Dash looked over at the two men on the other side of the entrance who raised their weapons, ready to step into the firing line.

They'd breached many places like these over the years and knew exactly what to do.

Dash ripped the pin; on the other side of the doorway, Portland pushed what was left of the door back with the barrel of his AR-15 and Dash tossed the grenade into the house.

But as he did so, its twin suddenly appeared on the porch in front of them, rolling across the threshold and onto the concrete step.

TWENTY FIVE

Dash and Piccadilly reacted fast and protected their eyes and ears in time but the flash-bang took Portland completely by surprise, and he delayed a fraction too long covering up before it went off.

After it detonated, he staggered back and knelt against the wall, momentarily out of the game as he tried to recover his sight and hearing. Undeterred, Dash took the lead, pushing back the remains of the flimsy, shot-up door and entering the house.

The cop and Bernhardt weren't in the hallway anymore. As he walked in he stared down the sights of his assault rifle, checking out an open sitting room on his left; behind him, Piccadilly continued forward towards a closed door straight ahead.

The South African immediately put a stitched burst of gunfire diagonally across the wood and kicked it back.

All he saw was smashed glasses and crockery.

No sign of the two men.

Behind him, Dash had cleared the sitting room and was now focused on the stairs, keeping his assault rifle trained on the space above.

If in an ambush situation, try to get to higher ground.

They were upstairs.

In the guest bedroom at the top of the stairs, Bernhardt was struggling to open the window, the two men having locked themselves in after Archer had thrown the flash-bang from halfway up the flight, getting into the room just as another stun

184

grenade went off below, buying them some vital seconds.

'Come on!' Archer hissed, keeping his MP5 on the closed door and standing out of the field of fire. *'Open it!'*

'It's jammed!'

Cursing, Archer turned, moved forward and yanked at the mechanism, releasing it. Hearing a creak of a footstep on the stairs, Archer looked out of the window and saw the roof of a garden shed within jumping distance. They could use it to get to the top of the wall on the side of the house and jump into the alleyway he'd used earlier.

Hardly ideal but their only option.

'Go!' he whispered, pushing Bernhardt forward.

The former soldier started climbing out, jumping onto the roof of the shed then clambering up onto the wall. Looking back at the closed door, Archer didn't waste a second, quickly manoeuvring through the window too and leaping out onto the roof of the shed with a *thump* that made the flimsy wooden frame shudder with the force of his landing.

Ahead of him, Bernhardt dropped down into the alleyway and disappeared out of sight.

Moving fast, Archer hoisted himself up onto the wall and went to follow.

Then he suddenly heard the door to the guest bedroom smash open.

Looking down the sights of his assault rifle, Dash saw the blond cop crouched on the wall, completely exposed.

He pulled the trigger, firing through the open window, but the man reacted fast and leapt over the wall, the rounds just missing him by a hair's breadth, the gunfire tearing into a tree opposite and coughing leaves and bits of bark into the air.

Cursing, Dash didn't waste a second. He turned and ran back down the stairs as he reloaded with a fresh magazine, Piccadilly waiting for him at the bottom of the flight as he hurtled towards him.

'They went around the back!'

Pushing Bernhardt ahead of him, who'd injured himself on landing and was struggling to move at any speed, Archer moved along the alleyway as quickly as he could to the back of the house.

As they emerged onto the street Archer suddenly stopped dead, staring in disbelief at Cobb's Mercedes across the road.

There was a strip of cloth now hanging out of the fuel tank, and the lower end was alight. To their right, the youths he'd seen earlier had backed up down the street having heard the gunfire but curiosity had clearly got the better of them and they were still standing around to see what happened when the car blew.

'Get back!' Archer shouted, pushing Bernhardt to the left and watching the flames catch hold of the cloth.

A second later the Mercedes exploded, the two men recoiling from the blast.

Recovering first, Archer glanced back at the alleyway, knowing the gunmen would appear at any second. As he desperately looked around for some kind of solution, he noticed opposite that the alleyways ran alongside every other house.

Grabbing Bernhardt, he pulled him back into the alley adjacent to the one that ran beside this one as the car burned in front of them. Even from across the street the wave of heat from the wreckage was intense, fifty thousand pounds gone up with one strip of cloth and a lighter.

Crouching beside Bernhardt in the second alleyway, Archer snapped back as two of the gunmen suddenly appeared, quickly joined by the third. The men were silhouetted by the fire on the street and fanned out, searching for their prey with what looked like AR-15 assault rifles.

'Shit!' he whispered. *'Shit!'*

He and Bernhardt were stranded.

TWENTY SIX

Standing on the opposite side of the road from the burning car, Dash, Piccadilly and Portland quickly checked up and down the street, searching through the sights of their automatic weapons. They saw a load of frightened teenagers cowering behind a car down the street to their right, but there was no sign of Bernhardt or the cop.

'*Shit!*' Piccadilly said, standing in the middle and looking left and right. 'We lost them!'

'No, we didn't,' Dash replied, looking at the burning Mercedes, the only vehicle near Bernhardt's house. 'I saw that car outside the ARU HQ earlier. The cop must have come in it.'

'So?'

Doing a 360 degree turn, he scanned the road around them. 'So they're still here. They can't get away.'

Then he froze in sudden realisation.

Turning, he sprinted back towards the alley.

On the street the other side of the house, Archer and Bernhardt raced out of the other alleyway and up to the BMW the three gunmen had arrived in. As Archer hoped, they hadn't locked the car, and when he jumped into the driver's seat he saw the keys were still sitting in the ignition, the driver not bothering to take them in the rush to breach the house.

As Bernhardt pulled the passenger door shut, Archer twisted the key and the engine burst into life. Up ahead was a cul-de-sac, so they needed to turn around to get the hell out of here.

But before they could move, he saw the three gunmen running down the alleyway twenty feet to their left, coming straight for them.

'Shit!' Archer said, slamming the car into reverse and stamping his foot down.

Realising he'd left the keys in their car, Dash hadn't made it out of the alley before he heard the engine roar into life.

With the other two hot on his heels, they sprinted out onto the street to see their BMW reversing hard down the street to their right, the blond cop behind the wheel and Bernhardt beside him.

'Son of a bitch!' Dash shouted, opening fire with his AR-15.

'Get down!' Archer shouted, gunfire ripping into the windscreen and the sun visors as he reversed, the front of the car eating the brutal onslaught of gunfire.

As they roared backwards, Archer yanked the handbrake on and spun the wheel, swinging the car round and then taking off to his right, heading towards the exit to the next street. The gunmen had each emptied a magazine into the front of the vehicle, but the onslaught didn't stop the BMW, the front of the vehicle riddled with bullets as they swung out onto the next street, the rear eating some rounds too as they escaped.

Trying to put as much distance between them and the three gunmen as possible, Archer put his foot down, evening shoppers standing around uncertainly, wondering what the noise of gunfire was about.

'You OK?' he asked Bernhardt as they sped down the street.

189

The former soldier didn't answer, twisting round in his seat to check behind them.

Archer went to speak again but then disaster struck.

The BMW suddenly started to stall.

He pumped the accelerator, but the engine didn't respond and the car continued to slow. Swearing and quickly checking his rear view mirror, Archer changed down and tried to rev the engine to coax a response, but it was no good. The car drifted to a halt right there on the main street, having taken too much punishment from the AR-15s.

Fighting with the unresponsive car, Archer checked the rear view mirror again, waiting for the three gunmen to reappear.

He knew they'd be coming.

'C'mon!' he said, begging with the engine. 'Not now!'

Smoke started rising from the bullet-riddled engine.

It wasn't going anywhere.

'Shit!'

As soon as he'd seen the two men disappear, Dash didn't waste any time chasing after them on foot. He'd immediately turned and headed for the house next door to Bernhardt's, the other two following close behind as they each reloaded their assault rifles with a fresh magazine.

Striding up the path to the front door, he shot the lock and kicked the door open. Entering the house, he quickly found the woman he'd seen at the door earlier cowering in the sitting room, talking frantically into a telephone.

Walking over and pulling her to her feet, Dash threw her against the wall with vicious strength then stepped back, aiming his rifle straight at her. She screamed and sank to the floor, cowering against the wall in pure terror.

'Where's your car?' Dash shouted, keeping his sights on her head.

She didn't reply, just whimpering in fright. He fired a burst, putting three bullets into the wall two inches from her head, and she screamed again, covering her head with her hands, looking as if she was about to pass out from fear.

'Where's your car?' he screamed at her.

'G...garage,' she stammered.

'Keys?'

'My...bb...bag!' she whispered.

Standing beside Dash, Piccadilly saw a handbag on the floor by the sofa. Grabbing the bag, he immediately upturned it, spilling the contents all over the floor. He saw the keys lying amongst all the other paraphernalia and bent down to pick them up. As the woman started to sob hysterically, Dash stepped forward and hit her hard over the head with the butt of the assault rifle, one savage blow hard enough to knock her out cold.

Once she slumped to the floor in an unconscious heap, Dash turned and strode back outside. As the other two joined him, all three could hear sirens approaching in the distance. The garage door was locked but Dash took it out with one burst from his AR-15 then ripped the door up. There was a Volvo parked inside, the rear window now with three bullet holes in it from the assault rifle fire.

The trio jumped inside the car, Dash behind the wheel, and he reversed it straight out onto the street.

A moment later he slammed the gearstick forward and the tyres screeched as they took off after the cop and Bernhardt.

Just a single street away, Archer and Bernhardt were already out of the wrecked BMW, taking cover behind the front of the car, kneeling side by side as Archer reloaded his MP5 quickly, ripping out the empty mag and replacing it with a fresh one from his vest. He was on the left, Bernhardt on the right, and as he hit the cocking handle forward on the sub-machine gun Archer desperately looked around for an escape route.

'Shit! We need another way out of here!' he said.

Searching around their position, Archer's eyes were suddenly drawn to a four-storey car park to their right.

Before he could say another word, there was a sudden squeal of tyres on tarmac in front of them.

Looking around the BMW, Archer saw a car slide out onto the main street, a silver Volvo with the three gunmen inside.

Recognising their previous vehicle slumped to a halt in the road, they immediately braked hard and raised their rifles.

'Go!' Archer shouted an instant later, pushing Bernhardt up and out into the street.

The former Para took off across the road, running as fast as his ankle would allow as Archer followed behind, opening fire directly at the Volvo as he ran and unloading the entire clip.

His gunfire tore into the front of the car, the three gunmen inside forced to duck as Archer and Bernhardt sprinted across the street, totally exposed. The magazine had thirty two rounds slotted inside and Archer used every single one, firing as he ran, the MP5 spitting out a stream of shell casings and buying him and Bernhardt the chance to make it across the road.

The weapon clicked dry just as they entered the car park; a moment later, the glass of the empty ticket collector's hut smashed out beside him from a barrage of close return fire as he and Bernhardt fled inside.

TWENTY SEVEN

Firing from the driver's seat into the multi-storey car park, Dash swore then pushed open his door, Portland and Piccadilly following, all of them dusted with broken glass and pieces of the car's interior. The street around them was now deserted, all the pedestrians and drivers of passing cars running or taking cover, and they stalked unchallenged across the road towards the car park entrance.

Just as they were about to enter there was the sound of sirens and tyres screeching on asphalt and a Met police car suddenly appeared down the street to their left. Portland spun immediately and opened fire, aiming at the front tyres and blowing them out. The vehicle braked, the officers inside ducking down as Portland focused his gunfire on the car, Dash and Piccadilly leaving him to it and moving inside the car park.

Stepping past the barrier and into the four-storey concrete structure, they saw the place was a sea of parked cars, scores of potential hiding places.

Bernhardt and the blond cop had disappeared.

Tracing with his assault rifle, Dash swore; they didn't have time for this but they dare not let this son of a bitch escape. He and Piccadilly moved further inside, looking for any sign of movement. Portland's gunfire continued from the street as he held off the police but Dash took no notice, focusing on the lines of cars parked in neat rows instead.

He paused and waited, listening. The ramp behind them was the only way out of here for a vehicle;

however, he realised the car park would most likely be connected to a shopping centre of some sort.

That meant their prey could also get away on foot.

As he turned and took a step forward, the sound of a car alarm suddenly reverberated around the car park, echoing off the concrete walls and coming from the level above.

He smiled in satisfaction.

'Go!' he hissed to Piccadilly, who was already running for the ramp.

Lowering himself back to the ground floor through the gap between the metal barrier and the floor above, Archer watched as the pair of gunmen ran up the ramp on the other side of the car park to the 1st floor, where he'd just set off the car alarm.

For the first time since this had all kicked off, he had a good look at the men and saw both were big, dressed in cargo slacks and t-shirts. One of them was Dash; he was easy to ID. His skin was terribly disfigured from horrific burns to his face and arms, and he also had a strip of tape over his nose, possibly Vargas' handiwork. The other guy was blond and built like a rugby player with wide shoulders and a thickly muscled frame.

To Archer's left thirty feet away, Bernhardt was still where he'd left him, hiding beside a 4x4 Toyota parked with its back to the wall. As the alarm on the level above continued to echo its shrill warning, Archer ran forward and joined him. Checking they hadn't been seen, he tried the driver's door of the Toyota more out of hope than expectation, but it was locked.

'Ready?' he whispered to Bernhardt, who nodded.

Without hesitation, Archer reversed his MP5 and smashed the driver's window.

The moment he did, a second alarm wailed inside the car park, an instant giveaway of his location, giving him just seconds to work. Moving fast, Archer reached through the broken window, undid the lock, then climbed inside and pulled a jack-knife from his tac vest. He ripped off the panel under the ignition as he looked back up at the car park for the gunmen to reappear.

As Bernhardt leapt in the other side, Archer found the three wires under the exposed panel and separated the two red ones, ripping off the plastic nubs on the end and touching the naked wires together.

Nothing happened.

'C'mon, c'mon!' he said desperately, trying again as the car alarm wailed.

The engine fired.

Archer slammed the gear into *Drive*, pressed his foot down on the accelerator and turned the wheel to the left as hard as he could.

The car lurched out of the spot with a screech, heading for the exit. Dash and the other man suddenly appeared at the top of the ramp, raising their weapons and letting loose another violent barrage, but Archer already had a head start on them. As the back of the car took some intense fire, he pulled a sharp left turn, ploughing through the lowered barrier and snapping it off.

Straight ahead of him was the third gunman, who was firing on the unarmed police down the street, keeping them pinned down. Hearing the car racing towards him, he swung round, but Archer jammed his foot down and pulled a quick sliding right, the side of the car smashing into the man and knocking him to the ground.

'Stay down!' Archer shouted to Bernhardt, straightening the vehicle and stamping his foot down.

This time the car wasn't shot to pieces, and they took off down the road at a furious pace, finally making their escape and heading off into the night.

Running out into the street moments later and seeing the tail-lights of the Toyota disappearing out of sight, Dash shouted a curse then turned and saw another Met police car had arrived beside the one Portland had shot to pieces. There was no sign of the occupants who were no doubt already out of the vehicles and taking cover, calling for back-up.

Dash's temper boiled over and he swung round to Piccadilly.

'Get us another car!'

As the South African nodded and ran back inside the multi-storey car park, Dash strode out onto the road. He could hear officers shouting at him to put his weapons down and get down on his knees, but he ignored them. One of them fired a warning shot, which meant the new car must have contained a Firearms Unit, forcing Dash to take cover behind a post-box beside him. He quickly reared up and returned fire with his AR-15, emptying the clip and keeping the cops pinned down.

Behind him, Portland had managed to get back to his knees after being hit by the Toyota and started firing again on the police, giving Dash the chance to reload as he hustled across the street and opened the

197

rear of their original car, the destroyed BMW. Inside the trunk was an equipment case; slinging his rifle, he unlocked the case and took out an M90 rocket launcher, which each car of his team was carrying in case of a situation like this. An anti-tank weapon, the M90 was light-weight, only thirteen kilograms when the warhead was slotted inside, and could only be used once, but it was designed to stop tanks in their tracks in combat situations, which meant static police cars were like target practice.

Slotting the rocket in place and arming the launcher, Dash nodded to Portland, who'd just reloaded and intensified his fire. Dash lifted the launcher to his shoulder, stepped out and aimed the M90 at the front fender of one of the newly-arrived firearms officers' police car.

Seeing what he was intending to do, the police officers scrambled out from behind their vehicles.

He fired and the rocket whooshed down the street, smashing into the front of the police car, shortly followed by a huge explosion destroying the windows on the cars and buildings around them. The blast ignited the other police car's fuel tank which resulted in a second explosion, levelling the two vehicles and injuring the officers nearby.

Standing in the middle of the street, Dash watched in satisfaction as the cars burned, everything suddenly quiet around them.

That would keep the police occupied for a while.

Throwing the now useless launcher to one side, he unslung his rifle just as Piccadilly swerved back onto the street with a stolen car. Stepping forward, Dash climbed into the front passenger seat, Portland getting gingerly into the back and pulling the door shut. A moment later the men took off in the same direction as the Toyota, leaving a scene of total destruction in their wake.

But without the cop and Bernhardt.

TWENTY EIGHT

Archer and the former Para made it back to the ARU HQ in twenty minutes or so, not a word said between them as both men recovered from the sudden, intense encounter with the gunmen. As he focused on the road ahead, Archer felt rough as hell; although his only injuries were some small nicks and cuts, the combination of the continual nagging worry about Vargas, his constantly-spiking adrenaline ever since they'd landed and jet-lag wasn't a good cocktail.

He also knew how lucky they both were to be alive and wasn't lowering his guard for a second until they got back to the relative safety of the ARU HQ. It was only through quick thinking, firepower and a bit of luck that they'd managed to make it out of there; consequently, he was driving on all his mirrors as well as constantly scanning both the road ahead and the streets they passed either side, just in case they got hit by another ambush.

These still anonymous guys seemed to be everywhere, and anticipating the ARU and NYPD's every move.

Beside him, Bernhardt was unhurt but silent as he recovered. As Archer made a final turn, the former soldier's phone made a sound and he withdrew the Samsung from his pocket.

'My girlfriend,' he said, as he tapped in a reply. 'Shit. Better warn her the house won't look the same when she gets home from work.'

Behind the wheel, Archer didn't reply, focusing on the journey and relieved to see the ARU HQ finally come into view. The barrier was back down, two Met police cars parked either side and their occupants talking to Wilson, who was standing just outside his hut in his tac vest and with an MP5 in his hands. They all turned and visibly tensed when they saw the damaged Toyota approaching, but when the car pulled to a halt Wilson saw Archer behind the wheel and moved back to his hut to open the barrier, reassuring the Met officers at the same time.

As Archer drove into the car park, he saw that all the ambulances and fire teams had departed, leaving behind the burnt-out, blackened shell of the upper half of the building, the mostly destroyed wall revealing the interior of the level from down below. He also noticed in a parking space on the left that Josh and Fox's ARU BMW had returned, parked up front by the building; like himself, they'd also clearly run into some trouble. It was sitting beside two other black BMWs that were undamaged, the task force cars that must have been returned from the council estate in Brixton where Porter and the guys had been ambushed.

The two intact BMWs highlighted the damage the third one had taken; it had been shot to pieces, the lights smashed and all the windows blown out, as if it had been put through a meat-grinder of gunfire.

'Jesus Christ,' Archer said quietly, more to himself than Bernhardt, as he pulled into a space and looked at the wrecked vehicle. 'What the hell happened?'

'That's exactly what I was going to ask you,' Bernhardt replied, leaning to the side and staring up at the destroyed 1st floor of the ARU HQ through the window. 'You're having a bad day.'

Once they parked, the two men stepped out of the Toyota and headed for the entrance, Archer bringing his empty MP5 with him and walking backwards for a few steps as he made a mental note of the Toyota's licence plate. The ambulances and fire crews might have departed since he'd been gone but the concrete was still stained with blood and littered with fragments of broken glass which crunched under their feet as they walked.

As they headed into the building, Archer saw Lipton was back at his desk, still in his tac vest and with his MP5 no doubt in the booth with him; the ARU guard nodded at the two men from the other side of his Perspex as they approached the screen.

'Good to see you back,' Lipton said, pushing a button and letting them in.

Archer nodded his thanks, taking the lead, and continued down the lower corridor until he entered the interrogation cell, Bernhardt right behind him.

Nikki, Chalky, Marquez and Josh were all inside talking; apart from Marquez they all looked pretty beaten up. Nikki's arm was in a sling, Chalky had the wound to his head and Josh looked as if he'd been put through the mixer too; he had small nicks and tears in his clothes as well as on his arms and face, blood also staining the left sleeve of his white polo shirt and one leg of his jeans.

They all turned as the two men entered, their quiet conversation coming to an abrupt stop.

'You made it,' Josh said, relieved. 'Trouble?'

Archer nodded. 'There's an understatement.'

Pausing, he looked around the room.

'Where's Fox?'

'Hospital,' Josh said. 'He took one to the body.'

'Shit. How bad?'

'We don't know yet,' Nikki said. 'He's going into surgery any minute. But now we're down to five.'

'What happened, Arch?' Chalky asked, looking at his friend and the newcomer beside him.

'Three guys ambushed us at the house. Did everything they could to take us out; one of them was our man Dash.'

He focused on Josh.

'Similar treatment?'

He nodded. 'Four of them came after us. Ambushed and boxed us in. We got off lucky, which is saying something considering Fox was hit. We should be dead right now.'

'Any sign of Beckett's kids?'

'We couldn't even get into the apartment. Some asshole was waiting in there with a shotgun. He blew the entire door apart.'

Archer thought for a moment. 'So that's seven men at least that we're dealing with.'

As he said it, the group's attention shifted to Bernhardt, who was standing silently beside Archer.

'This is Michael Bernhardt,' Archer said, the former soldier nodding to the group.

Chalky rose from his seat, offering him the chair. 'Please.'

Hesitating for a moment, Bernhardt then obliged, limping forward and taking a seat.

'Also, I had to use another car to get us out of there, Nik,' Archer said, checking the safety on his MP5 and then hooking the sling over his shoulder. 'We need to call the owner and let them know.'

'Plates?'

He gave them to her, and she tapped them into her computer. 'I'll get someone from the Met to drive it back.'

'It might need a trip to the repair shop first,' Archer said, glancing at Bernhardt.

'But you left in Cobb's Mercedes,' Nikki said. 'What happened to it?'

Archer remembered the moment the car exploded in Tottenham, a fifty-thousand pound fireball, and swallowed.

'That might need a bit of work too.'

TWENTY NINE

Before Bernhardt could explain any of his history with Dash, he needed to know the current situation and it took five minutes or so to brief him and bring him up to date. During the explanation, the five remaining police personnel took up various positions around the room, Nikki sitting at the desk, Chalky joining Archer by the mirror wall, Marquez standing to their left and Josh to their right.

Nikki gave the former Para sergeant the basics, then Archer added the details from the NYPD group's point of view.

Once he arrived at the gunfight they'd both barely just survived, he paused.

'And now, here we are.'

'So they kidnapped your colleague in Spain,' Bernhardt said. 'Detective Vargas. But now you think they're not traffickers, correct?'

Nikki nodded. 'Stanovich was used to lure us to a property in Brixton, and Payan was employed as a distraction to mop up the rest of us. To ensure it was a clean sweep, the real perpetrators strapped the TNT onto Beckett in an attempt to wipe out anyone left here.'

Bernhardt whistled. 'Shit. These people sure as hell don't like you.'

Nikki looked over at Archer. 'How did they operate on the street?'

'Slick as hell. They boxed us in, stayed calm; used a stun grenade when they breached the house. One of them held off the police on his own whilst the other

205

two came after us. They were using assault rifles too; AR-15s I think.'

'Same as two of our guys,' Josh said. 'And the other pair had semi-auto shotguns; Benellis.'

'They had more than that,' Nikki said, indicating to her laptop. 'I'm looking at the Met log. Seven of the officers who arrived as back-up for you guys in Tottenham have been injured. Apparently they were fired on with an anti-tank rocket.'

'What?'

She nodded. 'An M90 anti-tank weapon, straight into a Firearms Unit police car; took it out and the one next to it. Officers arriving at the scene shortly afterwards found the discarded launcher and every cop already there wounded.'

There was a pause.

'M40A5 rifles, AR-15s, Benelli shotguns, TNT and M90 rocket launchers,' Chalky said. 'Holy shit.'

'But what the hell are they after?' Josh said. 'Why go to all this trouble to try and kill us?'

'Did you recognise any of the men who ambushed you?' Nikki asked Josh and Archer.

'Never seen any of them before,' Josh said.

Archer nodded in agreement. 'Me neither. Well, apart from Dash, and that was only from an hour ago when we pulled his ID.'

He turned to Bernhardt, who was listening in silence.

'Dash; your old friend.'

'How did you know he was involved before he came for us?' Bernhardt asked.

'His blood was at the scene of the abduction in Spain. And our files say you two were checked into

206

hospital together in Kabul. That's why I came to get you.'

Bernhardt nodded, smiling ruefully. 'Yeah, that all rings a bell.'

'So you know him?' Chalky asked.

'I knew him. Past tense.'

'We need to know everything you can tell us,' Marquez said. 'How did you both end up injured?'

Bernhardt paused.

'What you say is important,' Josh said, noting the hesitation. 'Right now we know next to nothing about this guy.'

'Oh, don't worry. I'll tell you,' Bernhardt said. 'That son of a bitch just tried to kill me. I'm trying to figure out the best place to start.'

Across London, the fifty seven year old woman who'd employed Dash's team stepped out of the unfinished office on the 12th floor of the office building, having just removed her blood-spattered overalls and leaving a disturbing scene in the room behind her.

Now she was the employer of eleven men, but the loss was worth it. She hadn't hired these men to make mistakes and what she'd done to Finchley would focus the others. As she peeled off her mask, she smiled.

At least that was one less she'd have to pay.

Re-entering the main office to her right and tossing the mask to one side, she wiped her brow with a cloth and it came away smeared with red; despite the protective clothing she'd been wearing, flecks of the dead Australian's blood had sprayed onto her forehead, some of it also wetting her hair. She'd been right about doubting that the man could beat the Russian soldier's record.

He'd only made it to just below the knee.

Pulling the door closed behind her, she saw that her cell phone was flashing on the desk, not making a sound given that it was set to silent. Wiping her hands on the cloth, she tossed it to one side, walked forward and picked up the phone, seeing it was Dash. He'd gone to Bernhardt's house with Piccadilly and Portland; it was almost certain by now that the police would have pulled his ID from his blood and Dash had guessed that the remaining ARU and NYPD detectives would try to bring Bernhardt in immediately as he'd be their only lead.

She took the call. 'Yes?'

'I have some news,' Dash said. *'One of them showed up, just as we arrived.'*

'Who?'

'The detective's boyfriend.'

The woman felt a jolt in her gut. 'And?'

Pause.

'And?'

'He got away. He took Bernhardt with him; they must be back at their station.'

She closed her eyes. Her hand clenched tight on the phone.

'He took Bernhardt too?'

'Yeah. Don't ask me how. But it's a game-changer.'

The woman didn't reply, thinking.

Dash had a point.

'I spoke to Regent and Notting too. Apparently two others came for the analyst's kids in Kensington; the black NYPD cop and one of the ARU officers. They

*got lucky and made it out, but Grange was pretty
sure he hit one of them as they drove off. If so, that's
another down that we can finish off later.'*

There was a pause.

'We underestimated these people.'

'No, *you* underestimated these people.'

She paused.

'But it's OK. As your South African companion
said earlier, all this is good. Although only a couple
have died, which is a pity, a number of them have
still been removed.'

She looked at the blood-stained rag on the desk
that she'd used to wipe down her forehead.

'Working on the Australian just made me realise
my original orders may have lacked imagination; I
think I might have been too hasty. And this current
situation could very well work in our favour.'

'That's what I was thinking.'

As she'd been talking, the woman's eyes had been
drawn to some materials across the office.

Several flat-packed boxes and a roll of duct tape.

'Where are your men?'

*'Some out in the city, others at the safe-house with
you. All on standby.'*

'OK. This is what I want you to do.'

THIRTY

'In total, I was in the army for ten years,' Bernhardt said, as the five other people inside the ARU interrogation cell listened closely. 'Joined when I was twenty, left when I was thirty. Spent all of it with the Paras. Saw action all over the place, but I left six years ago after doing my stint. My choice, not theirs.'

'Why'd you leave?' Nikki asked.

'At the time, I thought I wanted to do something else. The army lifestyle is unique, but it was starting to get old. I was sick of long tours, constant danger and not getting paid enough for any of it.'

He smiled.

'But the grass is always greener, right? Soon after I left, I knew I'd made a big mistake. I hated civvy street and started going crazy without the action. Life out of the army was as boring for me as watching a game of chess.'

'But you didn't re-enlist?' Marquez said.

'No; I didn't. I missed the adrenaline rush and my mates but I was enjoying my freedom. But there was a way I could have both.'

'Let me guess,' Archer said. 'Private contracting.'

Bernhardt nodded. 'Correct. After calling up some old contacts and letting them know I was looking for work, I was called in to meet with a private security company based in Essex named *Shields Security*. At the time they had contractors working all over the Middle East and were always looking for well-trained men like me. By then, the industry was

210

booming too; the annual revenue of Brit security firms by that year was 1.8 billion pounds.'

'That much?' Josh said.

Bernhardt nodded. 'This was six years ago too, so the number's actually increased since then.'

'Where was all this cash coming from?' Josh asked.

'Once Saddam was toppled and the war in Afghanistan gathered intensity, the entire region needed restructuring, as well as needing specific training for some of their military forces. There were also big, big companies either wanting to stake a claim somewhere in the country or get to work rebuilding it; whoever they were, they all needed protection on the ground. Pay men like me the right amount of money and we'd do any or all of those things.'

'Mercenaries,' Chalky said instinctively.

Bernhardt gave him a look.

'Not all of us like that word; *private contractors* is better. Without us, the US and UK forces couldn't operate over there; we've been crucial in helping rebuild the region. Shit, a lot of contracts come from the American and British governments, seeing as ex-squaddies like me are cheaper to hire than the military.'

He smiled.

'And if one of us gets killed, they don't have to announce it on the six o'clock news. Anyway, after an initial assessment and interview, *Shields* offered me a role, and two weeks later I was working as armed protection for military convoys in Iraq. Wasn't a bad gig and was much better paid than the army, but I soon realised I was working for the wrong people.'

'Why?' Archer asked.

'*Shields* were sloppy and cut corners; God knows where our weapons came from, but they were shit. Old AK-47s that were unreliable, pistols that constantly jammed, insufficient amounts of ammunition. Some of the other guys they hired were hot-heads, actively looking for trouble. And in other firms, most newcomers to private security work are given specialised training, but I never got anything like that. *Shields* regarded it as too much of an expense and just relied on their employees' past experience.'

'But you were all ex-military,' Chalky said. 'This wasn't your first dance. You already knew what you were doing.'

'Private security contracting is defensive, not aggressive,' Bernhardt said. 'It's a completely different mind-set; to do it right requires additional training. In the army, it was seek and destroy, but for contractors it's protect your clients and get them to their destination as quickly and safely as possible. They get killed, you don't get paid.'

He paused.

'Anyway, once that first protection contract was up, I ended up joining another company where the work was much better paid and far more professional. In the next twelve months, I earned over a hundred grand, tax free.'

'Pretty good,' Marquez said.

'Sounds a lot, but that was only a fraction of what we should have been paid considering the constant dangers we were exposed to. By that point I'd been doing it for eighteen months; the nature of the work means you get to know the guys you're working with better than your own family, so after a while, a few of us decided to set up our own firm. There were eleven of us in total and we began operating by ourselves, using our inside knowledge to intercept contracts before they could be put out there for bigger firms to scoop up.'

'Were you all Brits?' Chalky asked.

He shook his head. 'I was the only one. The rest were from all over; South Africa, Saudi Arabia, New Zealand. Two of the lads were from Afghanistan.'

He paused.

'And your man Dash was one of them. In fact he was our leader.'

'Tell us about him,' Nikki said.

'He's an ex-ANA Commando. No wife, no kids. Tough bastard. He'd been in the Afghan army for a few years but had left like me and was looking to make some real money.'

'Did you like him?' Josh asked.

'Yeah, I did. Until today, at least.'

'His record is surprisingly clean,' Nikki said.

'He was good; very loyal. But fed up of not making any money.'

'What about his background?'

He shrugged. 'Aside from his army career, Dash never really talked about it. Said his father was dead, hadn't seen his mother in years and had a brother somewhere, but that was about it.'

'What kind of work did your new team do?' Josh asked.

'All sorts; some of it was more savoury than the rest. For the proper money, we were happy to do

213

anything, neutralise or capture someone for interrogation. Shit, for the right amount of cash, we'd have gone after Bin Laden himself.'

He paused.

'But then the beginning of last year came about, two and a half years into our operations.'

He paused, looking down at the burn scars covering his arms.

'And that's when the shit hit the fan.'

*

'In February, seventeen months ago, we'd just closed out a contract on four mid-level members of a Hezbollah cell,' he continued. 'The op was smooth, and our extraction equally so. But that night once we returned to Kabul to celebrate, there were two guys waiting there for us that we hadn't exactly expected to encounter.'

'Who were they?' Marquez asked.

'A pair from the CIA. Yeah, that was my reaction,' Bernhardt added, seeing the look on Josh's face. 'They were Americans in the Middle East looking for help, which kind of surprised us.'

'Why?' Marquez asked.

'Ever since 9/11, your homeland hasn't exactly been struggling for volunteers willing to pull a trigger. These guys had recently received some new intel and figured three prominent Al Qaeda figures were hiding out in a certain part of Kabul, laying low. Bin Laden was dead by that point but other members of the organisation were still out there and they were just as dangerous. A bit like the Hydra; cut off one head, two more appear.'

The group listened close.

'The CIA wanted our team to help them out; we were men who knew the area, the players, the culture, not trigger-happy inexperienced recruits who'd never even left their own State before arriving in theatre. In the past, they'd bombed the living shit out of the caves trying to kill Bin Laden, but this time figured sending in a team like ours would be more beneficial. Local knowledge goes a long way in a conflict on enemy soil.'

He paused.

'It was a smart move to approach us; we knew the area, were already tied up with the locals and had valuable connections; most of us could speak passable Arabic and some Pashto. US soldiers fresh from the homeland with a buzz-cut would never get anywhere near these guys. And the Agency made it very clear that it would be worth our while, and we figured they'd better, considering who we were going after. You know the deck of cards right?'

'Of course,' Archer said.

'Fifty two cards, fifty two of the most wanted men from the Taliban and Al Qaeda. The three guys they figured were out there in the caves were three of the Royals of the deck. Big targets, big bounties, big retaliation expected from the enemy if they were killed.'

He paused.

'They offered us seventy thousand dollars each and a cut of the bounty if we capped them off, so we went to work, doing what we could to find these bastards, talking to locals and slowly acquiring information. After a tip-off, we finally managed to pin down two of them, hiding out in a warren of caves in the countryside east of the capital. We

215

geared up and moved in; there was a lot of money at stake.'

'What happened?' Archer asked.

'We fired on the pair, but they took cover and retreated into the caves just as the sun was going down. Entering those bloody places is a nightmare. You're in enemy territory and they know those caves better than you know your own house, so we decided to call it in. We'd still located and pinned them down, so we figured that had to be worth some gold.'

He paused.

'We waited for a few hours, but never heard anything back. By then it had gone dark; we had a quick vote and decided to move in after them at first light to finish the job.'

He sighed.

'Turned out the Agency had other ideas. At dawn, just as we'd started to make our approach we heard an aircraft high overhead. We stopped to look up, thinking it might be an enemy carrier, but it wasn't.'

He blinked, stretching the translucent skin on his face.

'Then it happened.'

'What did?' Archer asked.

'They carpet bombed the entire hillside.'

THIRTY ONE

Silence followed.

Suddenly, the former soldier's scars made a lot more sense.

'Know what a daisy cutter is?' he asked the group.

'It's a bomb,' Marquez said quietly.

Bernhardt nodded. 'The BLU-82b weapons system. A fifteen thousand pound incendiary used to create an instant clearing for a chopper to land. It was built to flatten forests and take out entire townships. One of the largest and most dangerous conventional weapons ever created, and I can testify to that.'

He licked his dry lips.

'Twelve and a half thousand pounds of ammonium powder, aluminium and polystyrene slurry shit that needs to be dropped from six thousand feet above ground level for the pilots in the plane to be safe. Any lower, they're in as much trouble as anyone on the ground below. And that was our reward for finding the two Taliban targets.'

'Why the hell didn't they warn you?' Chalky asked, incredulous. 'Get you to pull out?'

'There was a lot of distrust back then, even with the American guys towards the Afghan boys who were on their side. They'd had some bad experiences with each other; suicide bombings once they'd infiltrated army bases, US soldiers fresh from Pendleton firing blue-on-blue and killing guys on their own side. The intelligence we'd acquired and radioed in was so valuable that I guess the importance of the targets outweighed their concern

217

for us. Wasn't the first time that kind of shit happened and won't be the last. And as I said earlier, that's why they hired men like us. Not only do we not make the headlines, but you also don't have to tell Ma and Pa back home that you took me out to kill the enemy.'

He paused.

'The US Army had already used the daisy-cutters to knock off some Al Qaeda and Taliban bases, and they'd dropped them on Tora Bora a few years back when intel told them Bin Laden was hiding out there. And we were right there on that hillside when they let go of that next one.'

'How did you survive?' Josh asked.

'It hit the top of the hill about two hundred yards from us. At that point, we were close to the entrance of one of the caves, but they were Taliban hideouts and not exactly a safe refuge. After the first blast, we didn't have any choice and just made it inside one of the warrens before the fire hit. Even so we still got caught and the impact caused a collapse of rocks inside the cave. Killed five of the guys instantly, the rest of us trapped inside. Burned and now buried alive; hell of a way to go.'

Silence.

'How did you get out?' Archer asked.

'I passed out and woke up some time later. The others were all dead; Dash and I were the only two left. We were both in so much agony that I can't even begin to describe it; so bad that I wanted to pass out again just so it would end. But I managed to drag myself over to the rocks blocking us in and packed them with our C4 and grenades. I pulled Dash back behind cover and blasted it. If it worked, we'd get out. If it caused another cave in, hopefully we'd die quickly.'

He paused.

'The blast cleared a big enough gap for us to get through and we just made it out before the cave behind us totally collapsed. It was nightfall, but the hillside around us was still smouldering with parts of it on fire. We were both severely burned, most of our clothes gone, patches of what remained stuck to our flesh. We went as far as we could off the hillside but we didn't make it far. The last thing I remember before passing out was knowing I was going to die.'

Silence.

'However, I came to a few days later and was in a hospital. It turned out some locals on the Western forces' side had found us and taken us to the doctor in the local town, who then transferred us to hospital in Kabul. They doped me up with a shitload of morphine so the next few weeks were a blur. Found out later over seventy per cent of my body was covered in burns.'

He paused to lift up his shirt. Just like his face, it was patchy, translucent and milky, all scar tissue. Even now it looked angry and painful, and that was after the wounds had healed as well as they were ever going to.

'Word had spread around the place about who I was and what I'd been doing, so they continued to treat me,' he said, lowering the garment. 'After four months of skin grafts and constant pain, I was ready to be discharged. Once I left the hospital, I spent some time recovering out there, holed up in a hotel in the city. I'd already stowed away a large sum of money along with my passport at a bank in the city

219

before I'd left for the job, so I used it to pay for everything and then book a flight home.'

He smiled.

'Look a little different to the way I did when I left mind you. UK Border Control grilled me for over an hour seeing as I didn't resemble my passport photo anymore.'

'When did you get back?' Josh asked.

'Five months ago.'

'But you have a house in Tottenham?' Archer said.

'Inherited from my grandmother. Was sitting there empty the whole time I was away.'

'What about Dash?' Chalky asked. 'What happened to him?'

'Two months into our treatment, I asked the nurse how he was doing. She said he'd left a few days earlier and no one knew where he'd gone. This was in April last year; until today, I hadn't seen him since.'

And just like that, his story ended; it was followed by a period of silence as everyone absorbed what he'd just told them. The former soldier's story had been hard to listen to, made more difficult by the graphic evidence on his face, arms and body.

Standing with his back to the mirrored wall, Archer looked at the ex-Para in the chair.

'I'm sorry that happened to you,' he said.

'Join the club.'

'You heard anything from Dash since you last saw him?'

'Not a peep and I didn't seek him out. I didn't want anything to do with that world anymore.'

'Well he's reappeared, back on the radar,' Archer said. 'You saw him as clearly as I did.'

220

Bernhardt nodded. 'Judging from what you told me, he must have realised you'd find his file and figured you'd pay me a visit. Guess he doesn't want me talking to you and telling you about the past.'

He sighed.

'Not that I know that much about him anyway. As I said, he always kept to himself.'

'And now he's got a new team after all your other guys were killed,' Chalky said. 'All ex-military, for sure.'

Bernhardt nodded. 'After seeing them in action, I agree. Trained killers. I know the type; I used to be one of them.'

'Do you think Dash could have switched sides?' Marquez asked.

Bernhardt paused. 'What; joined the Taliban?'

She nodded.

'Maybe,' he replied. 'Experiencing the daisy cutter isn't something that exactly endeared the US Army to us. But since he left the army, Dash wasn't a guy who liked to be tied down to one organisation; I'd say he's still doing contract work.'

'What about you?' Josh asked.

'I'd had enough of conflict for one lifetime.' He motioned at his arms and face, at the disfigured skin. 'No adrenaline rush is worth this.'

He paused again. Across the room, Marquez shook her head and swore, frustrated.

'So how the hell does this connect together?' she said. 'Did someone put a contract on Alice? And if so, why didn't Dash just kill her at the villa when he had the chance? Why come after us?'

She saw the look on Bernhardt's face.

'What?'

221

He hesitated.

'It might not be something you want to hear.'

'Go on,' Archer said quietly. 'Speak.'

'I know Dash. I know the kind of men he'll have hired.'

He glanced at Archer.

'But you've heard nothing from him? No ransom demands or threats?'

'None. Just a series of attacks.'

'Then maybe she's not the actual target; one of you is.'

The room suddenly went silent.

'And if that's so, I'd say it's almost a certainty that your colleague is already dead.'

At that moment nine miles south of the ARU HQ, Grange entered a UPS collection point with a package under his arm and a heavy black holdall slung over his shoulder, having come straight from the safe-house under fresh orders from Dash and their employer.

The place was closing very shortly, but there was no queue and he walked straight towards an open booth. There was a man sitting behind the desk and he smiled at the Canadian, who didn't return it as he slid the square box onto the counter.

'How can I help you sir?' he asked.

'A colleague of mine booked Express Delivery by phone earlier,' Grange said. 'As requested, she wants this parcel to be delivered by 9pm.'

'Do you have the booking details?'

Grange gave them to the employee, who checked the computer.

'That's fine, sir. Please confirm the delivery address.'

'The Armed Response Unit,' he replied, the square brown parcel on the desk under his arm sealed tight. 'It's a police station across town.'

THIRTY TWO

Inside the interrogation room at the ARU HQ, several pockets of conversation had quietly formed after Bernhardt's explanation about his past with Dash. Marquez was talking with him at the desk, clarifying certain details; Nikki and Josh had both stepped outside for a moment, Josh calling his wife to let her know he was OK just in case news reports from the UK had made any of the US bulletins and Nikki wanting to see if she could get her personal landline up and running again upstairs in Operations, despite the instructions from the Fire Chief.

Archer and Chalky were standing beside the mirrored viewing window; leaning against the glass with his back to the door, Archer noticed with relief that Chalky seemed much more with it than he had earlier. His navy blue polo shirt and jeans were stained with smoke and patches of dried blood, but nevertheless he was looking a lot better and appeared to be back in the game. He still had his Glock in his hip holster but was now wearing a tac vest at Archer's request, as was Marquez. Until this was resolved, he wanted anyone who might go outside wearing one of the bulletproof garments.

'How's the head?' Archer asked.

'Hurts like a bitch.'

Archer smiled. 'Good thing there's nothing in there to damage then.'

Chalky gave him a look; there was a pause and his expression changed. Archer knew what he was thinking.

'I hate to say it but he had a point,' Chalky said, folding his arms and nodding at Bernhardt. 'Your girl's been missing for almost a day, yet all these attacks on us are still happening.'

'You think one of us is actually the target?'

'I don't know. Maybe.'

Archer frowned. 'But if it's one of us, then why not go after that person individually? With all these weapons and tactics, Dash and his team most likely could have succeeded without going to all this effort.'

'Could it be all of us?' Chalky suggested.

Archer paused. 'Both Shepherd's NYPD team and the ARU?'

Chalky nodded.

'But why?'

Before Chalky could answer, Archer saw his friend's attention shift to something behind him; Archer turned as Nikki slipped back into the room.

'Landline's back,' she said. 'And I just spoke to the hospitals.'

'How's everyone doing?' Chalky asked.

'Fox is in surgery. Porter and the rest of the task force are already out and are now in the Critical Care Unit. All of them are doing OK. So far, Mason and Spitz are the only two fatalities.'

'What about Shepherd?' Marquez asked from across the room, halting her conversation with Bernhardt, having overheard Nikki's report.

'He's banged up but he should be OK, same as Cobb. The task force guys are at The Royal Marsden. Cobb, Shepherd, Fox and the analysts are at two other hospitals. Too many of them for one place to handle.'

225

'Guarded?' Archer asked.

Nikki nodded. 'Firearms teams on every entrance and ward. No one is getting near any of them.'

She paused.

'I also spoke to the sergeant now on site at Beckett's apartment. The boys weren't there. CCTV cameras show them being taken away earlier in the day by two men driving a black Ford. Met analysts are trying to locate them but aren't having any luck drawing the plates. I'll see where they're currently at.'

She walked across the room, Marquez rising and offering her seat. Nikki thanked her, then sat down in front of her laptop, using her good hand to get to work and peering closely at the screen as she tapped away.

'So whatever the motive is for all these attacks, our objectives remain the same,' Chalky said, as the separate conversations in the room merged into one. 'Number one is finding Vargas as well as Beckett's two boys.'

'And number two is to identify and track down all the men doing this,' Nikki said. 'Dash's new team.'

'Same thing,' Archer said. 'We find those three, we'll find their captors. And these guys will have a command post somewhere; that's probably where they'll be holding the hostages.'

'So let's start working up an ID list,' Nikki said. 'We've established at least seven men for sure as you guys were jumped about a minute apart.'

'There must be more,' Marquez said.

'Why?'

'Wherever they are, Beckett's two boys will need someone watching them.'

226

'And Vargas,' Archer said.

Marquez hesitated. 'If she's even here, Arch. It's been over twenty hours since someone last saw her. She could be anywhere.'

She faltered at the end of the sentence, catching herself, but the unspoken words *or dead* hung in the room, especially after Bernhardt's comment earlier.

There was a pause.

'The men who attacked you weren't wearing masks, were they?' Nikki asked Archer and Bernhardt. They shook their heads. 'Good. I'll get on the cameras and start trying to pull some identities.'

'That might be harder than you think,' Bernhardt said. 'I know Dash. The kind of company he keeps aren't exactly the kind of men you'll have police files on.'

'You never know. And right now, it's all we've got.'

As she set to work, Archer suddenly realised Josh still hadn't returned.

'Keep at it, Nik,' he said, stepping outside of the interrogation cell and going to look for his NYPD partner to make sure he was OK.

Across the city, Dash, Piccadilly and Portland were sitting inside the replacement car they'd stolen in Tottenham and reloading their weapons as they laid low inside another four storey car park. The Met would definitely already have the plates of this stolen vehicle by now and be looking for it, but they were staying put until Grange arrived with new plates.

He'd just called to confirm he was on his way, having delivered the package to the courier's service from their employer. Once he arrived they could switch the plates and then move around the city again without the risk of being apprehended.

The night was young.

And they still had plenty of work to do.

Considering what had just happened, the three men were surprisingly upbeat. Things hadn't worked out the way they'd planned in Tottenham, but they'd still worked out. Taken back to the police team's base, Bernhardt would no doubt be telling them all about his past and interactions with Dash in Afghanistan, but that wasn't an issue.

In the front passenger seat, Dash slapped a fresh clip into his AR-15 and pulled back the cocking handle, loading a round into the weapon as he glanced at his cell phone resting on his lap. Including himself, there were twelve men on his team, eleven now Finchley was gone. Over the past year or so, Dash had recruited them all; he was the leader, Piccadilly an old acquaintance and his second-in-command, Camden an old colleague too. The two Americans, Notting and Regent, had come as a pair, the same as Grange and Stockwell, two Canadian ex-army snipers. Portland, Finchley and Aldgate had come as a group, their backgrounds just as murky as the others, and Wood and Covent had come individually, ex British Army soldiers, both dishonourably discharged.

Each man had years of experience in combat and were willing to do anything for the right amount of money, the qualities Dash had most been looking for. The temporary call-signs they'd adopted today were standard practice to protect their identities, born from long-ingrained habits and a desire for anonymity that had helped keep them all alive; at some point, the police would be all over the phone calls between the group and Dash didn't want to give away any of their real names over the phone.

He smiled. His real name wasn't even Dashnan Sahar.

The police would most likely figure they'd be onto him by now, but they weren't even close.

Looking down at his hands, he saw that the gelatinous skin on the gap between his thumb and forefinger was red from handling the assault rifle. He'd been on strong pain-killers ever since he'd been burned last year but in the chaos of today, had forgotten to take a dose and now had a thumping headache from his broken nose as well as the usual aches that were starting to kick in. After the incident on the Afghan hillside, he'd been in almost constant, unrelenting pain and although he'd learned to live with it, the agony fed an ever-present anger in him, the embers of which had always been smouldering just beneath the surface. It was a family trait.

He'd been checked out of the hospital one night in April last year and when he finally got back to his feet a few weeks later, his intentions had changed. In the past, he'd been selective about the contracts he took, but since his betrayal by the CIA, everyone had been fair game and he'd put all his energies into gathering a team with a similar disregard for whom they were working.

Despite their efforts however, this operation hadn't gone anywhere near as planned.

That meant their work tonight was only just getting started.

As he considered their current status, he saw Grange suddenly appear through the doors of the shopping centre carrying a thick black holdall. The

229

man's real name was Vincent Baer, former Master Corporal in the Canadian Royal 22nd Infantry. Baer was good; Dash was surprised that he and his partner Stockwell, aka former Master Corporal Nicolas Gagnon, had failed in Hendon. In the contracting world the two men had excellent reputations, and Dash had approached them in Kabul in June last year when he was putting together his new team.

Leaving his weapon in the car, Dash stepped out to meet the sniper, glancing around quickly; several shoppers were walking towards their vehicles, but weren't paying them any attention.

'The package?' he asked.

'On its way,' Grange replied.

'The plates?'

Grange patted the bag. He glanced up at a camera mounted on the wall above them, but Dash shook his head.

'Already down. Let's do it.'

They waited for two cars pulling out of their parking bays further down the level to leave. Then the pair walked to the back of the stolen vehicle and kneeling down, unzipped the bag. It contained a Phillips screwdriver, adhesive tape, two sets of licence plates, a pistol, a stripped down assault rifle and a batch of fully-loaded spare magazines. As Grange pulled out a fresh licence plate, Dash grabbed the screwdriver and after flipping off the protective caps started unwinding the screws on the rear plate.

Whilst doing so, he glanced at his watch and realised Notting and Regent would already be in place to follow their fresh orders from their employer given the new intel they'd just received.

The plan she'd outlined over the phone was clever, her usual style.

And it was time for some more of the ARU and NYPD people to die.

THIRTY THREE

Archer found Josh down the corridor in the locker room, sitting on a bench beside the gun cage tending to a wound on his shin. He was holding some gauze against it, the white bandage stained red, and Archer stepped forward in concern when he saw what his partner was doing.

'You're hurt?'

'Just a ricochet,' Josh replied, lifting the bandage and showing Archer a superficial wound. 'Son of a bitch grazed me. It's OK.'

As Josh reapplied the gauze, Archer watched him for a moment, this end of the corridor quiet. He saw that someone had moved the NYPD team's bags in here from the cars outside. Placing his empty MP5 back on a rack in the gun-cage, Archer unzipped his tac vest, pulled it off and then changed t-shirts, replacing his dirty black one with a fresh white one from his holdall. When it was in place he then slipped the ARU vest back on over the top, zipping it up and all the time lost in thought, certain uncomfortable images reappearing in his mind now he had quiet and time to think.

Across the room Josh watched him. 'You OK?'

Readjusting his earpiece and strap mic, Archer nodded ruefully, unable to raise a smile.

'Yeah. I guess.'

'Forget what Bernhardt said. Vargas is still alive. She's more use to them alive than dead. And we'll find her. These men can't keep surprising us.'

'They're doing a pretty good job of it at the moment.'

232

There was a pause. His t-shirt replaced, Archer took a seat on a bench against the wall opposite his partner, keeping his thoughts to himself. Josh watched him in silence, knowing when something else was bothering him, and waited for him to speak.

'The last time she and I talked, we had a fight,' Archer said eventually.

'What about?'

'Her daughter.'

He paused.

'The kid's suffering. I think she needs help. Vargas doesn't agree; she thinks it could make it worse.'

Josh nodded. 'Did you try to apologise?'

Archer shook his head. 'That's the thing; I didn't. And she might already be dead.'

Pause.

'You know what the best thing about you is?' Josh said, breaking the silence.

Archer looked up. 'What?'

'You never give up. You could be fighting one man, ten men or an entire army, you'll never back down. You never surrender. You saved her life in that building; that's a huge thing. Not many people would have kept going against those kinds of odds.'

He paused.

'But you know what the worst thing about you is? You never give up. You're stubborn. And so is she. That's why neither of you have apologised. Unstoppable force and immovable object.'

Archer didn't reply; Josh lifted away the gauze he was holding to his leg. The wound on his shin seemed to have stopped bleeding and he placed the bloodied bandage to one side. He leaned back on the bench, looking down at the wound.

233

'I did the same thing once.'

'Held your ground?'

Josh nodded. 'With my brother. I was stubborn as shit. And I paid for it.'

Archer frowned, cocking his head, genuinely surprised. 'I didn't know you had a brother?'

'His name was Nathan. He was younger than me; three years. We had a big fight, back when I was a teenager. Nineteen years old, but already thinking I'd figured everything out. I wouldn't back down and neither would he. We both said some bad things; really bad. I left that night and went to North Carolina with some of my friends and wouldn't answer my phone. He tried to call me a couple of times; even left a message but I wouldn't listen to it.'

He swallowed.

'Later that night, he went out with his girlfriend to a concert and they got jumped on the way home by some gang members wanting their money. Apparently Nate tried to fight back, so they shot him four times.'

He paused.

'He was still alive in the ambulance, but never made it to the hospital. Lost too much blood. And he bled to death thinking that I hated him.'

Archer didn't move, staring at his NYPD partner.

'He died with us on terrible terms, something that he tried to fix but which I refused to. And I have to live with that for the rest of my life.'

He smiled.

'Shit, I thought I was a tough guy, that real men don't back down ever, but once he was gone I wondered how I could ever have been that stupid.'

He paused.

'Sometimes backing down's the right thing to do.'

Archer didn't reply. Josh looked over at his detective partner.

'Wherever she is, Alice is still alive; I'm sure of it. And I don't care how tough or well-trained these men are, we're going to take them down one by one until we find her.'

He fixed Archer's gaze, his face determined.

'But right now, we don't back down.'

Archer glanced at him and nodded. 'No. We don't.'

Another brief silence fell between the two men, Archer absorbing Josh's words. But before either could speak again, they suddenly heard the door down the corridor smash open.

It was followed immediately by the sound of running feet.

Looking at each other and frowning, both men rose as they heard voices talking urgently in what sounded like the interrogation cell.

Then the sound of hurried footsteps continued, coming their way.

Suddenly, Lipton arrived in the doorway.

'There you are,' he said to Archer. 'I think we've got a problem.'

'What is it?'

'There's a delivery outside,' he said. 'UPS. A package'

'So?' Josh asked, pushing down his trouser leg to cover his shin.

'It's an express parcel,' he replied, looking at Archer. 'And it's addressed to you, Arch.'

THIRTY FOUR

'What?' Archer said.

'It's addressed to Sam Archer,' Lipton said. 'Right here, at the Unit's address.'

Archer looked at Josh; then, without a word, they both walked swiftly out of the room.

As they moved down the corridor, Marquez, Nikki, Chalky and Bernhardt appeared out of the interrogation cell, clearly having been told and following the pair out of the building.

When they made it outside through the front entrance, the group saw a courier standing behind the barrier on the other side of the car park, holding a parcel. MP5 in hand, Wilson was right there alongside the man and wasn't letting him any closer; he was the only cop down there, the armed Met officers who'd been stationed there earlier now gone.

Stepping past Archer, Chalky immediately pulled his Glock and ran forward into the centre of the lamp-lit car park, aiming the weapon straight at the man. Josh moved out to the left and did the same, the two pistols trained on the delivery guy.

'Put it down and back away!' Chalky ordered, fixing his sights on the driver.

The man obeyed the command immediately, quickly lowering the box to the ground, his eyes wide with fear.

'Step back from the package!'

The man did as he was told until his back hit his van parked on the road behind him.

'On your knees!' Chalky ordered.

236

The man knelt down, clearly terrified. Standing with his back to the building, the concrete under his feet stained with blood from the triage operation earlier, Archer stared at the courier twenty five yards away. He was an inoffensive-looking wiry white guy somewhere in his late twenties; he couldn't have looked less of a threat if he'd tried.

But it had been a day of unpleasant surprises.

'Does he have ID?' Chalky called to Wilson, who was standing with his back to his hut fifteen feet from the delivery guy's van.

'He looks OK!'

'What's the order?' Chalky asked the courier. *'And keep your hands up!'*

'Special delivery!' the man called back, his voice shaking. *'Came in less than an hour ago and said it had to be here by 9pm for a Detective Sam Archer. You're my last call.'*

With Marquez stepping forward to join him, Archer checked his watch.

It was 8:57pm.

The driver went to wipe sweat off his brow with his arm but Chalky jerked his Glock, taking a step forward.

'Don't move!' he bellowed. *'Do not move!'*

'We need to call EOD,' Nikki said to Archer and Marquez, joining them where the triage area had been set up earlier as Bernhardt stayed back by the front door. 'We've already had two bombs go off today. This could definitely be a third.'

As they all stared at the package and Archer went to reply, a quiet ringing sound suddenly started to echo around the car park.

237

Archer, Nikki and Marquez each instinctively reached for their cell phones, Chalky and Josh glancing back in response to the sound as they kept their pistols on the scared and confused delivery man. As the other three withdrew their phones and checked the displays, they realised it was coming from somewhere else.

'Yours?' Archer called to Josh and Chalky.

Both men shook their heads. Archer turned back to look at Bernhardt by the doors, who was watching in confused silence.

'You?'

He shook his head quickly, the ringing continuing to echo around the car park.

'Where the hell is that coming from?' Nikki said.

'Wait!' Marquez said, closing her eyes and focusing her hearing.

The ringing continued.

Then she turned and looked up at the blown out windows of the 1st floor above them.

Without a word, she immediately ran back into the building.

Sprinting up onto the 1st floor, Marquez headed straight towards what had been the Operations area.

The ringing was louder now she was closer to the source; it was coming from a replacement phone sitting on the floor, echoing eerily in the quiet abandoned space. When Archer, Fox and Josh had been away, Nikki had located a spare phone from a maintenance store on the lower floor and reconnected it up here, wanting to have her particular land-line up and running again.

Moving towards it, feeling a slight breeze coming from the gaps in the walls of the Briefing Room to her left, Marquez reached for the receiver then suddenly paused.

If it's a bomb in the box, this might detonate it, she thought.

The ringing continued.

She waited, thinking, and looked outside through the gaps in the wall.

The ringing continued.

Taking a deep breath, she pushed the *Loudspeaker* button and took the call.

There was a pause. Marquez waited.

'Having a bad day?' a voice suddenly asked.

Marquez looked at the phone, surprised. It was a woman's voice, which somehow she hadn't been expecting.

'Who is this?'

'I take it my package just arrived?'

'What do you want?'

'I want Detective Archer to go and open my gift.'

'And why should he?'

There was a pause, and some shuffling down the receiver.

Then there was the sound of sobbing children. Marquez froze, the distressed sound cutting right through her.

Beckett's sons.

'Because if he doesn't, bad things are going to happen to these two boys. Very bad things. Detective Archer has sixty seconds before these runts lose their feet.'

Before Marquez could reply, a screeching sound suddenly filled the receiver. The unexpected noise startled her; she tried to place it, then realised it was the sound of an electric saw. It ran for several seconds, emphasising the woman's point, the banshee-like scream echoing around the level and chilling Marquez to the core.

Then it slowed and stopped, replaced by the sound of muffled whimpering from the two children.

'Fifty nine. Fifty eight.'

Standing down below, waiting for Marquez, Archer saw her suddenly appear at the edge of the blown apart wall, looking down at him and Nikki.

'Some woman just called!' Marquez shouted down to them hurriedly. 'She's the one who sent the parcel. She's got Beckett's sons as hostages.'

'You're sure?' Nikki asked.

She nodded. 'Yeah, I'm sure. She said you have to open the box, Arch, or she's going to start cutting them up with a power saw. She turned it on so I could hear she wasn't kidding. You've got one minute and counting to go open it.'

He stared up at her, then back at the package, as Marquez stood there. They were out of options.

And Beckett's sons were about to run out of time.

'Shit!'

Archer stared over at the box, waiting for him across the car park.

'She's counting down, Arch!' Marquez called from above, desperation in her voice as she looked at her watch. *'You've got fifty seconds!'*

He stood there for a moment, Nikki staring at him, her face fearful.

'What do we do?' she asked.

Archer didn't reply.

240

Then a beat later, he started walking towards the barrier.

He didn't have a choice.

Josh and Chalky were keeping their Glocks on the courier but had heard the exchange with Marquez and watched Archer walk in the gap between them, slowly approaching the parcel.

'Forty five seconds!' Marquez called from the blown-out 1ˢᵗ floor.

Chalky held the Glock double-handed, watching his best friend approach the package just the other side of the barrier, apparently sent by this woman Marquez had just spoken to.

Cursing, he stared at the box.

Christ, I hope that bitch hasn't seen Seven, he thought.

THIRTY FIVE

Bomb-disposal specialists call the approach to a potentially-explosive device *the long walk* and right then Archer knew exactly what they meant.

He'd walked across the ARU car park hundreds of times in the past; the distance from the front door to the gate was only twenty five yards or so, but this time it felt like a mile as he approached the box. As he walked towards the innocuous-looking package sitting there on the concrete, his mind worked at a hundred times the speed of his feet, conjuring up all sorts of images as to what could be inside.

Someone cruel enough to threaten to kill two children with a power saw had sent this thing.

He suddenly pictured Vargas, smiling at him.

Then an instant later, tied up, terrified and completely helpless.

'How am I doing, Lisa?' he shouted.

'Thirty seconds!'

Pulling a jack-knife from his tac vest, Archer stepped around the edge of the wooden barrier and popped the blade, now just ten feet from the package. By his truck, the delivery man stared at him, his hands still in the air, and to Archer's right Wilson was beside his hut, watching silently but his eyes wide.

Walking closer, Archer saw the box had a rectangular white label with his name and the ARU HQ's address clearly printed on it.

'Twenty five!'

Taking a deep breath, Archer stepped up to the parcel and knelt down beside it. The parcel was a

242

brown cube, about the size that held a large toaster, and seemed completely harmless sitting there on the ground in front of him.

'Twenty!'

Taking the knife, he drew in a deep breath then lay the blade gently against the side by some brown tape sealing the lid. He couldn't see wires or anything that looked like a trap. He paused to listen for a moment but couldn't hear anything either; he looked up at the terrified driver, who was watching him from his knees, his eyes bulging with fear.

'How heavy was it?' he asked.

'It was light!' the man said. 'Really light!'

'Fifteen seconds!'

Archer nodded.

Placing the blade at one end of the box, he cut through the tape, the knife sliding along easily as if it was cutting through butter.

It made it all the way.

The flaps either side lifted half an inch.

'Ten! Nine!'

The box was now open, but whatever was inside was still hidden from view. Archer took another deep breath and eased back the flap on the left side.

He saw there were two more flaps horizontally underneath the top two, concealing the contents.

'Five seconds, Arch!'

From their positions around the car park, the gathered group were watching in complete silence, everyone holding their breath.

He was out of time.

Pulling back the third and fourth interior flaps, Archer looked inside.

'What the hell?' he whispered.

It wasn't a bomb.

It wasn't a piece of Vargas.

It was a piece of A4 paper.

And the sheet was folded in half.

Reaching forward, Archer took it in his hands and opened it.

There was a message written there, five words, neat handwriting.

An eye for an eye.

From her vantage point up on the damaged 1st floor, a flicker of movement caught Marquez' attention from the building directly across the street.

Looking over, she saw two dark figures suddenly appear in one of the large office windows.

The moment she saw them, Marquez realised what this was.

Archer, Chalky and Josh were totally exposed in their various positions around the car park. They'd all just been lured out of the building.

Directly into firing range.

THIRTY SIX

'Get down!' she screamed.

At her shout, Josh and Chalky both went to turn in her direction, but a split-second later, two windows in the building opposite shattered as a pair of booming gunshots echoed across the quiet car park.

Both men took a shotgun shell to the chest and were punched off their feet, their pistols clattering to the ground as they were hurled back onto the concrete. A second later, Nikki screamed and dived for cover with Lipton behind the nearest car to their left, following Bernhardt as blasts tore into the wall where they'd just been standing, spewing brick-dust into the air.

As Lipton fired back at the two gunmen with his MP5, Marquez saw Josh and Chalky were both flat out on the ground, Archer taking cover, shielded by the courier's van. Wilson was racing to join him and only just made it as two more shells ricocheted off the concrete just behind him. Drawing her own pistol, Marquez fired at the two gunmen, more in an attempt to attract their fire than in expectation of hitting them at this range.

It worked and she took off to her left as shotgun fire ripped into the room behind her, muzzle flashes lighting up the dark windows in the building fifty yards away as the shells ripped into the open Operations area.

From his cover behind the van beside Wilson and the terrified courier, Archer realised what Marquez was trying to do. Pulling his Glock, he moved forward to

245

the front of the vehicle and fired up at the smashed-out windows of the office building, buying Marquez time to find cover before resuming fire.

Squeezing off two more rounds, he looked over his shoulder and saw Josh and Chalky both laid out in the car park. Josh was writhing in pain, lying in the middle of the space like target practice.

But Chalky was completely still.

With Archer and Lipton firing on the two gunmen, Marquez sprinted down from the 1st floor and used the opportunity to join Nikki, Lipton and Bernhardt just outside the front building behind the car. Reloading her pistol, she looked around the side of the car; Archer was trapped behind the truck and pinned down, not able to do anything to help the two men who'd been hit. She knew it was only a matter of moments before Chalky and Josh took another shell, stranded out there in the middle of the car park.

If they were going to survive, she had to do something.

Looking around desperately for anything she could use as a distraction, she suddenly realised there was a lull in the assault from above.

They're reloading.

'Cover me!' she told Lipton, who nodded.

Taking a deep breath, Marquez darted out from behind the car. She went straight for Josh, relying on Archer and Lipton to give her some cover fire, and they duly obliged.

When she made it to the grounded NYPD detective, she saw he'd been hit in the lower part of the vest, his face screwed up in pain, his breathing laboured as his huge hands clutched at his stomach.

Looking up at the windows, she saw the two gunmen hadn't reappeared, not yet realising she was a sitting duck.

She went to drag Josh but he was too heavy for her to move.

'C'mon!' she shouted. *'You have to help me!'*

Bleeding badly, Josh half-levered himself to his feet and leaned on Marquez as they started to stagger back towards the building, Marquez expecting to take a shell herself at any second.

Firing his last clip at the two gunmen from behind the delivery van, Archer glanced over his shoulder and saw Marquez was horribly isolated as she helped Josh back, Lipton maintaining cover fire. She'd taken advantage in the lull of fire from the building to aid Josh, but Chalky was still out there in the middle of the car park alone. He turned to Wilson, who stepped forward to the front of the van with his own MP5, reading Archer's mind.

'Go!' he shouted, firing up at the two gunmen with the sub-machine gun.

A moment later Archer launched himself forward and sprinted out, running towards Chalky as Lipton and Wilson both fired up at the two windows, preventing their attackers from blasting Archer.

He reached his best friend, who was unmoving on the ground, blood coming from his mouth, his body limp. He'd taken the shell on the upper portion of his vest, the fabric and tools there ripped apart.

'Oh shit, Chalk!' he said.

Grabbing the shoulders of his tac vest, Archer quickly dragged him unceremoniously towards the front door of the building, Chalky's boots scraping across the concrete as Archer moved as fast as he could. A blast smashed out a window on the car protecting Lipton to Archer's right as they passed it but undeterred, Lipton maintained his fire as Archer focused on getting Chalky to the safety of the building.

Up ahead, Marquez and Josh made it inside, one of the doors shattering behind them from a shotgun shell.

'C'mon!' Nikki shouted to Archer, hidden from view just inside the doors, waving him forward.

They entered the building just as two shells hit the brickwork above his head but Archer didn't slow, dragging his best friend down the lower corridor into the heart of the HQ and out of the line of fire as Lipton reloaded and remained where he was, defending the entrance.

Marquez and Bernhardt carried Josh into the interrogation room, followed a moment later by Archer with Chalky, laying him down on the floor as Nikki entered the cell close behind.

Chalky was unconscious and not moving; Nikki ran over and knelt down beside him as Marquez tended to Josh. Standing above Nikki, gunfire still echoing down the corridor, Archer stared down at his best friend's limp and unresponsive body, then at Josh across the room, and an ice-cold rage swept through him.

'Look after him!' he told Nikki, turning and running out of the cell, heading down the corridor to the locker room.

Once inside, he immediately grabbed the MP5 he'd used earlier, slamming a fresh magazine inside

248

furiously. Vargas' kidnap had lit a fire inside him, but watching two of his closest friends get shot had just poured two barrels of gasoline onto the flames. Moving with a speed borne from years of training, he grabbed two spare mags then turned and ran out into the corridor, sprinting down towards the entrance.

Marquez appeared in the doorway as he came down the corridor. She knew immediately what he was planning to do and without a word took off with him, pulling her Glock.

Inside the interrogation cell, hearing Archer and Marquez run off, Nikki was checking Chalky with her one good hand but he was unresponsive.

'He's not breathing!' she said, unzipping his tac vest to begin CPR as Bernhardt knelt beside Josh and watched her.

THIRTY SEVEN

In the office building across the street from the ARU HQ, Notting and Regent were sprinting down the stairs heading towards the ground floor. The parcel had been the perfect bait for an ambush, drawing the remaining cops out of the building just as planned; the two ex-US Army soldiers had managed to take a pair of them out, but the bitch across the street in the Operations area had seen them and shouted a warning before they could drop the others.

The two men went down the stairs two at a time, needing to get the hell out of there before the cops arrived and sealed the building off. There was no fire exit in the stairwell, which meant they'd have to go out through the lobby, but the Benellis were plenty persuasive and would ensure a trouble-free escape.

Smashing open the door to the ARU's lower corridor, Archer and Marquez saw Lipton by the doors, his MP5 in his hands still aimed up at the building across the street. He wasn't firing though and neither were the two enemy gunmen.

'I think they're gone!' he said.

Archer and Marquez immediately raced outside, not delaying for a second. Making it across the car park without being fired on, the pair ran past the barrier and the delivery van with Wilson and the courier still beside it, sprinting across the street towards the office building from where the shots had been fired.

Ripping open the glass door to the building, they raced inside, just as a stairwell exit ahead to their right smashed open and the two guys appeared.

The gunmen reacted fast; each was carrying a black semi-auto shotgun and the man closest to the two cops turned and unloaded an entire handful of shells in quick succession, smashing apart the glass where Archer and Marquez had just been standing as they hit the floor behind a reception desk. There was a ferocious onslaught from both shotguns, spraying Archer and Marquez with fragments of wood and glass and forcing them to stay down, but then it suddenly stopped, the shots continuing to reverberate around the lobby.

Risking a look around the side of the desk, Archer caught a brief glimpse of the gunmen disappearing through a revolving door, heading straight out to the street.

Pushing himself to his feet, he took off after them.

Notting and Regent raced across the road towards their car parked on the other side of the street as the few people around them screamed and ran, having heard the gunfire and then seeing the armed men erupt out of the building.

Notting jumped inside the vehicle and fired the engine as Regent turned back, aiming his Benelli at the lobby and giving his companion the chance to start the car.

'Get inside!' Notting shouted, putting it into gear.

Bursting through the revolving door, Archer and Marquez sprinted out onto the street but dove to the left immediately as another shotgun blast exploded into the glass behind them.

Across the road and to the right, one of the gunmen was standing by a car, his partner already behind the wheel; the guy on the street went to fire again, but his shotgun clicked dry. Dropping the weapon, the man's hand flashed for a pistol on his hip, whipping it out of the holster. As the guy did so, Archer lifted his MP5 and put his sights on the man's chest, but he couldn't shoot.

'Move!' he shouted to a couple of stunned pedestrians, who were standing behind the gunman and in the line of fire. *'Get out of the way!'*

He couldn't pull the trigger; there was too great a chance he could hit one of them. However, the gunman standing by the vehicle had no such concerns and as the pedestrians scattered, he squeezed off some silenced rounds with the Ruger, Archer and Marquez both rolling behind a pillar outside the office building as the glass doors behind them were smashed to pieces, showering them both as the man unloaded with the handgun, not caring if he hit anyone else.

As Archer drew the man's fire from one side of the pillar Marquez snapped round the other side and squeezed off a round with her Glock, hitting the gunman in the leg.

He shouted in pain and staggered back, dropping his pistol and falling onto the road in front of the car.

Inside the Audi, Notting saw Regent go down but he wasn't hanging around.

Taking off the handbrake, he immediately put his foot down and floored it.

Running forward, Archer and Marquez watched as the man in the car ran straight over his companion, crushing him under the wheels as the car ploughed on and sped away.

As Marquez moved towards the man on the ground and checked for a pulse, Archer ran forward but watched the other man turn the corner and disappear out of sight. As Marquez grabbed the remaining man's weapons, securing them, Archer suddenly remembered Chalky and Josh.

Turning, he sprinted back the way he and Marquez had come, racing back through the building lobby and out the other side towards the ARU car park.

Inside the interrogation cell, Nikki was desperately performing CPR on Chalky as Bernhardt tended to Josh and Lipton finished speaking to an emergency operator, having called for an ambulance. Laid out on the floor, his damaged tac vest unzipped to allow access to his sternum, Chalky wasn't reacting to Nikki's efforts.

Suddenly, Archer ran back into the room, kneeling beside her and placing his MP5 down in one movement.

'Where was he hit?'

'The upper chest. He's not bleeding; I think the force of the impact stopped his heart!'

Doing the CPR with just her good hand, Nikki started to slow, running out of stamina. Archer immediately took over, locking his hands and pushing down on his best friend's sternum as Bernhardt looked on and Lipton returned his attentions to Josh, who'd recovered his breath but was hunched over in pain.

Chalky's body jerked with each push but there was no response, no sign of life.

'C'mon, Chalk!' he said. 'Stop messing about.'

He continued to pump his chest. Archer then pinched his nose and breathed into Chalky's mouth as Nikki looked on helplessly, then resumed the CPR.

But Chalky's body just jerked lifelessly under Archer's clenched hands.

'Don't you die, you son of a bitch!' Archer said to his best friend, pushing harder and harder.

He kept performing the CPR for a minute or so, refusing to quit.

'Arch,' Nikki whispered.

He didn't hear her, continuing.

Chalky still didn't respond.

'Arch.'

Tears spilling down her cheeks, Nikki put her hand on Archer's arm.

He slowed, taking deep breaths.

Then he stopped altogether.

Rocking back on his heels, Archer stared down at his best friend in disbelief.

Chalky was gone.

THIRTY EIGHT

Kneeling beside his best friend's body, Archer couldn't take his eyes off him. Tears were streaming down Nikki's face as she clutched onto Archer's hand, staring at Chalky's corpse too.

He was dead.

As they all knelt there in silence, Marquez ran into the room to join them and stopped in her tracks when she saw Chalky.

She covered her mouth, realising what had happened.

Then Archer suddenly got to his feet and ran past her out of the room.

Turning right, he sprinted down the corridor into the locker room.

Once inside, he started pulling out all the drawers under the benches in the room in a frenzy.

The first few were filled with tools, rags, some spare vests, but he couldn't see what he was after.

'*Shit!*' he shouted.

It had been moved since he'd last been here.

'*C'mon!*' he shouted in frustration, ripping open another drawer.

Then he found it.

Grabbing the item, Archer ran straight back down the corridor and raced into the room, the others frozen in a tableau, still in the same places where he'd left them. Dropping down to his knees beside Chalky's body, Archer ripped open the case, revealing the defibrillator that every police unit in the city was required to have on site. Switching it on, he pushed up his best friend's polo-shirt, waiting for the device to charge.

It did.

'Clear!' he shouted, pushing the paddles onto his chest.

Chalky's back arched.

Then he hit the ground again with a *whump*.

No response.

Archer waited for the paddles to recharge then did it again.

'Clear!'

Nothing.

There was no response.

Beside him, none of the others spoke.

'C'mon!' Archer shouted at his best friend as he used the paddles again.

His back arched and he dropped back down.

'Fight it, Chalk!'

The paddles charged and he used them again.

Chalky's back arched.

He didn't respond.

'Arch, he's gone,' Nikki said, crying.

Archer charged the paddles and pushed them down again.

'He's gone!' Nikki shouted at him, Archer's refusal to acknowledge Chalky's death tipping her over the edge.

'No he's not!' Archer screamed, charging the paddles for a final time.

He pushed them down onto Chalky's chest.

His body arched and fell back to the ground.

But he didn't respond.

Staring at him, Archer sat back on his knees again, panting as he looked down at his closest friend, unaccustomed tears filling his eyes as the defibrillator hummed quietly beside him and he shook with emotion.

He was gone.

Chalky really was dead.

I failed.

His mouth open, Archer stared at his friend, Nikki sobbing behind him. Across the room, Marquez was kneeling by Josh, her own eyes welling with tears, Lipton and Bernhardt staying silent.

I'm sorry, Chalk, Archer thought, blinking as unaccustomed tears rolled down his face.

I'm so sorry.

Then Chalky suddenly stirred.

As Nikki gasped, Archer almost went into cardiac arrest himself. Lifting his shoulder as Nikki and Lipton both moved forward in disbelief, Archer supported his friend as he started to take sharp panicked breaths, Archer propping Chalky up as he sucked in air, grabbing at Archer and Nikki, blinking rapidly as he regained consciousness.

'It's OK, Chalk!' Archer said. 'It's OK. We're here!'

Chalky couldn't reply, continuing to take deep gasps as he clutched his best friend's arm, blinking and breathing. Archer and Nikki looked at each other in pure relief as the sound of sirens came from outside, back-up arriving.

'God damn it,' Archer said, looking down at his best friend as Nikki clutched onto them both. 'Don't you ever do that to us again.'

THIRTY NINE

Less than ten minutes later, Archer and Marquez were standing in handcuffs in the middle of the car park watching an ambulance carrying Josh depart, the siren blaring as it headed off down the street. Wilson had been taken along with them, having been clipped in the leg by a ricochet in the shootout but not badly wounded.

Less than twenty seconds after Chalky had been revived, two paramedics had suddenly arrived inside the interrogation cell; one had attended to Josh and the other treated Chalky, giving him oxygen while Nikki talked them through what had happened. Moments later, a Firearms Unit had arrived en masse and after Archer and Marquez had headed outside to meet them and explain the situation, they'd both been put in cuffs until their identities could be established.

They were now standing in the car park with two officers beside them, two others walking back across the car park having just checked out the building opposite and their sergeant approaching as he wrapped up a phone call concerning the body of the dead gunman a street away.

With Josh and Wilson's ambulance now on its way to hospital and the threat of the two men with shotguns gone, Nikki appeared from the building and marched across the car park towards Archer and Marquez, carrying some papers in her good hand, the other still contained in the sling.

The Firearms Unit sergeant stepped forwards to meet her. Although these officers were always professional, Archer knew this particular sergeant of old and there was no love lost between him and the Unit. Named Haskins, he'd applied to join the ARU several times but had never made it past the final interview stage; consequently, he'd developed a large chip on his shoulder against Cobb's team and would always run interference with their field work if he possibly could.

'Show's over, sweetheart,' Haskins said.

He smirked at her, holding up Archer's and Marquez' NYPD badges as Nikki approached him.

'And you're in deep shit,' he continued. 'You've been allowing non-licensed people to run around the city with weapons. Do you have any idea the trouble-'

'No, you listen to me!' she interrupted.

Her unaccustomed ferocity took the man completely by surprise and stopped him in his tracks.

'In the last few hours, I've watched almost every member of my Unit get taken out,' Nikki said. 'Not only are two of my friends dead but the sons of one of my co-workers and a kidnapped NYPD detective are still missing and quite possibly dead by now.'

She slammed the wad of papers in her free hand into the surprised man's chest.

'These are official authorisations, signed by Director Tim Cobb giving these people the temporary right to bear arms in this country between the dates specified. We're a para-military organisation that works under our own protocol, but then again you should already know that considering how many times you've tried to join us. Tell me Sergeant, do you really think Director Cobb would allow unauthorised personnel to operate out of his

HQ and run around the city armed without his express permission?'

Haskins didn't reply.

Not pausing for a moment, Nikki pointed to the vehicles across the car park, rigid with pent up fury and frustration.

'So thank you for your support, Sergeant. Truly, I'm touched. But I suggest you take the cuffs off my colleagues, get in your cars and leave before you really piss me off.'

She stepped in close, her eyes blazing.

'And if you call me sweetheart one more time, you'll join the remainder of my task force in the Critical Care Unit. Are we clear?'

Archer and Marquez grinned at that, both watching Haskins who didn't know how to respond, knowing he'd been wrong-footed.

Haskins didn't move for a moment, Nikki staying where she was and glaring at him.

Then eventually, he turned to his team, some of whom quickly hid smiles after listening to the exchange.

'We're leaving.'

He swung back to Nikki and motioned with the papers.

'And I'm going to check these out. Make no mistake. If there's even one word missing that invalidates them then I'll be coming right back.'

'Good luck with that,' she said as she wrenched the authorisations back off him, not prepared to let them out of her sight. 'I'll email you a copy.'

Turning, she watched as Haskins' men removed the handcuffs from Archer and Marquez then climbed back into their cars.

After the teams had departed, leaving just a solitary ambulance team behind, Nikki turned to the NYPD pair, taking deep breaths and looking shaken.

'Are you OK?' Marquez asked.

'I feel sick.'

'You did great,' Archer said, glancing around them and feeling exposed standing there in the lamp-lit car park surrounded by office buildings and anonymous windows. 'But let's continue this inside.'

A minute or so later, the trio were back inside the interrogation room, re-joining Chalky, a paramedic and Bernhardt.

Chalky was sitting in one of the chairs, his breathing back to normal, his tac vest still open but his polo shirt now pulled back down over his torso. The bulletproof garment had saved his life, absorbing the shotgun blast, but the front of it looked pretty tattered, the fabric torn, the tools slotted inside dented and chipped.

Nikki and Marquez immediately moved across the room, making sure he was OK. Standing by the door and noting the paramedic was packing up his gear, Archer frowned.

'You're leaving?' he asked, puzzled.

The man nodded, looking at Chalky. 'I wanted him to come with me just for a final check but he told me what's happened today. I guess he'll be more use to you here than in hospital.'

'But his heart just stopped,' Nikki said, beside Chalky with her hand on his back. 'Doesn't he need an ECG or something?'

The paramedic shook his head. 'I just did one. As expected, he's fine. The force of the shotgun shell

261

put him into cardiac arrest, but you restarted his heart with the defib kit and it's working just fine. He's perfectly healthy; totally back to normal.'

Clipping up his bag, he saw Archer looking doubtful.

'Believe me, it's as good as if it never happened. I wouldn't leave him here otherwise. He didn't sustain any broken ribs or collarbones, so although he may feel a bit shaky for a while, he's good to go.'

He turned to Chalky.

'You're a lucky man.'

'I've heard that before,' he replied.

The man slung his bag over his shoulder, then nodded to the room. 'Stay safe. Whatever this is about, I hope you resolve it.'

The others nodded in acknowledgement and the man departed, pulling the door closed behind him.

'You OK?' Archer asked Chalky once the paramedic had left.

He cracked a half-hearted smile. 'I could use a holiday.'

'You should go to the hospital, Chalk,' Nikki said.

Chalky shook his head, looking at her injured arm. 'You stay, I stay. I'm not going anywhere. And you heard the man; I'm as good as new. Well, almost.'

As she smiled, listening to the exchange, Marquez focused on Bernhardt, who was standing across the room watching in silence.

'Are you hurt?'

He shook his head. 'I'm fine.'

He looked at Chalky.

'The guy was right. You're a lucky man.'

Satisfied Chalky wasn't about to pass out or suddenly drop off his chair, Archer glanced at the people around him. Not including Bernhardt, they were now down to just four; Nikki, Marquez, Chalky and himself. Nikki was working at fifty per cent and Chalky had taken a hammering.

However, everything had suddenly become a lot clearer.

Looking at Nikki, Marquez and Chalky, Archer remembered the message inside the parcel outside addressed to him.

Vargas' kidnap.

The bombs in Brixton and here.

The sniper attacks.

The ambushes.

All of it was now starting to make sense.

'So what now?' Chalky asked quietly from his seat. 'We're getting demolished by these people.'

'At least we've got one less to deal with,' Marquez said.

'He's dead?'

Marquez nodded. 'I shot him; his buddy finished the job driving over him to escape.'

'He's already on the way to the lab,' Nikki said, as she took a seat at the desk and looked at her laptop screen. 'Hopefully they can get an ID for us. Whatever the case, as you said, at least that's one of them down.'

'What about that phone call?' Chalky asked, thinking back to the parcel sequence. 'From the woman? Can we trace it, Nik?'

Nikki shook her head in frustration. 'To do that, I need to be connected to the phone-line during the call. It all happened so quickly, I didn't even think about it.'

263

Bernhardt turned to Marquez. 'Any noise in the background? Anything distinguishable?'

'Apart from the power saw, not much. That really dominated proceedings.'

'What about the parcel?'

'Forensics took it to the lab and are working on it,' Nikki said. 'Dusting the whole thing for prints and checking for DNA. It's going to take a while though; this isn't CSI Miami. I doubt we'll find anything and if we do it's probably because they want us to.'

'Someone must have dropped it off for delivery and signed a form,' Chalky said. 'Can we check the depot cameras or the UPS log?'

Nikki sighed, motioning to her injured arm. 'I can try. I'm working as fast as I can. Normally I've got two hands and an entire team working on this stuff.'

'Wait, what was inside the box?' Bernhardt asked, looking at Archer, who'd gone quiet.

'A piece of paper,' he replied. 'A4, folded in half. Five words, hand-written.'

'What did it say?'

'*An eye for an eye.*'

'*An eye for an eye?*' Nikki echoed, looking at Archer. 'That sounds like revenge.'

He nodded. 'Yes. It does. And now I know what this is all about.'

The group looked at him.

'The kidnap and all these attacks on us haven't got anything to do with Vargas. They never did. They're not after her.'

He paused.

'They're after me.'

FORTY

'Wait a minute,' Nikki said. 'You're the target?'

He nodded. 'Yes. I am.'

'But you said in Hendon that the two snipers had their sights on Lisa and Fox?'

'They did. And that reinforces my point.'

'How?' Chalky asked. 'Why would they kill them and not you?'

'Remember when you all said that I should take command of this operation?'

Nikki looked at Chalky and Marquez, then nodded.

'What was the main reason why?'

'You were the one person who'd worked in both teams,' Chalky said. 'Us and your NYPD group.'

Archer nodded. 'My old team and my new team. Brought together then viciously and repeatedly attacked. *An eye for an eye.* That's a personal message.'

He paused.

'For some reason, the woman who called and sent the parcel is pissed at me. She kidnapped my girlfriend and all day has been trying to wipe out the people I've worked with here and in New York, the men and women I care about most.'

He glanced at Marquez.

'The snipers were going to take you, Josh and Fox out around me. But not me. Not yet.'

'But you said the three men who ambushed you at Bernhardt's were trying to kill you?' Nikki said.

Archer shook his head. 'Something about that's been bothering me. One of them had a clear shot at my head when I was about to jump over the back

265

wall but he dropped his fire, aiming at my legs. That's been puzzling me ever since; these guys are too good to make mistakes like that. I think he was trying to wound me. They wanted to take me alive.'

Across the room, Bernhardt frowned.

'How can you be so sure it's about you?' he said. 'This sounds like a lot of guesswork.'

'Firstly, Vargas is my girlfriend. Secondly, whoever this woman is, she knows my name and that I'm back today, otherwise how did she know to send the package? I don't work for the ARU anymore, so why send it here?'

He looked at the others in the room.

'Thirdly, the people in these two teams are my closest colleagues and friends. I can think of no other reason why someone would target us all specifically when we were pulled together. And last of all, why else would NYPD detectives be targeted so fast in London? We've been in the city for less than four hours. No one else knows we're here. It's all way too much of a coincidence.'

Nikki stared at him for a moment, realising that he was right.

Then she looked down at her screen as the machine beeped.

'Forensics have pulled a hit on the dead gunman who got run over,' she said. 'They've attached his file. It's from the US Army database.'

With Archer's statements lingering in the air, the team all moved forward to look as she opened it.

'Staff-Sergeant Ronald Needs; thirty four years old, ex-US Army, been out for eight years. Worked as a contractor in the Middle East for a variety of different companies. Blackwater, Dyncorp, Airscan.

His record isn't great. Beat two theft charges, but when he was still serving he was arrested for assault; stabbed two guys in a bar fight in Louisiana. The army got rid of him after that, so he went solo and travelled out to the Middle East by himself looking for work.'

'A gun for hire,' Marquez said. 'A perfect new team-mate for Dash.'

'And his buddy ran him over without a moment's hesitation in order to escape,' Archer said. 'Not a scrap of loyalty. These guys are brutal.'

'He was using a Benelli M2 and a silenced Ruger 22/45 pistol,' Nikki said. 'Serial numbers on both trace back to just last year. Fresh off the line and expensive, the Benelli in particular. These weapons and the amount of ammo they've been using means someone with very deep pockets is bankrolling this.'

'The woman on the phone,' Marquez said. 'If you're right about her calling the shots Arch, then she must be the one who hired them.'

Nikki paused, thinking. 'If this is a personal vendetta then this man's friends will keep coming back for us until we're all dead. That means we need to get everyone involved in the Unit under protection.'

'You said all personnel at the hospitals are under armed guard?' Chalky said.

'Yeah, but we need to think past members, as well as present. We don't know what triggered this or how far back it happened.'

Across the room, Chalky frowned; then he suddenly looked over at Archer.

'Mac,' they said simultaneously.

'Who's Mac?' Marquez asked.

'He was the sergeant of the task force here for the first year,' Chalky said. 'Once the team was up and running, he retired and left.'

'Where does he live?' Archer asked.

'Putney, across the River,' Nikki said, typing with one hand as she pulled up his address and phone number. She paused, trying to withdraw her phone, and Bernhardt stepped forward to help her. 'I'll get on to him.'

She tapped in the number, then pushed the button for loudspeaker.

The ringing filled the quiet room, all of them waiting.

But no one picked up.

The call rang through to the answer machine. Nikki quickly ended the call and tried again just in case he hadn't made it to the phone in time.

As she did so, Archer turned to Chalky. 'We need to get him back here and under protection immediately; should be pretty straightforward. Are you up to it?'

Chalky grunted and rose. 'Definitely. Could use some fresh air.'

'I'll come with you,' Marquez said. 'I'm not staying behind this time.'

Archer nodded.

'Armoury first, guys. Before you go anywhere, I want both of you wearing intact vests and carrying weapons.'

'Damn right,' Chalky said, unzipping his damaged tac vest as he and Marquez headed for the door. 'Until this is over, I'm sleeping in one of these damn things.'

Across town, Dash, Piccadilly, Portland and Grange were waiting in their car in the car park when Dash's phone rang.

He took the call immediately. 'And?'

'The package worked,' Notting said, the sound of a car engine in the background. *'Drew them all out of the building but they reacted fast. We put two of them down though.'*

'Dead?'

'One probably, another possibly.'

'The golden boy?'

'Still standing. But there's a negative.'

'Which is?'

'Regent's down.'

'How?'

'He got shot and caught under the car as I drove off.'

'But you put away two of the cops?'

'Yeah.'

'That's what matters. He knew the risks.' As he spoke, Dash suddenly felt his phone purr as a new message came in. 'Where are you?'

'Getting the hell out of the area. The cops will have tagged my plates.'

'Don't take any risks; we don't want you tailed. Pull over, switch them and keep your phone close. I just got another message, so I'll call you back.'

'Copy.'

Dash hung up and opened the text message. As he read it, he frowned, but then his eyes widened.

'What is it?' Piccadilly asked.

Dash passed the phone to him and fired the engine. 'Call Notting back right now and put it on speaker.'

As Piccadilly redialled the American, Dash took off the handbrake and looked in the rear view mirror at Portland and Grange as he pulled out of the parking spot.

'You two, reload your weapons. We're in business.'

Back at the ARU HQ, Chalky and Marquez walked down the corridor, both carrying a Glock, an MP5 and each wearing one of the tac vests. Chalky had a fresh, undamaged one over his navy blue ARU polo shirt and jeans, and Marquez had strapped hers over her white t-shirt, stowing the Glock in the thigh holster already secured around her right leg.

They paused inside the shot-up reception, checking their gear and adjusting the ear pieces to their radios, then looked out at the now quiet car park, both of them glancing up at the sea of office windows surrounding the police HQ.

'Ready?' he asked her.

She nodded, hitting forward the cocking handle on the MP5.

They both took a deep breath, then moved out into the car park, checking left and right as they headed straight for one of the Unit's two remaining BMWs.

FORTY ONE

Now Chalky and Marquez had departed, Archer, Nikki and Bernhardt were left alone inside the interrogation room, Archer's and Nikki's focus now purely on finding the three hostages. They'd had a proof of life when Marquez had heard the two boys on the phone call, but they hadn't heard a peep from Vargas since she'd been kidnapped. If Archer was right, the woman who'd sent the package clearly wanted him to suffer.

And with Vargas missing for almost a day, her chances of survival weren't looking good at all.

Standing across from Nikki and Bernhardt, Archer felt exhausted, unnerved and confused; the message on that piece of paper inside the box was also running through his mind on an endless loop.

An eye for an eye.

But whose eye was that?

If this was specifically targeted at him, it must have been something he'd done personally. He'd pissed a lot people off since he'd been a cop, but if it'd been from his time in New York then they'd have gone for him there; the fact that members of the ARU were targets too meant it had to be something from when he was an officer here. The list of potential candidates was huge given the amount of operations the ARU had been swept up in, but the apparent ex-military status of the enemy gunmen could be a clue. He'd encountered a team of Special Forces soldiers in the past on an operation; could the woman have cared about one of them?

271

'Who do you think she could be?' Nikki asked Archer, guessing what he was thinking.

He shrugged. 'We'll find out soon enough. Whoever she is, at some point she'll want me to know what I did.'

'Josh broke a couple of ribs but he's OK,' Nikki said, studying her screen. 'They're running an x-ray to make sure nothing else is damaged.'

Archer nodded. 'Glad he's OK. Scared the hell out of me.'

'Me too.'

In the silence that followed, her laptop beeped, alerting her to another message. She clicked it open and read whatever came up on the screen.

Archer saw her expression change immediately.

'What?' he asked.

'Damn it,' she said, reaching for her phone and starting to scroll quickly for a number.

Four miles south of the ARU HQ, Chalky and Marquez were on their way to Mac's house when the software already synced into Chalky's phone inside the car started ringing.

Keeping his right hand on the wheel, he pressed the button and took the call.

'Yeah?'

'Turn back,' Nikki said. *'Now.'*

'Why? What's wrong?'

'It's a wasted trip.'

'Why?'

'Mac's not in the country. He's in Portugal on holiday. Met operator was calling his family; his daughter just answered and told him.'

'You're sure?' Chalky asked.

272

'Positive. He's not in the UK. If he's going to get protection, we need to get on the phone to the Portuguese police. So come back; we need you here. Until we figure out more, none of us should be out and about in the city unless it's absolutely necessary.'

'OK,' he said. 'We're on our way.'

Ending the call as they were just approaching a small roundabout up ahead, Chalky took the fourth exit and started moving back down the road they'd just driven up.

'Saves us another task, I guess,' he said.

Marquez nodded, checking the passing streets either side of them.

Neither of them noticed a silver Audi with freshly changed plates making the same turn on the roundabout and slide in behind them twenty yards back.

The call finished, Nikki tapped away on the keypad, studying her latest feed as Archer and Bernhardt watched her in silence.

'That's one less potential target to worry about,' she said, as Archer nodded, thinking.

'How are you doing on tracking their cars?' Bernhardt asked.

'Some Met analysts have been checking the CCTV, but there's been no response.'

'They'll be changing the plates constantly so we can't trace them,' Archer said.

Nikki went to reply, but suddenly paused.

She looked at Archer, who'd gone still too.

Listening.

'What's wrong?' Bernhardt said.

273

Neither responded.

Chalky and Marquez had left the door slightly ajar and they could both hear a noise echoing down the quiet corridor.

Faint and distant, but recognisable.

The phone upstairs.

It was ringing again.

FORTY TWO

As they drove back to HQ, a brief silence had fallen between Chalky and Marquez.

Looking out of the window to her left, Marquez was watching the unfamiliar city streets passing by. It seemed to her that London was like New York's older, polite cousin, busy and intense but with shorter buildings and cooler tempers. It was quieter too; people didn't drive on their horns here or constantly shout on the street. She'd never been to London before and so far the jury was out on whether she'd ever want to come back.

Today hadn't exactly been the most pleasant of welcomes.

Watching all but two of Archer's old ARU team go down had been hard, but seeing Shepherd and Josh being taken out had been even worse. Both men were like family to her, as were Vargas and Archer; she'd already been totally invested in this case, but now her determination had risen to a whole new level to find out who was doing this and bring them to justice.

Staying quiet, she pulled her cell phone from the slot on the vest she was wearing and sent a quick text message to her sister, who was watching her daughter for her whilst she was away. As she tapped away on the phone, Chalky took a right turn; the traffic was pretty light and they were making good time as they continued on their way back to the station.

The quiet of the car and the darkness of the streets were somehow calming, the brief respite of the

275

intensity of the last few hours welcome to both of them.

Pushing *Send*, Marquez returned the phone to the vest and glanced at Chalky. 'How's the chest?'

'Sore. Think I've had enough punishment for one day.'

He smiled.

'I take any more of a beating, people will start thinking I'm Archer. Just not as ugly.'

She laughed, looking out of the window again, the city rolling past.

'I've never been here before,' she said.

'England?'

'Yeah.'

'Shit, you've been missing out.'

'Clearly,' she replied.

He glanced over at her and smiled. 'It's good to finally meet you. Next time I'm in New York you should come out with us. I was over there for New Year with Arch and Josh.'

She smiled. 'Oh, I heard all about it. I think it's taken seven months for Josh's liver to recover.'

Chalky grinned, then paused. 'How's Archer doing over there?'

She thought for a moment. 'I've been a cop for over a decade. I started out in the Bronx and worked up through two different divisions to the Counter-Terrorism Bureau. But he's one of the best I've ever worked with.'

She glanced over at him.

'He surprised a hell of a lot of people too. We all found out about the strings that had been pulled to get him working in the Bureau. Then of course he walked in and as soon as people saw what he looked

276

like a lot of them made up their minds on the spot, figuring he'd be a waste of space. My old partner was one of them. Turned out they were all wrong.'

She smiled.

'Sort of ironic, having a guy being judged on his looks for a change.'

'Yeah, his face is a burden,' Chalky said, smiling as they pulled up at a red light. 'But your people weren't the first to underestimate him.'

He sat waiting at the light and turned to look at her.

'But I meant how's he doing?' he asked. 'Personally?'

She paused. 'I think he struggled at first. Wasn't easy for him to come into the Department the way he did. Not with his accent and the favour Franklin gave him by fast-tracking him into the Bureau. He keeps a lot of things to himself, but you could tell it was hard. I think he missed you guys.'

She paused.

'But in the last few months, he's looked more settled. I think he's finally happy.'

'Because of Vargas?'

'I think she's got a lot to do with it.'

Chalky didn't reply; Marquez glanced over.

'You all miss him.'

Chalky didn't respond, his silence speaking volumes.

'He'll come back,' she said. 'One day.'

'But not for a while. It sounds like he's doing a pretty good job over there.'

'Yeah, he is.'

Chalky paused. 'Today's been a nightmare. Two of my colleagues are dead. The rest are all in hospital.

277

But the strange thing is, a small part of me doesn't want this to end.'

'Why?'

'Because when it's over, Arch goes back.'

He smiled, shaking his head.

'Jesus Christ, I sound like a bad rom-com. People hear me talk like this, they'll start getting ideas.'

'He's your best friend. It's OK to miss him.'

She paused.

'I made it into the interrogation room just before he left to find the defibrillator. When you weren't breathing, he wouldn't give up; he's the one who brought you back. Everyone else thought you'd gone and had given up. So take it from me, he cares about you just as much as you all care about him.'

Chalky looked over at her, but didn't speak. The red light in front of them turned green.

Staying silent, Chalky moved forward and then took a left down a side street.

As Marquez started to say something, she glanced in her side mirror for the first time in a while and then stopped abruptly.

Chalky glanced over at her quickly then checked his rear view mirror.

There was a silver Audi with blacked out windows turning left, following close behind them.

'Recognise it?' Chalky asked.

She nodded. 'I think so. Same model that the gunman ran over his buddy with.'

She peered closer.

'But the plates are diff-'

The end of her sentence was lost as suddenly a black car pulled across the end of the road in front of them, stopping with a screech of brakes. It appeared out of nowhere, completely blocking their path, and forced Chalky to slam on his brakes.

The action threw him and Marquez forward, their seatbelts locking and preventing them from being catapulted through the windscreen; a moment later, they saw the doors on the car ahead open and four figures in khakis and shirts step out.

One of them was Dash.

Each man had an AR-15 assault rifle and all four weapons came up simultaneously, aimed at the ARU BMW.

Back at base, Archer and Nikki had sprinted upstairs, Archer carrying Nikki's laptop as they raced across the damaged 1st floor into what was left of the Operations area.

They were now by the phone sitting on the floor, which was still ringing. Archer quickly opened the laptop as Nikki plugged a wire into the phone from her laptop and then started typing as fast as she could, the fingers on her free hand flickering across the keys as she pulled up the tracing program, peering in close to see what she was doing.

'Hurry, Nik!' he said.

'We're there!' she said, hitting a last key, the tracing software on the screen, ready to be activated. 'If it's her, keep her on the line for one minute. That's all I need.'

They both looked at the phone, which continued to ring.

Then Archer pushed *Answer*.

He didn't speak, waiting. In the silence, he glanced at her laptop and saw the trace had begun, the red numbers ticking down as the map of London appeared, a pulsing red circle over the grid.

00:57.

00:56.

He continued to wait, listening.

Then he eventually broke the silence.

'It's you, isn't it?'

'I recognise that voice. It's the man himself,' the female voice said. *'The prodigal son has returned. Have you enjoyed your homecoming?'*

He glanced at Nikki, who checked the screen.

00:53.

00:52.

'I've had better.'

'I'm sure. But tell me Sam, how does it feel?'

He paused.

'How does what feel?'

00:48.

00:47.

'Knowing that PC White, Detective Marquez and Miss Carter are all about to die?'

Archer hesitated; he glanced at Nikki, whose eyes had widened in confusion.

Before either of them could react, they heard a footstep crunch on some broken glass behind them.

It was followed a half second later by the quiet *click* of a pistol's hammer being drawn back.

FORTY THREE

'Holy shit!' Marquez shouted as the four men opened fire with the AR-15s.

She and Chalky both threw themselves sideways into the gear well as automatic gunfire riddled the car, the brutal echoes of the assault weapons filling the street and the muzzle flashes lighting up the night. As the bullets tore into the car, Marquez and Chalky were showered with debris and glass, the quiet of a few minutes ago completely shattered.

'Hold on!' Chalky shouted, stamping his foot down on the accelerator as Marquez stayed down, reaching for her MP5 which was stowed beside her right leg in the foot-well.

The car suddenly leapt forward, the sudden move surprising the gunmen who were forced to stop firing and leap out of the way as the BMW ploughed forward and slammed into the blocking car, knocking it slightly off kilter. The impact activated the twin airbags, but they were shot out almost immediately and instantly deflated as their tops each caught a bullet.

Staying low, Chalky grabbed hold of the gear lever, slammed it into reverse and pushed down on the accelerator again, holding the wheel level and steady. The car sped back as Marquez sat up, taking the safety off the MP5 and firing on the four men ahead, shooting through the smashed windshield and forcing them to take cover. Emptying the magazine, she risked a quick look behind and saw they were heading straight for the man who she and Archer had shot at earlier, the man who'd escaped in the car and then run over his partner, the ex-US Army soldier.

Chalky kept reversing and smashed straight into the Audi, the lone gunman only just jumping out of the way in time but managing to unload with the shotgun, two shells blasting into the back of the car and a third taking out Marquez' headrest as she ducked.

Using the car like a Dodgem, trying to batter his way out, Chalky switched the transmission to *Drive* as Marquez reloaded then fired at the man behind them, the guy flinging himself to the ground behind his car.

'Go!' she shouted.

The BMW shot forward as Marquez turned her attention back to the gunmen in front of them and opened fire through the shattered windscreen. As they sped forward towards the blocking car, Chalky suddenly twisted the wheel to the right, causing the BMW to smash into the rear end of the gunmen's vehicle, hitting it hard like a battering ram.

The force of the impact smashed a severe dent into the front of the BMW but also spun the blocking car to the side, giving the BMW just enough room to escape through the gap.

Chalky kept his foot down as they shot forward; beside him, Marquez reloaded for the last time then changed hands and fired with her left through the rear windshield at the five ambushers, the barrage not hitting any of the gunmen but forcing them to stay down and giving her and Chalky a chance to escape.

Taking a hard right turn, Chalky sat straight up and sped on as Marquez' MP5 clicked dry.

'Shit, I'm out!' she said.

'Take one of mine!' he replied, checking his rear view mirror to make sure they weren't being pursued then shifting his attention to the road ahead, squinting through the smashed-up windshield.

Both of them were bleeding from small cuts from the flying glass; wiping blood off her temple, Marquez pulled the magazine from her MP5 and replaced it with one that she took from Chalky's vest.

'God dammit!' she said. 'I've had enough of this shit! Where the hell did those guys come from?'

Before Chalky could answer, they heard the sound of rubber on tarmac, and the two cars suddenly skidded around the corner into view on the street behind them.

'Burn it!' Marquez shouted, slamming the stock of her MP5 forward and turning to fire as Chalky floored the accelerator.

On the ARU HQ's blown-out 1st floor, Archer and Nikki had slowly turned after hearing the pistol being cocked behind them.

They were looking at Bernhardt.

He was standing ten feet away, holding Josh's Glock in his scarred hand, aiming it directly at them.

Behind the gun, his dark eyes were expressionless, half-concealed by the milky scar tissue surrounding them, like two dark pebbles half-submerged in sand.

'Surprise,' he said.

'Are you there, Camden?' the female voice called over the loudspeaker.

'I'm here.'

'I'll leave it with you. You know what to do. Kill her; I want him alive.'

283

Then the call went dead.

Looking over her shoulder slowly, Nikki glanced at her screen. The trace had frozen at *00:23.*

Just over twenty seconds from knowing this woman's location.

'Your friend and the NYPD bitch aren't coming back,' Bernhardt said. 'Right now they'll have more holes in them than a sieve.'

He smirked, looking at Archer.

'Such a shame. All that effort to bring him back from the dead only to lose him again.'

'You're one of them,' Nikki said. 'Part of Dash's team.'

Bernhardt grinned. It stretched the damaged skin on his face, tightening it.

'Yes, I am.'

'She called you Camden.'

'My call-sign for this operation. We all have them.'

He smiled, looking from one to the other.

'I admit, I'm surprised you've lasted this long but you've been more than helpful. Not only did you bring me into your base, you gave me the chance to see your old sergeant's address right when I helped you with your phone. Remember?'

Nikki didn't reply.

'And it's amazing what a simple text message can do.'

'You told them where Marquez and Chalk were going?' Nikki said. 'But they tried to kill you too.'

'No,' he said, looking at Archer. 'You were on the money about that. They were trying to wound your friend here to take him alive on the boss' orders. Our employer was very specific about that. I didn't have

284

time to get to my weapon inside the house and I've seen men on the same side get killed before in the process of eliminating a target, so I decided to allow myself to be rescued and taken with you. I did try and slow you down though.'

He smiled, lifting his foot and rolling his ankle easily, with no pain.

'And this all worked out for the best, right? Adapt and improvise. You brought me right into the centre of your operation. Now Dash knows everything: how many of you are left, who's carrying what weapons and what you know. Which isn't a lot I might add.'

He focused on Archer, seeing his hand inching towards the Glock in the holster on his thigh.

'Take it out, finger and thumb, and toss it.'

Archer didn't move. Bernhardt suddenly fired, Nikki jolting and screaming at the sound, the bullet putting a hole in the blackened wall two inches from Archer's head.

'Last chance.'

Without a choice, Archer complied, slowly taking the pistol out and tossing it to the floor a foot to his right.

'You said you left that world behind after you got burned,' Archer said. 'But that's bullshit, isn't it.'

'Oh, everything until then was true,' he said, 'But you're right, I didn't leave. I've been working with Dash ever since. You think after someone did something like that to us that we could just walk away?'

'You said you came back five months ago.'

'That was bullshit, same as that girlfriend I was texting in the car; I've been in constant contact with Dash and our employer ever since you brought me

285

in. Three weeks ago was the first time I've been back to this shithole of a country in years, and that was only because of you.'

'Why is this about me?'

'You were getting close downstairs. But you'll find out soon enough.'

Bernhardt licked his cracked lips, his tongue flicking out and catching some white stuff that had gathered on the edges of his mouth.

'How many of you are there?' Nikki asked, desperately trying to buy them some time.

'Enough.'

'But not that great though are you?' Archer said. 'Two unsuspecting police teams and still you only manage to kill three guys. And one of those was your own man.'

Bernhardt paused. His eyes narrowed.

'You're not making this easier on yourself.'

'Who is she?' Archer asked. 'Who hired you?'

'Jesus, you're a disappointment,' Bernhardt said. 'I heard so much about you. You're supposed to be this shit-hot hero cop, and you still haven't figured it out?'

'So why don't you tell us?' Nikki said.

He turned the Glock on her. 'No point. I'm going to kill you. And I'll be doing you a favour; some friends of mine are going to be here any minute, the ones who just killed your friend and the Latina bitch. They haven't had any female company for a while.'

Keeping the pistol on Nikki, he flicked his dark eyes to Archer and smiled.

'Well, not counting your girlfriend of course.'

Archer didn't reply. Bernhardt looked back at Nikki.

286

'Then once you're dead and we've worked the hero detective here over a bit, we're going to take him to see our employer.'

He focused on Archer.

'Then she's going to kill you, but not after she's had some fun. And while she does that, we're going to pay the hospitals in town a visit and finish off the rest of your friends. And as you said downstairs, you get to die last. After all of your friends are gone. The woman you just spoke to on the phone has it all organised. And believe me, she's an expert.'

Standing together, side by side, Archer didn't reply; neither did Nikki. They kept their focus on the former soldier.

Making sure they didn't look at Lipton, who'd just appeared from the stairwell behind Bernhardt.

Bernhardt shook his head and whistled through his teeth, turning his gun on Nikki.

'Time's up. I wouldn't want to be you right now, my friend,' he said to Archer.

'And I wouldn't want to be you,' Archer said, as Lipton raised his MP5.

The ARU guard aimed the sub-machine gun straight at the back of Bernhardt's head.

But then part of the damaged floor under his foot gave way.

Bernhardt heard it and whirled around, moving like lightning.

Lipton had lost his balance, his foot caught in a hole, but fired at the same time as Bernhardt. He took a round in the arm as he hit Bernhardt in the leg, both men recoiling from the impact of the gunshots. As Lipton fell back, dropping his weapon, Bernhardt rode the shot to his leg and aimed at the guard's head, but suddenly heard movement behind him and spun back.

Archer and Nikki had split either side, going left and right. Aiming for the analyst as he needed to take Archer alive, Bernhardt fired again, Nikki screaming in pain as she took the round in the leg.

Hitting the blackened, debris-ridden floor to his right as Nikki was shot, Archer scooped up the Glock and aimed from his side in one double-handed smooth motion, putting the sights on the gap between Bernhardt's dark eyes as the man turned to look at him.

He saw them widen for split-second as he looked at Archer, realising his mistake, the former Para's gun still aimed at Nikki.

Then Archer pulled the trigger.

FORTY FOUR

The round hit Bernhardt in the forehead, killing him instantly as the back of his head blew apart.

Almost on his feet before the ex-soldier hit the floor, Archer ran over to Nikki, who was slumped on her side and clutching her thigh in pain, blood pooling out from the gunshot wound. Putting his Glock down, Archer clamped his right hand over the entry point, feeling the underside of her thigh for an exit wound. There was nothing there and blood wasn't pulsing out which meant the bullet was still inside but her femoral artery hadn't been hit.

Holding her thigh, blood wetting his hands, he searched for something he could use to bandage or tourniquet the wound. One of the female analysts had left a cardigan, which was now lying among the debris on the floor. The garment was singed and dirty, but it was better than nothing; he ran over, grabbing it then returned and wrapped it above the wound tightly, using it as a tourniquet.

'Stay awake, Nik,' he said, looking her in the eye. 'Don't fall asleep.'

Behind him, Lipton had struggled back to his feet. Turning, Archer saw the guard move over, stopping on the way to kick Bernhardt's Glock away from his motionless hand, clutching his left arm with his right hand and blood staining his fingers.

'Jesus Christ; thanks, Lip,' he said. 'How did you know?'

'Heard a gunshot; thought I'd better come investigate.'

Archer looked at his arm. 'How bad is it?'

289

'I'm OK,' he said, checking the wound on his arm, his palm stained with blood. 'He just clipped me. Son of a bitch.'

'We need an ambulance and armed back-up right now!' Archer said quickly, looking at Bernhardt and remembering what he'd said. 'Some of his friends are coming for us.'

Lipton nodded then turned and moved quickly back the way he'd just come, clutching his arm as he headed for the stairs to make the call. As he left, Archer turned back to Nikki, who was saying something quietly.

'What?' he asked, listening closely.

'Call...her back,' she said quietly.

'Huh?'

She looked over at Bernhardt's body. 'Call her back. Use...his phone. We...can trace.'

Archer stared at her for a moment, then he realised what she was saying. Rising, he retrieved Bernhardt's Samsung from his pocket, then picked up Nikki's laptop and ripped out the connection from the land-line, carrying both computer and cable back towards Nikki.

'Will it fit?' he asked, kneeling beside her.

She nodded and he connected the cell to the laptop. As it synced with the software, she slowly reached over and starting typing on the keypad, Archer checking over his shoulder as she tapped away and listening hard for the sound of any cars.

The attempted trace they'd performed moments ago showed up on the screen, stuck on *00:23*.

'Wait; this is a different call,' he said.

'Doesn't matter,' she said, wincing in pain. 'Same number that called us. It'll...close out.'

He took Bernhardt's phone with a blood-smeared left hand, scrolled until he recognised the same number that had flashed up on the land-line display and pushed *Call*, holding the phone to his ear.

It rang several times, Archer looking over his shoulder as it did so, willing someone to answer.

Suddenly, he heard something in the distance.

The roar of car engines.

And they were approaching fast.

The ringing suddenly stopped, as someone answered; looking down, Archer saw the trace immediately continue.

00:22.

00:21.

'Is it done?' the woman asked.

Archer waited.

00:19.

00:18.

'Camden, is it done?'

'She's dead,' Archer said, doing his best to imitate the dead man's voice.

As he spoke, he could clearly hear the sound of cars getting closer.

They were almost here.

Grabbing his pistol, Archer willed the trace down.

00:16.

00:15.

'What about the golden boy?'

'He's still alive,' Archer said, looking at Bernhardt's corpse. 'But wait a moment.'

Suddenly, there was the sound of tyres screeching to a halt as someone pulled into the car park outside.

C'mon! he silently shouted at the computer screen, the trace not yet finished, the numbers ticking down agonisingly slowly.

'What's wrong?'

'I hear something.'

00:13.

00:12.

He heard car doors open and slam, and footsteps running across the car park.

'What the hell are you doing?'

'I think someone else just arrived.'

'It'll be the others. Bring Archer to me.'

'Right now?'

'No, next week. Of course right now.'

The running footsteps entered the building, continuing down the lower corridor, heading to the interrogation cell or the gun-cage.

They were here.

00:07.

00:06.

C'mon, Archer screamed in his head, willing the trace to go through as he looked over his shoulder.

C'mon!

'I need a car,' Archer said, improvising fast. 'I'm stuck at their station.'

He cursed himself, realising that in concentrating on the arrival below he'd spoken in his own voice.

There was a pause.

'You're not Camden.'

Pause.

'That's you, Archer, isn't it?'

Archer heard footsteps running up the stairs.

'I was going to kill your girlfriend in front of you, but I'm just going to kill her right now instead.'

Archer froze.

Vargas was wherever this woman was.

00:04.

00:03.

'And my men will bring you back. Even if Bernhardt couldn't. So know that your girlfriend is about to die, Archer. And there isn't a thing you can do to save her. How does that feel?'

00:01.

And the call went dead.

Staring at the phone, Archer heard the sound of running feet coming down the corridor and spun immediately with his Glock, ready to fire.

Chalky and Marquez suddenly ran into view. Both of them were bleeding from cuts to their head and arms and were carrying their MP5s, reloading the weapons quickly with fresh magazines. As they raced onto the level, both of them stopped dead when they saw Bernhardt's body laid out on the floor and Nikki leaning against the wall beside Archer, bleeding out from the wound to her thigh.

'What the hell happened?' Chalky asked as Marquez ran into the Briefing Room, checking the car park outside.

'He screwed us,' Archer said. 'He was one of them!'

Lipton suddenly reappeared, staggering slightly now as the pain kicked in and clutching his left arm. 'Back-up's on the way.'

Before any of them could reply, there was the screech of cars pulling into the car park.

'They're here!' Marquez shouted from the Briefing Room, raising her MP5 to her shoulder.

293

As Lipton slumped back near Nikki, Archer and Chalky immediately ran forward into the half-destroyed Briefing Room. As they joined Marquez and looked through the gaps where the outside wall used to be, they saw two cars had pulled up below, driving straight through the open barrier now Wilson was gone.

The five gunmen were already out of the cars and had seen the trio on the 1st floor, aiming four AR 15 assault rifles and a Benelli shotgun up at them.

'Down!' Archer shouted, as the men below opened fire.

Across the city in the 12th floor of the office building, the fifty seven year old woman stared at the phone in her hand. Then she quickly called Dash.

The moment he answered, the sound of close-quarter gunfire filled the receiver, the woman holding it back a half-inch from her ear.

'Holloway?' she said. 'Where are you?'

'Their HQ! His friend and the Latina girl made it back.'

'Enough mistakes!' she screamed. *'Kill them! Kill all of them!'*

Hanging up before he could respond, livid with rage, she rang another number, calling someone four floors above.

'Aldgate? Are you with the woman?' she asked as he answered.

'She's right here.'

'Cut her throat!'

FORTY FIVE

At the ARU HQ, the fire-fight between Archer, Chalky and Marquez and the five gunmen in the car park was brutally intense. The three police officers had the higher ground but they were outnumbered and were taking a ferocious onslaught. Neither side was giving an inch, and after a day of surprises and hit and run attacks, the two opposing teams were now confronting each other head on.

This was it.

And someone was going to lose.

After firing off a few more rounds from his Glock at their attackers, Archer turned and ran back into the Operations area as Marquez and Chalky maintained their rate of fire with their MP5s. Well back in the room, protected from the gunfire, Nikki was still propped against the wall where Archer had left her, bleeding from the gunshot wound to her thigh but gritting her teeth as she managed to tap the keys on her laptop, Lipton slumped down against the wall ten feet away and holding his arm.

'Did the trace work?' Archer asked as he knelt beside Nikki, far enough away from the Briefing Room that she could just hear him over the noise of the gunfire.

She nodded, looking at her screen.

He twisted it round towards him and saw a red circle drawn in tightly on the map.

'*451... South Bank,*' she said quietly.

As the gunfight behind them raged on, he went onto street view and quickly searched for the address, the anonymous woman's statement that she was going to kill Vargas giving his actions a new urgency.

'Got it!'

'What…is it? Nikki asked weakly.

'An office building.'

'Then that's where she'll be.'

Archer stared at the image of the tall building where the call had come from.

Exactly the kind of place that had been giving him such terrifying nightmares ever since that night in Harlem.

The woman had said she was going to kill Vargas immediately.

That meant they both had to be inside.

Inside a mid-level office overlooking the Thames on the 16th floor of 451 South Bank, the large Australian mercenary watching Alice Vargas on the floor beside him put the phone back in his pocket and leaned back in his chair, savouring the moment. He'd felt his arousal build all day thinking about what he was going to do to the detective before he killed her and he'd just been given the green light from the boss.

His call-sign was Aldgate, but his real name was Corporal Craig Wheeler, a former Australian army soldier; he'd been dishonourably discharged a few years ago but like an iceberg, the officers who'd been involved in his court martial only knew about what they'd seen on the surface. Wheeler thrived on theft, intimidation and rape, but had messed up four years ago; he and two other men, Finchley and Portland, had gang raped a female private. Despite the threats they'd made if she told anyone what happened, they'd chosen the wrong victim and the bitch had gone to the Military Police, getting him and the other two arrested. After serving four years in military prison and then kicked out of the army, the three men had become soldiers of fortune, working as a trio and selling their skills to whoever paid the highest price.

Last year he, O'Connor and Weaver had been fighting for the Taliban against the US and UK forces, but they'd been recruited by Dash to join his new team and had since become wealthy men. Dash's squad had been hired by a variety of international organisations, their speciality carrying out tasks which other contracting firms wouldn't touch for various reasons, mostly ethical, and they were good at what they did. Wheeler was a perfect member; he didn't possess so much as an ounce of human compassion; he couldn't care less about anyone other than himself and never had.

Leaning back in his chair, he smiled. This particular operation was the kind of thing that he dreamed about. It had been put on the table six weeks ago; the woman currently down on the 12th floor offering Dash and his men fifty grand a head in US dollars for the gig which they'd accepted without hesitation. Her orders had been simple and specific.

She wanted some cop called Sam Archer's NYPD team lured here and then destroyed, along with every member of the Armed Response Unit, some counter-terrorist police team formed in the last few years. However, there was a stipulation.

This asshole Archer was to be saved till last.

As Dash had relayed the operational brief, Wheeler hadn't asked why; he couldn't care less. He'd be getting paid well for the gig and that was all that mattered. He'd had a great day, doing nothing but sitting around here in the office on the 16th floor with his feet up as he watched the detective on Dash's orders, all whilst the others had been running around town trying to take out the counter-terrorist police force and getting shot at in return.

Tilting back in his chair, he looked down at the dark-haired woman on the floor, 3rd Grade NYPD Detective Alice Vargas, who was staring at him with wide, fearful brown eyes.

She was lying lengthways, her feet closest to him, her hands bound behind her back, her feet wrapped with duct tape, a strip over her mouth and a stain of dried blood running down the side of her face. She was still dressed in the grey shorts and top they'd kidnapped her in, revealing lots of tanned skin that Wheeler had been lusting after all day.

He'd been under strict orders not to touch her until told to do so; usually, that wouldn't have stopped him but he hadn't dared disobey this particular boss.

However, his patience had finally paid off.

On the ARU HQ's 1st floor, Marquez and Chalky were unleashing a ferocious barrage on the men below but hadn't managed to put any of them down. Given their military training, their attackers were slick and knew what they were doing, staying low and not offering any real opportunity to get hit.

Marquez was down to the last mag for her MP5 and Chalky was already out, emptying his Glock down at the enemy. The men had parked on either side of the car park, the guy with the shotgun positioned behind the Audi on the right and the four others with assault rifles behind the car on the left. Their fire was violent and constant, bullets and shotgun shells pounding into the already-damaged Briefing Room, an onslaught which wasn't showing any signs of easing despite the men surely knowing police back-up could arrive at any moment.

Clearly, they'd had enough of the subtle approach.

Running forward to join Chalky and Marquez again, Archer motioned at them to pull back. As they moved, all three ducked as another blast hit the ceiling just above their heads and showered them with plaster.

'Vargas is in an office building across the city!' Archer shouted over the mercenaries' gunfire, the three of them crouching on the floor. *'I need to get over there right now!'*

'You can't get out that way!' Marquez replied, jerking her head towards the car park whilst quickly reloading her MP5. *'They'll cut you to pieces!'*

'What about the chopper?' Chalky said, bleeding from a cut to the side of his head.

'I thought of that, but Mason and Fox are the only ones who can fly it, Chalk!' Archer replied, as Marquez rose and moved forward, opening fire on the two cars below and keeping their attackers at bay. *'One's dead, the other's out cold in hospital!'*

'I qualified four months ago, Arch!'

Archer paused. *'You did?'*

Chalky nodded, looking over his shoulder. *'But what about Nikki?'*

'She and Lip can come with us.'

'She's too badly hurt to move!'

Archer looked back at the gunshot lead analyst in Operations and swore as Marquez fired on the mercenaries again, emptying an entire clip, the shell casings spraying out of the weapon. Chalky was right; Nikki wasn't going anywhere.

'I'll stay,' Marquez said, dropping back down and reloading with her final clip.

'Alone?' Chalky said. *'No way!'*

'You said back-up's on its way,' she said, ducking as the ceiling took more gunfire. *'I can hold them off until it gets here!'*

The two men looked at her.

'Go!' Marquez shouted, rising and firing a three round burst into the car park again. *'Just get me some more ammo!'*

Archer and Chalky looked at her for a moment, then turned and ran out of the room and towards the stairs, Archer going down as Chalky headed in the opposite direction, heading straight for the roof.

As Archer hit the bottom of the stairs and sprinted down the lower corridor towards the gun-cage, the sounds of gunfire echoing down the hallway, he heard the anonymous woman's words echo in his mind.

Know that your girlfriend is about to die, Archer. And there isn't a thing you can do to save her.

FORTY SIX

Lying on the office floor inside the tall building across the city, Alice Vargas looked up at the large man guarding her and knew her time was up.

She'd been here in the room all day, bound with the same duct tape from when she'd been abducted in the villa bedroom. After she'd closed her eyes and just been drifting back to sleep, a meaty hand had suddenly clamped over her mouth. She'd fought like crazy, thrashing and managing to break one guy's nose with her elbow, but two others had quickly restrained and gagged her, one of them hitting her over the head to daze her and stop her struggling.

After they'd subdued her and dragged her off the bed, the last thing she'd seen before they injected her with something was the man with the broken nose opening two vials of blood, pouring the contents onto the bed.

Then everything had gone black.

She'd woken up here hours ago, in some kind of office building. She'd been lying on the floor for hours, the same man watching her; she was still dressed in the grey shorts and crop top she'd slept in, and had felt his lecherous, sleazy eyes on her all day. They hadn't given her any food or water, and her whole body ached with fatigue.

The man guarding her had taken a phone call moments ago; she couldn't hear what the other person had said but she saw from the satisfied look on his face and his body language that this was it. Just like that ordeal four months ago in Harlem, she was trapped in another building, but this time, she was alone, Archer not here to help her.

And if she was going to survive, she had to do something right now.

She'd already come up with a plan, which she'd been working on for hours. As a result, she'd changed the angle at which she was lying about an hour ago, moving slowly and subtly enough that the guy in the chair hadn't noticed.

Right now, the man grinned as he leant back in his seat, reaching into his pocket and pulling out a closed flip-knife.

'Bad news, bitch,' he said. 'I've been told to cut your throat.'

She saw his gaze move to her legs and slide upwards again, his eyes lusting over her body.

'But there's no rush; I'm thinking we should do some other activities first.'

Snapping her legs up to her chest, Vargas suddenly kicked out as hard as she could into the chair leg closest to her.

The force smashed the chair out from under the man, taking him completely by surprise, and he hit the floor hard. The heavy fall knocked the wind out of him; in a flash, Vargas immediately hooked her bound feet around his neck and locked her bare calves tight, squeezing as hard as she could, gritting her teeth under the strip of duct tape as she strangled him.

Ironically, the tape around her ankles helped, acting as a brace and she used it to exert as much pressure as she could, adrenaline, fear and anger giving her extra strength. Starting to suffocate, the man fought back, twisting hard and grabbing at her legs, trying to prise them apart, but the tape they'd used to bind her kept them tight.

She twisted over so she was lying face down and tightened her legs even more, using all her pent-up anger and fear as she choked him to death, her face taut with effort as she strained and used every ounce of muscle strength in her lower body. The man continued to tear at her legs but she felt no pain, his resistance growing weaker as his oxygen ran out.

Vargas maintained the pressure despite her muscles screaming out in protest. This was her one and only chance.

If he got out of this, she was dead.

He went limp as he passed out but she kept squeezing until her legs felt as if they were on fire, not daring to ease off the pressure. When she was as sure as she could be that he was dead and not feigning it, she turned back on her side and slowly released the pressure, unhooking her legs from around his head, waiting for the lactic acid to go but not taking her eyes off him, ready to whip her legs back into place if he so much as twitched.

Sucking in oxygen through her nose, she pulled her knees in tight, trying to bring her bound hands back under her feet so they were in front of her body again. However, she couldn't manage it with her ankles strapped together. Shuffling over to the dead man's body, she reached behind her until her fingers made contact with the man's closed flip-knife, which had fallen out of his hand onto the floor by his leg. Lying on her side and flicking open the blade, she reached back then slowly and carefully began to saw through the tape around her ankles, taking long breaths through her nose and trying to regulate her breathing.

She sawed for almost twenty seconds, feeling blood wet her hands as the knife cut into her skin, but then the tape suddenly gave way.

Ripping her feet apart, she dropped the knife and tried to bring her hands under her feet again.

This time it worked and she could pull her legs through one at a time.

With her bound hands now in front of her, she ripped off the strip of tape across her mouth, taking deep breaths for the first time in twenty four hours. Turning and picking up the knife again, she held the hilt tightly between her teeth, then brought up her hands and carefully used the blade to start sawing through the tape around her wrists.

Working the blade through the duct tape, gripping the blade hard between her teeth, she looked over at the closed door to the dark office, desperately trying to cut through the binds before anyone else came in. Kicking the man off the chair had made a loud noise.

And she didn't know how many more of his friends were in the building.

FORTY SEVEN

Working her hands as fast as she could, blood running over the tape and down her fingers, she finally made it through the binds. Pulling her wrists apart, she tore the duct tape away and climbed to her feet, taking a moment to let the circulation flow through her arms and legs again, flexing her wrists and ankles, getting the blood pumping into every capillary of every muscle and clearing the lactic acid.

Turning, she saw the dead man wasn't carrying a pistol, but he had his cell phone tucked in the pocket of his trousers. Moving forward quietly, her feet silent on the bare floor, she knelt down warily and checked his pulse just to make sure, but there was nothing. She pulled out the phone. It was a Nokia, T-Mobile the provider, no password enabled to prevent her from making a call. Looking down, she saw she there were three bars of service.

Keeping her eyes on the door to her left, she backed over to the window and glanced outside, trying to figure out where the hell she was. Although it was dark, she immediately saw Big Ben and the Houses of Parliament illuminated on the other side of the River.

Holy shit.

I'm in London.

Turning away from the window, she quickly dialled Archer's number, watching the door and keeping the knife in her other hand as she closed her eyes and took a deep breath.

Across the city in the ARU gun-cage, the sounds of the gunfight between Marquez and the five men in the car park continued to echo down the corridor as Archer grabbed all the gear he would need to assault the office building.

He slotted two fresh flash-bang grenades into his tac vest then pulled the MP5 he'd used earlier in the day from the rack. Beside the guns was the ammunition, thirty two rounds magazines. Laying two MP5 clips back to back, he taped them high and low then slotted the double-clip into the weapon, tucking two more into the pouches on his vest and needing as much ammo as he could carry. He figured this office building where the call had originated would be the mercenaries' safe-house, and he didn't know how many of them would be waiting for him inside.

As he reloaded his Glock, tucking it into the holster on his thigh, his phone suddenly rang. Pulling it from his vest, he looked at the screen.

It wasn't a number he recognised.

'Hello?' he said, grabbing his MP5 and heading for the door.

'Arch, it's me!' Vargas said.

Archer froze in his tracks. 'Where are you?!'

'I'm in London in some office building. There was a man guarding me. I just killed him, but I'm trapped. I don't know how many more of them are here but I need help. Are you in New York?'

'No, I'm in London! We all came to find you. I think I know where you are; what floor are you on?'

'I don't know. I'd guess somewhere in the teens. Quite high up, looking at Big Ben.'

South Bank, Archer thought.

306

She's definitely inside.

Pause.

'Hang on, I hear someone.'

He waited, not moving a muscle.

'Alice? Vargas?'

She didn't reply.

And the call went dead.

Turning, Archer put the phone back into its slot on his vest, knowing she was still alive giving him even greater urgency as he took four more magazines from the rack. Then he ducked out of the room and sprinted down the corridor towards the stairs. Vargas was still alive, but she was trapped and would be totally outnumbered.

Taking the flight two at a time, he ran back down the blackened charred corridor into the Operations area. Marquez was still in the Briefing Room, still managing to pin the gunmen down, firing her MP5 one round at a time to save ammunition.

Running into the room, he joined her.

'Here!' he shouted, laying the four magazines he'd brought from downstairs in front of her.

She grabbed one immediately and reloaded fast, hitting the cocking handle forward as more return fire ripped into the wrecked room. Ducking as bullets tore into the ceiling, the two looked at each other for a brief moment, knowing it could well be the last time they saw each other.

Then Marquez nodded.

'Go get her,' she said quietly, Archer hearing her through a break in the gunfire.

Squeezing her shoulder, he turned and was about to run down the corridor when he saw Nikki was beckoning him over weakly with her good hand.

307

Pausing, Archer moved over towards her as Marquez resumed her cover fire on the men below.

'Just hang on, Nik,' Archer told her, kneeling down. 'Back-up's going to be here any minute!'

'I...know who she is,' she whispered.

Archer paused. 'What?'

'I know who the woman is. The woman...who's doing this.'

She paused.

'I ran her voice...recording through all our systems. And there...was a match. An Interpol...file...It's...recent.'

She paused again, gunfire filling the gap.

'She's a former mujh...mujahedeen fighter. She...has two sons...One of them...is called Dashnan.'

'Our Dashnan?'

She nodded. *'He must...have changed his surname...when he joined...the army.'*

Archer didn't reply, staring at her, waiting for more.

'The woman's husband...and Dash's father...died...a few years ago.'

She took a breath, gunfire continuing from behind.

'His name was Khalid Farha.'

Archer suddenly froze, staring at her.

His blood turned to ice.

'Her full name's Talia Farha,' Nikki finished. *'She's Dominick Farha's mother.'*

FORTY EIGHT

Standing by the windows overlooking the River Thames on the 12th floor of the South Bank office building, Talia Farha looked out at the city beyond, waiting for the return of the mercenaries under her command who would be bringing Sam Archer to her.

The man who'd killed her son.

Talia had been a fighter her entire adult life. Although she was Saudi by birth, she'd left the country on her twentieth birthday in 1978 and had never been back. An Afghan mujahedeen leader had visited her father in their house in Riyadh to discuss business, bringing two of his men with him as security. One of them was a man called Khalid Farha; seeing him in the house, Talia had immediately fallen for the soldier. He'd been good-looking but it wasn't that that had attracted her; he'd seemed tough, exotic and dangerous, his attraction not surprising for a young woman living a very restricted life in Riyadh.

Fortunately for her she was the daughter of a wealthy man and therefore quite a prize. He also came from a fairly prominent family in Afghanistan and with Talia's father's blessing, it hadn't been long before they had married. The pair had soon left for Afghanistan and a short time later, Talia fell pregnant with their first child.

Her son Dominick had been born nine months later and as soon as she'd set eyes on him, he'd become the centre of her world. The family had lived in Kabul for the next five years, but then Khalid had gone out into the desert to fight the occupying forces of the Soviet Union. Unwilling to be separated from her husband, Talia had gone with him, taking Dominick with her.

The conflict back then had been concentrated in the deserts and the inhospitable wilderness of Afghanistan, mujahedeen turf. The Soviet forces were on foreign soil and were in way over their heads. After just killing them became monotonous, the mujahedeen had started kidnapping the soldiers for sport, handing them over to their wives like Talia who had then tortured the prisoners, roasting them over fires, maiming them, killing them slowly, a piece at a time. She'd always possessed a cruel and sadistic streak and out there she discovered she could give it full rein.

Talia became very proficient at what she did, the captured soldiers' screams echoing across the plains and terrifying their comrades who heard them which was the intention. But then she'd fallen pregnant again and in 1984 had given birth to her second son Dashnan. Unlike Dominick, he'd been unplanned and to a certain degree unwanted, and his presence in the camp had been an inconvenience, a screaming baby's cries not exactly conducive to covert operations. Consequently, Dash had kept his mother out of the action for almost two years while she was forced to stay in the camp to look after him, the enforced inactivity only adding to her resentment. Dominick had never given her such trouble and had been a much quieter and easier baby.

Although, over time, she grew to care about Dash, in her eyes Dominick was always the favoured child. After those initial two years, Talia began to hand the toddler over to another woman to look after at night, going back out with the men. She enjoyed being on the frontline again where the action was, resuming her old activities with enthusiasm. Occasionally their victims were brought back to camp, and although Dominick, Dash and the other children had been led away before the torture started, they still heard every scream and smelt the stench of burning flesh.

Talia was adamant that the boys both get used to such things; she wanted her sons to grow up to be strong men she could be proud of, not cowards. In the early years, Dominick had covered his ears when the Soviet soldiers started to scream, but by the time he reached his ninth birthday, his hands no longer came up to block out the sound. Being four years younger Dash never managed it, and to Talia, his tears at the screams only highlighted his deficiencies in comparison to his brother.

In 1989 when Dominick was ten and Dash was five, the Soviet Union withdrew its forces and Khalid had wanted to take his family to live in civilisation again, his sons getting an education. Money had never been an issue for them as her family had been extremely wealthy and she'd not only come with an enormous dowry but had also inherited another significant sum with her brother when her parents were killed in 1991.

But then a few years later, 9/11 had happened.

And everything changed.

By 2001, Talia and her husband had been drifting apart after twenty years of marriage, and when she'd demanded to join him to aid the Taliban against the US forces he'd refused, their ensuing argument resulting in him giving her a severe beating. That night, she'd lain there running through various ways of killing him without attracting suspicion but then fate had intervened. Khalid had gone to visit her younger brother in Riyadh, and had never returned.

Like herself, her brother wasn't someone to cross, being the head of a drug cartel.

The timing was more than coincidental.

And it was a problem solved.

With Khalid gone, Talia had been free to do as she pleased and had chosen to go back out into the desert, joining the people she used to fight alongside and putting her old skills to good use. Her sons were old enough to fend for themselves by that point but even so, she saw them as often as she could, especially Dominick. Twenty two years old at the time, he'd left for Riyadh soon after his father's disappearance and began working for the cartel. Dash had still been in school and she'd left him to his own devices under the care of his paternal grandmother. Talia had fought with the Taliban for over a decade, but in April of last year after a long stint trapped out in the caves, her world had fallen apart.

She discovered that Dominick had been killed sixteen months earlier.

Whilst out in the wild terrain of Afghanistan, many of the Taliban fighters didn't have easy access to news or information on current events. However, word of an incident reached Talia involving Dash, who'd reportedly been caught in a US bomb strike but had somehow survived and been transported to a hospital in Kabul.

The pair hadn't spoken in a long time. She knew that he'd become a soldier, joining the Afghan National Army for a spell then fighting as a mercenary, but to her disgust, had allowed himself to be hired by the enemy. He'd changed his surname to

Sahar, apparently ashamed of his family identity because his parents had fought for the Taliban, so Talia had washed her hands of him.

She hadn't reacted initially when he'd got a message to her last April saying he wanted to see her, but after a few days had changed her mind and made the journey to the capital, more out of a sense of duty than anything else. Seeing him in the hospital bed covered in bandages hadn't stirred much of a response; they were fighting for two different sides and her feelings towards him had always been lukewarm at the best of times. However, that had changed when he'd told her his loyalties had shifted; maybe she could make something out of him after all.

Deciding to take over his remaining care, she'd organised his discharge from the hospital that night then set him up in their old home.

Standing there in the London office over a year later, Talia sighed.

She would never forget the moment when he said how sad it was about Dominick.

She'd thought he was delirious at first. *What are you talking about,* she'd asked him. Then he realised she didn't know, and informed her.

Dominick had been killed the year before, during some terrorist attacks on London over New Year's Eve and New Year's Day.

The news had hit her like a savage punch to the gut.

In the following months, Dash had recovered well, hideously scarred but still alive, and after regaining his strength he'd stayed true to his word about changing loyalties. Dash had set up his own

313

contracting team with Michael Bernhardt, recruiting men whom no one else would touch, and they started working on specialised contracts, everything from assassinations to trafficking drugs. Talia had gone back out into the desert to re-join the Taliban but the grief she felt at what had happened to Dominick haunted her.

She'd always been a violent and sadistic woman but the loss of her favourite son had totally unhinged her. She couldn't move on; no matter how much pleasure she took in taking it out on the enemy, she was always left with a feeling of dissatisfaction.

Whoever they might be, they weren't the person who'd killed Dominick.

As the feelings festered inside her, she finally had enough and left the desert in March of this year, eleven months since she first found out Dominick was dead. After travelling to Kabul and spending a day sat in front of a computer, she'd accessed enough archived newspaper reports to find out exactly what had happened to her boy.

It turned out Dominick had been the mastermind behind those attacks in London, but the situation had ended with him being shot in the head. With Talia's wealth and contacts, it was relatively easy to find someone with the necessary skills to hack into the London Met official reports and she'd quickly learned the identity of the man who'd pulled the trigger.

Sam Archer.

A policeman in the Armed Response Unit.

As she'd stared at the name on the screen at the beginning of this year, her battles for the Taliban

314

against the US and UK forces suddenly faded into total insignificance.

This man became her complete focus. He'd killed Dominick.

For that, he was going to die.

The hacker had accessed the London Met police records but Sam Archer's file had no longer been on the ARU database. It looked as if he'd either been transferred or possibly even resigned, which was unlikely considering his age, but the hacker had then simply searched the man's name on an internet search engine.

A hit had come up in *The New York Times* immediately, a recent news report from just ten days before.

Hero cop and US Marshal survive Harlem building siege.

The article then went on to name the officer involved.

3rd Grade NYPD Counter-Terrorism Bureau Detective Sam Archer.

The moment she read it, Talia's heart had skipped a beat.

That was why she couldn't locate him.

The son of a bitch was in New York.

FORTY NINE

Three months ago, she'd been about to kill him.

She'd flown to New York without any difficulty, having travelled from London on a fake passport with neither the US or UK border controls having a clue who she was or her connection with the Taliban. She'd then tracked Archer down and had been watching him for almost two weeks before she decided to make a move.

On a bright afternoon, she'd tailed the detective from his apartment and followed him into the city on the subway, watching him head into Bryant Park on East 42nd Street. He'd taken a seat in the courtyard there beside a dark-haired woman she hadn't seen before, both watching some kid playing on the grass nearby. After a brief conversation, Archer had stood up and moved over to a stall to buy a few cans of soft drink and Talia had stepped up immediately behind him, gripping the hilt of the knife jammed in her pocket.

She'd longed for this moment, the chance to bury all three inches of the blade into his neck and watch him die. She'd already spotted several cops in the immediate area and knew there was every chance they would shoot her once she killed Archer, but she didn't care.

Her precious son was dead and this man had killed him.

But standing there trembling with rage, the knife in her hand and his neck exposed, she couldn't do it.

Not because she'd changed her mind.

Not because of fear.

But because it was too quick.

Letting go of the hilt, she'd let the knife drop down into the pocket of her light coat. He'd turned away from the stall, carrying three cans of Sprite, and had smiled at her as she'd stepped back out of his way.

Without hesitation, Talia had instantly walked away, leaving Archer and his female companion alone in the courtyard of the Park.

Her cruelly inventive mind immediately set to work.

It was time to plan something far bigger.

Sam Archer had suffered before; Talia had read that much in the files she'd been obsessively accumulating on him. His father had been murdered a couple of years ago and his mother had died of cancer, both of which she'd been pleased to read about, deriving some comfort from picturing their son's pain at both their deaths.

Apparently he had a sister too, a lawyer who lived in Washington DC, but Talia couldn't locate the bitch as hard as she tried; she'd called her hacker back in Kabul and put him onto it, but it seemed the woman had got married and changed her name, her exact whereabouts unknown.

Not wasting any more time on her, Talia focused on her brother and his friends. Sam Archer had more lives than a cat; judging by the reports Talia accessed, he'd found himself in some extremely dangerous situations but had come through all of them. Suicide bombers, bank robbers, Neo-Nazi terrorists, Special Forces soldiers from Kosovo; they'd all failed to take him down. It sickened her that he was obviously highly regarded whilst her son had briefly dominated the headlines, but only as an evil monster whom the world was well rid of.

Sam Archer had taken so much from her that a quick death was far too merciful.

He deserved to suffer, to watch everyone he cared about die before he joined them.

Then Talia had an idea.

She'd hire Dash's team to do it.

By the time the men had agreed to the terms of the contract and had all arrived in the city three weeks ago, Talia had already paid for a six month lease on the 12th and 17th floors inside this office building, using a fake identity, bank accounts and a series of fake references, bank-rolling it all with some of her substantial fortune. She'd been informed that workmen hadn't finished renovating much of the place but she said that wasn't an issue; in fact it was just what she'd been looking for, the floors between the two she'd hired totally out of action due to the renovations.

An anonymous space big enough from where she and Dash's team could work.

The building was empty today given that it was a weekend; despite that, there would usually still have been some activity from other businesses, but there was no one here due to the fact that many of the floors were closed. However, over the past few weeks, Dash and his team had set up shop here and accumulated weapons from an old contact of Bernhardt's.

Dash's man Piccadilly had then come up with the plan of attack. It was a good one, luring Archer's NYPD team here to London then ambushing them

318

and the ARU at the same time. Nevertheless, getting the New York police group over here in the first place was the main challenge.

How could they do it without attracting suspicion?

Kidnap was the answer. Talia and Dash's team all knew the way police teams worked; the abduction of a fellow cop was almost as serious as one getting shot, especially in the States, whose military prided themselves on the *no one gets left behind* bullshit that continued to get so many of them killed. They guessed the same would apply to the police force, which was something to exploit.

And Archer's girlfriend was the perfect target.

As Dash's team had gathered in London and waited on standby on Talia's orders, she'd stayed in New York and waited patiently, observing Archer and his movements, looking for a chance to take the woman Vargas.

An opportunity had presented itself eight days ago.

In a car down the street, Talia had been watching Archer's apartment when his girlfriend had suddenly stormed out, striding up to 30th with a bag and hailing the next available taxi. Talia had followed her to JFK, and after leaving the car in the short stay area she quickly relocated the woman inside the Terminal and watched her check in for a flight.

She'd made it to within earshot of the desk and heard the airline employee tell the woman that her flight left at 12:05. Looking up at the board as the woman passed her, she checked the departures.

12:05 to Malaga was the only flight that matched that particular time.

She was going to Spain.

Calling Dash, he ensured that Wood and Covent were already in place before the girl landed and they'd tailed her from the airport south to some coastal town called Nerja, watching her step out of a taxi at a villa by the beach.

She was isolated, unprepared and unarmed.

Ready to be taken.

Ordering Wood and Covent to watch the female detective's movements and report back to him, Dash and his team soon identified two men they could use as donors and bait, two Eastern European scumbags who had records for trafficking which Dash knew would get the detectives' colleagues running over here hotfoot from the States.

Once two other small safe-houses were arranged, a place in Hendon and a run-down apartment in Brixton, they were ready to go.

Two nights ago, they'd abducted the two Slovakians and transported them to Hendon and Brixton, forcibly taking samples of their blood before injecting them with sedatives; Dash had then gone to Spain in Talia's hired private jet to join up with the two other men, the trio kidnapping Archer's girlfriend to bait the trap. The bitch had fought back and busted Dash's nose, which they hadn't allowed for, but they'd left the traffickers' blood on the sheets as planned to spoon feed the NYPD before flying back to the UK.

The blood samples had worked, luring the NYPD search team to London, but getting them here had been the easy bit.

Killing them had proved to be a whole lot more difficult.

The news reports and Dash's calls had kept Talia up-to-date all day as each successive officer or detective went down, but to her knowledge only two of them had died. Maybe some of Sam Archer's luck had rubbed off, like fairy dust or some other shit.

However, a quick death meant no pain, so Talia was able to take some pleasure from the fact that they were all suffering at the loss of their two colleagues and that so many were lying injured in hospital.

She knew all about the two teams; Lisa Marquez, Josh Blake, Danny White, Ryan Fox and Mike Porter. Tim Cobb and Matt Shepherd. The analyst Nicola Carter. Some of them had been involved in that operation that had taken on Dominick and his cell of suicide bombers.

But as well as that, they were all Sam Archer's colleagues and close friends.

And just for that alone, they were all going to die.

Talia hawked and spat on the office floor as she thought of someone else that Archer cared about, the bitch upstairs, Alice Vargas. Talia had been observing Archer for a while and had seen the female detective with him constantly; the pair had somehow survived that situation she'd read about inside the Harlem building and were clearly more than just colleagues.

And now, just as he was happy, she was going to take that from him.

She smiled, picturing Aldgate upstairs with the woman; she'd be dead by now, bled out like a stuck pig, her boyfriend soon to follow.

She'd make sure Archer saw her body before he died.

321

The day Dominick had been killed he'd been the ninth member of his cell to die, and the post-mortem said he'd been shot through the right eye, Sam Archer the man who pulled the trigger. Her mood darkening, Talia looked down from the window at the city below, waiting for Dash and his men to return with her son's killer.

An eye for an eye, you son of a bitch, she thought.

FIFTY

At the ARU HQ, Chalky had got the black
Eurocopter going, the rotors on the vessel gathering
speed fast. The angle of the building meant the bulk
of the helicopter was hidden from the gunfire from
below, but the spinning rotors pinged as they took a
round every now and then, Marquez still unloading
on the five mercenaries below and giving Chalky and
Archer a chance to lift off.

Bursting through the door to the roof, Archer
stayed low and ran over to the vessel, his MP5 in his
hands and spare magazines slotted into his vest.
Pulling open the cabin door behind Chalky, he
jumped inside then dragged it shut.

'Let's go, Chalk!'

Down below, Dash saw the rotors of the ARU
chopper now whirring in a blur.

The return fire from the police building was now
only coming from one person, the Latina NYPD
detective. He knew how cops like this operated;
they'd never leave someone behind in a situation like
this, which meant Archer and his friend would only
depart for somewhere or someone absolutely crucial.
There was no sign of Bernhardt either, which meant
he was either restrained inside or dead.

The office building; it had to be.

They must have found his mother's location
somehow.

As the others fired up at the woman on the 1st floor
who was pinning them down, Dash looked across at
Notting, who was firing his Benelli with a litter of

empty red shells around him; he'd arrived in the same Audi that he'd started out with earlier in the day and Dash remembered he had a spare M90 in the trunk, each car equipped with several, the team taking no chances.

Notting squeezed off two shells, then looked to his right, hearing Dash shouting to catch his attention.

'What?' he called back.

'M90; take it out!' Dash ordered, pointing at the police chopper.

It was just starting to lift off the roof.

As the vessel climbed into the air, there was a sudden smash in the cabin and Chalky jolted, falling against the door on his left.

Seeing his friend get hit, Archer leaned over and helped him with the stick, fighting to keep the aircraft level.

'Chalk!'

Gritting his teeth, Chalky heaved himself upright, gripping the gear stick hard and continuing to control the chopper as it climbed into the air. Looking down, Archer suddenly saw one of the gunmen from behind the silver Audi aiming something directly up at them from his shoulder.

It was a rocket launcher.

Down in what was left of the Briefing Room, Marquez had seen it too.

Letting loose with a volley of fire to buy her a brief second, she sighted her MP5 on the mercenary as he aimed the M90 at the vessel.

She couldn't see his head.

But she could see his arm.

As Dash watched from behind his car, Notting was suddenly thumped back, shot in the shoulder.

At the same moment, the heat-seeking rocket whooshed out of the launcher, ploughing across the car park and exploding as it hit a car parked on the far side. Taking cover from the explosion but feeling the intense wave of heat, Dash swore, looking up at the ARU helicopter as it disappeared into the night unscathed, no doubt heading for the office building. He emptied his assault rifle at the vessel, but it was already out of range as it flew off across the city and out of sight.

He turned to the three men beside him.

'You stay here with him!' he said to Grange, pointing at Notting then up at the building. *'Kill that bitch before back-up gets here then get back to base!'*

As Grange nodded, Dash turned to Piccadilly and Portland.

'You two, with me!'

Looking around the car park, he saw one of the police 4x4 BMWs sitting in a bay to his left.

'Cover fire!' he shouted.

As the other three men opened fire, he ran towards the vehicle and tried the handle, but the car was locked. He went to break the glass, but a burst of gunfire from the Latina cop suddenly smashed out the window by his head, taking him by surprise and causing him to duck.

Reaching through the blown out window, he sprung the locks and opened the car, then jumped inside and after a few seconds, hot-wired it. As the engine fired, he reversed the car around, the rear taking some fire but the angle momentarily protecting him in the front seat.

He pulled to a halt as Piccadilly and Portland both ran across the car park, jumping into the car. Not wasting a second, Dash floored it and they took off, speeding down the street and back towards their base in the office building by the Thames.

Now alone in the Briefing Room, Marquez fired down into the parking lot, watching three of the mercenaries take off in a stolen ARU BMW, speeding out of the car park and leaving two men behind, one being the man she'd just shot in the shoulder.

However, the son of a bitch reappeared with a pistol aimed in her direction over the side of the car, and at the same time, the uninjured man fired up at her.

She went to return fire, but the sub-machine gun suddenly clicked dry. Pulling the trigger three more times, as if the act might cough up another bullet, she quickly stepped back and reached to the ARU vest she was wearing, but her hand met nothing but empty space. She looked down at the floor, grabbing the magazines that were lying there, but they were all used. Despite the extra clips Archer had brought her, she'd already gone through all the bullets keeping the attackers at bay.

Ducking as enemy rounds ripped into the ceiling above her head, she dropped the MP5 and pulled her Glock, firing back. Sensing the balance was shifting slightly in their favour, one of two men edged out from behind the car to try and get a clearer shot but Marquez fired again, a double-tap that ricocheted off

326

the metal beside his head, just missing him but forcing him back behind the car.

She fired again to reinforce the point but then fell back as the slide on the Glock stayed back.

She was out of ammo.

'Shit!' she said, looking around in desperation. She could hear sirens way off in the distance but they were still too far away.

She, Nikki and Lipton would be dead before back-up got here.

The two men below reared up again and fired a barrage at the upper level, realising the defensive fire had stopped and Marquez threw herself back onto the burnt, damaged floor, looking towards the stairs down the corridor to her right.

She needed to get to the armoury for more ammo.

Swearing again, she turned and ran across the room, stopping by Bernhardt's body to pull the magazine from the Glock he'd been holding and slot it into her own pistol. Then she moved over to Lipton; helping him to his feet, she half-carried him over to the Briefing Room and unslung the man's MP5 from his shoulder, putting it into his hands.

'Whatever you do, stop them from getting inside!' she ordered.

Lipton nodded and started to fire down at the two mercenaries, but Marquez saw the two gunmen had taken advantage of the brief lull in the return fire and had almost made it to the entrance, ducking down behind another car much closer to the door. Now Marquez would never make it to the armoury; from their field of fire facing the stairs, they'd cut her in half.

Cursing, she turned and ran across the floor towards Nikki, who was slumped against her desk, her laptop beside her, lying in a pool of blood from her leg.

'Is there any more ammunition up here?' she asked.

Nikki shook her head. *'All…downstairs.'*

Knowing she had seconds to come up with something, Marquez looked around frantically for anything she could use as Lipton continued to fire with his MP5. Running across the room, she moved into Cobb's office, thinking the boss might have a weapon or something inside his desk. All the filing cabinets had been knocked to the floor but his heavy desk was still upright, bolted to the floor.

Racing behind it, she pulled open his top desk drawer but saw no weapon, just an unopened bottle of Glenmorangie whiskey.

Looking at it, she thought for a moment, then suddenly remembered seeing Lipton smoking outside earlier when he was by the front gate with Wilson and two Met cops.

I just hope he didn't ask for a light, she thought, grabbing the bottle.

She ran back into the Briefing Room as Lipton continued to fire on the mercenaries below, not inflicting any damage but managing to stop the two gunmen from getting inside the building. He'd run out of ammo for his MP5 and was now firing his Glock, blood running down the side of his arm from the gunshot wound.

Kneeling beside him, Marquez ripped a strip off a tattered, smoke-stained piece of now unrecognisable clothing she'd found on the floor, stuffing it into the bottle. Then she tipped the Glenmorangie upside down, wetting the lower end of the rag.

Beside her, Lipton's Glock suddenly clicked dry and he dropped back.

'I'm out!'

'Lighter!' Marquez demanded.

Clutching his left arm, he tilted his pocket towards her and she reached forward, taking out a plastic lighter.

Sparking a flame, Marquez lit the rag, ducking from a sudden burst of assault rifle fire.

Then she rose and quickly threw the bottle down at the car twenty feet from the entrance as hard as she could.

The makeshift Molotov cocktail exploded on impact, the two gunmen jerked back but not affected by the blast, protected by the other side of the car.

'Shit!' Lipton said, who'd hauled himself up beside her to watch. 'You missed!'

Ignoring him, Marquez suddenly pulled her reloaded Glock.

And she aimed the sights at the car's fuel tank.

She fired twice, putting a double tap into the side of the car, and then dove back with Lipton as petrol spilled from the ruptured tank onto the flaming Molotov cocktail on the concrete beneath.

The blast that followed a second later was huge, resulting in a massive fireball as the car's fuel tank went up.

Lying on the blackened floor, hearing the car thump back onto the concrete as it landed after the blast, Marquez rose carefully to her feet and edged towards the damaged open edge of the building, one bullet left in her pistol.

Both gunmen were dead. They were sprawled either side of the burning car with their weapons on the ground beside them, the car they'd taken cover behind burning like a pyre. The flames crackled in the sudden quiet after the gunfight, the sirens of approaching police cars growing louder as they turned into the street, the car park a sea of empty shell casings, broken glass and cars shot to pieces.

It looked more like a warzone than a police station.

Turning back, she saw Lipton was OK and then ran across the level, re-joining Nikki and kneeling to check her leg.

'Are…they down?'

'They're down.'

As Nikki looked at Marquez, they both heard cars arrive in the car park outside, back-up finally here.

'That…was a nice move,' Nikki said. 'How did you…'

Marquez grinned, as the sound of car doors opening and closing joined the crackling of the flames from the burning car, the flashing lights on the police cars reflected off the windows of the buildings around the car park.

'You see some interesting things growing up in the Bronx,' she replied.

FIFTY ONE

High above the city, the black ARU Eurocopter
swept through the night sky, heading straight
towards 451 South Bank, a tall looming structure by
the River Thames that Archer now knew held
Vargas, Talia Farha and God only knew how many
more paid killers intent on ending his life.

In front of him in the cockpit, Chalky was hanging
in there, breathing hard through the pain and
bleeding badly from the gunshot wound but gritting
his teeth, knowing he had to get them to the building
and land safely.

Seeing the building approach, Archer felt his heart-
rate increase, thumping with adrenaline as he looked
at the epitome of his nightmares for the past four
months.

With Chalky injured, he was going inside alone.

As he took a deep breath and focused, he realised
Chalky's arm would need attention before he left
him to look for Vargas. Looking around the cabin, he
saw a cloth stowed in a compartment in the rear of
the vessel beside him and pulled it out. It wasn't
particularly clean but it was going to have to do;
making a small incision with the jack-knife from his
tac vest, he ripped it in half, looking over at the
building again as he did so.

They were almost there.

Dominick Farha was the first man he'd ever had to
kill, the leader of a terrorist cell who'd unleashed
mayhem on London with his eight-person team on
New Year's Eve two and a half years ago. It had
been the ARU's first major operation and Farha had

331

been responsible for an unforgettable series of events. Archer had put him down a split-second before he cut another man's throat and had shown him as much mercy as Farha had afforded all his victims throughout that day.

Archer had felt zero remorse since and hadn't lost a wink of sleep over what he'd had to do; Farha had been as evil as they come. Considering what he'd done to the city over the previous twenty four hours, taking him out was a public service. But that one action that day had unleashed all this, and was why Vargas had been kidnapped.

It had never been about something she'd done.

Everything today was about him.

Finishing ripping up the rag, he looked up and saw they were only fifty yards from the building. Pulling out his phone quickly, he tried the number Vargas had called him from again but no one picked up.

As the helicopter finally came to a halt and they hovered over the office building, Archer grabbed a support rung and moved to the left window. Up front, Chalky used all his remaining strength to keep the vessel steady, his breathing becoming increasingly laboured as he gritted his teeth and focused on the controls.

Looking down, Archer couldn't see anyone or any anti-personnel mines on the roof, but he knew from past experience the kind of welcome that could be waiting.

'Should...I land?' Chalky asked.

'Do it!'

Chalky moved the stick and the chopper started to descend, Archer ripping his door open and tracing with his MP5, looking for any sign of a welcoming committee.

There was no-one there.

The chopper touched down on the roof. Archer jumped out a moment later, clearing either side with his sub-machine gun, his heart thumping with adrenaline. When he was satisfied they weren't about to be attacked, he turned back, opened the cockpit door and immediately caught Chalky as he toppled towards him.

He steadied his friend then took one piece of the cloth he'd grabbed from the back of the vessel and packed it over the gunshot wound.

'You're having a bad day, mate,' he said.

'I've had worse,' he mumbled back.

Archer tied the other strip over the top, holding the wad in place as he cinched it tight.

'Just stay here and stay awake,' he said.

Noticing Chalky didn't have his Glock, Archer pulled his own and passed it to him. He pointed at the closed access door to the roof to their left.

'Just in case you get any company.'

Chalky nodded, taking the pistol, his eyes hazy. Then, despite the pain, he suddenly smiled.

'Just like…old times,' he said, quietly.

Archer paused. Then he smiled briefly too.

'I'll be back soon.'

Chalky didn't respond, focusing on staying awake.

Archer then turned with his MP5 and ran across the roof towards the entrance to the building.

Nine storeys down, Vargas was desperately fighting for her life with an armed man who'd just walked in through the door to talk to his companion.

While she'd been talking to Archer she'd heard someone coming into the office next door and after quickly ending the call had moved quickly and silently across the room to the side of the door.

There'd been the sound of movement next door; nothing had happened for some time, just the occasional sound of sniffing. She'd waited, gripping just the dead man's knife, her heart racing, wondering what he was doing and beginning to think she was going to get away with it.

Then the door had suddenly opened.

Carrying an assault rifle, the man was relaxed when he walked into the room, not expecting any trouble.

Until he spotted his dead buddy's body lying on the floor.

Before he could react, Vargas had appeared from around the door and buried the knife into his thigh, the man screaming in pain and dropping his AR-15. Vargas had gone for the weapon instantly but the man had thrown himself into her, knocking her to the ground as he pinned her down. Vargas was now trapped underneath the man as he tried to strangle her, his strong hands clamped around her throat.

'Bitch!' he shouted, crushing her windpipe.

Suffocating, Vargas trapped his right arm by holding his tricep and forearm then hooked her left foot past his right foot and pushed up with her hips. The man was so blinded with pain and rage he was taken by surprise as suddenly she tipped him onto his back. He immediately fought back, trapping her in an arm-lock and trying to dislocate her elbow, but she quickly grabbed the knife still buried in his thigh with her left hand and twisted it as hard as she could.

The man shouted in pain, immediately releasing her arm; she saw her opportunity and pushing herself up, dived for his AR-15 across the room. Clutching his leg, the man saw what she was doing and lunged after her, grabbing her ankle, but her fingers curled around the weapon and she spun round in one smooth motion, firing a single shot from her back.

She hit him straight in the chest as he reared up and he dropped instantly with a heavy *thump*, the gunshot echoing around the office floor as the man lay still across her bare feet.

Panting hard, Vargas kicked her legs out from under him, keeping the assault rifle trained on the man as she rose. Staring down through the sights, she saw blood pooling out from the guy's limp body.

He was dead.

Up on the roof, Archer didn't hear the gunshot due to the noise of the chopper.

As he approached the door, he felt his heart pounding as he forced the waves of claustrophobia down, focusing on getting to Vargas and taking on anyone who tried to stop him.

He had no idea what was waiting for him in this building.

Armed men.

An ambush.

Anything.

But Vargas was here somewhere.

And he was going to get her back alive.

Grabbing the handle, Archer took a deep breath and eased the door back as gently as he could, his MP5 aimed at the gap in case someone was waiting the other side.

It was dark, and he couldn't see clearly. It seemed no-one was there.

Edging his way through the door, he closed it behind him, the noise of the chopper suddenly gone. He quickly scanned the dark stairwell below with the MP5, tense, waiting for his eyes to adjust.

There was another door down the flight, the entrance to the top floor of the building.

Gripping the sub-machine gun tight, Archer moved down through the darkness towards it.

FIFTY TWO

He walked down the few steps slowly, arriving outside the 25th floor fire escape door.

Easing it forward, he stepped out straight into a huge office space covering the entire floor, each work station separated by a screen.

His heart thumping, memories of being trapped in a building with men hunting him all flooding back like a burst dam, Archer narrowed his eyes, forcing the thoughts back and focusing down the sights of his MP5.

The entire place was quiet.

Just as Archer arrived on the 25th floor office space many floors up, the ARU BMW Dash had stolen screeched to a halt in front of the building.

Pushing open their doors, he, Piccadilly and Portland leapt out and ran across the courtyard towards the entrance, moving inside quickly and securing the door behind them. As Portland finished bolting the door and Piccadilly reloaded his AR-15, Dash dialled Aldgate, who'd been left with the detective. None of them were hindered by anyone behind the front desk; the guard had been shot dead earlier and dumped in a maintenance closet.

'Shit,' Dash said. 'He's not picking up!'

His assault rifle fully loaded again, Piccadilly moved to the two lifts and pushed the button. As one of them descended and the numbers above the doors ticked down, Dash tried Stockwell's number, aka Nicolas Gagnon, one of his two Canadian snipers.

'Stockwell, where are you?'

'On 17 with Covent. We're prepping the workspace for the boss. You get Archer?'

'Where the hell is Aldgate?'

'He's watching the girl on 16 but wasn't answering our calls. Wood just went down to check on him.'

Dash swore as the lift arrived in the lobby. 'Both of you, get up to the top floor now! Archer escaped from the ARU by chopper; he's coming for her.'

'You want him alive?'

'Just get to the roof and kill that son of a bitch!'

As the doors to the lift opened, Dash and Piccadilly stepped inside, pushing the button for 16, the floor where the detective was being held, Piccadilly holding the door momentarily so Portland could join them as he finished locking the doors.

'Cops are coming!' he said, turning and running over from the front doors to join them as he reloaded his AR-15, the distant sound of sirens in the air.

'I'll handle them,' Piccadilly said, jabbing the button for 3 as the doors closed.

On 16, Vargas pushed herself back to her feet, the AR-15 in her hands, then grabbed the cell phone she'd dropped in the fight. Tucking the phone into the pocket at the back of her shorts, she moved over to the man she'd just shot and took a spare magazine for the assault rifle. He had a pistol too but she had no way of carrying it so she'd have to leave it, but the AR-15 was more than she'd had all day and she felt a damn sight more confident with it in her hands.

Kneeling, she rolled the man over and saw his eyes were open, his body limp, staring vacantly up at the ceiling with a stream of blood leaking out of the side of his mouth. She yanked the knife out of his leg and wiped it on his torso, then folded it shut and put the blade in the back pocket of her shorts along with her phone. Checking his pockets for anything else, she found a pack of cigarettes, a lighter and a half-empty bag of cocaine which explained what he'd been doing outside and the time delay.

She then crept to the door of the large office and stepped out into the space beyond. Archer said he was on his way; all she had to do was hang on until he got here. As she walked across the dark empty space of the main office floor, the AR15 buried in her shoulder, she suddenly froze in mid-step.

The two lifts in front of her had digital red lights above each.

And the floors where each cart was located was changing.

Both were heading up.

Swearing, she raced across the floor towards the stairwell door, pushing it open and sprinting down the flight, pulling her stolen cell phone and calling Archer as she ran.

On 25, he was walking through the empty office floor, tracing either side, all his senses on high alert as he searched for any sign of movement.

Suddenly he felt his phone vibrate on his tac vest. He answered quickly, his left hand snapping back down to hold the stock of the MP5 as he used his earpiece and Velcro throat mic.

'Hello?' he whispered.

'It's me!' Vargas said.

'I'm in the building.'

'What? Where?'

'On 25. Where are you?'

'Get to the stairs! There're people in the lifts coming for us!'

Just as she spoke, one of the two lifts suddenly arrived in front of Archer.

And a moment later, the doors started to part.

FIFTY THREE

Before they could open all the way, Archer was already running. At the same time, he pulled a flash-bang with his left hand, ripped out the pin and threw it at the parting doors as he took off across the level towards the stairwell.

The two armed mercenaries who were in the lift saw him the moment the doors parted, but the detonation bought him a few valuable seconds. The pair covered up as the grenade went off but then assault rifle fire hammered into the wall behind him a split-second later as Archer ran through a gap between some of the cubicles and dove to the floor.

Hitting the deck, Archer didn't have a line of sight but traced the direction of fire and let rip with the MP5 through the thin screen of a cubicle, hearing a shout of pain and a muzzle flash of uncontrolled fire as one of them took a hit. Archer unleashed the MP5 again in the same direction and the fire ceased.

He went to get back to his feet but another burst over the top of his head forced him back down, small pieces of the cubicle falling down onto him.

Below, Vargas had moved down a floor to 15, trying to find a safe refuge where she could hide and give Archer time to get to her.

Like the one above, this entire floor was being renovated, full of bare wood, transparent carpentry sheets and unfinished areas. Hearing the gunfire from above, she was clearing the large space with the AR15 when she heard a noise from a closed half-painted door to her right.

Taking two steps forward, keeping her assault rifle trained on the door, she snapped the handle back and kicked it open with her bare foot.

Two boys were lying on the floor, trussed up just as she'd been earlier, their eyes wide with terror as she burst in. Quickly checking the small office space, she ran forward towards them, using the knife she'd stabbed the man upstairs with to cut away their binds.

'Stay quiet!' she whispered, removing their gags as gently as she could.

They both nodded, signs of tears dried on their faces, but did as they were told.

Hearing a noise, Vargas dropped the knife and suddenly whirled around, grabbing her assault rifle and aiming it at the lifts outside in the main floor.

She waited.

No one came.

Vargas paused for a moment, then turned back and saw how scared the two boys were; putting the AR-15 down, she hugged them both, one of them starting to sob quietly, holding onto her tightly. She held onto the boys for a moment longer then released them, looking at each in turn and putting her finger to her lips. Once they both nodded, understanding, Vargas picked up the assault rifle, turned and led the way cautiously out of the office, the two boys following right behind her.

Clearing the open plan space, she quickly headed towards the stairs, turning to make sure the boys were with her. She wanted to use the lift but the number display above each meant she might as well shout *here I am* to anyone hunting her.

One of them was on *25*, the other a floor above her on *16*.

She could still hear the sounds of gunfire coming from somewhere above; she desperately wanted to get up there to help Archer, but she couldn't go up, not now she had two boys with her.

Backing up from the stairwell, she stood still for a moment, trying to work out the best plan of action.

But in that short time, she never saw the lift from 16 move down a floor and arrive behind her.

On 25, Stockwell ducked as the blond cop let off his own stream in his direction then saw him make a run for the stairwell door, smashing it open and racing through it as Stockwell fired back, spraying bits of wood and plaster into the air around the doorframe.

As he stood up to follow, he saw Covent slumped in a bloody heap by one of the cubicles.

'Son of a bitch!' he shouted, immediately sprinting towards the door after the cop.

The Canadian sniper kept his assault rifle in his shoulder as he went through the door, immediately starting down the stairs seeing as they were on the top floor and with nowhere to go but down.

It was the last mistake he ever made.

Archer guessed the gunman would expect him to go downstairs and so had stood behind the door, waiting for it to open.

Now behind the mercenary as the door closed, he fired with the MP5, hitting him as he moved down the stairs, killing him instantly. Going down the flight would be what ninety nine per cent of people

343

would have done, but Archer had had some recent experience of building warfare.

The gunfire echoed all the way down the stairwell as the guy hit the deck, instantly telegraphing Archer's location. Reloading fast by reversing the double-taped magazine in the MP5, Archer pulled his phone and pushed *Redial,* tucking it back into the slot, taking deep breaths and keeping his MP5 trained on the gap in the stairwell, waiting for anyone else to appear as blood started to pool out from the dead gunman's body slumped half a flight below.

The call connected.

'Where are you?' he asked quietly, sucking in oxygen, watching the gap in the stairs. 'Alice?'

'I'm on floor 17,' she said after a pause, her voice slightly strained.

He paused for a moment.

'Hang on,' he told her. 'I'm coming.'

Hanging up, Archer moved forward, stepping over the dead mercenary, and headed down the stairs.

On 15, Dash grinned after the call ended, looking at Portland who had his pistol to the woman's head as he gripped her hair from behind, the two boys standing there helpless beside her. Once they'd found Aldgate and Wood's bodies upstairs, they figured the woman would move downstairs and had arrived on 15 to find her standing right in front of them with her back to the lift, the two brats beside her.

With the bitch under Portland's control, her AR-15 dropped to the floor, Dash ran for the stairwell,

344

ripping open the door and disappearing into the flight.

Archer was on his way to 17.

Little did he know what would be waiting for him.

Watching in desperation, Vargas went to shout but the big man guarding her hit her over the head with the side of the pistol, staggering and dazing her slightly, the two boys beside her whimpering in fear.

Archer was walking right into a trap.

FIFTY FOUR

Moving out into the stairwell, Dash paused for a moment, listening.

He couldn't hear footsteps on the stairs above him, but he knew Archer was coming.

Moving up to 17 quickly, keeping to the walls so he couldn't be seen from above, Dash slid inside the prepared torture floor quietly, taking up a position the other side of the door so he would be shielded when it opened.

Aiming his rifle at the wood, he grinned. Although he knew his mother had always preferred Dominick, Dash and his older brother had been close and he'd been just as pissed as Talia about his death; he was going to enjoy this.

As he waited, he quickly pulled his cell and called Talia, holding his assault rifle with his right hand and the phone with his left.

'What the hell is going on up there?' she said. *'I can hear gunfire.'*

'Archer's here,' he whispered. *'He came by chopper.'*

'Bring him to me.'

'I'm on 17,' Dash whispered, focusing on the door. *'Check your camera; I'll put him down then we can have some fun. Payback time. Piccadilly's holding off the cops downstairs. We can use the chopper later.'*

He ended the call, hitching his assault rifle and focusing on the door.

The previous cases in Sam Archer's file had suggested that he was impossible to put down.

But that luck of his had just run out.

On the 3rd floor, Piccadilly had already opened fire through one of the windows on the police cars that had gathered below in the front courtyard. The officers had been caught by surprise and had quickly ducked for cover as the South African opened up with the rifle, but he still managed to hit two of them.

Watching them go down and the others scatter, he saw a black truck approaching. It turned into the car park below and he saw SCO19 printed on the side, the other main counter-terrorist police unit in London. Grange and Stockwell had killed four of their officers earlier in the day, so they'd no doubt be in the mood for revenge.

They could bring it on.

Reloading, Piccadilly, or former SA Army Sergeant Danny Heydrich, aimed at the truck and fired, blowing out two of its tyres just to make a point.

No one was coming in to save Archer or his girl.

Just inside 17, Dash waited for the door to open, aiming his assault rifle where Archer's legs would be.

He strained his ears, listening for the sound of his footsteps.

Nothing.

Suddenly, however, he heard a strange sound coming from the stairwell.

He frowned, trying to work out what it was.

Then he looked down.

Smoke started to seep under the door.

347

It swirled into the open space around him, forcing him to cover his mouth with his left hand.

Focusing on the door, he waited.

But it didn't open.

Losing his patience and guessing this was some kind of trick, Dash reached for the handle and eased the door open carefully, allowing more of the smoke to pour into the room.

Moving cautiously around the door and tracing with his weapon, trying to figure out where the smoke was coming from, Dash felt it wash over him, the black stuff rendering him momentarily blind.

Blinking hard and trying to clear his vision, he looked for Archer.

Suddenly, the building fire alarm system kicked in, the noise shrill and distracting as it echoed through the building. Stepping forward, Dash moved out into the flight, peering up the stairwell and aiming his rifle where he expected Archer to appear.

Then he felt the muzzle of a gun jam into his neck from his right.

'Drop the gun,' Archer ordered, his MP5 under the man's ear.

Dash didn't react.

'Drop it,' Archer repeated, pushing the sub-machine gun harder into his neck. The man complied; through the smoke from the grenade Archer had set off he saw it was Dash, Dominick Farha's brother. Archer had known immediately from Vargas' voice on the phone and the way she spoke that something was up and he'd been right.

It had been a trap.

348

He'd ripped off a smoke grenade in the stairwell to conceal himself and confuse the enemy then had moved down the stairs fast, taking up a position below the 17th floor door; just as before, he'd guessed which way any gunmen hiding inside would turn once they opened the door. And he'd been correct

Archer pushed Dash onto the 17th floor, checking left and right through the smoke for any more of the mercenaries.

Then Dash made his move.

He jerked the gun free from his neck, using his left arm to smack it out of Archer's hands as he fired, then immediately went for the suppressed Ruger on his hip. As he grabbed it, Archer hit him with a hard uppercut, forcing the bigger man to drop the gun; dazed and full of fury, Dash grabbed Archer by the throat and propelled him back, slamming him into the wall by the 17th floor stairwell door which had closed beside them.

His eyes burning from the smoke, the fire alarms echoing around the building, Archer pulled at the guy's forearm but it was like a forklift was holding him in place and squeezing his throat. He needed to work for a joint lock or chokehold to take him out, but he was pinned to the wall, unable to move or breathe. Feeling the walls closing in, his oxygen running out, Archer kicked out as hard as he could in a last ditch attempt and managed to hit Dash in the groin.

The Afghani former soldier shouted in pain, letting go. Archer threw a hard right hand that smashed into Dash's jaw, mashing his teeth against his lips, and in the same movement ducked low, tackling Dash back onto the floor. Moving like lightning, Archer hooked his right arm behind Dash's head, threaded his right forearm across his throat then put his right hand on his left bicep and tipped Dash onto his side, tightening the squeeze in a D'Arce choke.

Caught before he could react, Dash tried to struggle out, but he was trapped. Archer gritted his teeth and applied as much pressure as he could, blood leaking from a cut under his right eye. As he choked Dash towards unconsciousness, a red light mounted on the ceiling above a table to his right suddenly caught his eye.

It was attached to something big and metallic that resembled a bee's nest. Archer blinked, blood staining the side of his face.

It was the biggest nail-bomb he'd ever seen.

And there was a small webcam stuck right beside it.

On 12, having stayed where she was as Dash's team hunted down Vargas and Archer, Talia stared at her laptop screen, the detonator for the device resting on the desk by her right hand.

She'd seen the two men enter the room, but nothing had gone as expected, a brutal fight now ending with Archer having the upper hand. Looking at the two men on the screen, she could see Archer staring at the camera beside the bomb she'd planned for him to beg her to detonate after she'd worked on him on the table below.

The detonator was beside her hand on the desk. She could kill him right now.

But if she did, her remaining son would get caught in the blast.

Staring at the nail-bomb and the red light, Archer released the half-conscious Dash, not taking his eyes off the lethal device. He rose and quickly yanked the dazed mercenary to his feet, holding him in front of him by his collar, then pulled a jack-knife from his ARU tac vest and put the blade to Dash's throat.

He stared at the camera, the floor around them empty and silent.

Now upright, he glanced through the smoke at the bare wood workman's table to their right.

He saw a number of wickedly sharp metal tools laid on the surface alongside some duct tape, syringes and strips of cloth, makeshift tourniquets.

A power saw was there too.

It was a torture spot.

His torture spot.

Looking up at the camera beside the nail-bomb, he stared into the lens.

Reaching for the detonator, Talia quivered with rage as she stared at the screen, her finger beside the button.

Archer had the knife to her son's throat, holding him in front of him. According to the Met police report, Dominick had done just the same with someone else before this man had shot him in the head, a complete role reversal.

She saw Dash staring at the camera, bloodied but confident, knowing his mother was watching.

Archer didn't move, staring at the camera and the huge nail-bomb with the glowing red light beside it. Dash tried to struggle out of his grip but Archer

351

added extra pressure to the knife to his throat, keeping him still.

Archer then started to slowly back away from the nail-bomb towards the door, taking Dash with him, keeping his eyes on the light.

Down below, Talia screamed in frustration and fury as she made her decision.

Archer was fifteen feet from the stairwell door, the fire alarms shrill and constant.

Then the light on the nail-bomb suddenly turned yellow.

FIFTY FIVE

Two floors down, Vargas and the two boys heard the explosion through the fire alarms, taking them completely by surprise as the noise reverberated around the building. Vargas instinctively recoiled, but then felt the big mercenary's hand clumping in her hair, impassive and threatening as he held her in place.

'Your boyfriend just died,' the man holding the gun to her head whispered into her ear, his accent Australian. 'And you're about to join him, bitch.'

She didn't move, his words sinking in.

Archer's dead, she thought.

Archer's dead.

As the man holding the gun flicked off the safety, Vargas suddenly felt one of the boys slide something into her hand.

The knife.

He must have picked it up earlier after she cut their binds.

The mercenary hadn't noticed the movement, not paying any attention to the two little boys who were no threat to him. Vargas flipped the knife open and carefully reversed it in her hand.

A moment later, she suddenly stabbed backwards as hard as she could.

The blade jammed straight into the man's groin and he screamed in pain, instantly releasing her and staggering back with the knife embedded where his thigh joined his torso. Not hesitating for a second, Vargas grabbed her assault rifle from the floor, tossed it into the lift, then clutched the two boys'

353

hands and pulled them after it, hitting the button for the ground floor.

She pushed them both to the side, covering them as the doors started to close.

Clutching his groin, the man staggered round and fired with his pistol, but the bullets hit the far wall of the lift, Vargas keeping the boys back out of the line of fire as the doors shut.

Reeling in pain from the stab wound, Portland pulled the knife from his leg, blood flowing from the wound.

'Bitch!' he shouted, throwing the knife to one side and stumbling towards the stairwell. As he did so, he pulled his phone, needing to call the others downstairs to get them to push the button and stop the lift.

'Yeah?' Piccadilly said.

'Where are you?'

'3rd floor keeping the cops back. Where the hell is that alarm coming from?'

Portland ripped open the door to the stairwell, lifting the phone to his ear and waving smoke out of his face, his thigh on fire from pain.

'Forget that. Listen, the bitch is on her way do-'

Shooting the man in the chest with a burst from his MP5, Archer watched him take the burst and get thumped back, falling to the floor. He was unharmed from the nail-bomb but the cut under his eye from his fight with Dash was leaking blood as he carried his MP5 with the last clip inside, Dash's suppressed Ruger 22/45 shoved into the holster on his thigh.

When the light had turned yellow he'd instantly dropped his knife, spun Dash round to face him and threw himself backwards, dragging the other man down with him. As they'd hit the floor Archer had tucked his knees under Dash and gripped his collar hard to hold him in place.

Dash's eyes had suddenly widened in realisation.

And a split-second later, the nail-bomb detonated.

The blast had destroyed everything in the room, raining nails down with lethal force onto tables and chairs, the deadly hail annihilating furniture, penetrating the walls, the floor, everything; nothing escaped.

Archer had been underneath Dash, gripping the inside collar of his shirt as hard as he was clenching his eyes shut, his knees bunched up against the man's chest.

He'd waited for pain, but it never came.

Then he'd opened his eyes and looked up at the mercenary through the smoke.

He'd gone totally limp, blood leaking out of the side of his mouth. Archer had loosened his grip on the man's collar and Dash had immediately sagged to one side, slumping down face first, a dead weight. As Archer eased himself out from under him and rolled to his feet, his Converse crunching on pieces of debris, he saw that Dash had scores of thick nails protruding from the back of his body and head.

He'd been killed instantly.

Looking grimly up at the camera through the smoke, knowing who'd be watching, Archer had turned and retrieved his MP5, running out onto the stairs and heading downstairs. After checking 16 and finding two dead bodies, he'd been on his way to 15 when the door to the floor had suddenly opened and one of the guys who'd ambushed him at Bernhardt's had staggered out through the smoke, talking on his phone and bleeding from a wound to his thigh.

Archer had fired instantly, watching the man take the rounds and fall to the floor. Not wasting a second, he jumped over the man and edged out onto 15, clearing the space.

But Vargas wasn't there.

He pulled his phone and called her, waiting, but she wasn't picking up. *Shit!* He thought, sucking in air, looking around the deserted, quiet dark office floor as blood leaked down the side of his face.

He turned and looked at the two lifts, checking the digital displays above.

Where the hell is she?

Piccadilly was still on 3, having just taken Portland's call and pausing for a moment from firing on the arriving police below. The call had ended mid-conversation, cut off from the sound of gunfire, but Piccadilly had heard enough.

He was by a maintenance access box, which he opened and pulled a switch, killing the fire alarm which was driving him nuts, the building suddenly quiet again. Turning, Piccadilly saw one of the lifts ticking down towards them and pushed the button, stepping back with the assault rifle and aiming it directly at the doors.

It arrived, and the doors parted.

A second later, he unloaded with the assault rifle, the bullets ripping into the cart as he emptied the clip.

Once it clicked dry, he stopped and looked.

There was no one there.

Unknown to the South African mercenary, the lift had made one stop on its way from 15 to 3.

On the 12th floor.

This office floor looked to be almost completed, the floor carpeted, the walls painted. Vargas was standing very still, looking straight ahead, her AR15 still in her hands but staring out of the corner of her eye at the nail-gun which was aimed at the side of her head.

'Drop it,' the woman holding it said quietly.

Vargas didn't move.

The nail-gun suddenly swept down, aimed at one of the boy's heads.

'OK,OK,' Vargas said, tossing the assault rifle forward. 'But let them go. I'm the one you want.'

Pause.

'Very well.'

Vargas looked down at the two boys. 'Go!'

They didn't move.

'Go! Use the stairs!'

They stared at her for a moment then took off, running to the stairwell doors and disappearing out of sight, the frame swinging back behind them.

Now alone with the woman, Vargas watched her walk round in front of her, the nail gun trained on her face.

She saw she was older, somewhere in her late fifties or early sixties, and short but incredibly menacing.

Vargas had never seen her before.

'Who are you?' she asked.

'Someone who wants you to die.'

357

Vargas didn't reply.

'I've been trying to decide all day when to kill you,' the woman said, pressing the nail-gun against Vargas's head. 'And I'm glad I waited. Now you're going to die in front of him. Call him.'

'He's already dead.'

'No. He isn't.'

Vargas didn't move but felt a sudden surge of hope.

'Last chance. You do this, you get a few more minutes of life.'

Knowing she had no other option, Vargas withdrew her phone, and went to push *Redial*.

'No need for that,' a familiar voice suddenly said from her right.

FIFTY SIX

Turning, the two women saw Archer standing in the doorway to the stairs.

Blood leaking down the side of his face from the cut under his left eye, he moved forward, his MP5 in his shoulder, aimed straight at Talia as she kept the nail gun on Vargas. When he'd been standing on 15, he'd seen one of the lifts stop on the 12th floor before it continued below, and guessed Vargas could be here. Out of the corner of his vision, he saw the hope on her face.

It was the first time he and Alice had been together since she left New York last week after their fight.

But this was no time for a reunion.

His sights on the older woman's chin, his finger on the trigger, Archer didn't take his eyes off Talia Farha.

She looked to be somewhere in her late fifties or early sixties, her skin wrinkled and leathered, her dark hair streaked with silver. She was small but her lack of height was more than compensated for by her intimidating presence.

She stared at him with hard eyes that glittered with venom. Her two dead sons had been killers, but just by looking at this woman he could tell that her spawn had only been a pale imitation of the original.

As she kept the nail-gun trained on Vargas but stared at Archer, he had a sudden flashback to two years ago. He'd looked into those same obsidian eyes just before he shot her son through one of them.

359

'Guess we've come full circle,' he said, keeping his MP5 on her. 'This was the last thing your kid ever saw too.'

'Don't you dare mention him,' she snarled, the nail-gun rock steady and still aimed at Vargas.

'You shouldn't have come after me,' he told her. 'I never would have known you existed.'

'You shot my son.'

'Considering what he did, he got off easy.'

'I'm going to kill you.'

'I can't see that happening,' he said, his MP5 trained on her, his finger white on the trigger.

'You shoot me, I blast your girlfriend,' Talia said, her nail gun against Vargas' head but her eyes on Archer. 'Drop your gun.'

Archer stopped, eight feet from her, his MP5 trained on her chin. The office space was rectangular, no cover nearby save for the stairwell behind him and the door to a second office to his immediate right.

And Talia had the nail-gun pointed up close at Vargas' head.

'I'm going to start with your toes,' she hissed at Archer. 'Then your fingers. Then your lower legs and arms to the elbow. I'll cut out your eyes and your tongue. I'll give you shots of adrenaline to keep you alive.'

Archer went to reply but then he saw her eyes suddenly flick to the lifts to his left.

One of them had just arrived.

Instinctively, Archer followed her glance for a split second.

But by the time his attention swung back to Talia, she'd already pulled the trigger.

Anticipating the move, Vargas was already on her way down as Talia ducked and fired, the nail missing the top of her head her by a hair's breadth.

Archer fired a second later, hitting Talia in the arm and knocking her around in a pirouette to the floor as the lift doors began to open. Pushing herself back to her feet, Vargas ran towards Archer as a blond man with an AR-15 appeared out of the lift.

Archer saw he was the last member of the trio who'd attacked him at Bernhardt's house with Dash and the other guy, both now dead upstairs. The man saw Archer turning his MP5 onto him and threw himself back into the lift as Archer fired, the bullets tearing into the space where he'd just been standing as Talia clutched her wounded arm then reached for the nail-gun beside her on the floor.

Grabbing Vargas' hand, Archer turned and took off through the door to the office immediately to their right, kicking it shut behind them. A moment later, gunfire ripped into the wood, spraying pieces into the air as the pair threw themselves to the floor inside the other room.

As Archer rolled and fired back through the door, buying him and Vargas a few seconds, Vargas froze and stared around her in horror.

Firing again, Archer glanced at her then followed her eyes.

Workmen had left plastic sheets covering the walls.

But instead of sawdust they were liberally spattered with blood.

There were pieces of a human being shoved in a heap across the room. Beside it was a body, a man missing the lower half of each leg below his knees, pints of blood having leaked out and covering the floor, partially dried and sweet to smell. It was the most sickening and stomach-churning thing he'd ever seen, even outdoing a scene her son had left the police in the bathroom of a house they raided the day before Archer shot him.

Swallowing, Vargas looked at Archer, horror written all over her face, and their attention quickly snapped back to the door as more gunfire ripped into it.

Archer went to return fire, but then his MP5 clicked dry.

Cursing and tossing it to one side, he drew Dash's pistol.

Outside, Piccadilly was covering the door. Clutching her wounded arm, which was hanging uselessly by her side, Talia moved over and joined him, holding out her uninjured hand as Piccadilly passed her his Ruger.

As she took the weapon, Talia felt a surge of sheer anticipation.

Archer and his girlfriend were next door.

And they were trapped.

FIFTY SEVEN

Crouching in the blood-spattered office beside Vargas and holding Dash's pistol, Archer desperately looked around for another way out. There wasn't one, and the handgun was all he had apart from a flash-bang, a smoke grenade and a knife.

The man next door had an automatic weapon, ammunition, both exits covered and no doubt a pistol for Talia.

There was no sign of back up yet either.

'Shit!'

'What do we do?' Vargas said frantically, still staring at the blood-stained transparent sheets and the body parts. 'Sam?'

Cursing, he looked around desperately. Behind them was a bathroom, obviously servicing the main office beyond as well as this one when it was in use, and to their left was a load of workman's gear, tools, bags of nails and a small rubbish bin with some old food wrappers visible inside.

There was nothing.

As Vargas backed away further from the door, her grey nightclothes dirtied and stained with dried blood, Archer suddenly paused.

Looking at the rubbish bin and nails to his left, he thought back to his flight from New York to London earlier in the day.

And his conversation with Marquez about fear.

In the main office, Piccadilly suddenly let rip on the door with his AR-15, blowing pieces of it apart. It was returned a second later, rounds from a silenced

363

pistol hitting the door, which was exactly what he and Talia wanted, knowing the pair trapped inside would eventually run out of ammo.

All they had to do was provoke Archer into firing until his guns clicked dry and the return fire would cease.

Kneeling inside the bathroom as Vargas fired at the door with Dash's pistol, Archer frantically pulled open the doors under the washbasin and found some cleaning products lined up inside.

Including an industrial-size container of bleach.

Grabbing it, he moved back into the room, then rummaged through the rubbish bin, praying he'd find what he was looking for.

If he didn't, they were going to die.

Seconds later, his heart skipped a beat. It was there.

Reaching inside, he withdrew a rolled up ball of foil from an eaten sandwich, just as Vargas fired the last round and the slide on the pistol stayed back.

'Rip this into smaller pieces!' he told Vargas quickly, passing her the ball of foil.

Puzzled but doing what he said without question, she dropped the pistol and after quickly unravelling the ball, started tearing up the aluminium wrap. Realising they needed more time, Archer saw the gunfire had blown a hole into the upper part of the door; he pulled the last stun grenade from his pocket, ripped the pin, stalked forward then popped it through the hole, both of them covering up as the flash-bang went off.

Using every precious second it bought him, Archer unscrewed the bleach, instantly getting a hit of the harsh chemical smell. As Vargas continued to rip the foil into smaller pieces, Archer grabbed a bag of nails the workmen had left behind.

He then tipped them all into the bottle as fast as he could.

Talia and Piccadilly had just been advancing on the door when the stun grenade had come through, taking them by surprise and giving them no time to cover up.

As they waited for their senses to return, Talia smiled through the momentary discomfort.

Archer's return fire had stopped.

He was out of ammo.

With the whole bag of nails now inside the bleach, Archer scooped up the strips of foil Vargas had prepared and stuffed them inside. As soon as he fed the last piece in, he screwed on the cap and shook it frantically, starting the chemical reaction.

Moving forward, he placed the bottle in the centre of the room then took a smoke grenade from his vest, ripping the pin and laying it beside the bleach.

Walking forward silently, both Talia and Piccadilly approached the door, just as there was a crack and a hissing sound.

Smoke suddenly started to drift through the gaps in the shot-up door.

She grinned. They'd used a smoke grenade to hamper visibility, but all they were doing was delaying the inevitable by a few seconds. They'd unwittingly taken cover inside the room Talia had used to kill Finchley; she smiled at the irony.

In front of her, Piccadilly kicked the damaged frame back. Smoke was filling the space, making it hard to see. The fire alarm didn't start again though, which meant it must have been disabled.

Walking forward with the South African, both of them undeterred by the smoke grenade, they traced the gloom with their weapons.

Searching for their prey as the smoke grenade *hissed* and filled the silence in the room.

Inside the bathroom, Archer joined Vargas inside the shower stall and covered her, closing his eyes as her fingers gripped onto his tac vest tightly.

He willed the chemical reaction between the foil and bleach to speed up.

C'mon!

Clutching his vest, Vargas held him close as smoke flowed into the room behind them.

C'mon!

As Talia and Piccadilly moved through the smoke, brushing aside the transparent sheets spattered with Finchley's blood, the South African mercenary's foot suddenly hit something as he stepped forward.

He glanced down, Talia pausing just behind him, her gaze followed his.

There was a large container of bleach sitting on the floor beside the grenade.

Puzzled, Talia glanced at the South African, who shrugged. Shifting their attention, they focused on the bathroom to their right. The rest of the office was empty.

Archer and Vargas would be in there.

366

In the smoke, Piccadilly turned to Talia and nodded, smiling. But as she went to react, she suddenly saw movement out of the corner of her eye. He saw her expression and turned back to face the bottle of bleach.

The container on the floor suddenly expanded.

Like a balloon about to burst.

FIFTY EIGHT

Inside the shower stall and shielding Vargas, Archer heard the blast and two screams as boiling hot bleach and the nails he'd dropped into the fluid exploded outwards from the chemical reaction in a makeshift nail-bomb. Waiting a few seconds longer, Vargas holding onto him tightly, Archer turned and saw no one had entered the bathroom.

Smoke continued to drift into the room from the grenade.

He looked back at Vargas, who stared up at him, her eyes wide with confusion. Rising and pushing open the shower door, Archer crept cautiously towards the door of the smoke-filled bathroom. As he edged towards the entrance, completely unarmed, he peered round and saw the blond man from the lift on the floor.

He was dead, his skin and clothing covered with burning chemicals, nails buried in his face, neck and torso, his eyes open as the bleach bubbled on his burned face.

However, Talia was nowhere to be seen.

Grabbing a hand towel from the bathroom, Archer pulled off the dead man's shoes, passing them to Vargas behind him. She wouldn't need them for long, just to walk over the floor out of this office. As she slipped them on distastefully, Archer reached forward and scooped up the dead man's AR-15, his hand protected from the bleach on the grip by the rag.

All the while, the office continued to be clouded by smoke from the grenade.

And he couldn't see Talia anywhere.

Checking the clip and then tracing through the gloom, Archer took a deep breath then led the way as they walked through the aftermath of the explosion towards the door to the main office, holding their breath from the noxious fumes. With Vargas behind him, covering her mouth, they both moved slowly, Archer scanning the room with the assault rifle as he searched for Talia.

He could see the transparent, blood-covered sheets closest to him had been partially ripped by the explosion, the air stinking with the smell of burning chemicals, parts of the sheets smoking from the boiling bleach.

Checking that the main office beyond was empty, Archer stopped in the open doorway, unable to see shit through the smoke.

Vargas joined him, covering her mouth as she too searched through the thick smoke.

Where the hell was Talia?

Suddenly, there were two quick muzzle flashes from the other side of the small office.

Two rounds from a suppressed pistol pounded into Archer's chest. His vest absorbed the impact but it caught him off guard and knocked the wind out of him, throwing him back into the main office floor through the destroyed open door behind him. Fortunately, the rounds came from a .22 pistol, not a shotgun so he recovered fast and snapped up the AR-15 to return fire.

But through the swirling smoke he saw Vargas standing very still.

And Talia's outline right beside her.

He also saw she had her pistol jammed into the side of Vargas' neck.

'Drop the gun,' Talia's voice ordered.

This time, there was no chance she'd miss. Archer had no choice.

He let go of the assault rifle and it hit the floor.

A moment later, Talia swept the gun off Vargas and shot Archer again, hitting him in the vest and knocking him back another step. Vargas jolted as the pistol fired then Talia prodded her forward, pushing her into the main office. Reaching Archer, she turned and they both saw Talia more clearly as she walked towards them through the smoke.

She looked like something out of a nightmare.

Her face, arms and body had been hideously burned by the bleach. Several thick black nails were buried in her left side, drawing blood.

One was also embedded through the side of her left eye.

Standing there, Vargas beside him, Archer stared at Talia. Her skin still burning from the boiling chemicals, with her pistol pointed right at them, Talia stared straight back, blood leaking from the nail jutting out of the side of her eye. She must have been in excruciating pain; how she was still standing was beyond comprehension. The guy next door must have partially shielded her from the blast.

'You said earlier that this was the last thing my son ever saw,' she hissed at Archer, aiming the Ruger directly at him. 'I guess as you said, we really have come full circle.'

She hawked and spat blood and saliva at him, the bleach burning into her skin as Archer braced himself, ready to launch himself forward with his back against the wall. Pistols could miss; his vest had already absorbed three rounds from the Ruger and if he moved fast he could get to her before she could put him down.

However, keeping the pistol on him Talia suddenly knelt down and scooped up the AR-15 Archer had dropped, tossing the Ruger to one side, the bleach on the weapon immediately burning into her hands.

And Archer knew he was going to die.

Now just six feet from the pair, Talia lifted the assault rifle into her shoulder and put the sights on Archer's forehead. From this range with an automatic weapon, it was a done deal.

'Just do me one favour,' she said, aiming at his head. 'When you see Dominick, tell him who sent you.'

'Tell him yourself,' another voice suddenly added.

Keeping the AR-15 on Archer and Vargas, Talia's head swung round in shock.

And propped up in the stairwell door with Archer's Glock in his hand, Chalky pulled the trigger and shot her between the eyes.

The moment she took the round, Talia was thumped backwards, the assault rifle flying out of her hands as the bullet hit her right in the middle of the forehead. As the rear of her head blew apart, she fell to the floor in a heap, the single gunshot echoing down the stairwell behind Chalky.

Then everything was quiet.

Staring at her dead body, Vargas beside him, Archer stood still against the far wall for a moment, absorbing what had just happened.

Then he looked over at his best friend, who lowered the gun and slumped down to the floor in the doorframe.

Archer quickly moved over to him, Vargas going to Talia and kicking the weapons near her away.

'Christ, am I glad to see you,' Archer said, dropping to his knee by his friend.

'Thought you'd end up…needing some help,' Chalky said, his face pale from blood loss.

He turned his attention to Vargas as she joined them, forcing a smile.

'Finally we meet. Now I see…why he's gone to…all this trouble.'

She smiled back as she knelt down and gripped his free hand. Archer turned his attention to Chalky's arm and the makeshift bandage he'd tied on earlier which had slipped down.

Adjusting it, he looked at his friend and smiled.

'You left it pretty bloody late, didn't you?'

'You know I like…to make an entrance,' Chalky replied, grinning weakly.

Turning, Archer looked over at Talia Farha's dead body, the mother of the first man he'd ever had to kill. As he did so, the trio heard distant shouts of *police* from down the stairwell, back-up finally here.

He looked back at his friend. 'Thanks, Chalk.'

'After what you did for me…earlier…I guess now…we're even,' Chalky said.

With smoke still swirling around the office floor, the three of them waited there by the stairwell door for back-up, finally out of danger, Dash, Talia and their entire team gone.

'Yeah,' Archer said. 'I guess we are.'

FIFTY NINE

Three days later, the sun had just come up on a bright July Tuesday morning in London. A patched up Director Tim Cobb was standing on the far side of the car park outside the ARU's HQ, watching a team set to work ripping apart the upper floor of the burnt out building. Porter, Shifty and two of the other guys were standing beside him, all watching the men work in silence.

They all looked as if they'd been in a war, which in a way they had. Although Mason and Spitz had died, Porter and the other guys had been standing a bit further back, which had saved their lives. All the surviving task force officers had needed to have nails removed from their bodies, the wounds cleaned and bandaged, and all had wanted to be released from care immediately, thinking the operation was still on-going. Cobb had done the same of course, demanding the hospital discharge him, but quietened when he was informed that it was over; he'd suffered cuts to his face and body and still had a mild concussion, but was otherwise OK.

As they recovered in hospital all day Sunday and yesterday, the men had been updated on everything that had happened in the time since they'd been put out of action. They'd been stunned to discover the person behind all this death and destruction had been the mother of Dominick Farha, a man most of the ARU team remembered very well. Once SCO19 had cleared the building on the South Bank, they'd found the bodies of eight more mercenaries and a legendary female mujahedeen fighter called Talia Farha who'd been on a number of wanted lists of several countries for a long time.

Once their prints were run, it turned out five of the dead men were presumed to have died already in previous conflicts and the others had all dropped off the radar long ago, soldiers of fortune whose luck this time had finally run out. They were wanted men with a variety of nationalities; the UK, US, Canada, Afghanistan, Australia and South Africa. It quickly became apparent that Talia Farha had used several other aliases over the years; given the sophistication of the operation and the secrecy the entire group had operated under it wasn't surprising that someone as good as Nikki hadn't been able to identify who they were until it was almost too late.

In the extensive debriefing since Saturday, the Met had pieced together exactly why 3rd Grade Detective Alice Vargas had been kidnapped and why the attacks on their Unit and the NYPD team had followed. The abduction had never been about Vargas' past, but Archer's; laying a false trail had been a master stroke, luring the ARU and NYPD teams together and then unleashing the two bomb blasts and sniper attack to kill them all.

Months of planning had gone into the efforts to wipe out the entire ARU squad and the NYPD team, saving the man himself for last, the man who'd shot her son.

However, like many before her, Talia Farha had underestimated Archer.

And she'd paid the ultimate price.

Given the meticulous preparation and execution, Cobb and co knew they were lucky to have lost only two men but nevertheless, Talia, Dash and their team had all but destroyed the ARU HQ as well as several cars and had left a bloodbath inside the office building by the Thames, parts of which had only just been approaching the end of a long renovation.

Considering what they'd been up against, losing two of their people and four SCO19 officers was tragic but they knew it very easily could have been so much worse. The six who'd handled the operation when everyone else had gone down had truly outdone themselves. Stanovich, Payan and a guard inside the South Bank building which the mercenaries had used as a base were the other casualties of the day, but only one of them would be mourned.

Watching the demo crew work, Cobb smiled, proud of the way his team had handled affairs after he'd been injured and put out of action; he was particularly proud of Nikki, who'd stayed on despite having a broken collarbone and being shot. Her car had been totalled too, blown up in some kind of Molotov cocktail to kill two of the mercenaries, but Cobb figured she had a pretty fair case with the insurance company.

As a workman dislodged some masonry, the last piece of the Briefing Room wall crumbled away, falling to the concrete below in a cloud of dust. The five men all watched it drop in silence.

'To be fair, I never did like the colour scheme,' Shifty suddenly said.

As one, the group all turned to look at him.

After a pointed silence Porter spoke.

'Guess we're going to have to relocate for the next few months.'

Watching the men ahead work, Cobb nodded, then suddenly frowned.

Still thinking about Nikki's insurance case for her car, he shifted his attention from the building to the car park, looking left and right.

'Wait a minute,' he said.

'What's wrong, sir?' Porter asked.

'Where the hell is my Mercedes?'

*

Across the city, Archer took his boarding pass from the woman behind the check-in desk at Heathrow Terminal 5 and thanked her. Dressed in a clean pair of blue jeans and a grey t-shirt, he had a new pair of sunglasses resting on his head that he'd had to remove when she checked his passport.

He noticed her looking at the black eye he was now sporting after being hit by Dash.

'What happened?' she asked, smiling curiously at him and looking at the shiner.

'Saturday was a rough night.'

Her smiled faded, her look of interest changing to something more like disapproval, but before she could reply, he gave her a broad smile and turned away.

Scooping up his bag, he walked towards Josh, Marquez, Shepherd, Vargas and Chalky, who were standing there waiting for him, Vargas stepping towards him.

Now fully complete again, the NYPD team was heading home.

'All done?' Shepherd asked, as Archer joined them and put his arm around Vargas. Shepherd had a bandage around his head from a bad cut after the explosion from Beckett's bomb vest, but apart from that he was fully recovered.

377

Archer nodded. 'Club Class, here we come. I could get used to this.'

'Joys of the Bureau's budget,' Marquez said to Chalky.

As he smiled and went to respond, he felt his cell phone go off and pulled it out, reading a new message. He looked up at Archer and smiled.

'Uh oh. You're in deep shit.'

'What?'

'It's Port. Apparently Cobb just found out what you did to his Mercedes; said it's just as well you're leaving the country. If you stand outside, you might be able to hear him shouting from here.'

'What did you do to his Mercedes?' Shepherd asked, looking at him.

'I'll tell you on the plane, sir,' Archer said, checking their Departure time on the board above.

Confused but leaving it for the flight, Shepherd then turned to Chalky, offering his hand.

'Thank you for everything you and your colleagues did for us. I won't forget it.'

Chalky shook it. 'Pleasure. Glad it worked out and you're all safe.'

Marquez stepped forward and hugged him, then Josh offered his hand.

'I'll see you soon,' he said, as Chalky shook it.

Turning to Vargas, Chalky went to shake her hand but she stepped forward and hugged him too.

'Thank you,' she said.

'You too,' he said quietly.

'For what?'

He didn't reply. A moment later, the group gathered their things and moved off towards the security points, giving Archer and Chalky a chance to say goodbye.

The two friends stood there facing each other; then Archer chuckled.

'It's just as well I'm leaving. Most people don't ever get blown up, shot and have their heart stop in their entire lifetime, let alone all in one day.'

'Piss off. Lucky bastard. I go through all that and you only get a black eye.'

Archer looked down at himself.

'Shit, you're right,' he said, genuinely surprised. 'I didn't end up in hospital.'

'Don't speak too soon. You're not on the plane yet.'

Archer laughed.

There was a pause as they stood together in the large hall.

'Christ, I'm getting sick of these goodbyes,' Chalky said.

'Yeah; me too.'

'When are you gonna come back?'

'Some point again this year.'

'No, I mean really come back.'

Archer paused. 'Not yet, mate. I've got a good going thing over there.'

Chalky nodded, watching the rest of Archer's team walking towards the security checkpoints, their backs to him.

'Yeah; you do.'

Archer glanced at his friend and smiled. Then the two friends hugged quickly, and stepped back.

'Enough of that,' Chalky said. 'Don't want people getting the wrong idea.'

Archer laughed. 'I'll be back again before you know it. I promise.'

'Don't hurry. Need about twelve months to recover from this visit.'

Archer grinned then turned and headed for the security points, his team standing there waiting for him. As he watched him go, Chalky smiled.

Make it soon, Arch, he thought.

Re-joining the rest of the NYPD group, Archer and the team walked towards the checks, handing over their boarding passes and passports one by one. Josh, Shepherd and Marquez went through first as Archer and Vargas waited behind, Archer's arm around her shoulder and her own arm around his waist. Neither of them had needed to apologise to one another since they made it out of the office building, their fight from last week long forgotten. Sitting there with her and Chalky on the 12th floor as they waited for back-up to arrive, Archer had also realised that all of his choking claustrophobia and fears from that night in Harlem were gone, banished.

And he had a feeling that now his nightmares were gone for good too.

'Ready to go back?' he asked Vargas, looking down at her.

'I can't wait,' she said, looking up at him. 'But can I ask a favour?'

'Sure.'

'Let's never go into a tall building together ever again.'

He laughed. 'Deal.'

After she kissed him, Vargas then went through the checkpoint, Archer the last to go. He stepped forward, offering his boarding pass and passport.

As the official behind the desk took them, he opened Archer's passport and glanced up but then paused, seeing Archer's black eye.

'Someone hit you?' he asked.

He nodded. 'Afraid so.'

'Looks like you came off second best, mate.'

Archer shook his head and grinned.

'Not really. You should see the other guy.'

THE END

###

About the author:

Born in Sydney, Australia and raised in England and Brunei, Tom Barber has always had a passion for writing and story-telling. It took him to Nottingham University, England, where he graduated in 2009 with a 2:1 BA Hons in English Studies. Post-graduation, Tom moved to New York City and completed the 2 Year Meisner Acting training programme at The William Esper Studio, furthering his love of acting and screen-writing.

Upon his return to the UK in late 2011, Tom set to work on his debut novel, Nine Lives, which has since become a five-star rated Amazon UK Kindle hit. The following books in the series have been equally successful, garnering five-star reviews in the US, UK, France, Australia and Canada. The Sam Archer series has had over a million books downloaded worldwide and each title is currently being adapted into audiobook format.

Tom spends most of his time back and forth between the US and the UK. He can be contacted at http://www.tom-barber.co.uk/

Return Fire is the sixth novel in the Sam Archer series.

Follow @TomBarberBooks.

Read an extract from

Green Light

By
Tom Barber

The seventh Sam Archer thriller.
Now available on Amazon.

*****

PROLOGUE

The nineteen year old woman was in her apartment when her cell phone started to ring.

Although she'd been expecting the call, the shrill sound still made her jump. Out of communication for the past month, nevertheless she knew that word would have got out about where she'd been. She also knew that certain people would be more than pissed about it. She'd cost them a lot of money.

And with what she was about to do next, she was going to cost them a whole lot more.

Breaking off from her hasty packing, she walked across the room and picked up the phone. She wasn't leaving the city by herself; she had an accomplice, a friend she'd known less than a year but someone who'd done more for her in that short period of time than people she'd known her entire life. That friend had left her just under an hour ago, saying she'd call when she'd packed her own things and was ready to leave. The blonde girl had never been so excited or so nervous at the step they were about to take.

This was finally it.

Glancing at a clock across the room which read *9:45pm*, she pushed the green button then trapped the phone between her ear and shoulder as she walked back over to her bag.

'I'm almost done, babe,' she said. 'Are you ready?'

'Where are you?'

The girl froze, midway through tucking a pair of jeans into her holdall.

The voice on the other end wasn't the one she'd been expecting.

'I said where are you?'

'Uptown,' the young woman lied, stuffing the jeans into the bag then zipping it up. 'I'm getting back to work.'

'Bullshit. I always know when you're lying to me. You're at home, aren't you?'

Pause.

'I'm leaving,' the girl said, dropping to one knee and pushing her arm under the mattress.

'No, you're not.'

'You'd better believe it,' she replied, withdrawing some dollar bills folded in half, which she tucked into her back pocket. 'And you can't stop me. Not anymore.'

She heard a laugh down the end of the phone, which infuriated her.

'Try anything and I'll go straight to the cops,' she threatened angrily, hooking the bag over her shoulder then turning off the light in her bedroom and closing the door behind her. 'I'll tell them everything I know. All the things you're doing here. Everything.'

'Are you threatening me?'

'You bet I am,' the blonde girl replied, moving to the apartment's front door and unlocking it. 'So you can take this as a final goodbye. I'm leaving.'

'No, Leann. You're not.'

ONE

Three hours earlier it had been a normal mid-September evening in New York City. The streets were busy but not unusually so, the temperature pleasantly warm as commuters made their way home after a day's work while others headed into the city, some to start evening shifts, others to hit the town and meet friends.

However, in Brooklyn the usual sounds of the city winding down for the evening were suddenly interrupted.

A black Ford 4x4 with tinted windows slid around a corner, police fender lights flashing and siren wailing, other vehicles pulling over to give it room to pass. The car was heading north-west, being manoeuvred skilfully through the streets, the engine gunning as it propelled the 4x4 forward.

The Ford rounded another corner then headed towards the Atlantic Avenue entrance to the subway station fifty yards ahead, the last stop between Brooklyn and Manhattan. However, traffic was far thicker near the transport hub and the vehicles in front of the police car had no room to pull over; despite its flashing lights and siren the Ford was quickly forced to slow.

Before it had come to a complete stop, the front passenger door flew open and a young blond man in light blue jeans, white t-shirt and a black bulletproof NYPD vest leapt out.

'Go!' 3rd Grade NYPD Detective Sam Archer shouted to the driver.

Slamming the door, he raced through the gaps in the queuing traffic and sprinted off up the street towards the subway. Behind him, the 4x4 pulled a fast U-turn, taking off for the Brooklyn Bridge fifty yards ahead, leaving behind a sea of startled onlookers.

Six feet tall, a hundred and eighty five pounds and fast on his feet, Archer dodged his way past pedestrians, heading straight for the subway. Those who saw him coming did their best to get out of his way, others who were not so alert taken by surprise as he forced his way through.

'Move! Move!'

As he reached the entrance, Archer went for the far right of the stairs, taking them two at a time, the balmy heat of the New York September suddenly intensifying, the air thick with humidity. Cutting his way through the commuters, he vaulted the ticket barrier turnstile, an MTA employee in a glass cabin shouting as she spotted him.

Ignoring her but pausing for a moment to check the directions for a certain train line, Archer took off again towards the Manhattan-bound Q line, twenty yards ahead and down another flight of stairs. As he raced on, he heard the screech of brakes coming from the platform, followed by the sound of doors opening.

The train had already arrived.

Reaching the stairs to the N/Q platform he hurtled down them, willing a late arrival to hold the doors. Passengers who'd just exited the train were flowing up towards him, making his progress even more difficult, forcing him to fight his way through.

He could see the train waiting with its doors open.

387

Leaping down the last four steps, Archer hurled himself towards the nearest carriage as they started to close, managing to get his hand in the gap. Using all his strength to wrest them back open, he forced his way through and squeezed inside.

Stumbling into the carriage, he quickly regained his balance as the doors clicked shut behind him.

A beat later the wheels bit down onto the rails and the Q train lurched onwards towards its next stop.

Half a mile above the train, the two detectives Archer had left in the 4x4 were speeding across the Brooklyn Bridge, their flashing blues and siren assisting their progress as they cut and weaved through the Manhattan-bound traffic.

Trains on the New York City subway could reach speeds of 60mph and had the advantage of a clear run to their next destination, something Detective Josh Blake knew he couldn't match as he negotiated his way across the Bridge, drivers ahead unaware of the urgency of the situation as he flashed past them. Sam Archer's NYPD partner, Josh was a thirty one year old black guy built like a bodybuilder or line-backer, his usual calm, relaxed demeanour understandably absent at that particular moment as he gripped the wheel tightly, turning a sliding right and just missing another car.

Beside him sat Detective Alice Vargas, twenty nine years old and half his size, black-haired, brown-eyed, tanned and slender, a beautiful woman with an inner toughness which frequently took people by surprise, many of whom judged her purely on her half-Brazilian, half-American good looks. Having climbed over into the front seat after Archer left, she was holding her cell phone to her ear with her left hand, her right hand gripping hold of the arm support as Josh approached the end of the Bridge.

'Talk to me Vargas!' their team Sergeant, Matt Shepherd, ordered. *'Did you make it to the train?*

'Traffic was too heavy, sir! We left Archer trying to get on board.'

'Did he?'

'I don't know. We haven't heard from him.'

'Where are you?'

'On our way to Canal Street.'

'We're already here but we might not be able to stop that son of a bitch in time. Get to Union Square right now. Back up's already on its way!'

Somewhere below the Bridge, Archer was already making rapid progress through the Q train. The service was moderately full, not overcrowded, twenty or so people sitting or standing inside each carriage. At this hour most people were leaving the city, not entering it, but there were still way too many potential fatalities here on the city-bound service.

As he moved through the train, Archer rapidly scanned each person as he passed, his hand lingering near the Sig Sauer P226 pistol resting in its holster. He couldn't see the suspect or the bag anywhere.

Up ahead, the doors to the carriage suddenly whooshed open and an MTA employee in glasses and a blue uniform appeared and started walking towards him. Moving forward quickly, Archer met him halfway and pulled his badge from his hip.

'I need you to stop the train right now.'

'What? Why?'

'Just do it,' Archer ordered quietly, looking around, aware that they were in earshot of those immediately around them. 'And get everyone towards the rear of the train as quickly as you can.'

As the man pulled his radio, Archer turned to the carriage, showing his badge to everyone inside. The vest strapped across his torso had already attracted the attention of more than a few.

'Ladies and Gentlemen, I'm Detective Sam Archer, NYPD. We have an incident on board; I need you all to start moving towards the rear of the train immediately.'

As people looked at him uncertainly, hearing what he'd said but not immediately reacting, some who were listening to music quickly realised there was something unusual going on and pulled out their headphones.

'Why?' a woman asked.

'As I said, we have an incident. For your own safety, everyone please go, right now!' he ordered, not wanting to waste any more time. *'And tell everyone you pass to do the same.'*

Picking up on his urgency and his tone of command, people started to do as they were told, standing up and moving towards the other end of the train. Beside him, a workman picked up his toolbox as he rose from his seat. Archer grabbed his shoulder.

'Got pliers? Or a knife?'

The man nodded, thankfully not using up valuable time asking questions; he put the box on the bench and opened it up, passing over a small set of pliers. As he took them, Archer glanced at a green and white plaid shirt hooked across the box and pointed to it.

'Can I borrow that too?'

The man nodded; taking the garment, Archer quickly pulled it on and did up the buttons, hiding his NYPD vest as the workman walked down the train. Watching him follow the others, Archer rolled up the sleeves on the shirt then realised the noise level had changed.

They'd just entered Manhattan.

At Canal Street, Matt Shepherd and the fifth and final member of his Counter-Terrorism Bureau investigation team, Lisa Marquez, were rapidly clearing the platform of passengers who'd just disembarked from a train on the Uptown-bound Q platform, working fast with the help of scores of back-up officers. A thirty two year old Latina 3rd Grade detective, Marquez was only five foot six and a hundred and thirty pounds but more than made up for it with her no-nonsense, commanding attitude.

'Let's go!' she shouted, herding people out. *'Move it!'*

People instinctively responded to her tone, making their way quickly up the stairs and out onto the street above. An MTA employee standing close by listened to a message coming over his radio then turned and looked over at Shepherd who was further down the platform, also directing people out.

'Control say it's not slowing down!' he shouted. *'It'll be here in under a minute!'*

Swearing, Shepherd turned and ran towards the front of the train standing in the platform, the driver peering out of his window anxiously, waiting for instructions.

'Get out of here right now!'

On the approaching train, Archer was starting to sweat. He'd cleared all but one carriage, sending people down towards the rear, but the suspect was nowhere to be seen.

He heard the doors open behind him and the MTA guy reappeared, having successfully shepherded the passengers down to the other end of the train.

'Why are we still going?' Archer asked. 'I said we need to stop!'

'I tried!' the man said. 'I called the driver but he's not responding.'

Archer looked at the man for a moment then turned and stared up towards the front of the train, focusing on the closed door to the driver's cab in the next and last carriage. Pulling his pistol, he approached the connecting link between his carriage and the first. As they thundered through Canal Street, he saw a blur of cops and emergency personnel on the platform, but he barely registered them.

Holding his Sig Sauer double-handed, he entered the front carriage; he had no trouble attracting the attention of the passengers this time.

'Everyone get out,' he said quietly. 'Go down the train as far back as you can go. Don't take anything with you.'

The frightened passengers made no attempt to argue, the drawn weapon having an instant effect as they scrambled past him. A few moments later both he and the MTA employee were alone, the connecting doors closing behind the last passenger to leave.

Now just the two of them, Archer checked the door to the driver's cabin ahead, looking for any cameras.

'Can he see u-'

Before he could finish asking the question, a burst of bullet holes suddenly appeared through the driver's door ahead of them. Archer instantly threw himself to the floor, dragging the MTA man down with him, and fired back twice with his Sig. Keeping down as another burst of gunfire came from the cab, Archer saw the door swing open, revealing the driver on the floor with his hands over his head, the suspect standing beside him and firing wildly with some kind of compact sub-machine gun, lighting up the cab.

Firing back and aiming high to try and put the gunman down but avoid hitting the driver, Archer scrambled up and pushed the MTA man towards the carriage behind them.

'*Archer!*' the MTA man's radio said, bursting into life. '*Archer, it's Shepherd, can you hear me?*'

As they moved into the second carriage and the doors closed behind them, Archer snatched the receiver just as the suspect let fly with another barrage of gunfire, smashing the glass out above their heads.

'*Suspect located; he's in the cab!*' he shouted as he pulled the other man down, his voice fighting to be heard over the wind now howling through the train. '*But he's got an automatic weapon; I'm pinned down!*'

'*The driver?*'

'*Still alive!*'

'*Have you found the device?*'

393

'It must be in there with them. I can't get near enough to find out!'

Up on street level, Josh and Vargas screeched to a halt at the top of Union Square on 16th Street, bailing out of their car and moving as fast as they could into the station, the place heaving with evacuating commuters coming the other way. Forcing a path through the crowd, the pair headed for the N/Q Uptown track where they knew the train would be arriving any second.

As they appeared, two cops standing with an MTA employee ran towards them, one of them holding a radio receiver.

'Your guy on the train found the suspect!' one of the cops told them. 'But he can't get near him. The son of a bitch is pinning him down with some kind of machine gun.'

As Josh grabbed the radio, Vargas heard the sound of the train approaching the Q rails below. Knowing they were out of time, she pulled her Sig Sauer and sprinted down the stairs that led to the middle of the platform.

As she reached the last step, the train roared into view and the brakes started to screech, the bomber arriving at his destination. Seeing the suspect in the cabin as the train ploughed along the track towards her, Vargas pushed two remaining members of the public out of the way and fired twice, straight at the driver's windows, the sound of the gunshots and splintering glass lost in the noise of the approaching train.

Holding on as the train ground to a halt, Archer went to fire into the cab again but then realised the sub-machine gunfire had ceased. Peering round his cover, he saw the suspect was slumped on top of the cowering driver on the floor.

Standing up slowly and stalking forward, his sights never leaving the gunman, he saw the man had been shot twice in the head. Seeing the blond man approach, the driver wriggled his way out from under the dead gunman, crawling over shell casings and broken glass.

Reaching the cabin, Archer saw two bullet-holes in the front window, the train only stopping because of the dead man's lever. The front of the Q train had moved through the 14th Street station and was now partially in the tunnel, dark gloom ahead illuminated by the occasional light; but Archer wasn't here to admire the view.

'Where's his bag?' he asked the driver quickly.

'What?'

'He must have had a bag. Where the hell is it?'

As the man stared at him, shocked and confused, Archer turned away to look around the cab. Fifteen feet behind him, the doors to the carriage were forced open, Josh and Vargas climbing inside with their weapons ready to fire and saw their team-mate in the cab.

'Arch!' Josh said urgently.

Archer didn't respond; instead, he dropped down, turned the dead suspect over and pulled open his jacket; frisking him down, he paused, then pushed up a sleeve.

The guy had cylinders of ball bearings taped to his limbs.

'Jesus Christ,' Vargas said quietly, bending down beside Archer.

Working fast, Archer patted down the gunman's torso and frowned. Quickly pushing up the man's shirt, he froze.

'What the-?' he whispered.

The suspect had fresh, angry-looking stitches covering his stomach; the skin was lumpy and inflamed, dried blood visible from the crude needlework.

The explosives were sewn under his skin.

****